Layla's Story

Persian Moon

Moon Trilogy – Book 1

GUITTA KARUBIAN

The characters and events in this book are fictitious and the product of the author's imagination. Any similarity to real persons is coincidental and not intended.

ISBN: 978-1-7330151-7-2

CONTENTS

DEDICATION

Women, Life, Freedom

I dedicate *Persian Moon* to you, the Women of Iran, shackled for too long to the dictates of a male-led regime with the primary motive of keeping a tight grip on repressive measures that deny your basic human rights.

I join women around the world, united with our brothers in justice, both Persian-born and otherwise, who feel your pain and your longing while in awe of your courage and your passionate bravery.

We are with you. We watch, cheering you on.

I pray you will prevail.

ACKNOWLEDGMENTS

I thank the many people who supported me in writing **Persian Moon.** As this was my first attempt at writing a novel, the generous encouragement was reassuring and vital.

Special thanks to Jessica Parks Clark for completing the initial editing of this book. The added glossary of Farsi terms used in the story, included at the story's end, was Jessica's idea and I think her for that, as well as for her labor in putting it together.

I also thank my children, siblings and extended family as well as my wonderful friends who so kindly read early drafts of the book for their edits and helpfulness.

And I thank you, the reader, about to begin Book One of the Moon Trilogy, *Persian Moon - Layla's Story.*

Women, Life, Freedom

"No story has power nor will it last unless we feel in ourselves that it is true and true of us… A great and lasting story is about everyone, or it will not last."

— John Steinbeck

"Every Persian child should feel able to count on the love of mother and find shelter and refuge in her arms."

— Shah, Mohammad Reza Pahlavi

PART I: IN THE BEGINNING

PROLOGUE TO PART I

THE ROYAL WEDDING

Soraya Esfandiary- Bakhtiari-Pahlavi

I arrived in Tehran in October of 1950 by royal invitation to be interviewed for the position of wife to His Imperial Majesty, Mohammad Reza Pahlavi.

His Majesty had been divorced from his first wife, Fawzia, for some time, and I gathered he was enjoying the company of many women. Nonetheless, to ensure the future of Iran would forever be intertwined with the Pahlavi name, His Majesty was obliged to marry and produce a male heir. His mother – a domineering woman – combed the world in search of a new wife for her son. She was shown my photograph, and the invitation followed.

My father, Khalil Esfandiary-Bakhtiari, had once been in some sort of business relationship with the royal family before he married Eva Karl, a German Christian and moved to Switzerland where we now live; however, at the time that I received the invitation to the Golestan Palace, I was attending school in England.

The little I knew of his Imperial Majesty interested me, and I wanted to know more about him. I knew that his father had crowned himself King, simultaneously naming his then twelve-year-old son Crown Prince. From that day forward, everyone – including the boy's siblings – were to address the boy as royalty. Several years later, the young teenage boy was pulled away from his mother's tight embrace to attend Europe's finest schools. There he became fluent in several languages; this we had in common. Apparently, all he lacked was a happy marriage and a male heir to his throne.

Arriving at the palace, I was tired and worn out from my trip and wanted nothing more than a bed. Yet I barely had time to arrange my toiletries before the shah's mother commanded my immediate presence.

As we sipped tea in her suite of rooms, my hostess barely hid her intense scrutiny of me.

She almost immediately complimented me on my green eyes; green and blue eyes are rare among Persians, and they find them particularly alluring. She then complimented me on my "perfect face." After some time, she declared me "charming" as well, and was delighted to see that "unlike that Egyptian girl," I was fluent in Farsi. The "Egyptian girl" was, of course, the Egyptian Princess Fawzia, the shah's first wife. The groom had had no say in the choice of his bride. His father had arranged his son's marriage to King Farouk's stunning sister in the hope of cementing ties between Iran and Egypt. The two first met on the day of their betrothal. He was twenty and she was seventeen.

I had seen many photographs of Princess Fawzia. She was an exceptionally beautiful woman with long, ebony-colored hair that fell in waves, framing a perfect heart-shaped face, rosebud lips, and intense, dark blue eyes set against a porcelain complexion.

But the handsome couple's marriage was rife with incompatibilities. Fawzia had never been comfortable in Iran. She had arrived with an entourage of one thousand people, as if bringing as much of Egypt with her as she could. I can only imagine how isolated she must have felt when the entire entourage was ordered to return to Egypt. She also had trouble with the Persian language so that even simple communication between husband and wife was difficult.

Beyond that, their religions clashed. Though both were Muslim,

Fawzia was a devout Sunni whereas His Majesty was a Shiite. That was another commonality we shared. And we had both been raised by Christian nannies; we were both barely observant.

Perhaps, the princess also believed that the Iranian court was beneath her. That would have been understandable. After all, she was part of a dynasty that had reigned for hundreds of years, while only seventeen years had passed since the successful military coup that had rendered her father-in-law Shah and her husband, Crown Prince.

As if all that wasn't bad enough, there had always been friction between Fawzia and her female in-laws. Soon after giving birth to their only child, the daughter they named Shahnaz, Princess Fawzia returned to Egypt and left her little girl in Iran with her father as dictated by Persian law.

Within two years of his marriage to Fawzia, the West, ever hungry for Iran's abundant oil, exiled his father, afraid that the country's oil fields and the railway connecting them might fall into the hands of Nazi Germany. As a result, at the age of twenty-two, the Peacock Throne and all its plumes passed to the young prince. He was now His Majesty Mohammad Reza Pahlavi, Shahanshah, King of Kings.

Meanwhile, the tie between Iran and Egypt did solidify. When shah's father died, the Egyptians mummified his body.

Decades later, when my ex-husband was exiled, it was Egypt that granted his family asylum, and where he passed.

That first evening at the palace, the shah's mother extended my invitation to include dinner.

His Imperial Majesty, Mohammad Reza Pahlavi, joined us, wearing the air force uniform he later told me he was certain had saved his life. He was wearing the uniform when he'd survived an airplane crash as well as the two failed attempts on his life. Survival convinced him that he was protected by a divine hand and destined for greatness. As ruler of "the greatest country on earth," well over two thousand four hundred years old, with a culture revered for its art, poetry and early contributions to civilization, he felt it was his right to finally choose the woman he loved and would marry.

I was immediately taken with the man.

His bearing was regal, and I was more than flattered by his attention. His Majesty was certainly handsome and charismatic enough to attract any woman he desired. That evening, in his mother's quarters, we enjoyed a lengthy meal, filled with pleasant chitchat, and I was surprised afterwards when the hostess excused herself, leaving me alone with His Majesty; it was totally against all protocol. In hindsight, I realize he had signaled his mother to leave us.

In any event, the two of us passed hours of pleasant conversation.

His Majesty spoke of his favorite past times, and we found we enjoyed the same sports, among them horseback riding and tennis.

At dawn, I finally made my way to bed in a trance, at once lightheaded, exhausted, and yet, feeling marvelous. The next morning, I discovered that after we'd parted, His Majesty had telephoned my home in Switzerland to ask my father for my hand in marriage. Papa later told me that the shah had said, "I have found everything I could want in Soraya, and I have lost my heart to her."

That same day, the shah presented me with a 24-karat diamond engagement ring, a hint of the ostentatious wedding that was to come. The royal engagement was announced.

Overnight, I became the toast of the country. The populace was kind. They spoke of me as "the emerald-eyed beauty." The media used complimentary phrases, speaking of my "movie star good looks" and "glamorous, jet-set style." They wrote that I'd won the hearts of the people.

It was not uncommon for a man of great stature to take a wife 16 years his junior. His Majesty was then thirty-four and it was said that I was eighteen; in fact, I was sixteen.

Though we planned to marry that December, it was not to be. I contracted the Spanish flu, the most lethal plague ever known. Consequently, our wedding date was moved to February. Yet, February came and I still weak Nevertheless, His Majesty, not willing to wait any longer, ordered the wedding arrangements to resume.

Masses of spring flowers were flown in on refrigerated planes from

The Netherlands, and the shah – not a man to pinch pennies when in love – arranged to have an entire Italian circus flown to Tehran to perform for our wedding guests.

On February 27,1951, the streets of Tehran glistened in white, the result of an unrelenting snowstorm. This was considered to be a favorable sign by His Majesty and his mother, both of whom were superstitious and preoccupied with the mystical.

My wedding dress was dazzling. Commissioned by Christian Dior, it sparkled with six thousand embedded diamonds. It had a never-ending train and a multitude of petticoats. My headdress, designed by Van Clef & Arpel, was also laden with diamonds. Added to all this weight was the white mink cape His Majesty draped over my shoulders to protect my still frail body from the cold. The sum of all this proved to be burdensome in my weakened state and, as a result, I could barely walk. Minutes before the ceremony was to begin, a dressmaker was called in with a pair of scissors. Yards of petticoats were cut off and the train was substantially shortened. Only then could I walk down the aisle to take my vows.

And so, our marriage began.

Outside the palace, Iran's political and economic conditions were deteriorating. World War 2 had brought disruptions everywhere. There were food shortages. Health care was inadequate. The country's oil revenues, which had been picking up, plummeted.

Furthermore, the cleric, always critical of the monarchy, found fault with me, believing I was a terrible choice to be the shah's new wife.

They complained that I was part European. And though my father was Muslim, my mother and the nanny who had raised me were both Christian; consequently, I knew almost nothing about the Muslim religion.

And, though attempts on the life of His Majesty had failed, key political figures had been assassinated, including two prime ministers.

The country was vulnerable.

1

THE DAY IT BEGAN

Tehran, Summer, 1951

The day had started out like any other summer day.

When I left the house, Maman had been standing on her bedroom terrace watching the crowds cheer His Imperial Majesty and Soraya as they exited Golestan Palace following their marriage ceremony.

As always, I went outside to play with the boys.

I'd never enjoyed playing with girls. They bored me with their dolls and silly tea parties. These boys were my best friends and I loved them all. Though I was the youngest among them, they accepted me as their friend and protected me like a little sister.

We eventually found ourselves in Jalil's garden. We decided to kidnap Tarzan, Jalil's rooster, and move into his basement. Underground and cooler than the living room directly above it, the basement was used as a summer living room. Now that summer's hottest days had passed, couches and tables had been pushed up against the walls and covered with odd fabrics. The small, tiled pool in the center of the large room, used to cool hot feet, had been emptied. It was the perfect place for us to play.

Our game was an old one. We made a circle around Tarzan, watching as the rooster jerked and pecked at the air. He shifted from leg to leg and then, predictably, started moving toward us. Whomever he came to would be ousted from the circle. The rules of our game did not allow us to move our feet, so instead, we screamed, waved our arms, wiggled, and made faces trying to scare the rooster away. Tarzan's helter-skelter path excited us and the ruffling of his feathers as he changed directions increased our howls.

Tarzan eventually tagged Jalil, our host and my favorite among the boys. Jalil made a sour face before he left the circle, pursing his full lips and pulling up one cheek before going off to pass his time investigate the room. The rooster was put in the center again and the game continued. Then Bijan, the long-limbed clown of the group was ousted. Hands in his pockets, he kicked up his foot as he left the game and joined Jalil.

I saw Jalil pick up a length of bright orange yarn nestled under a chair. The two boys put their dark-haired heads together and, having conspired to catch Tarzan, crashed the circle and began to chase the rooster. The game broke up as the rooster fled from his pursuers, knocking down the *ghellyon,* the water pipe that was set on the ledge of the now empty pool. When it fell to the floor, the poor bird hesitated, startled by the sudden noise. In that moment, the two boys had him. Bijan scooped the bird into his arms and held him while Jalil began to tie the colorful yarn around his legs. Tarzan's feathers trembled. His yellow talons, fringed with red, dug into Bijan's forearm.

I approached my two friends and gently admonish them. "You're frightening the poor thing, Bijan. Please, don't hurt him. Put him down."

Just then I felt a short, sharp pang in my abdomen and winced in pain. I'd felt several pangs like that throughout the morning and now I reproached myself for having eaten too many dried apricots and sour cherries the night before.

My cousin Bahman saw me grimace. "*Cheteh?* What's wrong? Are you okay?" he asked.

I nodded. Then, whether because of my admonition to him or because of Bahman's concerned tone, Bijan let go of Tarzan. The rooster fell to the floor and ran frantically around the room, ruffling his wings in indignation with the orange yarn, tied to one leg, trailing after him. I smiled, then saw Bijan's eyes grow big as he pointed.

"*Bebeen!* Look!" He covered his mouth with one hand. We all turned to follow his finger.

Majid, the most serious of the boys, gasped, "*Vye,* Wow!"

"*Khoon,* blood!" That was Cyrus, the oldest among them.

They were staring at *me*! I looked down, saw blood on my shorts, and froze. I had no idea what was happening to me. I didn't remember hurting myself. "What happened?" I asked. "Where am I cut?"

I'd never been told of the female cycle, but the boys knew what the red stain meant. Several of them had older sisters and they had most certainly talked among themselves about the mystery of a woman's monthly flow, in the way boys their age have always done. They had all been warned not to take freedoms with girls who had "crossed the threshold into womanhood."

There in Jalil's basement, they all understood what they were seeing, and soon realized that I did not. If the taboo imprinted in their young minds hadn't forbidden them from speaking of such things to a girl, I know the boys would have explained it to me. As it was, they stopped pointing and, one by one, turned away. Jalil's look lingered on my cousin Bahman, as if imploring him, as my cousin, to do something. Bahman shrugged his shoulders and shook his head.

Jalil approached me. "You have to go home, Layla," he said in a whisper. I made no move to go. He shook my arm. He must have seen the fear in my eyes then, for he let go of my arm and took hold of my hand with more tenderness than I had ever felt from him. "*Beeya,* come," he said. "I'll take you home."

"Why am I bleeding? Where am I cut?" I asked again. Jalil shook his head. "It's nothing. You'll be fine," he said.

As he led me up the stairs, I became aware of a warm, sticky feeling between my legs, so I moved tentatively. I had the strangest certainty that the blood was coming from *there*. I'd always been a brave girl. I idolized Joan of Arc who feared nothing. I was never afraid to do whatever the boys did. Yet now I was frightened and puzzled by Jalil's vague reply.

I tried hard not to sound scared. "Jalil, I don't know why I'm bleeding." As I walked, I concentrated on moving my legs carefully, keeping them apart. If the blood was coming from *there,* what could be wrong?

"Don't cry, Layla. Your mother will take care of everything. Really. We just need to get you home."

Outside, the sun was bright.

We walked the length of the wooden veranda alongside the fishpond. Usually, I'd stop and talk to the goldfish, remarking on the weather or greeting them with *Saalom.* That day, I paid them no attention. We hurried along, cutting across the expanse of Jalil's front yard, his mother's little purple flowers no more than a blur of color through my tears. The whole time we walked, my friend never let go of my hand. *Poor Jalil!* All he could do was echo hollow-sounding reassurances.

"I promise you'll be fine. Don't worry Layla, your mother will take care of you."

When we finally crossed the low, decorative wrought-iron railing that bordered my house and arrived at our front door, Jalil threw the door open without bothering to ring the bell and ran inside calling out my mother's name. "Zahra Khanom!" I remained at the threshold, standing as still as a statue with my legs pressed tightly together, resenting the sweet fragrance of the red hybrid tea roses that climbed up the raw marble stones of my house. I was repelled by their deep color for they only intensified my preoccupation with the blood on my shorts.

I saw Jalil pass through our dining room and head toward the hallway. "Layla needs you," he announced. "She's very scared. She's bleeding."

"Bleeding?" I heard my mother's hurried steps, her narrow heels hitting the wooden floor between silk rugs. Maman would probably take call for the doctor. When she came to the doorway, I was still standing outside, holding onto the white doorframe with one hand, the other hand on my stomach, afraid to move. She saw my teary face and my swollen eyes filled with fear. Then she saw the blood on my shorts and her look of concern evaporated.

She turned to Jalil. "Did anyone else see her like this?"

What a strange thing for Maman to ask! Stranger yet, Jalil didn't answer truthfully.

"No, Zahra Khanom, only me." He answered with a bent head. If his eyes had not caught mine and held them on their way down, I would have blurted out that in fact five other boys had witnessed my predicament. As it was, I kept silent, puzzled by my friend's lie.

Maman nodded. "*Khoobeh,* that's good. Thank you for bringing her home. You can go now. Don't tell anyone about this."

She dismissed my friend and called for Fotmeh, our new house servant. The girl, close to my age, came running, hugging a soapy pail in one hand and a metal brush in the other.

"Bring me a towel. Quickly," Maman said. "Then fetch clean clothes for my daughter and put them in my bathroom." She turned back to Jalil who hadn't moved from his spot, his hands pressed into his pockets. "Leave now, Jalil. If anyone should ask where Layla is, say she has a headache – no, better yet, say you don't know. Say nothing."

I looked from my mother to Jalil unable to understand why they were both lying. Just before leaving, Jalil called out, "Zahra Khanom, would you like me to call for the doctor?"

"No. Now go!"

The door closed behind Jalil, and Fotmeh hurried back holding out a large towel.

Maman took the towel, passed it between my legs and handed me the gathered ends.

"Hold this tightly," she instructed me. She led me down the hallway past my father's study, past my room and turned the corner to the staircase. "*Beeya*! Come!" She said.

I told her I didn't have a headache. "Of course, you don't," she answered. "Be careful not to touch anything."

My mother ascended the staircase like a queen to her throne, while

I struggled to hold on to the ends of the thick towel in one hand, gripping the mahogany banister with the other, and trying to make sense of what was happening. I was bleeding for some unknown reason and had sharp stomach pains, yet I didn't need a doctor, and everyone was lying.

To add to the puzzle, Maman was leading me upstairs! I hadn't been there in a long time. Only the master bedroom and bathroom were upstairs. As I followed her into my parent's bedroom, I felt a layer of serenity wrap around me.

We entered the master bedroom. When I was a small child, my father, whom I affectionately called Babajon, would often romp with me on their big bed like a child himself, while Maman either went to sit on their bedroom balcony or, more often, went downstairs. There was the chair where Babajon used to sit with me perched on his knee while he read the newspaper. A recent copy of that day's paper lay on the small table with a photo of the on the front page, smiling. There was my mother's dresser, with her ivory jewelry box, painted with cat hairs. It sat alongside the ornate silver frame holding a photograph of my deceased maternal grandmother whom I respectfully called Khanom Bozorg, Grand Lady. I had only vague memories of her, always with my cousin Bahman perched on her lap. Today, as always, the old lady's eyes followed my movement through the room. Her piercing eyes looked right through me, and I sensed she wasn't at all happy with what she saw. I tore my eyes away from the photograph.

"Be careful. Make sure you don't touch anything," Maman said.

I followed as though in a dream as my mother led me into her bathroom, her inner sanctum. I'd always been forbidden to go inside. The room was bright with light bouncing off the mirrors. I caught sight of my glaring image, my red eyes and pale, my tear-stained face.

"Maman, *chera?* Why am I bleeding?" Maman looked me up and down then simply sighed. "Make it stop, Maman," I said.

She pointed to the corner of the bathroom floor. "Put your clothes there, then hurry into the shower and wash yourself."

How could Maman see the blood and remain calm?

I did as I was told and turned on the shower. When I saw the first spray of water hit blood and tur pink, my knees began to shake.

I poked my head outside the shower. "Maman *jon,* am I bleeding from my stomach? If I don't go to the hospital and the doctor doesn't come here, how will you make the bleeding stop?" I held my torso tightly with my arms crossed while I waited for her answer.

Maman had been looking at herself in the mirror, adjusting her gold earrings. "From now on, you'll bleed like this for several days each month."

I stared at her in utter panic. "*Chera*? Why? What's wrong with me?"

In the mirror, Maman saw my face drained of its color. She smoothed the collar of her fashionable, pale-peach silk blouse. "What a silly question," she said. "There's nothing wrong with you."

"*Pas chera?* Then why? Maman, I don't understand. If I'm not sick..." She said nothing. "Maman *jon!* Please! Don't make me do that," I begged. My hands were clasped at my chest, my eyes glued to her. "I really don't want that to happen, Maman," I sobbed.

She turned from the mirror to face me. "Hush, child! No one has asked what you or I want. You'll get used to it. Now hurry!"

"No Maman! I won't bleed!" I shook my head wildly and stomped my feet. Water splashed outside the shower.

"Layla! Have you gone mad? You are really trying my patience." My mother spoke as if I was a spoiled child in the midst of a temper tantrum. She resumed eyeing herself in the mirror, making sure no water had sprayed onto her delicate blouse. I rubbed my eyes under the sopping hair that had fallen around my face. Then Maman left the bathroom.

I was beside myself with confusion. *Why did she leave?* I stood still and prayed as hard as I could that she would come back; I needed her. I stood under the spray with my fists clenched, staring at the bar of soap on the small shelf until, after what seemed like an eternity, she returned.

"Maman, *bebakhsheed,* excuse me, I'm very sorry I made you angry."

"It was Allah's wish that I be blessed with a daughter and not a son. It is not for you to make apologies for Allah's wishes," she said.

Fotmeh entered just then, head down with fresh clothes for me. I saw her peer first at my naked body then at the bloodied shorts on the same floor she scrubbed every morning. Embarrassed, I stepped into the midst of the water and turned my back to her, trying to hide my body and my tears from her curious eyes.

Maman must have noticed my discomfort in Fotmeh's presence, and I suppose the last thing she needed just then was another complication for she stepped in front of Fotmeh and growled. "Why are you standing here when there is housework to do? Have you cleaned the dining room yet today? *Borro,* go!" Fotmeh turned and ran as though running from a devil *jen.*

Poor Maman! I had behaved badly and yet she made Fotmeh leave for my sake. I forced a smile onto my face. "I love you, Maman."

"Of course, you do, Layla. I love you, too. Now come out and dry yourself. Hurry up. I haven't all day." I did as she directed, still in a daze. She continued, "At some age – I suppose for you, this age – every woman begins to bleed for several days every month."

"No, Maman!" I was horrified anew and my tears flowed.

My mother turned my face up to hers. "Stop arguing and pay attention. Since the beginning of time, girls everywhere have gone into their moon cycle, and now, so will you. Rich or poor, pretty or plain, we all bleed every month whether we want to or not, and you are no exception. We all get used to it."

The vastness of what she said captured my imagination. "*Every* woman?"

"Yes."

My tears stopped. "Does Fotmeh?"

"No, not yet." Maman shuddered. "But I imagine she will soon enough."

"Did Khanom Bozorg bleed?"

"Yes."

"Did Joan of Arc?"

"I'm certain she did if she was a woman."

"Maman, do *you* bleed every month?"

"Yes. I told you every woman does. Now you do too, and I expect you to stop acting like a baby about it from this moment on.

"Watch what I'm doing and learn." Maman reached into a cabinet and brought out a big blue box marked, Kotex.

She sat on the closed toilet lid. "Whining and carrying on like a spoiled child! You have no idea how lucky you are to have nice pads like this," she said as she showed me how to attach the white pad onto my underpants with two large safety pins. "When I went into my moon, we had to use strips of cotton cloth."

"I'm sorry, Maman."

"*Aye*," she said, remembering. "And I was forbidden to bathe or shower while I was in my moon. They thought it would cause an infection. So, I had to wait until my cycle ended, then go to the *hammom omoomi*, the public baths." She stood. "Even *my* family didn't have bathrooms like this, Layla. You must appreciate how lucky you are. Most other people still use the common baths. You have no idea what they're like." Maman sounded a little angry, so I didn't remind her that Babajon's mother, Nanah Joon, Dear Grandmother, once took me to a public bath.

Maman smoothed down the rich fabric of her skirt, her broad palms gliding down her slim thighs, and glanced over at the pile of my soiled clothes then quickly turned away."Hurry now and get dressed," she said.

While I dressed, the white pad between my legs feeling bulky and awkward, Maman washed her hands in the sink.

"Maman, why do all girls have to bleed to become women?"

"So that we can have babies."

I mulled over that. I had never considered there was a price to pay for motherhood.

"You are to change your pad often and always stay clean, Layla. It's important that no one should ever know you are in your moon. Do you understand?" I nodded. "Wash your hands. You can finish dressing in your own room." She touched my shoulder. "And Layla, this was an exception; *never* come into my bathroom again. Fotmeh will put a blue box like mine in your bathroom for you to use."

"Yes, Maman."

Though my mother was finished with our mother-daughter conversation, I was not. Her last admonition hadn't made any sense to me. While washing my hands, I spoke to her face, reflected back to me as she arranged the walnut-brown curl at her temple and the hair that fell just below her ears. "Maman, if all girls bleed then everyone must know."

"They do. But that doesn't mean they need to know *when you* are in your moon." She spoke as if her words were too obvious to have to say.

"Why must I keep it a secret?"

Maman sighed and turned away from her own reflection to face me. "Because this is an intimate thing, Layla, the sort of thing a decent girl keeps to herself. It's simply no one's business." Then she shook her head ever so slightly, certain that now the matter had ended.

My mind was wrestling with the fact that I'd already done something wrong. I'd already disobeyed Maman. Six boys knew I was bleeding because I hadn't expected the blood. *How could I have known to keep it from them?* "Maman *jon*, you knew for certain this would happen to me?"

"For the last time: It happens to all girls."

"Then why didn't you tell me? I would have known why I was bleeding and ..." I couldn't finish the sentence. Maman was slow to answer, as if sensitive to any suggestion that she may have shunned her responsibility. I hurried to add, "I only mean that–"

"Layla, I am your mother and I know what's best for you. You were too young to understand. Now you are a young lady."

I might have pursued the subject if at that moment Maman hadn't reached out and embraced me. I was so jarred by her rare show of physical affection that I couldn't speak. I felt her soft blouse against my cheek, smelled her scent and felt her arms around me. Just as I was beginning to relax in her arms, it was all over. She held me at arms' length and gave me a smile that was as rare as one of her hugs. Maman didn't smile very much; I think she was afraid it would create wrinkles. The smile was like those I got from Babajon, something akin to pride. I was pleased, especially after having made her so angry.

Holding my shoulders, she said, "*Mobarrak!* Congratulations! You are no longer a little girl. Today, you took a big step. You're becoming a woman."

At last I understood. The monthly blood was a good thing. It pleased Maman for it meant I was no longer a child. My heart leaped in excitement and I felt a surge of importance. Maman led me out of her bathroom and through her bedroom. On my way out, my eyes fell on the photo of the pompous old woman staring at me. I was determined not to let her spoil my day.

Downstairs, Maman found Fotmeh and instructed her to prepare two cups of hot *chai,* Persian tea, sweetened with *nabot,* crystallized sugar. She was to serve one cup to Maman in the dining room and one cup to me in my room where I was to rest. The tea would settle my stomach. Immediately after serving tea, the servant girl was to wash my clothes and Maman's bathroom towels – separately – then scrub down her bathroom, again.

2

OUT IN THE WORLD

Alone in my bedroom, Maman's words buzzed around in my head: *Women all over the world … a young lady now ... becoming a woman … mobarrak!*

The look that accompanied those words and my mother's embrace combined to turn my anxiety into exhilaration and transform my tears into a smile of excitement. *I was becoming a woman!*

There was a lot I didn't yet understand. I only knew I was embarking on a new phase of my life. I stood in front of my full-length mirror and peered at my face to see if it looked any different; it didn't. I examined myself down to my feet, then stood sideways and studied my body's reflection in profile. Nothing looked different. I lifted my blouse and looked at my young breasts, touched the smooth skin and felt the slight swelling. There was a new sensitivity there, especially at the nipples. The feeling gave me chills and I quickly pulled my blouse back down.

I turned my radio on to classic Iranian music and began to dance. I was in front of the mirror, swinging my hips from side to side in time with the percussive rhythm of the *tonbakr,* when I saw Fotmeh standing in the doorway, watching. The servant girl stood with a cup of *chai nabot,* tea sweetened with rock candy, set on a tray, looking at me as though I was stranger than anyone she'd ever seen, unsure whether to enter.

I couldn't blame her! First, she'd seen me in the living room crying and carrying on, then acting shy and meek in Maman's shower, and now here I was, laughing and wiggling my hips in front of a mirror. I blushed, realizing that had she come a moment sooner, she would have caught me with my blouse up.

I'd been curious about the girl since she arrived at our house just a short time ago. She was the youngest house servant I'd ever seen, not much older than me. I'd tried to befriend her, but she consistently avoided me. I resolved to try harder to be nice to her. Now that my crisis had passed, I felt bad for her. Maman had yelled at her because of me, and her mother probably wouldn't be with her when she came into her moon. I thanked her and took the tray. She turned and walked hastily away. My attempt to befriend her would have to wait.

The smell of the steaming tea, the scent of the jasmine blossoms left to dry with the black pekoe leaves, kissed my senses. I sipped the hot drink, savoring its sweet fragrance and felt its warmth spill into my mouth. When I'd emptied the cup, I went to my window and leaned out into the mid-afternoon of a beautiful day. The *chai nabot* had calmed my stomach and renewed my energy. I could smell the jasmine that grew along the trellis on the side of our house. The sun still shone through the branches of the mulberry trees.

It was a day for children to be outside. I longed to tell my cousin, Shireen, who prided herself on being three weeks older than me, what had happened. I could just picture her face when she heard the news that I had transformed into a woman before her. "It's not fair!" she'd scream. Unable to wait a moment longer, I left the house.

On my way to Shireen's house, the sound of the rushing current of the *joob* waters running along the side of road seemed to play a melody and I found myself humming along.

Babajon had explained that the water of the *joob* originates from mountain snow then finds its way into trenches along all of Tehran's streets. It becomes increasingly dirty as it moves along, yet, until recently, households would divert this water into basement reservoirs and boil it to use for everything except drinking.

I couldn't imagine using it at all in the wonderful house that Babajon had designed. Though our home was not overly large, it had conveniences hard to find in my country at that time: electricity, gas for our fireplace, a water heater, running water and and bathrooms, when most homes in Iran still had outhouses or, at best, toilets that were no more than a hole you squatted over. Our new house had two indoor bathrooms, both with sit-down toilets. We also had showers and porcelain bathtubs at a time when many Persians still washed in water they took from the *joob* or visited a *hammom omoomi,* public bath. Earlier, I'd decided not to remind Maman of the day Naneh Joon had taken me to one. I understood – and appreciated – having my own clean, private place to bathe at home.

A little over a year earlier, after a night spent at my grandparents' home in central Tehran, my dear Nana Joon and I headed downtown after breakfast with a change of clothes in a bundle. At the entrance of the *hammom,* Naneh Joon paid a fee, and we were each given a long sheet called a *longi.* I was a mix of embarrassment and awe as we undressed in the communal dressing room along with women of all ages.

It was the first time I'd seen Naneh Joon naked. She was so different than my large, imperious, and harsh maternal grandmother. My father's mother was a gentle soul, quiet and comforting. She was thin, small-boned and slightly forward bent. Her breasts fascinated me, and I tried not to stare. They, too, were thin and draped down over her ribcage. She set our clothes on the wooden ledge that ran the length of the dressing room and directed me to wrap myself in one of the *longis.* Then she led me to the pool, ripe with the communal dirt of women who had soaked there before us. I closed my eyes, dropped my sheet and followed my grandmother into the grey film-covered water.

Afterward, I lay on my *longi* on the tiled floor as an old woman exfoliated my entire body, scrubbing with a *keeseh,* a coarse mitt. Dead skin fell on the white sheet in a profusion of short black worms.

Finally, we stood under one of several sets of faucets that lined one wall and Naneh Joon helped me rinse off. When we were again dressed, she bought me a drink of *khok sheer*, sweet, watered rocket seeds. That drink was my favorite part of the *hammom* experience, most refreshing after the hot humidity of the bathhouse.

I arrived at Shireen's door. Their manservant told me my cousin had gone shopping with her mother, so I left a message that I had stopped by and would come by again later. Then I turned back toward home, remembering this was the same path I'd taken earlier with Jalil. I thought back at how scared I'd been then. I was happy that Jalil had cared enough about me to walk me home. I decided to go to his house, thank him, and apologize for being such a crybaby.

I stopped in my tracks. *Jalil knew*! I realized that he must have known exactly what the blood was. That's why he was so anxious to get me home to Maman ... and why he'd lied to her! He knew she would have extremely upset if she knew the other boys had seen the blood. After another step I stopped again. *Why, of course! They all knew!* No wonder they'd all been so strangely silent! I would let them know I was okay. Hopefully, they were all still at Jalil's house.

"It's Layla!" It was Majid's voice.

The boys were in the empty lot across the street. I assumed they had been chasing Tarzan and had forgotten about him when they spotted me. Jalil headed my way and the others followed behind him. They surrounded me.

"Layla? Are you okay?" Jalil asked. He sounded so concerned that I had to chuckle.

"I'm fine." I smiled. Jalil grinned, relieved. "You were right," I said lightly. I touched his arm, aware of the thin film of sweat on his olive skin. "It was nothing to be scared about. Thanks for taking me home."

The other boys milled around me with curiosity and concern apparent in their eyes. Yet, when we made eye contact, they pulled their gaze from mine and put their hands in their pockets or awkwardly crossed their arms.

I walked away and started across the street, then reeled back around and gave them what I hoped was a dazzling smile. I settled a hand on one hip and haughtily sashaying my hips from side to side the way I'd done at home in front of my mirror, I said, "*I* am a woman now." With hips lopsided and my finger pointed, I added, "and don't any of you men forget that."

Six befuddled faces gawked back at me. I threw my head back and laughed, then clapped my hands in excitement. "Come on," I said. "Let's go find Tarzan." I turned and started across the street to the bushes, aware of the new feeling of a pad between my legs and trying to ignore it.

"It's okay to play with us?" Majid called from the sidewalk.

His question made no sense to me. "Don't worry, you won't catch it," I shouted back.

"Does ... um, does your mother know you're here?" he asked.

This time I didn't bother to answer him. If Maman didn't see me in my room, she'd know I was out with the boys.

"Come on." I said. "We can't let Tarzan roam around willy-nilly. Let's find him and take him home. First one to find him wins." With that, I stuck my head into the foliage and began looking for the rooster. The boys hesitated for only a minute before joining me in the hunt.

3
THE OTHER SIDE OF THE MOON

I was the one who found Tarzan.

I lifted the rooster and was about to call out to the others that I'd won when I heard my name being called by Abol, my family's manservant. I could see him standing in our driveway across the street, wearing his usual long, loose white shirt, loose black pants tied at the waist with a thin drawstring, and *guivehs,* cloth slippers with soles made of tire rubber. And there was Fotmeh, scurrying about our front garden, her flowered kerchief wrapped around her head, wearing an apron over one of my ill-fitting hand-me-downs, and shielding her eyes from the sun as she looked up and down the street.

I let go of Tarzan and cupped my hands. "I'm here," I called out. I jumped around and waved my arms until Abol spotted me. When he saw me, he put up his small fat hand, palm facing me, to signal that I should stay where I was, then disappeared into the house. A moment later he returned with Maman, pointed to me, and retreated into the house.

Maman headed toward me like a guided missile, moving fast, despite her high heels and her narrow skirt. The boys scampered into the thick brush. *How strange,* I thought. This was the first time Maman had come outside to get me. I wondered why. When she got closer, I could see she looked angry.

"Child, what are you doing?" She grasped my shoulders. "When did you leave the house? Why did you leave your room?"

I shrugged within her grip. I couldn't imagine why she asked such silly questions. "I went to Shireen's house."

Maman's hands slid down to take hold of my arms. She glanced around quickly. "Shireen isn't home," she said. "She's gone out with Haideh."

"I know, I found out when I got there."

Maman spoke, her tone sharp. "Why didn't you come home?" She hadn't yet seen the boys. She looked around again, slower this time. "What are you doing here?"

"Playing," I said, wondering how she could not know.

That's when she glimpsed Majid and Cyrus in the nearby foliage. She gasped, then grabbed me high up on one arm by my armpit and began to drag me across the street toward our house.

"Maman, what are you doing? I'm okay. Really … I don't need to rest. I want to play … Maman … You're hurting me." She just kept moving silently, towing me along as if I were a slow *khar,* a donkey.

When we passed through the gate that encircled our front garden, Maman brushed past Fotmeh before finally letting go of my arm. Her eyes were fiery. "What is the matter with you, girl? Have you lost your mind? What is in your head? Do you insist on going into your moon and ruining your family's impeccable reputation all in one day?"

My heart was pounding. "Maman, what have I done?"

"How dare you act as if you don't know?" As angry as she was, Maman, probably afraid someone would hear, managed not to shout.

Just then Abol came to the front door to say she had a phone call and ask if she would come inside to take it.

"Don't you dare go past that gate again, do you hear? Stay! You do as I say!"

I could only nod. She left me standing there baffled, and hurried inside, Fotmeh following behind her like a puppy running after its mother.

I crumpled and fell onto the grass with my back against the railing, feeling its iron bars dig into my back, but not caring. *What had I done to upset Maman so*? Hunched down on the ground in fear and confusion, with my hands at my temples, I felt a small rush of blood run onto the pad so new to me. The sound of the approaching boys lifted my head. They didn't see me. Before I could call out to them, I heard them talking as they passed our house.

"I told you we shouldn't have played with her," Majid said.

"We were only going to let her help us catch Tarzan. But I guess you're right. We should have listened to you." It was Cyrus' voice.

"Poor Layla!" That was Jalil.

I sat bewildered, without the slightest idea what they were talking about. Fotmeh opened the front door and called my name. "Layla Khanom, your mother wants you this minute."

I jumped up and ran inside.

Maman was waiting for me, still fuming, a cigarette set between her lips, though Babajon doesn't like her smoking. Taking my hand firmly in hers, she dragged me into my bedroom and slammed the door shut. My heart was racing; Maman did not slam doors.

"What have I done, Maman?"

Maman bent down so her steely dark eyes were only inches away from mine. "You dare ask what you've done? How dare you? Didn't I just finish telling you that you are no longer a child?" She paused. I swallowed.

"*Alhamdo le'llah,* Allah be praised, our luck is that Jalil is the only person that knows you've crossed into your moon. Don't you ever again dare try that! Do you hear me?" She took a deep drag of her cigarette as if sucking out oxygen she needed to survive.

"Try *what*, Maman?"

"You mean you still don't know? How can you possibly not understand?" Maman's eyes searched my room as though hoping to find the words she needed there and came blazing back to me. "You may not be with a boy!"

I wasn't sure I'd heard right.

Maman repeated herself, uncharacteristically loud this time. "*Baalegh shodee.* You've come of age. You may no longer be in the company of a boy alone, unattended, unchaperoned." She looked at me sternly, still speaking loudly. "Do you understand me?"

I was incredulous. "What? Why? I said nothing to them about my moon and my pad was still clean. Really."

She took a short, hurried puff of her cigarette and began to pace, taking small quick steps across the honey-colored silk rug, her heels stabbing the pink and green flowers. She reached the flowered border then turned back and called out for Fotmeh. The girl's knock on the door came so fast, she must have been standing right outside my room. Maman opened the door and handed her the cigarette. Fotmeh took the cigarette, bowed and backed away. Maman closed the door and resumed pacing.

I sat on my bed, petrified, watching my mother and waiting. This was as angry as I'd ever seen her. I spoke to her back, attempting to calm her down. "We were only playing, Maman *jon*."

Maman stopped her pacing. She turned and looked at me and her eyes seemed to quiver. "Playing? You were playing? *You* play, my daughter while *they* linger around you. Boys get excited until soon, they take advantage of you."

"Maman, my friends would never do anything bad to me."

"You silly little girl! You know nothing about boys. Don't be stupid! They would take advantage of you, as they would of any girl dumb enough to let them! They'll win your trust then take advantage of you. If you're lucky, you won't become pregnant from their games."

"*Pregnant?* From playing games with Jalil and Bijan?"

Maman stormed at me. "Yes. Yes! Pregnant!" She threw her hands up as though helpless, something Maman is not. "And if you don't get pregnant, you're *still* ruined. Be so much as seen with a boy and people will say you're indecent. You'll be labeled *dokhtareh kharob,* a damaged girl, and no one will care at all about you anymore – everyone will spit on your head. Either way, you lose everything."

Though I was filled with fear and completely confused, I didn't dare ask any questions. I didn't want to anger Maman further.

"I will not let you disgrace this family. Your future and our family's good name could be lost just like that." Maman snapped her fingers. "How dare you jeopardize all that."

"I would never do that, Maman."

"All it takes is for you to be seen alone with a boy one time – even just *one* boy."

"Can I play with them when I am not in my moon?"

Maman turned to me disbelievingly. "Are you kidding? Have I raised a jackass? Or an idiot? You may never play with boys again!"

I couldn't believe my ears. Was Maman telling me I'd just lost all my friends? I whispered the names. "Bijan? Majid? Cyrus? *Jalil?*"

Maman heard me. "Yes! Yes! YES! BOYS! *All* these boys of yours!

"I tried to keep you from going off to play like one of them a long time ago – when decent girls stop. You refused to play with girls, like Shireen and the others. Do you know how many times women told me I shouldn't be letting you spend time with Bahman's friends? My own mother! And your aunt, Bahia. Even that pig, Elahe. Still, your father permitted it. I couldn't say no to him. He is a *modern man*," she said mockingly. "He said it was *harmless*." Her voice crescendoed. "He said you would *outgrow* it. Well, it is not harmless anymore, Layla. You will stop. Now. *Immediately!*"

Not even Jalil? I was heartbroken but didn't dare speak.

Maman must have known she was asking a lot of me. She resumed pacing, slower now, her shoulders erect, her dark red lips set firm."I must make you understand," she said, "or you'll flounder, and all will be lost." She paused as if weighing the risks involved in continuing and making sure she wanted to take them. "I will tell you about myself without exaggeration or embellishment, so you understand."

There was another slight pause, then she told me this:

"I married your father when I was eighteen. He was twenty-seven and the most sought-after boy in all of Tehran. He could have married any girl. He had spent time studying in America, a college graduate. He was smart, handsome, and a most promising young man with great potential. His family was not wealthy, true ... still, they were highly respected."

This was the first time I'd heard about my parents' relationship before they wed, and I hung on her every word, fascination now rivaling fear, hopeful that sharing this information with me would calm my mother down and make her feel better, as it did me. "Of course, Elahe, his cow of a sister, had not yet married that mule Javeed, a man who proved to be a total failure."

Jila's father, Babajon's brother-in-law, my uncle, Javeed Khan, is a mule? A total failure?

"My family had far more wealth than your father's family, and I was considered a beauty, and–" Maman's long fingers went to her short brown curls. "Well, I was thought to be extraordinary." She paused a heartbeat then continued. "All of that on one side, do you think your father would have married me if he'd thought or suspected for an instant that I'd ever been alone with a boy for a moment? If he'd ever even heard such a thing whispered?"

I squeezed my eyes shut tightly and held my breath. *Please, please, don't say no!*

My mother's voice boomed. "No, he would not! He wouldn't have so much as looked at me." Silence followed the blow to my heart. That was as much of her story as she chose to share.

She shook a finger in my face. "No boys. Do you hear me, Layla?" She emphasized every word. "*You… may… no… longer… play… with… boys!*"

"Can I play with cousin, Bahman?" I whispered, too afraid to look at her.

She didn't hesitate. "Never alone. Only when you are with the family."

She looked down at me and spoke slowly, deliberately. "Layla, generations of our family have spotless reputations My family and your father's family are both highly regarded. You come from an esteemed lineage. I will tell you this: If you ever again risk your family's excellent name like you did today, believe me, for I swear on my soul and to the holiest Quran, you will live to regret it. You will be a decent girl! Do you understand?"

"Yes."

She opened my bedroom door. "You want to play? Play with girls. Is that clear?" I nodded as if in a bad dream. "Yes, Maman."

"I waited too long to separate you from the boys. Well, now. You are warned," she said under her breath. Then she locked eyes with me. "No boys."

Maman left me in my room and went back to her day, leaving me to go on with the remains of my life as best as I could. She no doubt believed she had fulfilled her motherly duty by setting explicit boundaries for me, ensuring that I would behave properly and do justice to the spotless reputations of the women who had preceded me.

When I again leaned out of my bedroom window, only the first glimmer of twilight showed in the summer sky, the crescent moon stepping up to take its place, and the leaves on the mulberry trees turning dark against the deepening blue skies.

The world seemed so peaceful and quiet. Yet, as I changed into my pajamas, I thought back on all that had happened to me in one day. My mother's words repeated themselves *"Women everywhere…"*

With my head on my pillow, I tried not to think about a life without my friends. Images flew through my mind, photographs I'd seen of Indian women dressed in rags, Greek women in flowing white togas, Japanese women dressed in those robes called kimonos, the various tribal women I'd often see outside the city carrying their babies in their colorful village garb, the women on the streets of Tehran and in the mosques, my teachers, my aunts, my two grandmothers, Joan of Arc … and as the list of women grew longer, a feeling of warmth crept over me and I felt a bond between myself and each and every one of them.

My mind drifted and I wondered: *Will I ever get used to this monthly cycle? Can I keep it a secret? What will I do without Bahman and his friends?*

Tears came to my eyes, for I dreaded a world without the boys I so loved. How could I say goodbye to them? I twisted and turned and tried to calm my anxiety without success. My life had changed so much in a day.

What would life be like now? What other surprises awaited me?

I recalled the new sensations I had felt when I'd touched my breasts while looking in the mirror. I slipped my hand under my pajama top and caressed them.

I liked the feeling.

4
MISS SALEH

My father, Hadi Saleh, was a gentle man.

He came to know illness, loss and terrible hardship; yet, though I know he suffered, I never heard him complain. He cherished a difficult woman, and I know he loved me. I think he felt we were alike, and, at least in some ways, perhaps we were.

My beloved Babajon was a self-made man. He founded Saleh Pharmaceuticals, the company that manufactured a family of products, including Galoo Cure, the single most popular cough and cold remedy in Iran, despite the fact that imported medicines were readily available. Later, the company began to import certain medicinal ingredients from abroad, a fact that was to have a profound effect on Babajon's life. He ran Saleh successfully for forty years until the day he was forced to leave it behind to save himself.

I was always happy to spend the day with Babajon at Saleh Pharmaceuticals. The complex, located on the way to Tehran's Mehrabad Airport on Karaj Road, was composed of a manufacturing plant, laboratories, and an office building.

Babajon would let me roam freely around Saleh. Everyone there knew me; many had watched me grow from the time I was a toddler. Everywhere I went at Saleh, I heard stories of my father's kindness.

"May your father's shadow never lessen," was the blessing I heard most often. There was the woman whose young daughter needed critical stomach surgery, which Babajon paid for; the man who couldn't work after his wife's untimely passing because he had to care for his children. Babajon kept him on salary and welcomed him back some six months later when appropriate arrangements for the children's care had been made. The smiles that greeted me at Saleh were mine by association.

Inside Babajon's personal office at Saleh, I would read my books, write poems and wander around the large room soothed by my father's voice as he spoke on the phone or conversed with visitors while sitting behind his desk.

Though Babajon had accumulated diplomas and certificates and both he and his company had been awarded various honors, there was no sign of these in his personal office. On the wall behind his desk hung family photographs: Babajon and Maman sitting with me as an infant in Babajon's arms, a scene of me and Babajon at Mount Damavand, both of us in skiing gear poised on the snowy slopes, and my favorite, a photo of Babajon seated between his mother-in- law, Khanom Bozorg, and Maman at the baccarat table in Monte Carlo. In the photo, Maman is wearing the emerald and diamond necklace Babajon had just gifted her to mark their 10th anniversary. They looked happy.

Another wall had been plastered with every award, honor and citation I'd received from the day I began school. There was also a picture of me at about 5 years of age standing by my father and wearing a white laboratory jacket so big on me that it trailed the floor. There were eight more photos like that set in a line. In each, I stand with my father at my side as I seem to grow into that same white jacket, while I simultaneously grew increasingly fascinated with science and, eventually, with the emerging field of microbiology.

One day, perhaps a week after I'd come into my moon and left my friends behind, I was delighted when Babajon invited me to spend the day at his office.

That morning, as Babak, our driver was pulling away from our house, I glimpsed our new neighbors for the first time. Parveen Shirazi immediately aroused my curiosity. She wore a *chador,* a long piece of cloth that covered her head and fell to the ground covering her entirely, exposing only her hands and face. She trailed her husband, Parveez Shirazi.

Of course, I'd seen women wear *chadors* before, but it was unheard of in our neighborhood. They had been commonplace, until the 's father had discouraged women from wearing them. The present continued to encourage western dress and many women transitioned, wearing a *roosaree,* a simple head scarf, instead of the *chador*. *Chadorees,* women who still insist on wearing the chador in public, gravitate toward their own kind, usually living in the villages or in small pockets of the city.

Encased in her black *chador,* Parveen Shirazi looked like a black crow as she moved along, following several steps behind her husband, one hand holding her chador closed at her chin, the other holding the folds of the cloth together at her torso and taking small steps with her head bent down. I wanted to learn more about her.

Babak turned the corner and soon the Shirazis were lost from sight. We traveled downhill on Niavaran Road, wound around curves, passing our old home and the odd mix of houses in various stages of construction as well as agricultural land and vacant lots. Before us spread the city of Tehran, its poplar trees tall and stately. Dirt roads were beginning to be transformed into asphalt streets with sidewalks of cement. Storefronts were still humble.

We descended into the morning traffic and entered the intersection of Jadeh Shemiran.

Though this was a major intersection, there was no traffic light; there were few traffic lights in the city then. Officers controlled the flow of cars and inevitably allowed Babajon's car the right-of-way. Added to the novelty of seeing a car driven by a chauffeur, our shiny new Buick, recently shipped from America, looked exactly like the Buick in His Imperial Majesty's stable of cars. The original U.S. license plates that came with the car and were still attached to it happened to be yellow and purple, the colors of Persian royalty. With Babajon and I seated in the back seat and our driver in front, we caused quite a stir in city traffic. Whenever we stopped, curious pedestrians would gather round to see if we were members of the royal family. I'd roll the window up and sit as straight as I could, hoping to look regal. Princess naz, the 's pretty daughter by his first wife, Fawzia, was my age, and I hoped to be mistaken for the Princess, although our coloring was totally different, and I looked nothing like her.

Babajon certainly looked important. Women must have thought he was handsome – they were always smiling at him. His paternal grandparents came from the deserts of Iran, in the area around Abadan where people tend to be darker, and he was far browner than Maman or me. His rich brown hair was thick and wavy, and he was always impeccably groomed, his hair trimmed every month and his mustache and nails well-clipped. That morning, he looked elegant in his Swiss-chocolate colored suit and the honey-brown tie that almost matched his deep-set eyes. The French cuffs of his white shirt were fastened with shining gold cufflinks. His wore his heavy gold watch as always.

Curious faces pressed against the back windows of our car and Babajon joined Babak in waving them away. "*Borro, borro aghab,* go, go back!" Though his tone was impatient, his smile was friendly, and his eyes were kind.

As usual, when we came to Maidoneh Shemiran, a square encompassing an open market selling fresh produce, there was a lot to see. Along the fringe of the square were donkeys and mules waiting to carry home the villagers who came from northern Tehran, wearing colorful *chadors* and carrying tight purses. Here, they mixed with the more urbane housekeepers and stylish housewives as the crates of watermelons and cantaloupes mixed with crates of tomatoes and onions. I could hear the vendors, mostly older men with beards of varying lengths, shout out their offerings while children ran about freely, ignored by mothers who were busy finding the food they wanted at the right price.

I saw a man in a pinstriped suit, several sizes too large for him, with a carnation at his lapel, sauntering around the edge of the stalls, eyeing the women from under his black, broad-brimmed hat. An almost toothless old man sat leaning up against a car, spitting out seed shells.

We passed slowly, aware of the vendors, the children playing and the distracted shoppers. Close by, I saw a heavyset woman walking away from the square, her flabby face bouncing with every step. She wore a soiled housedress and had bright pink slippers on. I could see the long black hairs of her legs encased under her nylon stockings. She carried a sack of potatoes over one shoulder and was sucking the juice out of an orange she held with the other hand. Both hands busy, she could do little to stop her scarf from slipping off her head, baring her Marilyn Monroe platinum-blonde bleached hair.

Maidoneh Tajrish, the second square we passed, was much larger. At that early time of day, the square was still quiet. But in an hour or two it would be crowded with people, and alive with a symphony of cries emanating from the stalls of men selling skewers of liver, kidney, chicken, and meat kabobs. On summer evenings, working class husbands and fathers would bring their families and a bottle of vodka to the square for an outdoor dinner; if they had a car, its hood would serve as their dining table. I rolled down my window and put my head out into the intense light of the morning sun.

We soon turned onto Pahlavi Avenue named for the royal family, a busy thoroughfare where buses and taxis wiggled in and out of lanes. Both sides of the new asphalt road had poplar trees planted at regular intervals with *joobs* running alongside them. There were private residences set like hyphens along the way, a multitude of empty lots, and a few small grocery stores interspersed among several smaller shops that sold knickknacks. I'd once been in one of those stores with Maman and Babajon when we had stopped to buy something on our way to their friend's home for dinner.

At Reza we turned right and continued west before connecting to Karaj Road, a primitive highway created from a mix of dirt and rough asphalt. With the city behind us, the desolate road bored me, and I couldn't get to Saleh Pharmaceuticals fast enough. I thought to ask my father why he'd built his business so far from our home. His answer surprised me.

"I'm a gambler."

"Babajon!" He may as well have said he was a cowboy! I'd hardly ever seen my father play cards, while Maman and her brother and sister played at every possible opportunity, at least once a week. And although he played *takhtenar,* also called backgammon, he never got excited when he played, never stood up to roll the dice and scream all kinds of things like his male friends and Dayee Mansoor did.

I smiled up at him. "*Shookhee meekoneed!* You're joking."

"You don't believe me!" He looked bemused.

"What game are you playing?" I asked.

He chuckled. "It's a land game." By way of explanation, he waved his hand loosely at the empty land we passed on both sides of the road. "See all this land? There's a lot of it and I've bought a lot of it. It's very cheap; it won't be cheap forever. This is the way to Mehrabad Airport and this road is a lifeline, one of the major arteries leading to Tehran from the west. See all these trucks and buses? They're taking passengers and provisions to Gazrin and other cities to the west." So far, it didn't sound like a game to me. I waited. "I'm betting that one day, other companies will realize the value of this location and want to build in this area like I did. Then the price of land here will go up. If I'm right and this becomes an industrial area, it will be very good for us," he continued. "Our land value – the land that Saleh is built on and the surrounding land we own – will appreciate nicely."

As it happened, my father won his bet but never collected his winnings.

We continued to travel away from Tehran, picking up speed. I put my head out the window and felt the hot wind blow my hair and press against my face, tugging at my breath and occasionally catching it. Babajon leaned over and pulled at my dress to get my attention, gesturing for me to sit closer. I was happy to nestle at his side. I looked up at him. He was looking at the road ahead and when he spoke it was about his work at Saleh.

"Layla, you know we make many different products that are meant to help people at Saleh," he said. Though he wasn't looking at me, I nodded, and he went on. "Well, there are a lot of employees that help me ... over one hundred. In exchange for their help, I pay them so they're able to take care of themselves and their families. It's very important that we treat these people well; that we deal fairly with them." His arm tightened around me as he looked down at me and repeated, "Very important. Do you understand?" I nodded again. This time he nodded in turn.

Babajon had rarely been so serious with me. There in the back seat of our car, I knew without a doubt that I far preferred his serious moods to Maman's.

"Fortunately," he continued, "business is very good. I have scheduled a meeting today with some people to discuss some possible ways I can help my employees beyond paying them their regular wages. I would like you to join us, listen to what we say and help me make the right decisions."

I was only too happy to be of help to him. "Of course, Babajon," I said.

Upon entering the Saleh offices, we were greeted by Maheen.

Babajon had paid for the stomach surgery Maheen's young daughter had needed. She notified Babajon that his visitors had arrived.

We passed through the hallway and entered the conference room. I saw the two men stand and greet my father, and my enthusiasm immediately vanished; I became shy. They looked dry in their matching black suits. Babajon introduced me, and they smiled as busy men would smile at a business associate's young child, expecting that I would soon go off and leave them to their business.

Babajon sat at the head of the long table and gestured for me to take the seat at the opposite end. I sat, making as little fuss as I could. I recall the look of surprise on the men's faces when my father said, "I've asked my daughter to sit in at our meeting so that she can hear what we have to say and help me decide what I should do." The men stared at my father. They looked at me, then at one another, then at Babajon again and back at me.

I was embarrassed and somewhat sorry I'd agreed to be there. I sat with my arms at my sides and stared at a spot on the table.

Babajon said, "Let's begin."

I listened to their discussion. Soon the two visitors seemed to forget I was there, or perhaps, they simply chose to ignore me. Early on, they suggested Babajon increase the pay of workers who performed better than others. Babajon talked of introducing what I now know amounted to a sort of profit-sharing plan. He made sure I understood everything, simplifying it all. When he'd heard everything he needed, he said, "I can't think of anything else. Let me ask Miss Saleh if she has any questions. Layla, is there anything else we should ask?" The men's eyes shot toward me like bullets.

I shook my head. I hated their sudden attention and wanted desperately to leave. Besides, I was hungry and ready for lunch. Babajon told them he would let them know of our decision after we discussed the situation. I slithered out of the chair. They smiled uneasily, nodding, "Of course, of course," and left.

It was over.

Babajon and I went to lunch. We ordered kabob. While we ate, Babajon asked if I had questions about the discussions, and I shook my head. Then he asked if I had any thoughts. I wanted very much to help him. "You want to let the people who work for you know you like them, make them happy," I said.

"Yes, that's right. That and encourage them to continue to do their best."

"Well, I think that if they work better, they should definitely get more money. That would make them happy. Otherwise, they might leave and go to work somewhere else, like when you told Maman that Abol would leave if we didn't pay him more." My father's bright smile and enthusiastic nod encouraged me to continue. "And you can give them other things, too. When I do well in class, I don't only get a 20 on my report card, I also get awards and papers to bring home and then you hang them up and that makes both of us happy … and Maman.

Maybe you can give them awards and papers for their families to hang up and make their families happy, too."

My father's eyes lit up. He reached over and held my face between his hands. He couldn't stop telling me what wonderful ideas I had and how smart I was. I was thrilled that he found my ideas to be of value. He said he would do exactly as I'd suggested. I tried to imagine the look on the faces of those two dreary men when they heard that! We celebrated with huge desserts that left us both with aching stomachs at dinnertime.

I've since thought back on that day, wondering why Babajon asked me to join him at that meeting.

I've decided that it was his way of bolstering my feelings of self-worth at a pivotal time in my life. The huge social consequences brought on by the physical change I was experiencing could not help but have a tremendous impact on my self-image. Babajon went out of his way to make me feel important.

As much as my father may have appreciated his daughter's intellectual advancement, my mother, Zahra Khanom, sought to stifle it. Maman believed education was only for boys; too much schooling did not become a girl of good breeding for it would make her less marriageable. She had always tried to hide my interest in the sciences from her friends. She blamed Babajon for encouraging my studies. The elegant Zahra Khanom fervently prayed that her daughter's interest in science and then – good heavens, microbiology! – would one day dissipate like a puff of smoke.

5
ZAHRA KHANOM REFLECTS

As I enter the room, I catch a glimpse of myself in the mirror and I'm again struck by my innate poise.

I seem to exude a sense of stately confidence. There is nothing coy in the way I hold my cigarette. I have never aspired to be coquette, and what some may consider to be arrogance is simply my belief that I need not embellish my charms for the benefit of others.

I'm glad Hadi took Layla with him today. I need time to relax without having to see my daughter pout around the house all day. Ever since she's stopped spending time with that gang of boys, she acts as though there's nothing to do. At least, I know that her moping around means that she finally understands what is expected of her. She knows she cannot be with boys.

I enjoy my husband's study, and I look forward to my time alone in this room. Hadi takes business calls and entertains his male visitors here. It is, like all the rooms in my house, large and bright. I sit facing the garden. I place the flowered ashtray I brought with me on the side table and inhale deeply from my cigarette as I look out the large, open window. At this hour, with the sun just so, the view is beautiful. The sun's rays play off the turquoise tiles of the fishpond and fountain. The flowers are abundant both in their color and beauty. Beyond the fountain, there's a view of the city and Golestan palace. I love this house, and these lush gardens surrounding it are the thing I love most. I smell the fragrance of jasmine, wisteria and honeysuckle heavy in the summer air, drifting in through the open window. I begin finally, to relax.

Hadi doesn't like me to smoke and loathes cigarette smoke, but he's at work with his darling Layla. Again! They won't be home until dinnertime, several hours from now.

I've never known a man to spend as much time with his daughter as Hadi does. He adores the girl! At times, the endless love Hadi has for our daughter actually makes me feel queasy. I don't think it's natural for a man to love his daughter that much. After all, my parents' attention and affection forever favored my brother, Mansoor, though I, the eldest child, had been a perfect daughter, and Bahia, the baby of the family, could be sweet.

I suppose I should thank Allah that my husband is what he calls "democratic," seeing no difference between having a son or a daughter. He has never so much as hinted that he would have preferred to have a son or that he feels the lack of one. When the doctors told us that I could not conceive a second time, his only thought was to comfort me. He has never suggested that he might have wanted another child. Yet despite his silence, I know I have failed him in the worst way.

Every time I stand in the confines of my bathroom and see my nakedness reflected back at me, I see the body of a woman who has failed to produce a male child. Surely every man deserves a son, and Hadi is a good man. The knowledge that he could have at least one strong son if he had married another woman makes me – though I would never admit it to a living soul – insecure. And that insecurity infuriates me for it is my sole shortcoming.

I suspect my husband showers Layla with the kind of love he would have given to the son he doesn't have. I certainly don't fault Hadi for loving Layla. I love her too; after all, she's *my* daughter as well. And she is lovely. I simply wish she were more like me, or at least more like her cousin Shireen and other girls I see. But she never was. Even as a young child, she'd rather have been swinging from a tree than coloring or playing tea party with the other girls. And, oh! How she loathed playing with dolls! Every single one she was ever gifted went right under her bed never to be touched again. She's never asked to try on my lipstick, and she doesn't even like shopping for pretty dresses. Why wouldn't I worry about her?

Yet Layla doesn't pout and complain like her cousin Shireen constantly does. The way she whined when she went into her moon was so unlike her! I never expected Layla to act like that. Nor had I expected her to enter into her moon quite yet. How old was I when my dear mother prepared me? I can't recall … I think I was definitely older than Layla … wasn't I?

Anyway, I don't like surprises and I certainly didn't enjoy dealing with her mess, nor did I like her unbecoming attitude, so like a sniveling child. And the questions she asked! She gets perfect 20s in every subject at school, yet she asked the silliest questions. Ah, such is my due for having a daughter!

Yet, in the end, I did a good job. I can't believe what a donkey she was to go out afterwards and find those boys. *Devoneh!* Crazy! So smart and yet so stupid! Hadi let her play with that pack far too long! I warned him. *Ensha'Allah,* God willing, hopefully, that's all behind us now. I'm certain she will behave properly from here on.

I'm actually delighted that Layla has come into her moon. *Mushallah!* Praise God! It's time she understood the privileges of being a woman, pampered in return for this monthly cycle, for the flower she will give to her husband, and for childbirth. She will learn, from watching me, the magic of being a woman, the power of it. Not all at once, of course; she is still too young to understand all that. But in time, she'll change. Perhaps we two will grow closer as she comes to respect and appreciate me more. Soon she may even prefer to go shopping with me rather than spending the day with Hadi. *Ensha'Allah!* God willing!

I *must* impress upon Hadi how important it is for him to stop encouraging Layla's interest in science. He's overly proud of her academic accomplishments. He thinks she's a marvel. Silly man! Whenever she brings home science awards, his face beams. He actually hangs all her citations on a wall in his office! How ridiculous! Really! Who cares?

There's no point in nurturing her academic interest. It will only stoke the fire, murky up her mind with unrealistic ideas. No woman of any class studies science! *Cheh begam?* What can I say? It's difficult to be a woman and far more difficult to be the mother of a girl like Layla.

I look around me and I am proud of my house. It is a testament to Hadi's superior standing in the community, his fine judgment and impeccable taste – all of which, of course, reflect well on me. Hadi built this house in the hills above our old Shemiran summerhouse. We would escape to that house from our home in the flats every year to avoid the city's sizzling temperatures. The Alborz Mountain Range unrolls into these lush, verdant, and naturally shaded foothills before continuing on to the flat land of the city where scorching temperatures of the dry summer months are unbearable. Hadi had been one of the first to move to the hillside year-round. As he'd predicted, others followed suit. As new construction began scrambling up the hill, he built *this* house perched even higher up in the hills in Niavaran, sold our home in the flats and rented out our home in Shemiran.

There was only one feature in the design of this house that was initially not to my liking: Hadi had insisted on doing away with the traditional wall that separates a house from the street. The short black iron railing at the boundary of our front garden is as much of a partition he would erect. My husband Hadi, The Pioneer, only laughed when I objected. "There is no one in these streets that we need to hide from, *omram,*" he said, calling me 'his life,' his term of endearment. "And look around you, *omram,* we have the gardens to separate us. Besides, what is the point of living on a hill with such lovely views of the Golestan Palace and all of Tehran if we are to block any of it off with a wall?"

I told myself that he would eventually relent and build the wall. Now, as I see the view of Tehran beyond the lovely gardens, I am content with the house the way it is.

I admire the décor of this room. I have furnished every room of my house with exquisite taste, and they are all impeccable; cleanliness has always been important to me. I check every room in the house daily to be certain everything is clean and in its proper place. I run my finger along the top of the exquisitely carved Spanish desk, a rare find I presented to Hadi when he'd finished building the house for me; it is free of dust.

The new servant girl is so good that I'm beginning to believe I've struck gold with her. Hadi thought she was too young to be our maid – I would guess her to be perhaps a year older than Layla. But I saw the benefits that came with her youth and fought to have her stay.

"Why, I bet she's not even thirteen," Hadi had said when he first heard of my plan to bring Fotmeh into our household. The girl's age was of little consequence to me. I remember that day well. It was a Friday, the start of the weekend. Hadi had suggested we spend the day in Vallian, the village I inherited from my father and now share with Hadi. As Vallian's *arbob,* lord of the land, of one thousand five hundred acres of fertile land and manage over two thousand five hundred *dehatees,* peasants who live in the village and farm the land.

"It will be a lovely day for a drive," he said. "Have Cobra pack us a picnic. We'll have lunch at the villa, just the two of us."

The next morning when the bread was delivered daily, fresh and still warm, I had Cobra pack a simple lunch for our picnic and empty baskets to bring fruit home in. We dropped Layla off at Shireen's house and set out on the road to Vallian.

I've always been fond of our villa in the village that sits atop the highest hill in Vallian.

Whenever the three of us spend a weekend there, memories of times I'd spent in the villa's many rooms with my own parents, my brother Mansoor and my younger sister Bahia come flooding back. Hadi is happiest when we spend a full week or more at the villa. He loves to tend to his herbs and vegetables in the garden there. I prefer short stays; I don't like to go too long without seeing my hairdresser and manicurist in Tehran.

That Friday, we drove past huts with sunbaked walls of mud and past roadside shops before stopping at the open stalls at the village square where we bought gifts of meat and produce for Ali and his wife. Those who recognized us as *arbob,* owner of the land they lived and worked on, scrambled to bow before us and kiss our hands as they always do. Purchases made, we headed for our villa and, as we drove away, our devotees, as usual, threw kisses our way and called out for Allah to protect us.

I had sent word to Ali, the caretaker of our villa in Vallian, that I'd been looking for a maid and was open to the idea of relocating a hard-working girl from the village. I was eager to know if he'd found a candidate. Though we arrived at the caretaker's small cottage at the foothill of our villa unannounced, Ali had heard our car approach and was standing outside ready to greet us. He was dressed as Abol dresses, in a loose faded shirt and baggy black pants held up with a colorful string and *guivehs,* shoes of woven cloth with soles made from rubber tires. He greeted us with a broad smile showcasing a broken front tooth. When our driver passed him the bags filled with our gifts of food, Ali took Hadi's hand in his, kissed it, then kissed his own fingertips and threw the kiss to the heavens.

"Health to you, Master Agha Arbob and to you, Khanom Arbob. May God remember you and walk alongside you both. Please come inside and bless our humble home." The villager was so excited that I was certain the man had smelled the envelope of money Hadi had for him in his suit pocket.

I loathe entering the hovel of a lowly *dehatee* and usually wait for Hadi outside. Nevertheless, that day I was anxious to know if Ali had found the girl I'd asked for, so I followed my husband inside. When we entered, Ali's wife – Gita or Gity, I can't be bothered with the silly woman's name – got up off the floor where she had been sitting with her daughters and carried the only chair in the house across the room, moving as fast as her heavy body allowed. It was an old, beat-up chair that had, like her, seen better days, not in this house. The woman greeted us and expressed her "undying gratitude" for our gifts of food. I turned away, repulsed by her dark mustache and the hair sprouting from a large brown mole on her chin.

"*Befarmayeed,* please, sit down," Gita or Gity, gestured. "May your feet rest on our eyes. *Cheh begam?* What can I say? You have brought light and many blessings to the home that you so generously provide for us. May Allah protect you for all the many kindnesses you have shown to our family. May He never shorten the shade you cast over our heads...." And so on.

Of course, I wouldn't dream of sitting on that filthy chair. "I do not care to sit," I said dryly. I was about to ask Ali if he'd found me a girl when Hadi beckoned him to a corner of the small room, leaving me alone with our hostess.

I couldn't bear to look her. When she offered me a cup of tea, I didn't bother to *tarroff,* to go through the ritual of graciously declining the offering several times as etiquette required so as not to impose. I simply didn't answer; she seemed not to notice.

As the peasant put water in a blackened pot to boil over coals, I eyed her five daughters sitting on the floor around their cloth *sofreh* having lunch, dipping *non* into the steaming pot of soup made from sheep fat boiled in water, seasoned with salt, pepper and turmeric. Black flies circled the pot waiting for opportune moments to land on its rim. I looked away from the vile scene and pretended I hadn't noticed that the five girls were staring at me. I was probably the only city woman, the only lady of standing, they had ever seen.

I turned from the girls to fix my gaze through the tiny window to the view of our car outside and was taken over by a feeling of devastation as the needling realization pushed its way into my consciousness that this lowly woman and I shared a common shame: neither of us had been able to present our husband with a son. That thought soon collided with the realization that this poor, ugly woman who had *five* daughters with another child quite obviously on the way lived little better than a street dog while I lived with every possible comfort and was loved by a man as wonderful as Hadi. I felt momentarily paralyzed, overtaken by waves of shame and gratitude.

Hadi returned with Ali trailing him. The lowly villager stood erect before me. I looked at his unshaven face and his dirty skin, tarnished by the hot sun. My eyes traveled from his cracked lips and broken tooth beneath his dark mustache to the dull brown eyes set under dark, bushy brows with hairs extending out towards me. He spoke demurely, subservience oozing out of him.

"Khanom Arbob." He bowed slightly. "I have done as you asked. I have the most perfect girl to work for your esteemed family." He said 'most perfect' almost dreamily as if speaking of a magnificent sunset. "You will find no one better for your purposes than my eldest daughter, Fotmeh."

Suddenly changing his tone, he called out a booming, commanding curt, "Fotmeh, *beeya*!" beckoning his eldest daughter, Fotmeh. She rose from the floor. He clicked his slippered heels together and bowed before me a second time, this time with his hand at his heart. "My daughter will sacrifice her soul if you allow her the chance to be your servant."

The young girl stuffed the last of her *non* between her dusk-colored lips and licked her palms, drying them against her sides before coming to stand by her father. She wore the typical attire of a *dehatee* girl, a loose dress over her *tomboon,* baggy pants. Her mud-colored hair fell out from under her soiled *roosaree,* the headscarf she wore in place of a full *chador*. She was dark, like her father, and barely came up to his chest. Her eyes looked sultry, as though her makeup had smudged, and her two brows almost joined. But what caught my attention was Fotmeh's forehead for it extended far above her eyebrows before reaching the dark hairline tucked under the *roosaree*. My mother had believed that a female with a high forehead brought luck to her household. I watched the girl wipe her mouth clean with the corner of her headscarf. Clearly, she had a lot to learn. I would teach her all she would need to know. She would be my maid.

Hadi looked at Fotmeh then at me and then at Ali with squinted eyes. "Are you joking?" he asked Ali. "Why, this child can't be much older than my own Layla," he said. "A maid? She should be in school!"

"She is fifteen, Agha Arbob." Ali said.

"Fifteen?" It was obvious my husband didn't believe him; nor did I.

Ali's wife joined us, carrying a metal tray with two chipped cups filled with tea. She set the tray on the table, close to Hadi. "To the soul of Mohammad, my daughter is fifteen!" she echoed, a closed fist at her heart.

"She must finish school." Hadi boomed.

"Agha Arbob, my child's school was lost in the recent floods," Ali said

"Well then, send her to school in the next village." Hadi said, forever encouraging education, and responding as though that was the obvious solution. "It's not so long of a walk from here."

Ali's eyes were cast down. "I have taken her there, Agha. The class is filled," he said. Then raising his gaze to Hadi, he said, "Besides, what better education can she have than to live within your esteemed shadow in Tehran? To live in the big city under the generous kindness of our Agha Arbob and his Khanom. She would forever thank God for her good fortune." He looked up as if expecting a sign from Allah that his prayer would be answered.

Fotmeh unexpectedly smiled at me, transforming her angular face into a moment of softness, then glanced at Hadi before quickly averting her gaze to the ground. When Hadi shook his head, Ali continued, "Please, Arbob Khan, understand me." He was pleading now. "There are too many mouths to feed here. If I had sons, it would be different. *Agha arbob,* they are all girls. Five of them."

"Don't I take good care of you and your family?" Hadi asked.

The man immediately fell to his knees in front of us and kissed Hadi's hand. "Oh, praise be to Mohammad and all his posterity, Agha, you are the most generous *arbob* in the history of the world, and my family is eternally indebted to you and Khanom Arbob for your kindness. But – *mushallah!* Allah be praised! – *another* child is now coming. *Ensha-Allah,* Hopefully, this one will be a blessed son."

I itched to speak my mind then, to say to this mulish man, "*Bee sapod!* You ignorant man! It's your own fault; why don't you stop? And why does your sheep of a wife continue to lie down for you?" Of course, I said nothing. I only wanted the man's daughter. Yet I had little use for a dimwitted maid. "What can your daughter do?" I asked her mother coolly.

It was the caretaker who answered eagerly, like a fish jumping out of the river to meet the fisherman's bait. "The last of the prophets, Mohammad himself, is my witness. I swear. Fotmeh can do anything. Fortunately, she takes after her mother and is quick to learn. She is strong and able-bodied. And she requires very little. You won't find any better."

Hadi turned to me, his squinting eyes brimming with curiosity. I read the silent questions he asked: *Why ask what she can do? You are not taking his proposal seriously, are you?* I met his gaze; I was taking it very seriously. My husband turned back to Ali then, shaking his head and waved his hand dismissively. "Enough of this talk. I'm sorry. The idea is preposterous. My wife and I will go to the villa now," he said.

Ali's face slackened with evident disappointment. His wife chewed her lip and slapped the top of one hand with the other in despair. She retired to the far side of the room and sat on the floor with her back against the wall and wrung her hands.

Hadi continued, oblivious to their distress. "Now, Ali, we've brought baskets to fill up with fruit. There might still be some peaches not yet overripe. Pick what looks good to you – figs and whatever else – and bring them to the villa where we will be having lunch." Ali bowed humbly.

My husband thought the conversation about Fotmeh was closed, but it wasn't. I wasn't about to let this opportunity go by. He didn't deal with our house servants, *I* did. I had the right to do as I pleased in that domain, and what pleased me was to try out Fotmeh as my maid. I said nothing more in front of the caretaker and his family.

We drove to our villa at the very top of the green, tree-filled hill. As always, the large house, set against the lush earth and the azure sky, looked inviting. I freshened up, then waited on the veranda that swung around the house while Hadi went to the kitchen and prepared a plate for the driver, then carried out our lunch on a tray. We drank wonderful wine from Shiraz with our lunch and enjoyed the view, now serene and unobstructed, almost totally green. Come nighttime, it would turn pitch black with only pinpricks of starlight and a handful of scattered lights to mark the village below.

When we finished our meal, I again spoke of Fotmeh. "Hadi, I want Fotmeh to come home with us." His look prompted me to add, "I'm serious."

"Have you gone mad? Did you see her? They're lying about her age. She's a child. I'll bet she's not even twelve."

"What does it matter?" I asked. "Their kind never has accurate birth certificates. She is as old as you or I guess she is."

"She should be in school," he said resolutely, taking a fistful of pistachio nuts out of the bag on the table.

"Didn't you hear what Ali said?" I asked. "She's finished with school."

He popped a pistachio nut into his mouth, expertly broke it open between his teeth and expelled the shells. "Then she should be with her family," he countered. "How can you think she could be a maid? She's so young. And what can she do? She has no experience."

"Exactly! That's why I want her, Hadi. You don't know my difficulties in training maids. First I have to *un*train these girls of the sloppy training they get before they come to me."

He continued enjoying the pistachios, assured he would convince me to change my mind. "The girl is just a child." He said again as if I hadn't realized the obvious. "We will find someone else from the village."

Had had set forth his objection. Now it was up to me to show him how sensible my view was. "It's her youth that makes her so pliable," I said.

I looked out over the expanse of green. "Hadi *jonam*, my dear, if she doesn't work out, we'll give her some money, bring her back here, and that will be the end of it. On the other hand, if she should work out, it would be my dream. I might very well never need to replace her. What do we have to lose?"

"What do we have to lose?" Hadi sat back on the divan, a hand on each thigh and stared at me. "Hah! What do we have to lose?" he repeated. "I'll tell you what. The girl is utterly naïve. She's also coming of age. What if you bring her under our wing and she goes looking for a boy? Or some boy in the neighborhood seduces her and she wants to give it to him? A girl like that, raised by illiterate parents like Ali and his wife! Woman, do you know what would happen?" He leaned towards me. "The girl will lose her virginity, and they'll blame you and me! We'd be blamed for disgracing her family." He pointed to the bottom of the hill. "*Omram*, these people are religious fanatics. Ali down there," he said jutting his chin towards the caretaker's hut, then made a circle over his head."and his brothers, his clan and the whole village will be at our door screaming. They'll rip her apart. They'll kill her to save face. And then, rest assured, they'll kill you and me as well, for allowing her corruption even if she's taken against her will; even if we try to stop her."

Hadi was right, of course. All too many village girls caught with a man are murdered in the name of family honor by those who profess to love them and that includes girls unlucky enough to be raped, despite stab wounds and obvious signs of attempts to defend themselves.

I weighed the potential longevity and loyalty of a young, competent servant that I could custom tailor and train, against the chance that the scenario my husband had just described would come to pass. I decided I was ready to take that risk.

"I will control her," I said calmly. "I can control our daughter, and I can control this Fotmeh. I want her, Hadi, get her for me." I went to him and brushed his forehead with a kiss. "Please."

"Woman, I think you're making a mistake. The girl will be the death of us or she won't work out."

"Then we will bring her home and spend a lovely weekend here," I said, ignoring his suggestion of death. The silence of concession broke with a long sigh signaling my husband's concession.

Just then, Ali arrived at the villa. The baskets of fruit he'd gathered on the grounds – peaches, plums and figs – were loaded on his donkey. "Does my humble caretaking of your home meet with Khanom Arbob and your own approval, Agha Arbob?"

Hadi's answer was to dig into his breast pocket for the envelope of cash he'd brought and hand it to Ali. The villager smiled broadly. But the news that his daughter would be accompanying us back to Tehran made him jubilant.

"I can see you and your wife are strained right now," Hadi said. "This needn't be a permanent change. Your daughter can return when her school reopens. Meanwhile, a stay in Tehran may be a good change for her."

"Allah is merciful," the man said, obviously thrilled. He stole a quick glance at me then kissed his fingers after touching his benefactor with them and bent down so low in front of his *arbob* that his nose grazed the floor. I was not surprised to see Hadi's embarrassment.

And, though he had acquiesced to my wish, I could read my dear husband's misgivings on the set of his face.

And so, that very afternoon Fotmeh was put in our car along with the baskets of fruit Ali had gathered for delivery to the Saleh home. The girl brought absolutely nothing with her other than instructions "to obey Agha Arbob and Khanom Arbob one hundred percent or never be seen by your parents again." She was to persuade us daily that she was worthy of our kindness. "Be loyal, faithful and obedient to your masters and praise Allah every day in all of your prayers that He has smiled down on you so magnanimously."

The ride to the city was Fotmeh's first automobile ride, and she could barely sit still in the car as we drove home.

Our neighborhood elicited gasps from her. Our house was, of course, unlike anything the village girl had ever even dreamed of. She stood in our foyer as if in a trance. I instructed her to strip and throw every item of clothing into the garbage, then bathe and shampoo twice. Afterwards, I dressed her in one of Layla's old dresses. She was accustomed to going barefoot and pleaded with me to let her forgo shoes. Of course, that was impermissible, but I allowed her to wear a pair of Layla's soft slippers temporarily – only as a transitional measure.

When I replaced her ragged and dirty *roosaree* with one of my own, least favorite scarves, the child first pressed it against her nose and inhaled deeply, caressed it and then cried tears of gratitude before delicately folding it into a triangle and tying it around her head. And when she realized the small room we were standing in was her bedroom, and hers alone, she swore she would do anything required to stay in this magical place forever.

Later that first evening, when Hadi brought Layla home and the village girl saw our daughter, she immediately retracted into herself like a jungle animal in sudden danger. That was a few short weeks ago. Since then, she has eyed Layla as if my daughter were of a different species. That's good. She's my maid and not here to become Layla's friend, though I know my soft daughter, who ignores class distinctions, will try to befriend her.

She has proven ideal at keeping my house clean. Of course, I won't let her know she's good. It is important that I keep her constantly trying harder, or she will forget her place and develop airs like the servants I've had before her. *No, not Fotmeh!* I won't let that happen.

I remove the ashtray from the room then reach for a bottle of perfume I have secreted in a corner of a bookshelf in the room. I stretch, reaching past the complete set of Rumi's poetry and past Hafez's complete '*Deevon*.' Hadi truly believes these two books written by the poet-mystics of Islam's Sufi brotherhood hold the secrets of life.

I find what I'm looking for on the top shelf and the shadow of a smile passes across my face. *Perfect! I'll show her the dust here and see what she has to say for herself.*

Pleased, I smooth down my skirt, and set out to confront Fotmeh, the dusty book held tightly in my hand.

6

BITTERSWEET

When I was young, I idolized Maman.

To me, Zahra Khanon was the ultimate woman: beautiful and composed, always elegantly dressed, and graceful. I knew Babajon adored her, and I genuinely believed she loved us both unconditionally. It wasn't until I was older that I came to truly know my mother. Then, there was much about her that I didn't like. I realized she was quite unsophisticated and that she was wrong about many things. Still, she was right about one thing: I did grow accustomed to my monthly cycle.

It was far more difficult to grow accustomed to the amputation of the boys from my life, and I was forever looking for ways to fill up the void left by their absence. I was to some extent distracted by my schoolbooks and homework, for I did love my classes. I also began writing poetry. My teachers said I showed talent. Once a week, I went to the movies with my cousin Shireen, not because I particularly enjoyed her company, but because we both enjoyed movies so much. Besides, spending time with her was convenient as she was my schoolmate, family, and lived only a few houses away. I accompanied Babajon to Saleh Pharmaceuticals as often as possible, and, as time went on, I spent more and more time in the laboratories there. Yet I always longed to be with my old friends.

There were entire days I didn't venture beyond the front gate of our house and wondered what adventures Bahman and the boys were up to. I yearned to share their unfettered freedom, running on rooftops, playing with stones, climbing trees, brandishing branches … and I wondered if any of them missed me as much as I missed them. In any event, neither they nor I could do much to change the situation. I had accepted the fact: That fateful summer day in Jalil's basement marked my inevitable separation from them. With the first trickle of blood, an invisible wall had sprung up between us and we stood on either side of it, unable to ignore it. So, when from time to time, I asked Cousin Bahman about his friends and he politely replied that they asked after me, I sent them my regards while keeping my distance, for I had changed. I had become a young lady, and my life had changed along with me.

One afternoon, Parveen and Parveez Shirazi, our new neighbors whom I'd first glimpsed when I was in the car with Babajon, invited my parents and me to their home for tea.

I was eager to find out more about the woman who wore the black chador. The fragrance of rose water permeated their home. Parveen Khanom wore the chador atop her street clothes though she was at home, because of the presence of my father, an unrelated male. Up close, her features, partially hidden, and yet framed by the black cloth, hinted at a beautiful face.

Parveez Shirazi seemed nice enough. He was obviously much older than his wife, olive-skinned, with a forehead that extended to the center of his scalp and a belly that obviously carried too much weight under his stretched white linen shirt. The couple had an adorable two-year-old son named Reza, whom Parveen Khanom affectionately called *mommy jon*. As soon as we arrived, Reza began pulling my hand, wanting me to play with him. I'd never before played with a toddler, and thoroughly enjoyed myself.

After that day, I returned to the Shirazi home quite regularly to play with Reza and later also with his younger brother Mohammad, born two years later.

I recall the first time I went to the house by myself and saw Parveen Khanom without her chador. I was in awe of her exquisite beauty. Her raven-colored hair framed a creamy complexion, and her small, delicate face was a perfect oval with a chiseled nose, rosebud lips, and enormous eyes the color of sable, fringed with dark, lustrous, curling lashes. She looked like the beauties I'd seen portrayed in the fresco paintings at the Chehel Sotoon Palace in Isfahan, the Palace of Forty Pillars, built when Isfahan was the capital of Iran and named for the 20 slender pillars on the veranda that double in the reflection of the pool situated before it. The women in those frescoes were defined by their grace and delicacy.

I came to admire Parveen Khanom, and developed a great affection for her. She was 20 years old when I first met her and was compassionate, good-hearted and universally loving. She was also devoutly religious, as evidenced by the chador, an anomaly at that time for city women. She always wore it when she left her home and always in the presence of men other than Parveez Khan. She read the Quran daily and prayed several times a day, fasted for the month of Ramadan, gave alms, and had made the pilgrimage to Mecca. Whenever I was at her home at prayer time, Parveen Khanom would quietly excuse herself while I busied the boys, then would reappear with an aura of such serenity about her that I wondered why my mother and father and I, also Muslims, did not pray daily. There was much I didn't understand.

She once told me, "I was sixteen when my blessed father married me to the honorable Parveez Khan who was then thirty-four – may it please Allah that I be sacrificed for him, may he live to be one hundred and may he never want for shade – and my kind husband has watched over me since the day I met my good fortune in becoming his wife."

She often traveled home to Shiraz to visit her family: her mother, her father who was an *ayatollah*, a Muslim cleric of the highest order, her three sisters and her two brothers, both *mullahs*, Muslim clerics. Shiraz, a beautiful city, famous for its many beautiful parks and gardens, is known as "the city of poets, wine and roses," and and the birthplace of two of Iran's most popular poets, Saadi, born around the turn of the 12th century, and Hafez who died in 1389.

It has always seemed odd to me that the work of both poets is filled with references to wine, which, if not forbidden by the Quran is definitely discouraged within the text; it is saved for consumption in Heaven along with access to an abundant number of virgins. One of Hafez's most popular verses begins,

Sit near my tomb with wine and music.
Feeling your presence, I shall leave my coffin.
Rise softly, moving creature; let me dwell on your beauty.

Hafez was a true believer of Allah. In fact, "Hafez" is an honorific title that denote one who has successfully committed the Quran to memory. I continued to wonder why such a religious man would use wine to symbolize life's beauty. Why not milk? or unfermented nectar? I wanted to ask my neighbor this question and others as well. *What, if anything, does the Quran say about the separation of the sexes? Is it specifically written that when a girl comes into her moon she must stay away from boys?* I didn't ask. In my childish embarrassment I was ashamed to admit that I didn't know the answers, and I was afraid that my ignorance of the Quran would reflect badly on my parents.

Playing with the two young boys became one of my life's delights. I taught them some of the games I used to play with the boys and did things with them that I'd never done before, like flying a kite. I think I had more fun with Reza and Mohammad than they had with me!

Despite all the time I spent with my neighbor, she remained a fascinating enigma to me. My curiosity about her was endless. *How could a woman as pretty as Parveen Khanom be content to hide her beauty from the world under a chador?* I tried to imagine cousin, Shireen, hiding under a chador or Maman covering her coiffure and stylish clothes under one. *Impossible!*

Having tea at the Shirazi home was wonderful. Though I was almost twelve when we first met, Parveen Khanom gave her servant instructions that tea was to be served in the salon as though I was an adult guest. The girl served us the jasmine tea I so loved from a lovely porcelain teapot set on a tray. The sweet blossoms grew on meandering vines all along Parveen Khanom's backyard and along our shared backyard trellis. Their strong fragrance was everywhere in summer. The tray also held hot water in a larger pot and two glasses in silver filigree holders, and set around the glasses were various sweets, including dates and rock sugar.

And so, the years passed. It was 1956.

Adults talked about Egypt's bold seizure of the Suez Canal. Dwight D. Eisenhower was re-elected president of the United States. Morocco won its independence from France and a young, bearded man named Fidel Castro began a revolution in Cuba. We kids were crazy about Elvis Presley's two hits and mimicked his swiveling hips as we danced to "Hound Dog" and his deep voice singing, "Don't Be Cruel." Tehran's moviegoers were lining up to see "Bus Stop" starring Marilyn Monroe. Photographs of the and his glamorous wife Soraya were everywhere with newspapers and magazines covering their visit to Russia.

Our household had received word that Fotmeh's mother had given birth to her sixth child, born after Fotmeh left home, another daughter. Now, with their seventh child, Allah had at last delivered the long-prayed for son. They named the boy Enayatollah, meaning 'God's mercy and blessing.'

"Maybe now they'll stop," Maman said when we heard the news. Fotmeh heard the comment but didn't react in the slightest. To mark the happy occasion, Babajon sent the caretaker and his wife what Maman thought was a too-generous gift of money.

I attended an all-girls' school.

At fifteen, the closest I came to boys were at chaperoned gatherings where, under the watchful eyes of teachers or parents, we would sit and talk in groups and dance at parties, apart in the Persian style, and closer in the European style, with adults literally at our elbows – cautiously, conservatively, barely holding hands.

As time passed, and we girls and boys began to burst into our sexuality like popcorn kernels exposed to heat, these gatherings became hotbeds of simmering hormonal activity. Everything – even the most innocent unintended touch of a hand or a lingering glance – took on a sensual subtext for us.

I became aware of subtle communication passed with a look or the subtlest movements of a pair of lips. A breath that happened to land on my neck while dancing would make my body tingle. If I saw one of my old friends at these events our early friendships took on a new patina, as if we were playing a new game that made us both shy.

Lunchtime chatter at school was usually all about boys. A boy we'd passed on the street, a stranger, might dare to make a sly or brazen remark to one of us girls walking by, like "May I be sacrificed for your beautiful ass." If we liked the boy, we'd giggle quietly. Whether we liked him or not, the next day we would report the incident over lunch to the other girls. Perhaps a boy in the bookstore or on a bus had stealthily handed a startled girl a scribbled note, "Meet me on the corner of such-and-such tomorrow at 8." She didn't go, of course. Nonetheless, she brought the note to school for us the next day to see and gasp over. Girls debated the cutest boy, the best-looking soccer player and the sexiest movie star.

Yet, despite all the talk and carrying on, from the day I'd come into my moon, I was never alone with a boy.

"Stay away from boys. They will ruin your life if you let them…they lose control…"

My mother's words gathered in my mind, lodged themselves in the deepest crevices of my consciousness, and eventually created a deep well of fear that was nurtured wherever women gathered.

Mothers would put their heads together with aunts and grandmothers, whispering to one another when men were near and shouting passionately to each other when they were not, hurling lurid curses back and forth about the woman who had most recently shamed herself. She was a *jendeh*, a whore...the worst of the *najess*, the filthy, and she'd been disgraced by her inability to stay decent, to keep away from men, and had utterly failed to be a *khanomeh sangeen*, a woman of proper deportment. The women chronicled the misery that befell the married woman seen in the company of another man, or the unmarried woman who had been eyed alone with a man.

There was a pattern to the demise of these indecent women. First, their sin was discovered – always, discovered. The sinner was thrown out of the house by her husband, left homeless and penniless, with no rights left to her under either her marriage contract or the law, and forever forbidden to have contact with her children. If the transgressor thought to return to her parents' home they shunned her too, for she had shamed not only herself but their name and them as well.

I wondered, *where did these women go*? My young mind imagined them being dragged along dirt roads lined with crowds calling them names on their way to death by stoning ... or, if they escaped that fate, wandering aimlessly, abhorred by good people wherever they went, and living worse than street dogs, in rags, hiding in dank cellars, emaciated and exhausted, not daring to sleep lest they be bitten by scorpions lurking in the dark or raped and beaten to death while they slept.

And I puzzled, *Why? Why did these women venture so close to the edge that they fell off?*

They had once lived lives as good as those of the women now gossiping about them. *Why did they let themselves get caught up in men's tricks? Were they missing some important component that better women like my mother had?* Though I knew Maman – and Khanom Bozorg and Naneh Joon – would ever come to such a fate – I didn't know *why*. I didn't know what made the sinners different from other women. And, as long as I didn't know the answer to that question, I harbored a sickly trepidation, for I didn't know what kind of woman *I* would prove to be. I didn't know if one day *I* would get caught in a net of temptation.

Would women one day share gossip about me, calling up my name in disgust, hurling ghastly curses at me and pitying my family?

The possibility that I might eventually prove to be indecent, *najess,* and shamed, shook me to my core and it was that fear that girdled me into tolerating all the rules of decorum appropriate to a young Muslim woman of my station and rigidly abiding by those rules without question and without protest.

It was made clear to me that only by remaining a virgin for my husband would I be assured of a secure future with a home and family, a place of respect in the community, and a lifestyle reflecting my family's worth. No one bothered to explain what "virgin" specifically meant. I only knew that it was vital to stay away from boys, so I assumed that no man other than my husband was to be alone with me, kiss me, touch my body or see me naked. I was to remain *baakerreh,* untouched.

I began watching Maman more attentively than ever, scrutinizing everything about her, in the hope of identifying the key to safety and survival. I came to appreciate how truly strong she was, how confident in her views. Her home was definitely *her* domain. She was adored by her husband as much as I imagined any woman could be. She always had her way with people. The only time she backed down was in disagreements with Babajon; I saw how she underplayed her strength around him. Yet, even though I couldn't recall her contradicting him, she usually managed to have her way with him in the end as well. She seemed infallible.

Was that her secret? And I had to wonder, would I ever be like her?

The cardinal rule was clear: I was to remain a virgin until marriage. I was determined to do that. My mother had adhered to this tradition as had her sister, mother, grandmother and great- grandmother before her, and there was every reason to believe that I would accept and pass on the torch of tradition, keeping it alive and sacred from one generation to the next.

What had not considered, was that neither my mother nor the others in my line had been where I would one day find myself.

7
SWEET SHIREEN

Forced to cut my cousin Bahman and his friends out of my life, I found myself spending more time with his sister, Shireen.

Like all my friendships with women in the years to come – except for my angel, Ferri – my friendship with Shireen was born of circumstance.

Shireen's mother, Haideh Khanom, and Maman were pregnant with the two of us at the same time and when we started school, Shireen and I became classmates. Shireen's father, my dayee Mansoor Khan, was Maman's brother. A year after we'd moved into our new home in Niavaran, Mansoor Khan built a home for his family on a large lot on the same street and we became neighbors as well.

I always knew that Shireen was different from me. What mattered to her was unimportant to me, but I was too young to foresee the impact these differences would have on our futures. Though I used to think I knew which of us was better off, I came to doubt myself.

Wearing one of her new dresses, Shireen was looking at her reflection in the mirror that lined an entire bedroom wall of her bedroom and was unhappy with what she saw.

"I am so fat." She was on the verge of tears. "It's not fair, Layla! We're family, how come you never gain any weight?

It wasn't fair when I got a bigger slice of cake. It wasn't fair when I – though three weeks younger – had gone into my moon before Shireen; not fair that I had grown inches taller than her; not fair when, having won first prize at the annual national science contest, I was one of 20 students invited to a luncheon at the Palace to hear a short speech given by His Imperial Majesty Mohammad Reza Pahlavi about the importance of education. And it was definitely unfair that I was thinner. I never told Shireen that I thought her far luckier than me in one respect: She had a brother.

Since the day I'd gone into my moon and stood before my mirror looking for outward signs on my body resulting from of change that had taken place within it, examining my body had become more or less a daily habit. Like watching a moving picture, one frame to the next, I detected the increments of my evolution from girl to woman. I isolated and acknowledged every new hair that sprang up on my pubis and was aware of every millimeter of new swelling that arose in my tender breasts. I noticed my arms take shape, a waistline form, and my legs develop a calf. A similar transformation was evident in the girls I knew. Still, in the last year or so, Shireen's body had seemed to rush into womanhood far faster than any of ours. Her ample hips and bosom were shapely beyond her years; at sixteen, she was voluptuous.

"You don't see yourself the way other people see you, Shireen," I said. "You have a lovely figure. You're beautiful." In our culture of swarthy people, Shireen's violet eyes and fair skin would prove to be valuable assets in her search for the husband she longed for.

Shireen pouted. She stomped over to her dresser, unwrapped a chocolate from inside a heart-shaped box and popped it into her mouth. *Shireen* means *sweet* in our language, so on some level, my cousin was her own worst enemy. Her undying penchant for sweets would lead to a lifelong battle with her weight.

Everything about Shireen was excessive. "I'm so fat!" She said, and bit into a chocolate-covered cherry. Syrup squirted out and onto her brand-new, white dress, leaving a thin stream of red, like blood.

Our horror was broken by Shireen's sudden burst of laughter. "Oh well, so much for this silly dress," she said. "I should never have let Maman buy it. It makes me look fatter than I am." With that, she took the dress off, crumpled it up and threw it in a corner of her room.

"*Beh jonneh man,* on my soul, Shireen," I marveled, "you are one of a kind."

She went back to her closet, brought out another new dress then decided against it and went back to rummage through her closet. "All my dresses make me look fat. Mama says it's because I'm only sixteen." She sighed. "She says it's just baby fat that will turn into curves. Well, you're 16 too, and you're not at all fat. It just isn't fair!"

I was accustomed to Shireen's whining. I lay back on her pink bedspread and eyed the crystal chandelier above my head. While she dressed, I scoped the room. "Shireen, you have so many things." Shireen didn't respond.

Most households were without a phone; they had to go to the post office to make a call. We had a phone in the hallway, one in the master bedroom, and another in Babajon's office that was also our library.

My overindulged cousin? She had a phone on her nightstand. Across from her bed on a shelf, sat a new record player, and next to that was an ornate brass birdcage, home to Shireen's new parrot, Haji Baba. Shireen wasn't yet comfortable holding the bird, so Haji spent most of his time in his cage. But she did expand his vocabulary. "Has Haji learned any new words?"

Shireen called out from her closet. "Not really."

Just then the parrot called out, "*Beraghks!*" It was a command to dance. We laughed. Shireen and I loved to dance, so it was not surprising that Haji had learned the word.

She had finally chosen a dress for dinner at home that evening and was now deciding on shoes. Lying there, I wondered why my cousin's parents pampered her so. The thought occurred to me that perhaps Shireen had some secret illness that prompted her parents to want to spoil her.

Shelves were cluttered with records, stuffed animals, six Barbie dolls dressed in full regalia and an army of dolls dressed in costumes from around the world. I never shared my cousin's interest in dolls. When we were younger, I couldn't understand how Shireen and the other girls could be content sitting quietly in unsoiled clothes playing with dolls and tea sets or coloring for hours on end. I craved the boys, always on the lookout for a new way to pass time and could barely tolerate the girls' lack of imagination, the way they repeated the same inane fantasies day after day with these lifeless pieces of plastic. I would immediately put every doll I was gifted under my bed where they were left, untouched – and there were dozens, for people assume that all young girls love dolls.

As I waited for Shireeen to complete her outfit, Boredom nagged at me. Her collection of dolls inspired me to write a poem comparing them to the girls who played with them. "I'm going home," I said, moving to get up off the bed.

She put her head out of her closet "No, don't go. I'm going to have Mama invite your parents for dinner."

Shireen bossed Haideh Khanom around in the same way she did everyone else, including me. I was impressed by Shireen's ability to manage us all, even if she often did resort to pouting until she had her way. She went to tell her mother of the plans for that evening, while I resigned myself to the fact that my poem would wait. Meanwhile, I continued surveying her room.

In a corner by the balcony door, was an oversized, white, wicker chair. On it were stacks of American and European magazines, some fashion magazines mixed in with Shireen's holy scriptures: Screenplay, Movie World, Hollywood Parade and Photoplay.

Ever since I could remember, my cousin had been totally infatuated with American movie stars and aspired to emulate the look of those she loved – in particular, Elizabeth Taylor or, as Shireen called her, *Liz,* as if she knew her. She'd read the latest news about the world-famous superstar splashed on the pages of her magazines and then recount them all to me with more gusto than dishing out gossip about our classmates.

She was in front of her mirror, turning her feet this way and that, examining her shoes when Haideh Khanom's melodious voice called from the foot of the staircase. "Layla *jon,* don't bother going home. Your parents will join us for dinner."

"Okay," Shireen called down to my aunt. Her hands traveled to her hair and all at once she jumped. "Oh, Layla, have you seen Liz's new hairstyle?" She grabbed the latest issue of Movie Fan magazine from the pile on the chair. Elizabeth Taylor was on the cover, her violet eyes aglow, and her dark hair glistening in a new short hairdo. Shireen turned to a page that she'd dog-eared. There was a half-page photo of Elizabeth Taylor and her husband, Michael Todd, sharing a table with Debbie Reynolds and her then still-husband, Eddie Fisher. Of course, we didn't know that it was a question of time before the popular singer divorced his famous wife and married Elizabeth Taylor following the tragic death of her husband.

"*Beh jonneh man,* on my soul, look at that," she said, holding up the photo. "Isn't her new hairstyle wonderful? I've begged my mother to let me cut my hair like Liz's ever since I saw this picture. She won't let me." Shireen mimicked her mother. *"It would be a shame to cut off your beautiful hair."* My Aunt Haideh's voice was warm when she spoke; Shireen's mimicry was only shrill. Abruptly, my cousin threw the magazine down, grabbed her long, thick, black tresses and pulled. "I hate this long hair." Her eyes shone with tears and her face was flushed. "I never get to do what I want," she said, flouncing on her bed.

I was amazed. I sat beside her and put my hand on her thigh. "*Shoo-khee meekonee?* Are you kidding? How can you say that? You've always gotten everything you've ever wanted, Shireen. Just look at this room. Look in your closet."

My cousin just stared at the rug, sliding her new shoes over one of the many flowers encased in dark green leaves embedded in the crimson silk rug. Arms folded at her chest, she shook her head and her ebony hair swung around, the thick waves shivering.

"No, I don't! I don't get to do half the things I want to. I didn't even get the shoes I wanted last Saturday because my Maman said '*the heel was too high,*' so, she got me these stupid ones instead." She rammed her short heels into the rug. "I can't pluck my eyebrows. I know that would make my eyes look bigger and you could see the color better.

And I can't wear sweaters unless they fall on me like a bag – I can't do *anything* I want." She turned to me. "God, how I envy Jila."

"Jila?" I repeated.

"Yes, Jila. Your father's niece. Your cousin; your Khaleh Elahe's daughter."

"You envy *Jila*?" Jila was my sole cousin on Babajon's side, the only child of my father's one sibling, his sister Elahe Khanom. Their family had left for America in the early 50s, a time when the trip was still thought of as daring as traveling to the moon. Jila's parents were humble, not nearly as wealthy as Shireen's, and didn't – couldn't – indulge their daughter. In fact, I recalled that as children, a substantial portion of Jila's wardrobe consisted of my hand-me-downs.

I couldn't think of a single reason for Shireen to envy Jila. Shireen spat out the answer as if it were too obvious. "She's growing up in America! She can do whatever she wants – anything – like those American girls."

My response was automatic. "Shireen, Jila may be in America, but she's still Iranian," In fact, I'd never given a thought to the lifestyle Jila might be having in the States. Yet, that comment stuck in my mind.

Shireen shook her head and retrieved her magazine from the floor. She flipped through it and came to another photo of the actress. She held the page only inches away from my eyes and jabbed her index finger at the dress *Liz* wore, fiery red with a plunging neckline.

"Just look at that dress. Isn't it divine? Why can't my mother get me a dress like Liz's instead of these ugly things she buys me or has made for me? They're all so unsophisticated." I'd heard all this before. The magazine fell, as she clasped her hands together in prayer and turned her eyes up to the chandelier. "*Khodah jon,* dear God, how I wish I were already married."

I giggled. "That's such a funny thing to say. Imagine if we were married now."

"Why is that funny?"

"Shireen, we're only sixteen ! Remember? We're still in high school. We're too young to get married. If you married now, you'd have to stop going to school to take care of a husband and a house."

Shireen wasn't kidding. She knew what she wanted even then. She got up off the bed and went back to her dresser. She dabbed some Chanel No. 5 perfume on her neck and wrists and the sweet scent of roses and jasmine filled the room. "You may be too young," she said, "but I'm not. Our grandmothers married when they were younger than we are. And don't forget, I'm older than you.

"And besides, I'm not like you," she went on. "You know I hate school." It was no secret that Shireen wasn't a very good student. Her best subject was English, thanks to her avid pursuit of everything American. "I'd have servants to take care of the house, like Maman does. And taking care of a husband? How difficult can that be? A grown man! I'm sure he can take care of himself."

Her mood changed again. "Oh, Layla, you have no idea how badly I want to marry." She twirled around with her arms raised up high. "I want to have a big wedding that no one will ever forget." She swooped up a magazine with a recent photo of the and Queen Soraya alighting from their royal airplane ready to meet French president Charles de Gaulle. Soraya wore an emerald green dress and a matching coat. "Look," she said, waving their images in front of my face. "Don't you envy her?" She clutched the magazine to her heart. "Imagine, marrying like she did, in the Hall of Mirrors in the Golestan Palace, all decorated with flowers flown in from the Netherlands, wearing a wedding gown with 6,000 diamonds sewn onto it." She sighed, then walked solemnly toward her mirror like a bride walking down the aisle – step, pause, step together – holding the curled magazine as if holding a bouquet of flowers in her hand. She turned to me. "Oh, Layla, just imagine. Wouldn't that be fabulous?"

"How do you know about her wedding dress?" I asked. "You and I were so young when they married."

"We weren't so young. It was 1951. We were eleven. And how could you not remember? It was all so wonderful."

"I don't remember a thing about it," I said.

"I remember everything. I remember jumping out of bed that morning. I saw all that snow and wondered if they'd call the wedding off. I was so excited by the whole thing ... I'll never forget a thing about that day. All my mother's friends, everyone everywhere, the whole city was talking about it. I don't know you could forget something like that. The flew in an entire circus from Italy. Imagine, a whole circus! And the most important people in the world were there."

"And you want a wedding with a circus flown in?" I asked.

Shireen was twirling again. "Oh, yes! Yes! I want to marry someone fabulously rich. I'd love to marry a man as rich as the and have a dress with diamonds and have flowers flown in and a circus. Why not?"

I smiled, picturing Shireen on the arm of his Majesty, the King of Kings, Mohammad Reza Pahlavi. I doubted the people of my country would open their hearts to Shireen as they had to the emerald-eyed beauty their king had chosen as his second wife

The royal couple seemed to be very much in love. Whenever I looked at photos of the shah as he smiled adoringly at his wife, I felt as if I was privy to an intimate moment. Soraya seemed to be in every way the perfect mate for the shah. She shared a love of the same sports as the shah and was as beautiful as any of Shireen's revered movie stars. She was worldly – a "jet setter" – and her European background and education were big pluses at a time Iran was struggling to hold its head high amongst the west. And she clearly cherished her husband.

I noticed my cousin hadn't mentioned love. "Why do you want to be married so badly?"

Shireen turned to face me. Her lower lip was pushed out. "So, I can do as I like! I want to live my own life. I want to wear sophisticated dresses, and go to nightclubs with my husband, and show Maman how good I'd look with my hair cut short like *Liz."*

"And do you think your husband will let you do whatever you want?"

A shadow passed across Shireen's violet eyes. "He'll have no choice." She grabbed my hand and pulled me off her bed saying, "Come on, let's go have some ice cream cake before dinner. Then I'll show you my new coat and we'll dance."

8
SHIREEN'S KHOSTEGAR

The following year, as Shireen and I embarked on our last year of high school, news spread in excited whispers.

Classmates were being visited by *khostegars,* suitors who called on them with marriage in mind. Shireen envied the classmates who told stories of having served tea to their male callers and his parents one day and the next day bragged that marriage negotiations were under way between the two fathers. Then Shireen announced that her parents would be hosting her own very first *khostegar* that very night.

The following day in school, we met at lunch.

"You're exaggerating."

It was the day after Ali, Shireen's first *khostegar* had visited. My cousin and I were in her room, and I was doubled over in laughter on her new violet bedspread while the could-have-been-bride recounted the previous night's events.

"Beh Ghoraneh Majid!" Shireen said. "On the holiest Quran, may I die if I am exaggerating. I went downstairs thinking I was about to see

my future husband, the man of my dreams. I guess I assumed he'd look like a young Cary Grant or Gregory Peck, or at least be nice to look at. When I came into the living room, *beh jonneh khodam,* on my own soul, I was looking at the ugliest boy I have ever seen."

"Why did your parents allow him to call on you?"

"Baba had never met him. His father had been boasting to Baba constantly about him. 'Oh, my Ali *jon* is so successful and so smart.' And his family is well placed. Baba said his uncle was an ambassador, so I guess he thought it might be a good idea."

"Tell me what happened," I said.

"Well, my mother was really acting neurotic. You'd think the shah was coming to our house. First, she told me to go downstairs and take Haji upstairs because he was calling out, *beraghks, beraghks!* When I came downstairs to take his cage, she was rearranging the flowers in the vase atop the piano for the twentieth time. She saw me and went nuts. '*Khodaya,* God! You can't wear that sweater,' she said. 'It is far too tight on you. We don't want these people to think you are coming from behind the mountains. Wear something more respectable. And wash off that eye makeup."

I started to object then realized that my father wouldn't allow it either. Besides, once I married this wonderful *khastegar,* I could do whatever I wanted. So, I headed upstairs to change and passed my father on the staircase. He took one look at me and said to my mother, 'I hope you've told your daughter to take off that makeup. She looks like Haji Baba.'"

I chuckled at Shireen's attempt to impersonate her father. Shireen gave me a stern look.

"Maman told him I was washing everything off except a little lipstick. Then I was about to go downstairs, but decided to sit on the staircase to watch, listen, and learn more if I could about my suitor. My mother was still re-examining the salon and switched the places of the several silver candy and nut dishes on the round brass table again. She'd already changed their places every time she'd passed by. Then she stood up straight and asked my father how she looked. She actually looked quite nice. She was wearing her French grey wool suit with red piping. My father eyed her and squinted, as if viewing her critically. 'You look perfect,' he said. 'They'd better not ask for your hand.'"

"That's so sweet," I said.

"Yes," Shireen agreed. "Sweet."

"Go on," I said.

"My mother kept asking him how the room looked, how everything looked, you know, if it was okay. 'Do you think the flowers look right? Do you think I should switch the two silver vases back around the way they were?' and my father kept saying everything looked fine. But she was still nervous."

"I don't blame her. It was the first time she was entertaining a *khostegar*."

"Well, anyway, my father went to the cabinet then and began to pour himself some vodka. 'I can't believe Abbos' boy has done so well for himself,' he said. 'Any man who advances as far as he has at such a young age can only have a very bright financial future.' I was thrilled to hear that and half-loved the boy already."

I smiled, knowing that coming from my cousin this was probably true. "Then I heard my mother say, 'Don't. They'll smell the alcohol on your breath.'"

"She really wanted everything to be perfect," I said.

Shireen shook her head. "My father paid no attention. He said it was fine. He said he and Abbos had had drinks together lots of times. Then my father said that the boy sounds almost too good to be true. Shireen looked at me then and sighed. "He was right."

Maman had my father turn around. She dabbed at his nape and adjusted his tie – which was already knotted perfectly."

"She really wanted everything to be perfect," I said again.

"I know," Shireen said. "In fact, my father had to remind her that Abbos was bringing his son to see me not them. He was actually quite funny. He said, 'Abbos has seen me dozens of times, he knows what I look like and how I knot my tie, and we don't want him asking for your hand.'"

"That is funny," I said.

"He took a second shot. Then he embraced Maman. *'Mobarak boshad!* May this merit congratulations, Haideh Khanom," he said. "A *khostegar* is coming to ask for your daughter's hand in marriage.' He began snapping his fingers and moving his shoulders back and forth, dancing to music that wasn't there.

"My mother smiled and then again turned her attention back to the room as if she'd just been reminded that important company was expected. She scanned the tabletops, and called out to Aflat, who was busy cleaning a small smudge off the mirror in the entry. Now Shireen spoke in a high, shrill voice. 'Aflat, where are the Belgian candies I bought? Bring the Belgian candies and put them on the table by the lamp. Check to see that the samovar is ready with hot water. And make certain everything is set on the tray for Shireen. Remember, she will serve only five cups.'" This the first time my cousin was to serve tea in the spotlight for the appraisal of a *khostegar*.

"But why only five cups?" I asked. The two sets of parents, Shireen, her brother Bahman, and the khastegar would have been seven.

"Because only his father was coming. His mother had passed away several years ago. And Bahman wasn't joining us, because it would look far too forward to have my brother present on his first visit, so there were just the five of us."

"I see. Go on."

My cousin sighed. "My mother kept asking my father if he was sure she looked all right. Then she asked if he was absolutely sure he had never met Ali. She said, 'In all these years, Abbos has never brought him to the Club?' But my father said he was sure he'd have remembered Abbos' son.

Then, Layla, the sweetest thing." I waited. "My father said, 'Haideh, do you remember my first visit to your parents' house? I can only imagine how nervous Ali is right now.' He reached for her hand and she put hers in his. They were actually about to embrace her when the doorbell rang." Shireen looked at me, shaking her head. They rose, straightened out their clothes and were ready welcome their guests.

"I ran back upstairs so I could make a grand entrance. I was floating on clouds. I'd be marrying at last! Everything I had ever wanted was about to come true. I would insist on a short engagement and an enormous wedding. I felt glorious."

I begged her to show me what Ali looked like again. The face she made was far more comical than his could possibly have been. She scrunched up her nose, lifted the left side of her lip and twitched her left eye. She looked so funny I couldn't help myself and fell back on the bed in gales of laughter. "Look at yourself in the mirror."

"I don't need to. I saw the original."

"Poor boy. Poor you," I managed to say. "What did you do when you saw him?"

Shireen's eyes stretched wide open and her hands went to cover her cheeks. "*Khodayah,* God! *Morrdam,* I died! I wanted to run right out of the room. My parents had never seen him before and they were as horrified as I was."

She shook her head and took a deep breath before continuing. "I sat down across the room for a while and tried not to look at him. *Khodayah,* God, I had to serve tea for the first time ever! And as if that wasn't hard enough, just as I walked up to him with the tray he snorted! He went –" Shireen snorted loudly "I almost dropped the tray. After that I excused myself 'to finish my homework.' *Beh jonneh khodam,* on my soul, I have never been so anxious to get to my school-work. He really was a toad. And when he spoke, he mumbled." She continued shaking her head.

"Poor Shireen." I thought she was taking the disappointment rather well and I was quite proud of her.

She opened the drawer of her nightstand and took out two pieces of *gaz,* that fragranced nougat candy filled with pistachios, and offered a piece to me. I could never resist *gaz.* "It's not fair! All our friends are getting married and I never will," she said, popping one into her mouth.

She was whining again, yet the dejection in her voice bothered me. "Shireen, don't say 'never.' You're not even seventeen. I'm sure you'll marry. What's the rush?"

"*Nemee-fahmee? Don't you understand?* I hate living under my parents' thumb. I hate having my mother tell me what I can and can't do. It's driving me crazy. And I'm almost seventeen!" She stood up and faced me speaking with such passion and conviction that I was taken aback. "I make a solemn vow here and now: I will be married before I'm eighteen. God is my witness, Layla, before I'm eighteen I will be living in my husband's house."

I just didn't understand Shireen. I had no interest at all in getting married.

9
I MEET MY ANGEL

I'll never forget the day my angel came to me.

That morning, Shireen had argued with her parents, wanting to stay home and nurse her cold one more day. It was one of the rare arguments she lost, and she complained all the way to school. "It's not fair! They treat me like I'm a child. I know when I should stay home!"

We arrived at school only seconds before the first of two late bells rang, signaling the start of the first class of the day.

I joined the rush to classrooms before the second bell rang, carrying my stack of books with my favorite school lunch in a paper bag, some paper-thin lavash bread, two small cucumbers, a tomato, ripened to perfection, and cold *kookoo sabzee,* a thick omelet of sautéed scallions and green herbs held together by eggs. I ran through the school's main building, across the plaza and into a small annex, flying like the wind.

The second late bell rang just as I reached my classroom. As I swung the door open, my lunch bag flew out of my hands and fell on the floor of the tiled hallway with a 'voosh.' Its contents fell out and scattered, the soft tomato, smashed. I bent down and was hurriedly cleaning up the mess when Ferreshteh's face appeared in front of me. The first thing I registered, was the incredibly thick, long, curly hair surrounding a small face; then the toffee-brown skin, the narrow dark-brown eyes, alive and intelligent, turned slightly down at the ends, and her graceful deftness when she took the bag that I'd picked up off the floor from my hand.

"Get to class," she said, her voice calming. "You're late. I'll take care of this." I hesitated. "I have a free class," she said, smiling kindly. "Go on, it's okay." I thanked this kind stranger and hurried to take my seat.

When class was over, she was waiting for me in the hallway. "Layla, since you've lost your lunch," she said, "I thought you might like to share mine. *Saalom,* I'm Ferreshteh Kohan. Call me Ferri."

I was surprised that she knew my name. A little over 200 girls attended our school; I didn't recall having noticed Ferreshteh Kohan among them and because I didn't know her, I used the polite formal form of address. "*Bebakhsheed,* excuse me, have we met?"

She shook her head. "I've been wanting to meet you," she said. "I happen to know we're the top two students in the school and they're deciding which of us will address the graduation class. You're the top student in the science program and I'm the top student in the liberal arts program. My passions are philosophy and history. Anyway, why don't you meet me in the plaza at lunchtime? You'll like what I've brought to eat. We can share it and talk."

After that day, I splintered away from Shireen and the other girls at lunch, as Ferri and I preferred to be alone whenever possible.

Ferri was as different from any girl I'd known as – well, as I was. Her name meant a*ngel,* and I came to love this thin, caramel-colored girl inside the mass of curly, dark hair.

My two friends, Shireen and Ferri, stood on opposite ends of a spectrum. Only their friendship with me brought them together. I still laugh to think how different Ferri was from Shireen.

Physically, Ferri was of a delicate build, thin and shorter than me, while Shireen was taller, all curves, and forever fighting her weight. They dressed differently, too. In school we wore uniforms, but outside of school, Shireen liked to dress like a movie star, striving to look alluring in sweaters and skirts, worn as tightly as possible under her mother's eye, along with stockings and designer shoes that matched her handbag. Ferri followed the fashion of beatnik Bohemia; the mainstays of her wardrobe were black pants or a black skirt and simple black sweaters; her look, serious and strong.

Ferri loved her books as much as I did mine, but she was far more knowledgeable about the world around us. She was well read in history, philosophy and current events and these things mattered very much to her. She taught me a lot about the world outside our country as well as the history and cultural heritage of Iran. She gave my life added dimension in so many ways. It wasn't long before I concluded that Ferri was not only a kind and loyal friend, she was also the most intelligent person I knew. Our friendship became invaluable to me, and I cherished our time together. For her part, Ferri told me that I was the one girl at school she felt comfortable around; that unlike the others, I was down to earth and had things to talk about other than *khostegars*. We soon became the closest of friends.

"I really like your parents, Layla.

"Your father's wonderful; he's so charming. I can't believe he makes Galoo Cure! My mother swears by it. We use it all the time. And he's obviously the reason you like science."

We were on the telephone just hours after Ferri's second visit to my home and the first time she had met Babajon. "My father's laboratories were my childhood playground," I admitted.

"You're lucky," Ferri said. "I've never spent much time with my father. He travels a lot."

I'd overheard Maman discussing Ferri's parents with my Aunt Haideh after her first visit to our house. Her own father had a reputation as a generous philanthropist who had donated handsomely to our school. Her mother was a beauty, thought to be given to opulent dress. I'd known her family was Jewish.

"Where does he travel to?" I asked.

"Oh, America, Canada and Europe. He exports Beluga caviar and has lots of salespeople. Still, he tells Mama it makes a difference when his customers see him paying them a visit every so often, since he's the owner and president of the company. So, he's gone a lot." I couldn't imagine what it would be like if Babajon were gone so much. She changed subjects then. "Layla, have you started writing your graduation speech?"

"No, why should I?" I said. "No one's asked me to speak."

"I told you, it's either you or me," Ferri said. "I'm getting mine ready just in case, though I'm pretty sure they'll ask you to speak as valedictorian."We both had perfect scores. "Why do you think that?" I asked.

"Well, I'm interested in history and philosophy. You're all about science, right? Layla, it's almost 1960! We're approaching a new decade, all about Progress. Since Russia launched Sputnik two years ago, the whole world has become science crazed. America is actually hoping to put a *man* in space! It's all science, science, science! No one cares about me anymore. I'm history."

We laughed at Ferri's pun. I adjusted myself on Babajon's chair, changing ears to the phone. "That reminds me, Ferri. I've wanted to ask you this since the first day we met. How did you know that we're both up to speak at graduation?"

"Well, the two of us are the only ones in the school who have perfect 20s."

"But how did you know that? I didn't. And how did you know my name and who I was? I didn't know you even existed." There was a pause long enough for me to inhale and exhale.

"You are one smart girl, Layla Saleh. Nothing gets by you. Okay, I'll tell you tomorrow."

"Why can't you tell me now?"

Ferri whispered into the phone. "Because I can't now. I promise I'll tell you at school tomorrow."

10

YOU WHAT?

The next day, I was held in suspense throughout my morning classes until I caught up with Ferri at lunch.

We sat alone and, as I hungrily opened my bag of food, I reminded her that I awaited her explanation. The explanation she gave me was hard to believe. My face must have reflected my utter astonishment. "You *what?*"

"*Sshh!* Quiet. Don't get so excited, Layla. We just talk."

"You just talk? You meet a teacher after school and just talk? A male teacher? Why don't you talk to him in class?" At that moment, I was sure that my smart friend was the stupidest girl in the world.

"I do. There's just so much to talk about. so much to learn. We talk about philosophy, history, politics–"

"Ferri, who cares what you talk about? You know that makes no difference. How can you? You must be out of your mind! Do you realize what you're doing? What you're risking? If anyone finds out, your life is over."

"Don't worry, Layla *joonie,* little dear," Ferri said. She smiled at me in an attempt to be reassuring. "Of course, I know. We're very careful." She took a bite of her drumstick as though she hadn't a care in the world while I sat staring at her, my appetite gone. The world had suddenly become a very dangerous place, and I was worried sick, frightened for my naïve friend.

"I shouldn't have told you," Ferri said. "Look at you, biting your lip. If you didn't know, you'd be fine. Now you'll worry for nothing." Our eyes met. She sighed. "Actually, I'm glad you know," she said. "I'm relieved *someone* knows, and you're the best person I can think of. You're the only person in the whole world I'd ever tell. Now I can talk to you about him."

She calmly finished her lunch, while explaining that she knew I would believe her and trust that their meetings were innocent. She was certain that I'd never share her secret with another soul. And then she went on about him. "He's absolutely fascinating. He was telling me about Mossadegh. You know, the last year that he served as Prime Minister – that was 1953 – Hamid was one of his student delegates at Tehran University."

"*Hamid?* You call Agha Amiri by his first name?" I was in double shock.

"He's asked me to; but only outside of school."

"Wait a minute." I calculated. "I know Agha Amiri is young, but he's that young?"

"He's the youngest full teacher at our school." I thought I detected a note of pride in Ferri's voice.

"Anyway, Hamid swears that Mossadegh was not a Communist, despite what we've been taught. Hamic thinks Mossadegh is a great man and that nationalizing Iran's oil to be in Iran's best interest. He was unfairly labeled a 'traitor' sentenced to death but that sentence was commuted. He's already spent three years in a military prison in solitary confinement, and he'll spend the rest of his life at home under house arrest."

What little I'd read about Mossadegh, had been in history class. In 1951, Mohammed Mossadegh was voted in as Iran's Prime Minister by the Iranian *majlis,* our Parliament. The shah, perhaps due to his youth and naiveté at the time, stood by, while it became obvious that his Prime Minister was becoming increasingly powerful. Our schools taught that he was a traitor who continually campaigned to erode the monarch's constitutional authority until the throne was almost powerless.

Ferri – or rather, Hamid – disagreed with this view and she went on. "Hamid says the U.S. and Britain joined to rid the country of Mossadegh because he'd tried to stop them from benefiting more from Iran's oil production than we Iranians did. He had the people behind him and soon had more power than the shah. In fact, the shah was so afraid of an uprising led by Mossadegh that at some point in 1953, he fled to Italy with Soraya and didn't dare return to Iran until Britain and the U.S. had arrested Mossadegh and put the shah back to the Throne to protect their interests in our oil. The two countries also promised enormous financial and technical support to the shah in exchange for a generous portion of Iran's oil. The U.S. created SAVAK, the agency that was to seek out those with anti-monarch sentiments. In exchange, Iran entered into a twenty-five year contract with the U.S. and Britain that expires in 1978."

Momentarily distracted from the terrible news she'd given me of her sinful meetings, I commented that I'd just learned more about Mossadegh than I'd ever known,

Ferri crumpled up her empty lunch bag. "Before Mossadegh was Prime Minister, he'd been an attorney, a politician, an author, and a member of Parliament, representing Isfahan. He is a great man who started many reforms, including sick pay for employees." She paused for a moment and nodded, as if completing a checklist. "I learned that from Hamid."

She stood up and looked down at me. "You know, Hamid in Arabic means 'admiration.'" I looked at her in wonderment. To me, Hamid meant 'danger.' But I said nothing. She tossed her lunch bag into a receptacle. "Anyway, Layla *joonie*," she said, flip as could be, "the thing is that Hamid and I just talk." I remained mute, looking at her. "Really, that's all. You have nothing to worry about."

As though it were possible *not* to worry. Over a drumstick, my new best friend had admitted two things to me, either one of which could be her undoing. If Ferri's support of Mossadegh was overheard by a member of SAVAK, that new CIA-created policing agency I'd been hearing about, she would likely be arrested and tried as a traitor, an enemy of the shah as had others who had supported the ex-Prime Minister. Of course, there was also the incredibly humongous matter of her meetings with her teacher. Apparently, I was far more anxious for her than she was for herself.

I doggedly continued to try persuading my friend to stop seeing Hamid – like Ferri, I soon found myself referring to Agha Amiri by his first name. I was unrelenting. I used every argument available; none worked. She acted as though I was overly concerned about the chance of rain on a cloudless day. I came to understand that the reason Ferri had joined so many after-school groups – the photography club, the chess club, the French club – was to provide ample alibis for the time she spent squirreled away with Hamid.

The news of Ferri's surreptitious meetings had me struggling with conflicting feelings. I was definitely frightened for her. I had no doubt that if their meetings were discovered, her life would shatter like a pane of glass hit be a bomb and when I imagined her being shamed and disgraced, my heart would fall to my knees. Yet listening to her talk about Hamid, I empathized with her. It was clear that she found him compelling – to some extent, that was how I felt about her. But I was disappointed in her bad judgment and careless ways.

Ferri knew the potential consequences of continuing her secret meetings. Why, I'd never dream of meeting with my science teacher alone, despite what gems he could pass me outside the classroom and he was Muslim like me, married, unattractive by any standard and well over sixty years old! No one could accuse us of doing anything irregular if we had met. That a girl of Ferri's age, family background and intelligence would dare to have clandestine meetings with a man was remarkable; that the girl was unmarried and Jewish, and the man, also unmarried, young, Muslim, handsome man made it exponentially more provocative.

Yet, paradoxically, I must admit that her confession also made her more intriguing to me. While I was frustrated by Ferri's stubbornness, I saw in that stubbornness, a certain bravery reminiscent of my hero who followed her heart's dictum though it led to being burning at the stake. I couldn't help but be in awe of my friend's determination and guile. I lacked Ferri's audacity. I could think of nothing I cared about enough to make it worth the risk she was taking.

And so, I flip-flopped back and forth, wondering if Ferri was strong or headstrong, courageous or foolish, daring enough to carve out her own destiny or stupid enough to carve out her own coffin.

In any event, Ferri changed my view of life. The discovery of her veiled meetings with Hamid had enormous impact on me. It brought home to me the realization that people and situations are not always what they appear to be. Day-to-day life could be full of hidden intricacies not apparent on the surface. She was forced to hide from the world the innocent fulfillment Hamid gave her. Hide from the world... *How could she? How could anyon*e? I was certain I never could do anything like that.

I was in the library, reading about experimental inoculations being administered in Europe.

Shireen approached. "Layla, of course you'd be here. *Beeya, bereem.* Come, let's go. Behesht Boutique has a dress in the window that is almost the identical purple one Ava Gardner is wearing in that photo with Cary Grant and I simply must try it on."

Sometimes my cousin was truly a nuisance. "I'm sorry, Shireen, I can't. I want to finish reading this, so I can talk to my teacher about it tomorrow. It's–"

Predictably, she pouted, interrupting me. "Never mind, I don't care. Whatever it is, I can't believe you'd rather read that than go with me. It's not fair! I want you to come with me. You're getting perfect 20s in all your classes. You don't need to study anymore."

"Shireen, I'll tell you what, I'll go with you tomorrow after school. Okay?"

"Don't bother," she sulked, taking a step back. "You never have time for me anymore. You're either studying or you're with Ferri. It's just not fair! You always have time for her. And when you're not with her, all you do is talk about her. 'Ferri says this' and 'Ferri says that.' Well, I don't care what she says. She took you away from me and I never get to spend any time with you anymore. It's not fair and I *hate* her!" She dug into her pocket and brought out a few sugarcoated almonds.

I was stung with guilt. It was obvious to Shireen that Ferri captivated me, and it hurt her.

Yet I couldn't help myself. Was it my fault that my cousin irritated me so with all her whining? That she bored me with her incessant shopping? Ferri was so dynamic, so full of interesting things to say.

Shireen's idols were Elizabeth Taylor and Marilyn Monroe while Ferri's were Aristotle, Kant and Nietzsche. Ferri revered the works of Da Vinci and Michelangelo whereas Shireen believed the greatest artists the world had ever known were Chanel and Dior. My cousin functioned in a material world of movie magazines, clothes and make up; Ferri lived in a world overflowing with ideas. In short, Ferri made a far more interesting companion; she never bored me.

Shireen was waiting, waiting and pouting. I closed my book. "Okay, let's go. Just know I have to come home right after Behesht Boutique."

11
SHOPPING WITH LAYLA

– Zahra Khanom –

I planned the afternoon out, shopping with her.

I had Fotmeh ready a bag with a pair of Layla's black heels and two bras, one strapless, one not, and had Cobra pack a snack of fruits and nuts in case she was hungry. I had notified Aynor, my Armenian dressmaker, to expect us at the end of the day. I waited in the car with Babak just outside the school gates to pick her up the moment classes let out. I was hoping that just for once Layla would act like a normal seventeen-year-old girl, so I could enjoy shopping with my daughter. I can't honestly say I was looking forward to our afternoon together.

As soon as Layla got into the car, she began a conversation with Babak, more interested in how our driver's twelve-year-old son had performed in his school play the previous evening than in where we were going.

But it was when we arrived at Jere's Boutique on Naderi Street, the fashionable women's clothing store, that I became truly angry. Layla didn't fly through the racks anxious to try on a dozen different things like a normal teenage girl would; no, not my daughter. I looked up from a silk blouse I was holding to eye my daughter dallying at the counter, smiling and chatting with the shopgirl!

Khodayah, God! I wondered what on earth my daughter could possibly have to say to this lowly shopgirl, and casually approached the two as though interested in the spring jacket hanging nearby.

"Thank you," the shopgirl squeaked. With the jacket held in front of me, I watched from the corner of my eye. The girl, dressed in inexpensive clothes unbecoming in a store of this caliber, had her arm extended out towards Layla who was toying with a brightly colored bracelet on the girl's wrist as though fascinated by large, perfect gemstones. "It was only eight tomans," the girl oozed, delighted by Layla's attention.

"It's so beautiful," the flesh of my flesh said.

I choked. *Eight tomans!* Less money than it cost for a package of lavash! The bracelet was a gaudy piece of trash. I turned away in disgust. *Why? Why did I, of all people, have a daughter like Layla?*

I had always assumed my daughter would be the kind of girl who would hold herself above others, appreciate class distinctions, and master the art of being coolly cordial to those beneath her; a girl who would value herself highly, proud of her lineage, with an appetite for the finer things in life. In short, I pictured my daughter to be very much like me. *What had I done to create this girl who was having small talk with a peasant, a shop girl?* It was ridiculous.

"Layla, have you found anything you like yet?" I asked, looking at my daughter without bothering to hide my disdain.

"Oh, I'm sorry, Maman. I'll look now." Afraid she had upset me, Layla smiled peevishly and moved to the racks of clothing with a buoyant stride.

"May I help you find something?" the salesgirl asked. Layla and I answered simultaneously.

"Yes, please," said Layla.

"No, thank you," I answered curtly. The girl retreated behind the desk. I abruptly replaced the jacket and turned to leave. "I've seen enough here," I said. "Let's go, Layla."

I left the shop with Layla following me out – but not before she gave the shop girl a smile, and whispered, "Bye, nice meeting you."

I had planned to purchase some lovely separates for Layla, as well as fabric for Aynor to fashion into dresses for her. Now, there I was, already in no mood to shop further with my daughter. It was always like that. Whereas my friends complained that their daughters bought too much and dressed too coquettishly – as Haideh complained about Shireen – from my point of view, these complaints were veiled boasts. Granted, Shireen had yet to learn the meaning of elegance. Still, I could barely recall seeing my niece in the same piece of clothing twice, while, if I failed to pull clothes out of Layla's closet, I think she would wear the same things forever.

Much as I would have preferred to end the afternoon at that point, I was obligated to make certain that my daughter had the appropriate wardrobe for the list of events on the horizon: the many parties clustered around graduation and the social events heralding Layla's availability for marriage. After all, one had to attract the right kind of son-in-law. Soon, *ensha'Allah*, God willing, I would be putting together her trousseau. Besides, I had a reputation to uphold. I couldn't let anyone think my husband was not able to afford the best for his wife and daughter or that he was miserly with us. So, I buried my anger and continued on with Layla.

"Take us to Georgette's," I said to Babak when we were again seated in the car. "Layla, I want you to look for fabrics for your dresses at Georgette's – and you are not to talk to any more shopgirls! Afterward we'll go to Aynor."

Georgette's Parchehs was the fabric shop known to carry Tehran's greatest variety of fine materials, including silks, chiffons and French Chantilly lace. I decided to let Layla first roam around the aisles while I searched for some black fabric for an evening dress Aynor would make for me and then search for fabrics to make Layla's dresses. I found some lovely black silk of excellent quality, then went to join my daughter.

How unexpected! I silently admired the rolls of material she nestled in her arms. Her chosen colors were perfect for her, her choice of fabric surprisingly discerning, and her eye for patterns, superb.

Armed with these purchases and feeling better about my day, we arrived at Aynor's shop to discuss designs for our new dresses.I have always been confident in Aynor's ability for I have found Armenians to be the most skilled of seamstresses.

When Layla disrobed for Aynor to check her measurements, I heard the seamstress exclaim, "*Vye*, wow, you've grown into a woman."

I looked up from fingering the black silk on my lap and was pleasantly surprised to see how Layla has matured since the last time I'd seen her clad in only a bra and panties. Both she and Hadi were tall. Layla was already a hair taller than me. Her breasts, though not yet large, were full. Her stomach was flat as a board. Her narrow waist gave way to hips that expanded gracefully, giving her a lovely shape before falling into long and shapely legs.

"Look at you," Aynor said. "Soon you will be a bride, *beh omeedeh Khodah,* may it be God's will, and we will be designing your wedding dress."

"*Ensha'Allah,*" I said. "May it be God's will." Layla had put her head down shyly. "Layla, say *ensha'Allah*."

"*Ensha'Allah,*" she repeated softly.

That afternoon, as Babak drove us home, I sat beside my daughter recalling her surprising success at the fabric shop.

I studied her, appraising her looks. Her thick chestnut hair fell down her back, and her exposed profile showed pleasing features. Her hazel eyes were wide and doe-like, set between thick black lashes that curled up toward naturally arching brows; her nose was straight and strong; her lips were full, rose-colored and curvaceous like her father's. *Khodaro shokr*, thank God, Layla had inherited my own high cheekbones. She had neither inherited Hadi's dark skin tone, nor my lighter one. The girl had a skin tone all her own that brought to mind the light from the sun as it begins to wane. I pictured my daughter's body when I'd seen it at Aynor's, and I wondered if Hadi had noticed what a beautiful woman our daughter was becoming. How could he not?

I thought about the life that awaited my young, attractive daughter, so full of potential for happiness. She was beautiful enough to have any man she wanted. I sighed with contentment, for though I hadn't been able to bear a son, I felt certain that Layla would no doubt marry a man Hadi would want for a son. Then perhaps, I could forgive myself.

I looked away from my daughter, set my eyes to the road ahead and allowed myself a thin smile.

12

THE CALL TO DINNER

Excitement among the graduating girls heightened like a fever running through the senior class as our last year of high school moved towards completion.

Dozens of gatherings would soon advertise our imminent availability into the marriage market. Girls gave extra attention to primping and preening themselves and most gave up even the slightest pretense of interest in their classes. But not me. I was filled with anxiety for I, too, was expected to marry soon after graduation. Maman had often said so; it was a certainty.

Aware that college wasn't in my future, I couldn't bear to leave high school behind. I was happy with my life as it was and in no hurry to become a wife. I'd always loved school. My greatest joy was in learning. There was a magic in school, a magic that could teach me everything I wanted to know and I wanted it to go on and on. I loved my books and teachers. I didn't want them cut from my life and make it as empty as when I'd come into my moon and had been forced to give up the boys.

With only two months left before graduation, Shireen was obsessed with finding a rich husband, Ferri was spending more time with Hamid, and I was – as usual – engrossed in my schoolbooks.

I was in my room studying when I was told I had a phone call from Ferri. She sounded unusually agitated. "You have to tell my mother I came to your house after school," she whispered into my ear.

I closed the door to Babajon's study and pressed the phone closer. "I can't. I wasn't home. Why?"

Ferri's voice was urgent. "I've already told my mother I was at your house. I had no other choice. I was with Hamid and lost all track of time."

I panicked. "Ferri, if your mother calls here, Maman will tell her we weren't even home until a little while ago. She took me to the dress-maker's again right after school. Why didn't you say you were at the Chess Club or some other after school meeting?"

"I got home far too late for any of those," Ferri said.

"This is terrible!" My mind raced. "Then say you were with Shireen."

Ferri's furtive voice became uncommonly shrill. "*Shireen?* You've told *Shireen* about Hamid?"

"Calm down. I haven't told anyone anything. I just know she'll help you."

"Shireen help me? Are you crazy? She'd be the first to spread the word that I'm seeing Hamid."

"No, she won't. Not if you explain that you just talk to him. She'll cover for you." Yet, even as I heard the words come out of my mouth, I knew they were most likely untrue.

"Layla, you honestly think Shireen would believe that I meet Hamid to talk about history and philosophy? Or care?"

I slumped in my chair. Ferri was right. Shireen wouldn't be sympathetic. She would no more believe that Ferri's meetings were innocent than would my parents or Ferri's parents. I also knew that if Ferri were found out the gossip that would surround her would, without a doubt, ruin her future – even if her parents miraculously did believe that their daughter's relationship with Hamid was purely innocent. Being alone with a boy could destroy a girl's future – unless her future was already formally tied to his.

"Don't tell Shireen where you were. Tell her you were buying a Chanel scarf to surprise your mother with. She'll understand that." Ferri was quiet. "You have to do something!" I said.

"I already have," Ferri said. "I've told her I was at your house."

Just then, Fotmeh knocked on the door and called out my name. "They're calling me to dinner, Ferri. Oh, what will we do? What if your mother calls my house?"

Ferri had no satisfactory answer. "Let's just pray she doesn't."

The aromas of dinner greeted me as I entered the dining room.

Though I normally found the scent of broiled saffron chicken and the sweet fragrance of basmati rice laden with black-eyed peas and raisins enticing, that night I had no appetite. My anxiety had made me light-headed, faint, and slightly nauseas. I felt a headache coming on. The last place I wanted to be just then was with my parents. I wanted to leave the house and come back the next day, and only if Ferri's mother hadn't called.

In an effort to act normal, I dutifully kissed Maman and then Babajon before taking my usual place at the oversized mahogany table. Fotmeh served the three of us rice with raisins and black-eyed peas, then chicken and left the silver platters on the table in front of Maman. I played with my food, trying to picture Ferri's household and what might be going on there, wondering if Ferri's mother would think to call Maman now, or now ... or now.

"How's my golden girl?" Babajon's voice interrupted my thoughts. I passed him a weak smile across the polished table.

The telephone in the hallway rang. Startled, I dropped my fork on my plate. It must have become obvious to my parents then that something was bothering me. I didn't usually jump like I'd been jolted by an electrical charge when the phone rang. It rang again and then a third time before Abol answered it. While waiting for Abol to appear with news of my fate, I kept my eyes on my plate, wriggled in my seat.

I wiped my clammy hands on my skirt. It took him forever to report on the caller, and as I waited, my blood seemed to drain out of me. Fortunately, when he finally did appear at the threshold of the dining room – *Khodah omresh bedeh,* God grant the caller long life! – his gaze was directed at my father. It was a business call for Babajon.

I said a silent prayer of thanks as my blood resumed its flow. My father directed Abol to tell the caller that we were at dinner and that he would return the call within the hour. My headache was now in full bloom. Though, for the moment, I was safe, I still feared that Ferri's mother would call any minute. I absently pierced the black-eyed peas on my plate with the silver tines of my fork.

"Are you ill, Layla?" Babajon asked.

"No, I'm just not hungry."

"She seemed fine this afternoon," Maman said.

"I am fine." I tried to sound natural and reassuring despite my feeling of anxiety.

"Well then, stop sitting there like a *dehatee* without manners. You're not a villager and you're not a child. Sit up straight in your chair. And for God's sake, stop playing with your food."

"Yes, Maman."

My father reached for the bottle of wine on the table and poured himself a drink. "Tell me about your day at school," he said. "Did you read that O. Henry story in English class?"

"Yes." I answered half-heartedly.

"And? What was it about?" he asked.

"It was about newlyweds who have no money to buy one another Christmas gifts."

Maman spoke up. "Now, why would someone write a story about poor people?" she asked cutting into her chicken. "What is there to say that's of any interest?"

"Maman, it was so sad. It's about self-sacrifice for love. They each sell the only thing they prize to buy a gift for the person they love, then discover that their gifts are worthless because they've both sold the very thing their gift was for." Maman shook her head dismissively.

"Zahra Khanom, I think our lovely daughter has been affected by the plight of the poor lovers." Babajon said.

Maman made a slight shake of her head. "Pathetic." Then it was quiet again, and I was once more lost in my worries until Babajon's jovial voice again broke into the silence. "I heard twenty-two American college students crammed themselves inside a telephone booth today in America – California. What do you think of that?"

I nodded absently. "I heard."

"Ridiculous," Maman declared.

"Tell me about science class," my father said. "Was it an interesting day?"

"Oh, yes." Before Ferri's call, I had been eager to tell Babajon all I'd learned that day in science class. Now that he asked, I connected back to that eagerness and turned in my chair to face him.

My father broke out into a smile. "Ah, the clouds have parted, and the sun is shining through."

"What Babajon?"I saw him flash a quick glance at my mother as he answered me. "Nothing. Go on, tell me about your science class."

"We learned how controlled experiments disproved the theory of spontaneous generation of life." Babajon asked me to explain. "Well, since the time of Aristotle, people believed that life could spontaneously appear from inanimate objects just by a wave of God's hand."

"That's silly," Maman said.

Babajon smiled and shook his head. "So?"

"In 1668, a man named Francesco Redi disproved that with a controlled experiment using maggots."

Maman looked up. "Maggots?" She looked disgustedly from me to Babajon, put her fork down, sighing in exasperation.

"Yes, Maman. He put rotted meat in three jars on a counter top; one sealed tightly, another open and the third, covered with gauze. No matter how long the jars stayed on the counter, no maggots appeared in the unopened jars."

"No maggots," Babajon said with a grand wave of his arm. "What did that prove?"

"That maggots don't just appear out of nowhere."

Maman sat looking at me, a sullen look on her face. "Must we really talk about maggots at the dinner table?" she asked Babajon.

I would have stopped then but Babajon's arm was up and waving again. "And what about this 'controlled experiment' you talk about?"

"A scientist wants the results of an experiment to be duplicated by others who run the same experiment. They want to eliminate as many unknowns as possible, so that the reasons for their results are certain. Redi published the exact procedure he used in his experiment. It was simple; those who copied it got the same results. He popularized the scientific method of experimentation made up of controlled observations and conclusions."

As I shared what we did in science class that day with my father, my headache lifted and my anxiety vanished; I forgot all about Ferri. Now my food was untouched because of excitement as I fed off the energy of my words.

I looked from my father to Maman and saw her subtle sneer. Unlike Babajon who gave me his undivided attention, Maman heard little of what I said. It wasn't that she lacked the ability to understand; it was simply that when matters that Maman had no interest in were being discussed, as for example science, her listening switch turned off. "Enough!" she commanded. "Spare me, please! No more. I do not want to hear about maggots at my dinner table."

"I'm sorry, Maman." I sucked in my lower lip. "Oh, and then after school, Maman *jon* and I went to Aynor's for fittings. Maman has chosen lovely fabrics for our new dresses."

"I'm sure you will look lovely in them," Babajon said. He tilted his head toward Maman and smiled. "As will Zahra Khanom."

Maman picked up the silver serving dish and set the largest piece of chicken on my father's plate. She set the dish down and rearranged the cloth napkin on her lap., taking advantage of the pause in the chatter to talk about something that mattered before resuming her dinner.

"Layla, I've decided to host a party celebrating your graduation on the last Saturday in May, a dinner party with seventy-five guests or so. Tables will be set up in the gardens. That's the night before the party at the Club. Ours will be first in the rash of graduation celebrations."

Maman's strategy of kicking off the social gatherings that would mark graduation with a party the night before the larger annual festivities at the Club, was brilliant. It would make her invitations coveted. "Thank you Maman *jon*. That sounds wonderful."

"Yes. I'll ask Vigen or Aref to come sing." These were the two most popular male singers in Tehran. "And perhaps I'll ask that young Googoosh to come as well. You may invite your Jewish friend; I'll be inviting her parents." I winced at the reference to Ferri. The thought that Maman would be speaking with her parents made me cringe, and I nodded without enthusiasm.

"Clouds again," my father muttered, observing me.

"Is something the matter?" Maman asked. "Have you and Ferri had a fight?"

"Oh, no, not at all," I said as brightly as I could. "Thank you for inviting her, Maman *jon*."

"Tell me more about school," Babajon went on. "Did they say more about the new microbiology program starting at the University of California in Los Angeles?"

I swiveled in my chair and faced Babajon again. "Oh, yes, it's for sure now. They will definitely be starting a microbiology program there next year by combining departments in the natural life sciences." I was so enthused by the subject my father raised, that I didn't realize Maman was not pleased that we'd returned to the subject of microbiology.

This wasn't the first time my father and I had discussed UCLA's upcoming microbiology program. It was the talk of the science world. The idea of being part of the program that would culminate in a degree in my favorite subject was heaven. I knew the closest I would ever get to heaven were these discussions about it with my father. UCLA was thousands and thousands of miles away. More importantly, college was off-limits for me and definitely not my destiny. I was now ripe for marriage and poised to fall off the tree. So, I relished even the chance to *describe* this academic utopia to my father.

"And they were telling us about the laboratory instruments that will be available –"

"*Beh jonneh babat*, on your father's soul. Please, enough! Layla, eat your dinner." commanded my mother.

Babajon put his elbows on the table and clasped his hands as if in prayer and said nothing. I turned back in my chair and pushed a forkful of rice into my mouth. Maman was heaping more rice onto my father's plate. "That's too much," Babajon said. She stopped, and he turned his attention back to me. "Of course, they'll have all the latest tools," he continued.

"That's what they say," I said.

Maman stood and set her napkin down on the table. She spoke accusingly though her voice was restrained. "I'll be all too glad when school ends and my daughter finally puts her mind to things more important than 'meecro-whatever.' That's not life."

Then she called for tea.

Still anticipating a call from Ferri's house after dinner, I couldn't fully concentrate on my studies. We received two more telephone calls that evening and with each, my heart stopped beating until I knew the call wasn't coming from Ferri's house.

***

That night, I had a terrible dream.

Maman and Maryam Khanom, Ferri's mother, stood in the midst of the bazaar wearing evening dresses. Maman wore a dark green velvet dress with the emerald and diamond necklace Babajon had gifted her on their anniversary. Maryam Khanom wore a rich yellow satin gown, a pearl choker and golden bracelets. Violins played in the background as the two women laughed, oblivious to the dirt, the vendors around them calling out their wares and the crowds, the sort of common people Maman would never approach.

All at once, the faces of the people in the bazaar mutated and became deformed. Maman turned into a wooden statue. Maryam Khanom let out a terrible scream. I followed their gaze and saw Ferri, huddled under a vendor's makeshift table, her clothes torn and ragged, her bare, bruised legs covered with scratches, and her shoeless feet, smeared with donkey dung. Her small face was pale, her curly hair was no more than a nest of filth and debris. She was weak and hiding from a band of men who were running around the bazaar and calling out to one another as they looked for her.

Then the bazaar was gone, and Ferri and I were in a damp, sunless room. From where I sat on a wooden chair in a cold corner of the dank room, I saw a scorpion idly testing its claws before making its way toward Ferri. Assured of its prey, it moved slowly.

Oblivious of the scorpion, Ferri was shivering as she leaned against a cracked wall, brown water oozing through it and into the room. I was terrified. I wanted desperately to save my friend. Though I struggled in vain to get to her, I found I was chained to the chair I sat on. I screamed out, "Ferri! Watch out! *Aghrab,* scorpion! Move away!"

Despite my screams, Ferri, delirious – whether from drugs or exhaustion – neither saw nor heard me. The scorpion climbed onto the heel of her filthy foot. I sprang up then, awake and in a cold sweat, my heart pounding. I tried to calm myself. I knew I could no longer bear this fear, this tension.

What if it was discovered that Ferri wasn't at my house that day?

I'd been afraid for my friend and I still was, but now I was afraid for myself as well.

What if her meetings were discovered and it came out that I'd known about them?

Lying went against my grain. I'd promised myself that I would do anything to protect Ferri and her secret, anything at all to protect my best friend from being found out. I would never allow her to spend even one night in a dark cellar in the company of scorpions. But now, I realized how vulnerable we *both* were.

I absolutely had to persuade Ferri to stop seeing Hamid before it was too late. The question, was *how?* Ferri was not an easy girl to convince. I wrestled with the problem until an unrestful sleep rescued me.

13
THE CHARLATAN

The next day, I waited anxiously to hear what had happened at the Kohan house.

When I finally met Ferri at lunchtime, she was as calm as ever. I was relieved, but curious. We walked toward our usual spot, side by side.

I couldn't wait another second. "I had nightmares last night and here you are, looking like the Goddess of Serenity." I said. "What happened at home?"

Ferri's smile was so broad, it barely fit inside her delicate face. "God was watching over me," she said. "While you and I were on the telephone, Rebecca fell off the tree she's always climbing and broke her leg." Rebecca was Ferri's nine-year-old sister.

"Oh, that's terrible! The poor girl! How is she?"

"She'll be fine," Ferri said. She was still grinning.

I stood in front of my friend, blocking her way. "Ferri, your little sister broke her leg! I would think you'd feel terrible."

To my astonishment, Ferri laughed. "It's only a slight fracture. Besides, you should see the little woman," she said as if speaking of a character in an amusing movie. "She's thrilled. And why wouldn't she be? You don't know how theatrical Rebecca is. Now she can moan about her broken leg. Meanwhile, she can't wait to show the cast off to her friends. She's staying home today, only to make her return to school that much grander." We sat at our usual table. "Mama is at home waiting on her and she has my poor parents promising to give her all kinds of things. I swear to God and all his prophets, by the time her cast comes off, Rebecca will own our house and everything in it." She looked up at me and scoffed. "Yes, Layla *jon,* I am sorry for Rebecca, but you have to admit, the timing was excellent. It was just what I needed, the perfect thing to distract my parents. I am forever indebted to my little sister."

I had to agree. "Well, *Khodara shokr,* thank God, she'll be okay, and you didn't get caught."

Ferri chuckled. "I thank God and Rebecca both, for saving me from my mother and father – and Shireen."

Despite myself, I giggled at her silliness before turning serious once more. "You have to be more sensible, Ferri."

She answered without hesitation. "Yes, I know. I will be."

"You mean you'll stop seeing Hamid?"

"Stop seeing him? No, of course not."

"Ferri, you can't keep this up. You almost got caught. You're taking too much of a chance. You're risking your whole future, and for what?" She didn't respond. "Am I overreacting?" I asked. "Maybe Jewish people are different. Maybe it's not a big deal if you're found out. Are Jewish people more like Armenians? I've heard they're more liberal when it came to mixed company."

Ferri rolled her eyes. "Are you kidding? We're as crazy as you when it comes to that."

"You don't… love Hamid… do you?" I asked.

Ferri had that faraway look in her eyes again. "No, not the way you mean. I love his mind. He's so *ja'leb,* so unique, so intriguing."

Was she lying to me? I wanted to believe my friend more than anything in the world. Yet, I had a nagging suspicion that there was more to their relationship than she admitted. Otherwise, it just didn't make sense. *Was she lying to herself? Was it possible that she was in love with Hamid and didn't know it?* Either way, I was sure she was on a road just one curve away from disaster, with no way of knowing where or when that curve would appear.

"Ferri, if someone sees you with him, they won't believe it's his mind that you love, nor will they care. They'll think the same thing that Shireen would. Do you understand that? Your future – and your sister's future – will be ruined."

"*Joonie,* no one sees us together." Ferri was no more changed by last night's close call than the bench we sat on.

"How can you be so sure?"

"We can't even see one another where we meet." She must have seen how frustrated I was. "Layla, I can't stop seeing him. Not now, not yet. Please, *joonie,* at least *you* can understand. As long as he's willing to teach me, I'll be there. History, philosophy ... I'm learning so much. Hamid explains it all in a way that's fantastic. He puts it all together and makes everything fit like pieces of a grand puzzle, like it's all part of one huge beautiful tapestry. Yesterday, he was talking about the effects of World War II on European philosophy and art." She rolled her eyes. "He's totally *ja'leb.*"

As I listened to my friend's resolve, I wanted to scream at her. I tried, for the umpteenth time to talk some sense into her head. "What do you mean you can't stop? Ferri, we're talking about your whole life, your future. You know that no one will marry you if your meetings with him are discovered. You'd be labeled a *jendeh,* a whore, may my tongue break and fall off; may I go mute for saying such things! And no one will marry your innocent sister either. Is it worth both your futures?"

"This *is* my future, *joonie.* All I care about is being the kind of teacher Hamid is. I don't want to recite lessons to students who sit there, bored to death. I want to excite them, to make them think about the world and what life is all about. I want to make history and art and philosophy all connect and come alive for them like Hamid makes it all come alive. I want to change their lives. To be the best teacher in the world." Ferri's eyes shone and her face was rapturous. I wanted to cry. She reached across the table and held my shoulders. "I know I'm risking a lot, Layla, but it's worth it to me."

"I'm really sorry, Ferri, but *I* can't do this. I've never lied to my parents and now I'm conspiring in your lies. And what do I do when your parents find out? What do I tell my parents or your parents? How can I tell them I knew and didn't stop you? Tell me, please, what do you really do when you're with him?"

The five-minute bell for classes rang as Ferri shook her head. "Listen, Layla. Let's not go to the library after school today. I'm taking you somewhere."

When school let out that day, Ferri and I found one another.

"Where are we going?"

"Where Hamid and I meet."

We took a bus toward the heart of Tehran then got off and walked for a few blocks, making turns this way and that off the main street until we were in a seedy area I'd never been. Ferri led me to a small storefront. We left the afternoon sunshine and descended a long staircase, passing a bearded man wearing a flat black beret and very narrow black sunglasses, holding a cigarette at the end of a long, white holder, and entered a black hole. Ferri took my hand and led me into the belly of the darkness. I felt a mix of excitement and curiosity. I heard footsteps as people passed by, and I wanted to see them, to know who else was here – and with whom. But as Ferri guided me along, holding my hand as we weaved through winding hallways, I could see nothing. Try as I did, all I could see were tiny oil lamps, set up high in alcoves around the walls, marking the various paths meandering around what appeared to be a cave. I gripped Ferri's hand. Still in total darkness, she suddenly stopped and pulled me down. I collided with a table.

"We're here," she said. "Sit down."

I cautiously felt around for a chair and lowered myself into it. My vision was as accustomed to the dark as it was going to get, yet still, in the blackness I could only make out the faintest outlines of human bodies. "Ferri, I can't see you."

"This is where I meet Hamid." Determined to make my eyesight work, I blinked hard, rubbed my eyes, opened them wide, and squinted. I saw no more than I had when I first sat down. "See? No one will see us together. Okay, we can leave whenever you're ready."

"Just don't let go of my hand," I said as we stood.

Ferri retraced our steps back outside into the sunlight, momentarily as blinding as the darkness inside had been. "So, *joonie,* that's what I mean when I say we're safe. See? We come in separately, and we leave separately. We meet at that same table or a second or a third. Happy now?"

"All right, yes, it's dark. But –"

"Dark? It's pitch black."

"Okay, it's pitch black. But it's not that simple. What about last night?"

"Stop worrying, Layla. I'll watch the time more carefully. I promised to be more careful. May I die if I'm not. *Be jonneh khodam,* I swear on my own life, I won't get caught." I wanted desperately to believe Ferri, for she was as unmovable as the tomb of Hafez. All I could do was pray.

On the bus ride home, I remembered to tell Ferri about the party Maman would be having to celebrate my graduation.

We discussed that for a minute or two, then exchanged notes about Lana, our classmate who had been absent from school for two weeks, and the rumors we'd heard about her mother. We were still talking about that when we got off the bus. We had walked a few blocks when we heard my name being called. We turned back to see Shireen running toward us.

"I've been chasing the two of you for blocks." She made an exaggerated show of catching her breath then rolled her lovely eyes in exasperation. "Where are you going?" she asked.

Ferri looked at me, passing me the burden of explanation. We were grateful that my cousin hadn't seen us coming off the bus, or she would have surely asked where we were coming from.

"Home," I said.

"You *must* first have a Coke with me at Hezbat's. I'm dying of thirst after that chase."

Again, Ferri cast her brown eyes in my direction. "We can't," I said, ad-libbing. "Ferri has a visitor and I have to work on a science paper."

Shireen pouted."Oh, don't be so grim. Whatever your science paper is about, you'll get a perfect 20 on it." She turned to Ferri. "Who's your visitor?"

Ferri straightened in discomfort. "My mother is waiting for me. My grandmother is visiting."

Shireen laughed. "Layla is always writing science papers, our mothers are always waiting for us, and our grandmothers are always visiting. You can tell them you were with having a Coke with Layla and me. We'll vouch for you and so will the waiter."

Ferreshteh was quiet, still gazing at Shireen's red shoes that matched the Chanel bag on her shoulder. Shireen didn't wait for our reply. She positioned herself between the two of us, intertwined her arms with ours and steered us across the street. "My treat."

14

THE FIGHT

– Zahra Khanom –

Hadi must have known he was setting off a bomb.

It was just weeks before both Layla's high school graduation and the party that was to catapult her into a wonderful marriage – and, he would remind me, days after she had won the national science award for the third straight year.

"I'm thinking of sending Layla to Los Angeles to attend the University of California," my husband said.

I thought he was kidding, but his stone face impressed upon me the dreadful truth that he was serious. All my alarms went off at full volume and we embarked on the single most defining argument of our married life. We argued in private, behind the closed doors of our bedroom as we had never argued before.

Where in God's name had Hadi gotten such an outlandish and irresponsible idea? I knew my husband's indulgence of our daughter was endless; still, this was ludicrous! *Utterly insane!* Out of the question! *How could Hadi even suggest that we jeopardize Layla's future?* He was fully aware that I would never agree to send our daughter away at this point in her life and certainly not to study! And definitely *not* in Los Angeles! I felt the blood rush to fill my chest, yet I spoke calmly. "College? I know you're kidding, Hadi *jon*." He was silent. "It's time for her to marry! Why, the whole point of our party celebrating her graduation is to officially put her in the queue of eligible girls. You know that."

"She'll marry after college."

I forced myself to smile and pointed out the obvious. "That's silly, Hadi. She'll be a year older. All the best prospects will have been taken!"

"She will be *four* years older, and there will always be excellent prospects for a girl like Layla. She wants college more than life itself."

"Four years!" My breath caught on the words and I collapsed into a chair. This was preposterous! Hadi must have lost his mind to suggest such a thing. We both knew that any girl's chances of finding a good husband diminished with every passing year. "Why you must be kidding. After four years, no one will want her."

"Woman," Hadi said, "You're wrong. Don't you see how people with marriageable sons grovel at our feet to be in our good graces? Don't you see the effect our daughter has on boys when she enters a room?"

"Exactly. That's why she will marry now. At seventeen and not twenty-one! By twenty-one her power will fade. The university is for girls who cannot find a husband." It frightened me to see my husband acting as if he didn't know that.

Hadi was suddenly overexcited. "*Azizam*, my dear, don't you see how she comes to life whenever she talks about science and microbiology? She almost bounced off her chair with excitement when we spoke about the program at UCLA. Her fervor surrounds her like an aura, her eyes dance, those flecks of gold become brighter, larger, and she becomes even more beautiful. Don't you see that?"

I had always known it was supremely foolish of my husband to encourage Layla's interest in science. Now my fear evolved into utter panic. "Hadi, I see you've forgotten that Layla is not a man. This is our daughter, Hadi! How do you think I feel listening to our daughter chattering on and on at the dinner table about germs and bacteria and maggots?" The idea was completely repugnant to me, and I shivered.

"Zahra, I've thought a lot about this. Her Western education, her time in the U.S., will only add to her value as a wife. She'll return home after college and marry happily."

His remark had a definite air of finality to it. I was devastated. *Could he have made up his mind before he'd spoken to me?* If so, it would be harder to bring my husband back to his senses. Yet that was exactly what I had to do.

I rose and went to him, took his hand, stroked it, and spoke to him lovingly. "Layla will marry and bear her husband's children" – I bit my lip – "Allah willing, they will be sons. College? What good will a college degree in meecro-whatever do her? It doesn't teach her what she needs to know: how to keep a husband and make him happy, how to entertain his family, how to keep a household running smoothly, how to furnish a house beautifully, how to deal with the servants with kindness, yet remain firm. That's what she'll need to know."

Hadi retracted his hand and slowly walked away from me. "Hadi *jon,* you should be encouraging the daughter you love to think about marrying well, living the good life, and doing her parents proud."

He spoke softly then, as though reflecting. "Layla is not like you or your sister, or my sister. She is not like Shireen and other girls. She will never be happy being no more than a wife."

I could have told him that was his fault. "That's the whole problem," I said. "Layla is already far too unlike other girls her age, uninterested in the things she ought to be interested in and far too interested in things she oughtn't be."

Hadi waved my comment away. "Our daughter has a wonderful and inquisitive mind. It should be nourished. Name one other child – girl or boy – who has won half the awards and medals and citations that Layla has won. She's won every science contest, every top honor."

He turned on his heel. "She *must* go to college."

My husband was speaking like a crazy man. *Was he really willing to go to this extreme to indulge our daughter's quirky interest in germs?* There was terrible danger here. "Even as a young child, her favorite thing was to come to work with me and watch what went on inside the laboratory. Soon she was asking question after question. Why, Layla has spent more time looking through a microscope than most girls spend with dolls."

None of this was news to me. Her father had encouraged Layla's scientific interest her whole life. And now this. I turned away. *How could he even think of doing this to me?* I would have thought it unthinkable. Yet, as I came to appreciate the extent of my husband's determination to send our daughter to college, I thought it best to compromise. If Layla stayed in Tehran, I could marry her off; plans could be altered, catastrophe averted. "Well then," I said, acquiescing. "If she must go to college, let her go to the university here."

"She must go to UCLA, woman!" Hadi boomed. I was shocked by his thunderous voice. He took a breath, then put his hands in his pants pockets, and spoke, impatiently. "They don't teach microbiology here. UCLA is the only place that teaches what she wants to learn."

The telephone rang, jolting me anew. Hadi strode back to the nightstand, sat on our bed and picked up the bedroom receiver. I wondered who would be calling at this late hour. When my husband heard the voice at the other end of the line, his face relaxed into a broad smile.

"Elahe *jon*?" It was his pig sister calling from California. *"Saalom, ghorbonne beram,* hello, may I be sacrificed for you," he said, delivering the traditional greeting of affection. Of course, he was treating the cow as lovingly as always. He continued, "Are you calling us in the middle of the night to break the news that your husband has finally thrown you out?"

The woman was so stupid, that after all these years she hadn't yet been able to figure out the time difference between Tehran and Los Angeles, yet Hadi only teased her.

I'd never felt anything other than coldness toward Elahe. Hadi's family had been below mine and, although my husband had become both financially successful and socially adept, the rest of his family remained embarrassingly below my estimation, particularly his sister and her husband. Elahe was grossly overweight and completely lacking in elegance and social grace. Worse, the woman had married a clerk, Javeed Forsati, a man common in every way, a complete embarrassment. Some ten years ago, Javeed had "decided to leave his job." I am convinced he'd been fired. The couple took their daughter, Jila – a sweet child – and left for America. Some thought them brave. To me – and others I respect – their leaving Iran was equivalent to shouting out "failure," utter and complete.

Hadi listened for a moment then said to his sister, "Yes, yes, that sounds excellent. How close to the school? Yes, of course, two bedrooms ... Wonderful. No, that's not a problem; I'll take care of that. Send me a copy of the lease. Layla will love being with Jila again ... Yes, yes of course, and she'll have family there ... Regards to Javeed ... We'll talk again and finalize it then ... Yes ... I know you will, thank you ... You'll have all that information. She'll be glad to see you there ... Of course. *Khodah 'hafez,* God be with you. Goodbye." He hung up and sat still for some time. I stood frozen behind the bed.

My already wounded heart suffered the fatal pang as I realized that the horrible deed was done. Hadi had begun looking for a place for Layla to live before he'd even broached the subject with me. All my arguments were completely meaningless.

Hadi turned and met my disbelieving eyes, answering my unasked question. He spoke without emotion. "I have contacted the school. I have had her transcripts sent along with letters of recommendation from the Headmistress as well as all her teachers. I have explained the situation to the head of the department at UCLA and he accepted certified translations of papers Layla had written for school in place of essays. They made exceptions because of the national awards she has won. That's how special our daughter is. She was accepted a long time ago. Her English will not be much of a problem. She already speaks English quite well. She can attend special English classes there though, of course, scientific terms are almost all in English anyway."

My mind raced. "Hadi Agha, please, don't do this. Layla is a girl. This is our daughter and our only child." I went and sat by his side on our bed. I put my arm around his shoulders hoping to reach his heart with my words. "My dream is for our daughter marry young and give us grandchildren. Isn't it your dream as well?"

Instead of softening my husband's heart as I'd hoped, my question aroused an unexpected anger. He stood up and turned to me with fire in his eyes. "Your dream? My dream? What is our daughter's dream? Would you, as a mother, deny her that? To ignore her hunger for knowledge is to starve her soul. She will never be happy like that."

Stunned, I felt the final stab of defeat. My arm fell away and my mind became numb. I couldn't absorb this. A short hour ago I could not have imagined this sudden turn of events: *My seventeen-year-old daughter going to Amreeka?* Absurd! *To college? For four years?* No! *And to California?* God help us.

Frantic, I forced myself to think despite my shock. I came up with a mother's final argument to keep my child at home where she would be guaranteed the shelter of an early marriage. Playing my last ace, I spoke as if cajoling a child.

"Hadi, please. Your time in Amreeka, in California, as a young man was different than your daughter's will be. Layla is a girl! Deny her dream? She should be having domestic dreams. We have her future to think of. Layla's future – our future – most assuredly depends on her remaining pure for her husband. Yet you talk of her going to California to live among people who have no decency and no moral code, people who have intimate relations without the blessings of Allah, like cats and dogs that roam the streets.

"Tell me this, Hadi: How can you send your beautiful, innocent daughter to a place where she will be exposed to such filth, where men will see her and pursue her for only one reason? Amreeka – California – is a sinful place. What will happen to her there? And what will become of her happiness? What will happen to our family name? What will happen to me? Tell me that, my dear husband and then let her go if you still can."

Hadi had been pacing as I spoke. Now he turned and walked right up to me, his face only inches from mine, eyeing me like a fox.

"Are you telling me, Zahra Khanom, that you have not done your duty as a Muslim mother? Dare you say you have failed to instill in our daughter the importance of decency and purity? That you have failed in your most important task as a mother before everything holy?"

I was speechless. I didn't know the man who stood in front of me. Registering the look of defiance on my husband's face, testament to a side of him I had never before seen, I was stunned and could only shake my head.

Not missing a beat, Hadi continued, his eyelids pinched. "Then is it that you believe Layla lacks integrity? That she lacks character? That she is weak and vulnerable to temptation? That though you have taught her well she's stupid and did not learn?"

I continued to shake my head as my dreams for our daughter faded away.

"I, your husband, tell you that our daughter is going to America. We will not discuss it further. We will surprise her at her graduation party."

I was totally beside myself, sick with distress. I had always respected my husband. He was a smart man. His business was a great success, his reputation was spotless, and he had been kinder to me than I would have expected a man to be, given my inability to present him with a son or even a second child. The home he had designed for me was a marvel and he'd given me a good life. He deserved my loyalty. I had no complaints at all – until now. This idea of sending Layla to California was a foolish mistake. I was absolutely sure of it. Yet, I could not defy my husband. I had to surrender or risk losing my husband as well as my daughter.

The next morning, alone in our bedroom, I sat holding the photo of my deceased mother.

I wondered what she would have done in my place. I stroked the cold silver frame and glided my fingers over the smooth glass tracing my mother's image, her commanding expression.

"Maman jonneh azizam, my dear mother, you taught me that a woman's place is in her husband's home. Many were the times Baba said I had an excellent head for business and that had I been a male he would have gladly bequeathed both the factory and his other business interests to me.

"He would laugh when I said I would do well. "My child," he would say, "a woman doesn't dirty her hands with that sort of thing," and it was enough that I had Vallian to look after. So, the businesses all passed to Mansoor who ended up selling them to our cousin for a fraction of their worth; my brother was far more interested in the law than in the business world. Now my husband believes it's acceptable for our seventeen-year-old daughter to shun marriage and live thousands of miles away so that she can study bacteria, surrounded by American filth and studying filth.

"What am I to think? What am I to do? He allowed her to play with boys far past the time of normal, healthy separation. Now, when she should be thinking only of readying herself for a husband, he speaks of her living amongst the sinful to study germs! Maman, I can't persuade Hadi. Nothing I say gets through to him. He is as immobile in his decision as any mountain and Mohammad himself could not make him change his mind.

"What does a man know of life's realities? Men are welcomed from the moment of birth as a blessing and live their lives as they wish. How can he understand that this is not his daughter's destiny? She will live to regret it. She will be miserable and so will I.

"A woman's destiny is to comfort a man, to ease his life and bear him sons. Our esteemed shah now divorces his beloved Queen because she is unable to provide him with a son even though he cries as he makes the public announcement, so great is his love for her. I am thankful to Allah that I have been spared such a fate as hers. Yet now, finally, I see the consequence of my failure, for my husband treats our daughter as though she were a son and cuts off my tongue, so I cannot object. He does not see what is in front of his eyes.

"Help me, Maman, I beg you. I am beyond knowing what to do. I will pray for Allah and your own sweet soul to help me."

I was a mass of repressed anger at both Layla and Hadi.

At her ripest time, the young, pure, innocent guarantor of my lineage was being sent to the land of immorality, delaying marriage for years.

She would be living in California, the very hotbed of sin, the home of Hollywood, where immorality is a way of life and portrayed as glamorous. *How could Hadi not see the danger inherent in sending her there?* Yet, when I asked him that very question, he had dared to put the responsibility of what could happen there on *me!* Not on him, not on her, not on Amreeka or that Godforsaken California, but on *me!* That I may have shirked my responsibility as a mother or that I may have failed as a mother to teach Layla the importance of decency and purity.

In my desperation, I would have run to Hadi's mother and pleaded for her help, begged her to help stop her son from allowing Layla to go off to Amreeka. Yes, I would have humbled myself before the woman who was so beneath my own dear mother. I'd have done anything to persuade Hadi to abort his plan. But I knew his mind was made up, and he would be furious with me if I'd gone to her behind his back to gain support for my position against him.

Having lost the battle against Hadi, I resolved to persuade Layla to decline the gift of a college education and choose to stay in Iran to begin the life she was meant to live.

To that end I began my campaign on several fronts.

At the exact moment in Iran's history when our shah was on the threshold of embracing the West and Tehran was opening its doors wide to all things western, I boycotted every American item I could possibly do without.

In my daughter's presence, I criticized U.S. culture and Americans for their gaucheness, their shallowness, and their lack of morals. "They are immoral beyond belief. They lack the wisdom of our culture. After all, what can you expect from a country that is two hundred years old? How can they compare to a civilization of almost twenty-five thousand years? Their country is filled with young girls having babies before marriage, women working outside the home and divorce."

I made certain to approach every girl we knew that was engaged, and every bride at every wedding we attended, to heartily congratulate both her and her mother, with Layla at my side. "Your destiny has been fulfilled," I'd say, "*Ensha'Allah,* God willing, I look forward to this glorious day to soon arrive for my daughter and myself." Of course, they would join in with a chorus of *"Ensha'Allah."* And though it wasn't easy for me to shine these women's shoes, I did. I also made certain that Layla got a good look at the diamond on every newly ringed finger, hoping that even she would like to have one on her hand.

It was highly probable that the disaster looming over my lineage was the result of at least one envious woman giving me the evil eye. To remedy that, I locked myself in my bedroom with the old *fallgir,* the fortune teller, and lay on my bed dressed only in a slip as she instructed, while she passed a raw egg rubbed with something, over my body. Then I held it in both my hands before she cracked it open over a cup. Late that night, saying nothing about it to Hadi, I stowed the cup containing both yolk and egg white the under my side of our bed. When morning came, the egg whites had turned gray and cloudy, a sign that the evil energy surrounding me had been trapped. I hurried, unseen, to the farthest southwest corner of our yard and, as directed by the *fallgir,* stealthily dug a small hole there and burying the raw egg while screaming out, "*Borro, Ensha'Allah lanat beshee, bemeerree!* Go! God willing, may you be cursed and die!"

I later wished she had broken at least one more egg.

Determined to eradicate all the evil spirits, I burned *esfand,* that aromatic gum resin. I put little more than two teaspoons in a small saucepan over a medium flame until it smoked and burned. It popped, proof that someone had given me the evil eye, wished me ill, or harbored jealousy.

I chanted, "May the evil eye burst," and walked through the house several times, holding the pan, filling every room with its scent and the smoke of the dark seeds. I even sprinkled some seeds in Layla's room while she was at school and put some in Hadi's desk drawer while he was at work.

Perhaps the most ambitious of my attempts was to marry Layla off as soon as possible, and thus make a trip to the U.S. unlikely, other than as a honeymoon. I reviewed the list of acceptable sons-in-law that Layla might agree to marry, reverting to the list of Bahman's friends, the boys Layla knew and played with as a child.

Jalil was at the top of my list. I recalled the day Layla had gone into her moon and Jalil had brought her home. He had obviously been concerned for her. I'd watched Jalil around Layla at gatherings through the years and surmised that his feelings for my daughter hadn't changed from that time – and I had to hope Layla still harbored affection for him. Jalil's qualifications for a son-in-law were excellent. The elder of two boys born to wealthy parents, he was not only available he was also presentable, respectable and uncontroversial.

It seemed rather simple. All there was for me to do was to encourage their engagement announced as soon as possible. Yet, if Jalil had been even remotely thinking of approaching us to ask for Layla's hand in marriage, he hadn't shown the slightest hint that he would be visiting us as a *khastegar* anytime soon. *How could I incite him to act?* I couldn't tell him Layla would be leaving for the States; Layla herself didn't yet know and I wouldn't dare upset Hadi's plan to surprise her. More importantly, a boy like Jalil would never dream of marrying a girl crazy enough to entertain the idea of going alone to Amreeka to attend college for four years! Good Iranian girls didn't do that.

I cagily invited Jalil's parents and four other couples of the same social circle to dine at our home the following week. "Please bring Jalil *jon* with you, there will be other young people here, they'll enjoy one another," I told his mother. The "other young people" were Shireen, Bahman and, of course, Layla.

It was a clear, warm evening with dinner served al fresco in the garden by the pools. After dinner, one of my guests, a singer of modest fame, was persuaded to warble classic mournful Persian songs to the delight of the other guests. A good time had by everyone except me. The very purpose of the evening was dashed early on when Jalil's parents entered, apologizing that he was not able to join us as he had been called to the northwestern city of Tabriz.

I doubled up on my remarks to my daughter about the ploys men use to manipulate innocent girls, how they trick them into doing things that they oughtn't.

I felt increasingly at a loss as Layla came closer and closer to receiving her graduation gift. I had no confidence that she would decline the offer to leave home for that godforsaken place.

And every time I saw Fotmeh's high forehead, I sighed.

15
THE GIFT

My parents surprised me on the night of Maman's graduation party.

With his arm around Maman and glee in his eyes, Babajon handed me his gift. He had one of my classmates ready to snap my picture at the moment that I opened the envelope and reached inside.

What a picture it was! There I sat, holding a plane ticket to Los Angeles in one hand and a letter of acceptance from UCLA in the other, both hands trembling, my eyes popping out, my jaw wide open, gaping at my parents. My father's face reflected all the pride he felt in bestowing this gift. I mistook my mother's cloaked eyes and lack of expression as her attempt to keep her dignity in front of our guests. I didn't care about appearances; I screamed, waved the papers in the air, jumped up and down, then hugged each of my parents tightly to me.

My friends were mystified. "*Cheeyeh?* What is it? What have they given you? What have you got there, Layla?" they asked.

Shireen took what I held in my right hand. It was the plane ticket to Los Angeles. "You're going to Los Angeles. Ooh, lucky you. All those movie stars. It's not fair! I want to go, too!" She took off in search of her parents.

Ferri, standing on my other side, took the letter of admission into UCLA from my left hand and began to read aloud:

"Congratulations on your admission into one of the finest universities…" she stopped, breathless. "Oh, my God, Layla, you're going to UCLA!" My friend's face was frozen in shock.

"Maybe Layla doesn't want to go?" Babajon teased.

"*Balleh, balleh, meerram!* Yes, yes, I'll go!" I was tearing now, nearly hysterical.

"Okay!" Baba boomed, using the American expression.

He threw his arms up, snapped his fingers, and at his signal, the band started playing "*Mobarak*," the traditional song of congratulations played at joyous occasions. I joined him in a traditional Persian dance, snaking my arms in the air, my body moving rhythmically to the Persian beat.

For the rest of the night, I remained in the center of the dance floor, my friends joining me as I danced for joy.

The next morning, I awoke to the miracle of the night before. I couldn't wait to find my parents and thank them again for what was unquestionably, the most wonderful night of my life.

I found them in Babajon's study. He was standing behind his desk. Maman was also there, sitting on a club chair.

"How did you manage to do all this without my knowing?" I asked my father. "I never even filled out an application."

– Babjon –

As my father explained the steps he'd taken to procure my acceptance into one of the best universities in America without my participation, I was overwhelmed by the strength of his aspirations and the measures he had taken for me out of his love.

"I am happy to give you this opportunity," he said. "Still, I don't want you to feel you must go. This is your future, Layla. I can only give you the choices. I can't make them for you. Only you can decide what to do.

"You can go to college in America and learn, fill up your mind with what it thirsts for, then return home to marry and fill up your heart with what it needs. Or, you can stay here, marry a nice young man and bear children at a younger age. Perhaps you can take some science classes at Tehran University if your husband allows.

"If you decide to go, you will room with your cousin, Jila. She lives near the school in Westwood. Jila has attended the university there for a year already and she will be a great help to you. You are smart, and your English is excellent. There are also English classes available to you there if you feel that is necessary.

"You can do this if you want to, Layla. I know you can. The question is, do you want to? I want you to think seriously about it. This is not an easy choice for you to make. It would be four years of your life. The most important thing is to do what is in your heart. Meditate. Go into your heart, then, give your mother and me your final answer."

My mother had sat erect this whole time, her face frozen. She had not uttered a word while my father spoke. Now I saw that she was wringing her hands in her lap.

"Maman, do you want me to go?"

Maman looked at my father and their eyes met, before hers traveled back to me and she answered, "No."

"If you go, your mother and I will, of course, miss you very much," Babajon said as he walked to the side of his desk. "It will undoubtedly be extremely difficult for her as well as for me to be without you. You, too, will miss your mother and perhaps miss me." He came around and perched on the other side of the desk. "You will no doubt also miss your grandparents, the rest of the family and your friends."

He picked up a paper clip laying on the desktop, played with it for seconds, and put it back down. "We both want you to be happy. That is the most important thing."

"Yes, Babajon. I understand." I flew to his side and kissed him, then bent over Maman's chair and kissed her. "Thank you both. I love you so very, very much."

For me, it was simple: I was going.

– Zahra –

When Hadi finished with what he had to say to Layla, I looked carefully at my daughter's young, fresh face to see if I could detect the effect of my husband's words.

The smile I saw there broke my heart.

The following evening the three of us went to the annual Club soiree. Though spoken of as a "Celebration of Graduation" it actually was meant to mark the official entry into the marriage pool of the girls who had just finished high school and not yet promised in marriage.

For my daughter, it was a goodbye party.

I hid my misery as best as I could from the mothers and fathers who approached to congratulate Hadi and me on the honors Layla received at graduation. These were fathers and mothers who would have soon been calling on us, lining up with sons, as Layla's hopeful *khostegars*. Had she stayed home, one of these couples would likely have been Layla's in-laws within the year.

"Congratulations on Layla *jon*'s graduation. I've heard the school gave her so many honors that they were forced to close down and send the students home for the summer." Laughter followed. It was the most terrible night of my life.

I asked my nephew if he knew where Jalil was. "Last I heard, Ammeh Zahra, he's sick and was feeling really rotten," Bahman said. "I guess he was too sick to make it."

I was about to be cornered by the overbearing parents of a handsome, deputy minister who'd had his eye on Layla; he was too old for my daughter.

I eyed the man I recognized as the father of a most eligible boy, holding a small plate of kabob, speaking to Hadi. I edged a bit closer to hear their conversation.

"Yes, no doubt. She's done splendidly well in her studies," the man said to Hadi. "Now comes the time for her to break many hearts and make one lucky man joyous." He bit into his kabob.

Though I didn't hear Hadi's reply, I saw the man's face move into disbelief and overheard his next words. "California? Four years?

You're kidding." A moment later, I saw the man walk away shaking his head.

I turned to see Layla standing nearby. She was so beautiful. The new dress – close-fitting at the bodice with a vermillion sash at the waistline – suited her perfectly, showing her slim yet shapely body. The soft fabric of a paisley pattern in green, vermillion and gold set off her hazel eyes, her long, lustrous, dark chestnut hair and her skin, the color of early dusk. She could be marrying a powerful man.

As the evening progressed, I saw how eyes followed my daughter as she passed by and loitered on her when she moved to the dance floor. She swayed her hips seductively, moved her arms with grace, smiling radiantly. She was compelling. With her happiness wrapped around her, she was positively glowing.

I saw all this and wanted to cry out. Instead, I made small talk with the other wives as Layla danced all night.

16
GOODBYES

I often wonder how different my life would have been if my father's love for me hadn't driven him to make the fateful decision that so altered the course of my life.

As the daughter of wealthy and prominent parents, I would have unquestionably been betrothed to a rich and prestigious Iranian almost immediately upon graduation and soon started a family.

Maman had not gone to high school. Her mother, Mama Bozorg, had married at thirteen and had become a mother within the year. As a young teenager, Babajon's mother, Naneh Joon, had married a man far older than herself with the promise that he would care for her. Consequently, I became the first woman in my lineage to graduate from high school. Then the seed of the impossible had sprouted in Babajon's mind and taken hold; I was presented with an opportunity undreamed of and I seized it.

I would be going to America. I would live in Los Angeles, California. I would actually be a student at UCLA, enrolled in their brand-new microbiology department. I, Layla Saleh, would be learning from the finest professors and using the finest laboratory equipment available in the world.

I'd be living my dream!

Suddenly, the days and weeks were tumbling by.

I was caught in an eddy of commotion and a jumble of emotion.

I was euphoric. I was filled with doubts. Unlike Shireen, I wasn't anxious to escape my parents. *How could I be happy so far apart from Maman and Babajan?* I'd seen them almost every day of my life. I'd be leaving home and all I'd ever known. Surely, I would be homesick. I wondered if I would be truly comfortable in my new surroundings.

I was scared. So many unknowns awaited me; dwelling on them made my heart pound. Then I would read about America's latest space plans or watch the newest Hollywood movie and the excitement of going would reignite. I was brimming and overflowing with excitement! I was about to embark on an epic adventure in America.

America!

It was comforting to know I'd be living with my Jila. Shireen had started me wondering about my cousin's life in America. Suddenly, it was only a matter of time before I would find out the truth.

I spent the time left at home with the people I loved. Dinners were shared with Babajon's parents, Naneh Joon and Agha Doctor, Maman's brother, Dayee Mansoor and his family, and her younger, childless sister, Khaleh Bahia, widowed three years ago when her husband died of influenza.

When I walked down my street everything took on a new importance. I observed my surroundings with a keen eye, hoping to etch these sights in my memory.

When had the lion's head on the pedestal in front of Khanom Bariot's home cracked?

Had Madame Elian widened her pathway by the side gate?

In the soft light of the late summer evenings, the beauty of the lush greenery that climbed up and fell over the walls enclosing the residential compounds seemed magnified. I inhaled the sweet smell of night-blooming jasmine, coming so alive as summer approached.

What would I smell on the streets of Los Angeles?

The days that I'd awaken in the only bedroom I'd ever called mine were rapidly being torn from the calendar. I sensed the end of a part of my life was near, a part that I would never be able to revive once I left home. How could I say goodbye?

I was so full of questions.

"I don't understand my own daughter," Maman said to me one afternoon as we chose clothing from my closets to pack.

She tossed a red cardigan on the bed. "You have everything you could want right here. *Beheshteh!* It's Paradise! It's heaven on earth. Then your silly father suggests that you do crazy things and you, 'Miss Smart Girl,' you listen to him and then you *do* those crazy things! I don't understand you."

She picked up the red sweater and dropped it back on the bed. "You have a wonderful home, friends and family; you could have a bright future with a decent man who would take care of you so that you can enjoy a good life. And what do you do? You get up and leave this Paradise to go to a godforsaken place to sit and learn about filthy little germs and bacteria!" She shook her head in despair. "Oh, Layla, why do you insist on going?"

I felt sorry for Maman. Her plans for me were not unfolding as she'd hoped.

"Maman *jon,* you're right. This is Paradise and I am so lucky to have it and it's all because of you and Babajon. And now you've me the chance to go to college in America. I love you both so much for that. And I promise you that I will have everything you want for me when I come home. You'll see."

"Not if you wait *four years.*" She sat down on my bed. "I only hope you find your senses and come home before you are too old to be wanted by anyone worthwhile."

"It really isn't fair! You're so lucky."

This time I agreed with Shireen. I *was* lucky.

Dinner had been cleared away and the two of us were sitting on the floor in our favorite corner of her living room, leaning against a couch. The adults played cards at the dining room table, and, as they played, the men continued the never-ending pastime of the wealthy, arguing the pros and cons of sending money abroad to a country where it – and their family – would be safe should the monarchy topple.

The shah had reclaimed his power with the downfall of his archrival, the popular prime minister Mossadegh. SAVAK, his secret service aimed at weeding out political enemies was now in existance. Still, Babajon, like many others, felt the shah's leadership position was not secure.

SAVAK had quickly come to be dreaded. No one knew who belonged to the organization. You could be complaining about the shah or one of his programs to your baker, co-worker, employee or guest and find yourself hauled off to prison that night. So, it was only in the most private circles that people dared to discuss any antipathy toward the monarchy, or even – as Babajon was doing – express the feeling that the country and its economy were less than stable.

Dayee Mansoor scoffed at Babajon's decision to begin sending some funds overseas. "You're overreacting, Hadi. There's no need to parcel one's wealth around the world."

I was interested in the conversation. Perhaps it was my friendship with Ferri that had awakened my curiosity to politics and the world around me. I wanted to sit at the table with them and listen to their conversation as Bahman was doing. But, Shireen was deaf to all but her own immediate thoughts.

For the umpteenth time that night, she said, "I just can't believe that your parents are letting you go to America," she squealed, "and you never even asked! How I wish I could get away from here."

My cousin's desire "to get away" still puzzled me. It actually nagged at me. I thought it was a sign of her maladjustment in what looked to me to be a happy household. Both her parents seemed to be reasonable; Bahman never complained.

"You'll be able to do what you want," she said. "Dance until dawn, wear what you like … " She'd clenched her fists. "Oh, it's so unfair!"

"Shireen, I'm not going to America to go dancing! I'm going to study." She didn't even hear me.

"That reminds me," she said after a bit more of pouting, "I have something for you." She reached into the built-in cabinet along the wall and presented me with a small, gift-wrapped box. Inside was a brown velvet headband embellished heavily with large turquoise stones separated by smaller coral stones. It was exquisite.

"It's beautiful, Shireen."

"Yes, I know. I had Maman buy it for you. You can send me something from California. You know my sizes in everything. My best colors are the same as Elizabeth's, greens and violet, purples and white."

She put her clasped hands to her chin. "Oh, to think you'll walk down the same streets as movie stars! When you see Liz, you must show her my picture. I'll bet she won't believe how much we look alike. And get her autograph for me. Have her sign, *'To my friend, Shireen.'* She'll probably sign it *'Elizabeth.* That's okay."

"Sure."

"*Ay, Khodah,* my God!" She looked around the elegant living room. "You're going, and I have to stay here in this godforsaken place. You are coming back to visit, aren't you?"

"I'll spend one month here every summer."

"Good. By your first trip home I'll be married. You'll see, I'll keep my promise. Be ready to come back for my wedding. I'll be married soon." She threw her arms around me. "I'll miss you so much. What will I do without you?"

I couldn't help laughing. "I'll miss you so much more. You have so many other friends."

"None of them are as close to me as you are, Layla, and none are as good to me." She suddenly became extremely shy. I'd rarely seen that side of her. She spoke softly, with a little smile. "And I forgive you for spending so much time with Ferri."

I was a bit thrown off by her uncharacteristic gentleness. "You'll be too busy looking for a rich husband to miss me," I said.

She suddenly brightened up. "Oh! Did I tell you about the Moloyeds?" I shook my head. My cousin reverted to the girl I knew, speaking excitedly. "How could I forget to tell you?" she asked. "I actually might marry into the Moloyed family."

"*Taymoor* Moloyed?" Shireen couldn't mean the heavyset man I was thinking of. That Taymoor was more than thirty years old.

"Yes, Taymoor. He's the second oldest brother and the only one still not married. I heard my parents talking. They didn't know I was listening. The Moloyeds have asked my uncle if I've been spoken for yet."

"Isn't Taymoor too old for you?"

"He's thirty-two. Oh Layla! Sometimes you exasperate me. You sound like my mother. That's what she says. You know Liz married a much older man when she was about our age. If Taymoor is actually as fabulously rich as I hear ... Besides, what's so great about a younger man?" She stood up and spoke in a wispy voice, shimmying up and down like Marilyn Monroe and quivering her lips. "Maybe I need a man with some *experience*." She threw her head back, laughing.

It wasn't funny to me. "Shireen don't do anything you'll be sorry for. Okay? Promise me that."

Shireen's "Okay" was too fast and easy for my comfort. "Let's go upstairs. We won't be able to dance again before you leave. Let's dance and dance until you have to go home."

We ran up the stairs to Shireen's bedroom where she immediately started up the phonograph and we began to dance.

"Shireen, what will you do when Taymoor is too old to dance?"

She shrugged. "Well, I have to marry within the year. I promised that before God. Remember? And he has to be someone really wealthy. And I have to dance. So, if I marry Taymoor, I guess I'll just *make* him dance," she responded.

Haji Baba continually repeated, "*Beraghks!* Dance!"

I was going to miss that parrot, too.

"Don't think that the bloom of youth lasts forever, Layla. Come home and marry before you become *torsheed,* before you pickle."

"Yes, Maman."

"And don't ever forget your upbringing."

"Yes, Maman."

"This is crazy." She shook her head and sighed.

The day I knocked on my neighbor's door to say goodbye, Parveen Khanom was wearing a blue cotton shirtwaist dress, and her hair was tied at her nape with a blue ribbon.

She invited me into her salon. As always, I sat down on one of the two velvet chairs facing the five frames holding gold-rimmed pages of the Quran. Parveen Khanom asked if I would prefer cold lemonade or *chai*. After I *tarroffed*, thanking her profusely for her offer, insisting that I wasn't thirsty and wouldn't dream of imposing on her, I agreed to a cup of chai. Her servant brought us the jasmine tea as usual, on a silver tray she set on the table between the two of us. There were small hand-worked silver dishes laden with dates, pastries, sugar cubes and pieces of hardened golden-brown halvah surrounded by thin slivers of almonds. With a piece of the halvah on my tongue, I took a sip of the aromatic jasmine chai. The halvah melted, and its consistency turned creamy, blending with the warm tea.

"So, my friend," Parveen Khanom said, "*Allah akbar*, Allah is great, praise Allah, you insist on leaving the men here in tears and going to a foreign land." Her smile was beautiful.

"I don't know how your parents can let you go, especially your mother, *Khodah umresh-shoon bedeh*, God grant her life! The party she gave to celebrate your graduation was lovely. *Daste-shoon dard nakoneh*, may her hand not hurt from all she had done, Parviz Khan and I enjoyed it immensely.

"It must be very difficult for her to see you leave. Your parents are obviously very proud of you. I expect you to do very well at school, *beh omeedeh Khodah*, may God allow. You have a great responsibility before you. To the Americans, you will represent all Iranians. Show the them that we Iranians haven't just been sitting around roasting pistachios and boiling rice for almost twenty-five hundred years."

Reza came running into the room, blowing on his toy trumpet. Behind him marched Mohammad, banging on the miniature drum that hung from his belt. By then, Reza was eight years old and Mohammad was four. Seeing me, Mohammad screamed out my name and dropped his drumsticks. He climbed onto my lap while his older brother, equally glad to see me, called for me to "come play."

"*Mommy joon,* Layla and I are talking." Reza promptly helped his little brother off my lap and we were left to ourselves again. "And you, Layla," my hostess continued, "aren't you nervous about going so far away from home, all alone?"

"Yes, a little."

"Yet you will go anyway. May God's will be done."

"I'm going to go to a *fallgir,* a fortune teller, to see what my future in America will bring," I said; I hadn't yet told anyone else.

Parveen Khanom shifted in her chair then said pleasantly, "Layla *jon,* one who puts their faith in Allah has no need for *fallgirs.* The Quran specifically advises us to stay away from *fallgirs. Whosoever goes to a fortune teller and asks him about anything, his prayers will not be accepted for forty days."*

I was again impressed by my neighbor's knowledge of the Quran and a bit embarrassed at my own ignorance of it. To think that she could quote passages like that! And then awe turned to frustration, for I had still not seen fit to ask this knowledgeable woman any of the questions I longed to be answered about our religion.

"Allah is great," she continued. "He will provide. Only what He destines for you will come to be, Layla. All you need are your schoolbooks and the Quran. Only study and pray. You need no *fallgirs.*"

I was on the verge of asking her all the questions I'd had about our shared religion, questions I'd kept putting off. But then, just as she finished speaking about *fallgirs,* her sons returned, asking their mother if I could now play with them.

"Go," Parveen Khanom said to me. "They will miss you more than you know."

"I will miss them at least as much."

When the time came for us to say our goodbyes, Parveen Khanom walked me to the door and held a copy of the Quran above my head reciting a blessing, then handed me the holy book. "I want you to have this with you in the foreign land," she said. "It will keep you safe."

I took the Quran from her, and a feeling of protection inexplicably washed over me. "Thank you for your kindness. I will pray for your family and remember all of you often and with great affection."

"It is I who thank you for blessing our home with your visit today. I wish you every blessing Allah has to give, and may He watch over you while you are away. May Allah hold you in his hand." We touched the two sides of our faces to one another's and kissed the air."Go with God. *Allah akbar!* God is great."

I did not visit the fortuneteller before I left. Nor did I follow Parveen Khanom's advice to simply "only study and pray" while in America. Perhaps I should have done one or the other.

"Layla, pay attention.

"You must remember who you are at all times. Stay away from boys. They will try to get close to you. You *must* not let them. You must not disgrace me. Do you promise me this?"

"I do, Maman."

My impending departure did not lessen my anxiety about Ferri.

I was afraid that in my absence, my angel's meetings with Hamid would be discovered and I wouldn't be there for her.

At our final lunch before my departure at a small *kabobee*, I presented her with a gift-wrapped box. "I suppose I'll never stop worrying about you and your alibis." I said. "I'm giving this to you to help ease my mind a little while I'm gone." As she unwrapped the package and opened the box, I explained. "I know you don't like wearing a watch but this one is special. The green hands glow in the dark so you'll always know what time it is, no matter how dark it is in the Charlatan. Hopefully, you'll never get home late again. "We laughed, and she thanked me as I helped her latch the watch onto her wrist.

"Now, let's talk about you for once *joonie*. You're the one who's going thousands of miles away."

"There's not much to say," I said. "I'm excited about UCLA and California and I'm nervous about going away, and you know I'll miss you a lot."

"And I'll miss my *joonie*. I promised you I'll always have a good alibi. I want you to enjoy your taste of freedom. You have your wings; go fly. But promise me that you won't fly so close to the sun that you burn and melt your wings like Icarus did."

"Trust me, Ferri, I have no intention of drowning in the ocean."

I left my angel, praying *she* wouldn't burn.

"Don't let your father's good opinion of me suffer. Don't disgrace me like that. Do you hear me, Layla? You do as I have taught you and stay away from boys. Far, far away."

"Yes, Maman. I will. I promise."

At last, I was ready to leave.

I had my visa. The immigration officials had stamped an exit visa on my passport after been presented with a letter from Babajon, my legal guardian as long as I was unmarried, stating that he permitted me to leave Iran.

I had my wardrobe. I'd been on numerous shopping trips and had made endless visits to Aynor. Maman had packed my several suitcases with clothes appropriate for a girl of my station to wear for almost every possible occasion.

I had completed both medical and dental check-ups. Maman had insisted that I be fully examined by both my doctor and my dentist before leaving, so that American doctors wouldn't interfere with my health.

Through it all, she had lectured and instructed me nonstop. As my departure date approached, her warnings only increased, and her list of instructions lengthened.

"Beware of Americans. Their culture, their thoughts and ideas are not like ours.

"We have come through a long and rich history, Lana. Amreeka is a baby that dirties its diapers."

"Yes, Maman."

"I know your father has put you together with Jila. All the same, don't spend too much time with her or her parents. They are below us. If they had been successful in Iran, they would never have left their home."

"Yes, Maman."

"Don't speak of our lives with Jila or her parents. Even if they ask, don't open up. They are jealous; *cheshm meezanan* – they'll give the evil eye."

"Yes, Maman."

"Never talk to strangers, guard your possessions, and lock your bedroom door at night."

"Yes, Maman."

"Don't be careless with money or valuables, watch them closely. If you need more money, call."

"Yes, Maman."

"Eat well. Try to find watercress and parsley, tarragon, cilantro and other fresh herbs and greens. Eat a lot of them."

"Yes, Maman."

"Be careful whom you let into your house and always offer your guests tea and cake."

"Yes, Maman."

"Eat a lot of pomegranates and figs, watermelon and quince – if they even have these in Amreeka. Make a list of things they don't have. I'll have Cobra gather them and your father will ship them to you."

"Yes, Maman."

"Remember: People judge you by the class you reflect, so always dress elegantly. Those cheap American styles are not for us. Always be chic."

"Yes, Maman."

"Write often and call regularly. Send pictures of yourself. And as long as you're doing that, enclose pictures of Elahe – she's probably still far too heavy – and let me see what your cousin Jila looks like."

"Yes, Maman."

"Don't walk in the streets at night."

"Yes, Maman."

"I know you like those American movies. Child, they all encourage indecent and immoral behavior. You are better off reading a book."

"Yes, Maman."

"For God's sake, do not befriend American shop girls and others of a lesser station. Be cordial to everyone and discerning of the girls you make your friends. I know there are less than ten Persians in Los Angeles and few, if any, are Muslim. Maybe there are some nice European girls there whose families we know."

"Yes, Maman."

"Most important of all, stay away from boys and men. Do not be caught alone with one. *Never* be in the company of a male alone, do you hear me? *Never!* Men will *do* anything, and *say* anything to seduce a young, pretty girl like you. You *must* guard yourself against their tricks."

"Yes, Maman."

"Remember what you have been taught by me. You are Layla Saleh. Remember always that your virginity, your decency and your reputation are all that you have; guard them as your most valuable possessions."

"Yes, Maman *jon*."

"Don't *Yes, Maman jon* me, daughter! Tell me you will do as I say."

"I will do as you say."

"And come home soon. Don't think you have to stay in that horrible place any set amount of time. You needn't stay four years. You needn't even stay one year, not even one month. As soon as you realize you've made a huge mistake, come home. Visit, see Jila and come back. You can always say you've been to America then."

"Yes, Maman, I will do as you say."

Though I didn't see a single tear, Maman wiped her eyes with a tissue before she turned away.

As fast as time went by, the last days seem to take forever.

Finally, the evening came that I was to leave the only country I'd ever known. Babajon and Maman held a Quran over my head as Parveen Khanom had, and I passed under it for good luck. We piled into two cars and, as we drove off, Cobra, Fotmeh, and Abol chased our departing car, sprinkling rose water on the road to clear the way for my safe return. I waved goodbye to them, and they soon disappeared around the curve.

At Mehrabad Airport, our caravan spilled out a pouting Shireen, her brother Bahman and their parents, along with my Khaleh Bahia, my teary-eyed grandparents, my overly excited father, my tense mother, and me.

Babajon checked in my three large suitcases and a smaller carton filled with bundles of Persian candy, tea and nuts, some for myself and some to give as gifts. When he returned to our group, he took me aside, embraced me, then held my shoulders.

"Layla, this is a happy day for me as well as for you. You have made your choice, and I am very proud that you were strong enough to follow your heart. You are a special girl. I know you will value your time in America. I want you to enjoy yourself."

I smiled and hugged him. "I will, Babajon."

"I know I don't have to tell you this. I will anyway. Don't think you can marry an American; the two cultures clash and a marriage between them won't work. Stay clear of the men there. Study in America, only that. Then come home and marry."

"Yes, Babajon."

Shireen ran up with one last reminder. "Don't forget Liz. *'To my friend, Shireen.'*"

Kisses, hugs, tears and last-minute admonitions finally ended.

I waved my last goodbye, threw my last kiss and turned to board the airplane that would take me to my future, a future that might have been sealed when I boarded that plane.

PART II: AMERICA!

PROLOGUE TO PART II

LAND OF THE FREE

America...How I wondered what awaited me.

In 1959, most Americans knew little of Persia.

Few Persians had immigrated to the States. As I set about discovering my new surroundings, I found Americans were curious about my unusual name, my accent, my country and me.

I think Americans first became aware of Iran in 1958, when photos of the shah's exquisite, emerald-eyed second wife, Queen Soraya, was splashed on magazine covers and they learned the heart-wrenching story carried by international newswires, "Shah of Iran Divorces His Queen."

Soraya became fodder for the news media and was one of the most photographed women of the Twentieth Century. She was often seen wearing large sunglasses after the divorce, likely to mask her sad eyes. In fact, she came to be known in Western press as "The Princess with the Sad Eyes." In May 1958, the banner that accompanied her photo on the cover of Life magazine read, "Banished Queen's Holiday."

The love story could have been made into a classic American movie:

The shah, king of an exotic, oil-puddled country, and the startlingly beautiful Soraya are deeply in love. They marry. They are happy. But the shah must have an heir if the Pahlavi dynasty is to continue, and Soraya has not yet become pregnant. She accompanies the shah on his diplomatic visits to the U.S. and throughout Europe, seeking out western fertility specialists, but nothing comes of it. She cannot conceive.

The shah's Royal Council exerts increasing pressure on the shah to remarry. The couple is devastated. Their happiness shatters. Their marriage threatened. Something must be done.

Options are considered. The shah is willing to abdicate, but it is impossible. Though he has half-brothers, the Iranian constitution allows only for his full-blood brother to take his place as monarch. Unfortunately, Ali Reza Pahlavi, the shah's sole full brother, died in a plane crash in 1952 on his way back to Tehran to join in the celebrations of the shah's birthday. Abdication is ruled out.

As a Muslim, His Excellency may take a second wife. His Majesty is prepared to do that – if he has Soraya's blessing. He proposes this to her, insisting that another marriage would serve the sole purpose of delivering a male heir to his throne. It is the only way to save their marriage. He begs her to consider this option. The young Queen refuses. She will not share her beloved with another woman.

On Feb. 14, 1958, she leaves Iran to return to her parent's home in Switzerland. She will never return to Iran. The shah sends envoys to Switzerland with instructions to persuade his life's love to change her mind and come back to him. Perhaps the shah himself follows her to Switzerland as well, to plead his own case. Soraya will not be persuaded. The marriage must end.

On *Norooz*, the Iranian New Year, March 21, 1958, and one month after Soraya's departure, a weeping shah publicly announces the royal divorce. He prefaces it with his heart rendering statement that, as he has shared his happiness with his people, so too he has chosen to share his heartache.

Soraya's statement to the Persian people is also aired. In it, she declares that she is sacrificing her own happiness for the sake of Iran's future. Her pictures are taken down in halls and from walls all over Tehran and around the country, leaving those of the shah to hang alone, once again.

The extensive media coverage given to the love story gone awry had familiarized Americans with the existence of Iran, though they know little else about my country. In time, the divorce no longer interests them.

Then, in 1979, the Islamic Revolution put Iran on the map again, in a way history will, no doubt, continue to find far more difficult to forget.

I suppose there is a lesson to be learned: In the competition to capture the attention of the masses, blood is apparently more memorable than love.

17
I ARRIVE

August 27, 1959 — Los Angeles, California

I had looked forward to coming to America, going to UCLA and seeing for myself the country I'd heard so much about; the origin of rock 'n' roll, the hula-hoop, hamburgers, telephones everywhere, movies, and so much more.

I look back and see how naïve I'd been to think I could view it all as if I were in a museum protected behind a glass partition, never realizing how greatly I'd be affected by the journey.

I was met at Los Angeles International Airport by my aunt, Ammeh Elahe, her husband, Javeed Khan, and my cousin Jila.

I'd last seen the three of them years ago, yet I recognized them even from a distance and spotted them before they spotted me. There were very few Middle Eastern families awaiting the arrival of passengers at

LAX back then, and my aunt and uncle's bearing stood out like a skewer of kabob on white rice.

As I got closer to them, it was apparent that both my aunt and uncle had aged. Javeed Khan seemed thinner, and Ammeh Elahe was heavier than I recalled. Yet Jila had hardly changed. She still had her mother's large lips and high-profile nose and her father's doleful eyes, all set in his round baby-like face. She was a shorter than me, slim, with hips that expanded like an open fan. Her long dark hair was held off her face with a headband.

I was genuinely glad to see them.

Ammeh Elahe spoke in short outbursts, embracing me between each sentence. She threw her arms around me. "Layla *jon, toyee?* Is it you?" She held me at arm's length and then hugged me to her again. "*Khodara shokr,* thank God. *Khosh amadee,* your arrival is welcomed."

We eventually stopped hugging, and when we went to the terminal to collect my luggage, I was surprised that Javeed Khan didn't ask for help from an airport porter. It was embarrassing to watch him struggle with the suitcases. I took hold of the handle of one and pulled, letting it skip behind me. Elahe Khanom managed the smallest suitcase and Jila was left with the bulky carton of food, leaving him only the largest suitcase.

"Welcome to America, our home! How was your flight? Was it too long for you? Of course, it was. Was it tiring? Oh, you must be exhausted! Are you all right? *Khodara shokr,* thank God, you're here."

Ammeh Elahe asked question after question, barely waiting for my answer and sandwiching it all between an endless string of thanks to God for my safe arrival.

"Maman *jon,* speak quieter," Jila said gently. "People are looking at us."

My aunt's eyes widened, and her elbows went up. "Jila, *fadot sham,* may I be sacrificed for you, let them look. My brother's daughter has come all this way. We haven't seen her for years. And you tell me to be quiet, so I don't annoy these foreigners?"

I smiled to hear my aunt call Americans "foreigners" in their own country.

Just before we exited the terminal, she instructed us to stop. "Let me look at my niece once more." Again, she held me at arm's length and looked me up and down. She clapped her hands. "*Mushallah,* well done. You really have grown into a beauty. Javeed, look at her. Jila, isn't she beautiful? *Mushallah!* May you be preserved from the evil eye. You're very pretty."

My uncle and cousin nodded in agreement (as if they had a choice). Ammeh Elahe grasped my hand tightly. "*Khodah shahed,* God is my witness, from the moment your dear father called to say you were coming, we have all been very, very happy."

We continued on our way. After a few steps, she asked, "How is my dear brother? *Khodah shahed,* God is my witness, I think of him every day."

"He's very well, thank you," I replied.

"*Alhamdo le'llah,* Allah be praised. *Ghorbonesh beram,* may I be sacrificed for him. I'm glad he's well. He is a special man."

She went on. "How wonderful that you are here. Of course, you should be with Jila! Am I not correct, Jila? You two belong together. After all, we are your family. And my Jila has been at UCLA for a year now; she knows everything about the school, an expert. Don't worry about a thing. We are here for you, and we will make sure you are fine. It will all be A plus." She continued on and on, never stopping her chatter.

Though the Los Angeles airport was far larger than Mehrabad Airport, it wasn't until we stepped outside that I was struck by how truly enormous LAX was. I realized that we had exited one of several terminals. The parking facilities were vast. We made our way to an older blue Ford station wagon, thankfully large enough to accommodate all my luggage.

"Excuse our car," Ammeh said lightly as my uncle loaded my suitcases into the back of the car. "There was some small difficulty with our new one, so we returned it and are looking for another."

Jila looked exasperated. "Maman–"

Ammeh Elahe had no interest in what Jila might have to say. "Tell me, how is Hadi *jon*?" she asked again. "May I be sacrificed for him. He is kind and wonderful and he deserves every bit of the success he has and more. He is well?"

"Both of my parents are fine, thank you, and they send all of you their love."

"Good. I'm very glad he's well," she replied. "So, he copes well." *Copes well with what?* "*Alhamdo le'llah,* Allah be praised. And my cherished parents? Are they well?"

"Yes, Naneh Joon and Agha Doctor also send you all their love." I answered. It was difficult not to notice that Ammeh hadn't asked after Maman.

We took our seats in the car and my uncle drove off as Ammeh said, "*Alhamdo le'ellah,* Allah be praised, *Khodara shokr,* thank God. How I miss my dear mother and father."

"Naneh Joon and Agha Doctor have sent things for you in the carton," I said, hoping she would take that to mean they miss her as well.

We drove the wide and efficient freeway, and I took in my new surroundings. There were endless stretches of open empty land punctuated by clusters of urban life. There were new freeways in various stages of construction. I was struck by how orderly the traffic was as compared to Tehran where drivers dared one another to be the more *zereng,* the more aggressive, right of way yielded to the most *zereng* driver. As a result, traffic there was haphazard, vehicles coming from and going in all directions at once. Here, drivers stayed in their lane and signaled before turning, stopped and waited at traffic lights. I didn't see a single head sticking out of a car window screaming insults.

And the whole time we drove, Ammeh Elahe talked and talked as if her mouth was the engine that powered the car.

"You will love Los Angeles," she said, wiggling this way and that in her seat, both hands on her black handbag. "Do you see how warm it is? We chose Los Angeles because the climate is so similar to Tehran's, hot but not as dry; though, of course, it never snows here. It's an endless summer," No pause, "and the foreigners – well, they're not Persian, but, nonetheless, they are generally very good-hearted. True, they don't think as we do, but many of them are nice. I know you will like them. Have peace of mind and put your energy into studying."

And she changed subjects again, craning her head to face me in the back seat. "Tell me, promise on my soul you'll tell the truth. What is our shah, Aalah Hazrat, His Majesty really like?"

I was surprised by her question that came out of the blue. "I don't know, Ammeh *jon*."

"But you met him. Don't be modest."

"I only met him once for a short while with a group of students. He shook my hand, and then we all sat down and had lunch. Afterward, the Minister of Education spoke to us and then His Majesty gave a short speech."

Ammeh was straining, trying to turn her heavy body around to face me as I sat in the back seat. It proved too difficult for her, so she spoke louder and waved her left hand around in my general direction.

"My dear niece, why do you belittle what you've done? *Eftekhar kon,* be proud! We are all very proud of what you achieved in school. Even though we weren't there, we know what you have done. Your father is very proud of you. You've been invited to the palace, Layla! You must have been very special, very smart to be invited to see the shah and have lunch with him. You must be proud of that. It is a great thing, a big thing. *Khoshgellan?* Is he handsome?"

"He's very distinguished looking."

"Is he still very sad?" she asked in a softer voice. Then, before I could respond, she slapped one hand on top of the other and went on, "What a shame. He and Soraya were so much in love." She put one hand on her husband's thigh. "You never forget true love. My heart breaks for His Majesty." She sighed. "How is he?"

"I don't know, Ammeh *jon*. I suppose he's well."

Jila patted my arm then and when I looked at her, she rolled her eyes and we both smiled.

My aunt, apparently satisfied, said, "*Khob, Khodah bozorgeh,* well, God is great!"

The entire time we were in the car, neither Jila nor her father even tried to get a word in as my aunt talked on and on. Javeed Khan simply drove, nodding when his wife said something requiring acknowledgement, while Jila, sitting alongside me in the back seat, would occasionally roll her eyes or smile. I returned her smiles, not meaning to be disrespectful to my aunt, but rather, eager to begin re-bonding with my cousin.

Ammeh Elahe nudged her husband's arm. "Javeed, there it is. This is where we get off."

Her husband nodded. The car swerved, as he traveled to the far right lane, then made his way to the freeway off ramp. After a few turns we were on a boulevard as wide as any in Tehran.

Ammaeh Elahe spoke. "We're going to stop for lunch. I hope you will like the restaurant, Layla. I know you are tired and hungry, but our home is not close. We'll eat and then take you and Jila to your apartment. You have a lot to do. You need to unpack.

"I see you've brought far too much clothing – no doubt your mother's idea. In any event, Jila will help you sort them out. You must rest. *Beh omeedeh Khodah,* with God's grace, you will visit us at our humble home often. It is your home now."

The restaurant was the largest I'd ever seen as well as the oddest, built in the shape of a circle. We were shown to a booth where Ammeh Elahe directed our seating arrangement.

There were items on the menu with names like "Malibu Melt," "Pasadena Pastrami" and "Beverly Hills BLT." I ordered a Hollywood Hamburger then excused myself and went to the Ladies Room with Jila. It was strange to hear fluent English spoken all around me. *Of course! I'm in America now!* I would soon become accustomed to it.

I was impressed by the cleanliness of the first American public restroom I visited. That level of sanitation in a public toilet was rare in Tehran. I counted five stalls, all with European-style toilets like we had at home, ample toilet paper provided. "Public toilets are definitely cleaner than those at home," I said as we washed and dried hands in the clean white sink with the soap and paper towels so generously supplied. I spoke in Farsi and Jila answered in English.

"Yes, but the poetry lags behind that of Hafez, Rumi and Khayyam," Jila said. "Come look."

We returned to the stall my cousin had occupied. There, written in elegant small print, someone had written, *Here I sit, brokenhearted, came to shit, only farted.* I knew what "shit" meant and now, through context,

I learned the meaning of "fart." It was the first English word I learned in America.

We returned to our booth, welcomed by my aunt's continuing monologue. She interrupted herself to welcome us back and let us know that our lunches were getting cold. My hamburger was as good as any I'd ever tasted, the French fries were crisp and the Coke, cold and refreshing. I ate hungrily.

"*Begoo,* do tell, how did your father convince Zahra to agree to let you come to Los Angeles?" Ammeh's latest question – as most – came out of nowhere. And, as I already had learned was her style, she continued on before I could respond. She spoke with an air of confidentiality and confidence. "She let you come here instead of staying in Iran and marrying? She must be very unhappy."

"I'm sure she'll miss me." Her look lingered on me. "She let me choose."

Ammeh knew Maman too well to swallow my answer whole. She raised her index finger and pointed to the ceiling. "I know my brother had a job convincing her."

I looked away and didn't answer, becoming increasingly uncomfortable by my aunt's apparent disrespect of Maman.

With lunch done, we continued our drive into Westwood. At Wilshire Boulevard, another wide thoroughfare, we made some turns, passed through an area of small multi-residential dwellings then turned again.

Jila nudged me. "This is Weyburn Avenue, our street," she said.

My heart fluttered as I tried to take in both sides of my new street at once. Javeed Khan parked, and as we took my suitcases out of the car, Ammeh again commented on the amount of luggage I had brought.

"Zahra has over-packed you. All this will never fit into your closet." She gestured to the suitcases. "You will have to keep most of your things at our house."

I stood at the door to my new home, then in the center of the smallest, most wonderful living room I'd ever been in.

Ammeh Elahe turned to me. "*Khodara shokr,* thank God, you are here safe and sound." She took her husband by his elbow and turned him to the door.

"Jila *jon,* see what your cousin needs, make her a cup of tea and let her rest. Give her the other key, help her unpack. We'll bring her home this weekend with her extra clothing to store at our house. Behave and be good girls, both of you.

"Call your father, Layla. Send him my love. Rest. *Khodah'hafez,* God protect you. *Khodah ham rahet,* may God be with you both. I must go now. I have a lot to do."

I would have thought she would go straight home and rest, too exhausted to do much. She kissed both of us on our two cheeks and threw us kisses in the air as she walked away, telling her husband that they would be stopping at the shoe repair and then the market before going home. Finally, she vanished with Javeed Khan trailing her, and I was left alone with Jila.

My cousin rolled her eyes. "She's gone," she said in a heavily accented Persian." Then she switched to English. "Okay, you were warned: The apartment is not much. Still, I love it and I hope you will, too."

She stopped and looked at me questioningly, "Layla, do you speak English?"

I answered in English. "My English is probably as good as your Farsi."

"No, it's better, thank God!" Jila said. We laughed and from then on, spoke only English. I preferred that as I needed to perfect the language.

"Let me show you the bedrooms. I hope you don't mind that I took the bigger one. I thought you'd like the room with a balcony. If you'd rather have the bigger bedroom, we can switch." I knew what "balcony" meant, so close to the French word; Persians say, *balcon.*

My bedroom was a bit closer to the living room. Hers was only a hair larger than mine. Entering my room, I went first to the balcony, a small space with barely enough room for a chair, and gazed at the street – my street! It was lined with trees, green and full. Compared to the tall, slender trees of Tehran, these were top-heavy; my second story balcony met their lowest branches. There were low buildings, duplexes and triplexes, up and down my street in both directions, and I could glimpse a triangular commercial block. I came back inside and looked around at what was to be my bedroom, my balcony, my bathroom, and my home for the next four years. The entire apartment was smaller than our salon at home.

"Well, what do you think?" Jila asked from behind me somewhere. "Do you like it? Is it okay?"

"I love it." I was only anxious to unpack then and there and make it mine. Once Jila and I lugged my suitcases into the bedroom, she sat on my bed while I unpacked and updated her on family and others whom she remembered from Iran.

"What about your cousin Shireen? How is she?"

"Shireen hasn't changed. She's the same girl you knew when we were all younger." I chuckled. "She's determined to marry a very rich man as soon as possible."

"Then I'm sure she will," Jila said. "She's always been very lucky." How odd that Jila would describe Shireen that way – not that I disagreed with her description. I didn't tell Jila that Shireen considered herself to be *un*lucky, or that she never seemed to be happy, or that she envied Jila.

Then my cousin surprised me. "Layla, I have to apologize for Maman. I'm sorry she was so rude. It's pretty obvious that she doesn't like your mother very much. I really have no idea why. I have no bad memories of Ammeh Zahra. I'm really sorry."

"She wasn't rude." I thought it better to deny than to share the feeling that her mother had been rude.

"My mother is really something," Jila continued. "You have to understand her. She's embarrassed. We don't *have* another car. We never did. She made that up. Baba's not doing well at all. He works for an aircraft company and I overheard him say he might be losing his job because the company isn't making money."

Neither would I tell Jila that Maman called Uncle Javeed 'a failure.' "I'm so sorry to hear that," I said, genuinely concerned. "What will happen if he loses his job?"

"Don't worry, we'll be fine. I just want you to understand my mom."

Then, decidedly more upbeat, she took hold of my wrist with her two hands and said, "I'm so excited you're here. I've told all my friends about you."

I sat on my bed. "What are they like? I mean Americans our age." At last, I would find out.

"You'll love them, and they'll adore you. I can't wait for you to meet them all. I'm sure you'll like all my girlfriends – well, most of them. And wait till the boys see you! You're gorgeous, Layla. You obviously got your nose from your mother's side."

My heart fluttered at the thought of boys. "Jila, you know I've never gone to a school with boys or really been around them."

"Well, you're going to now. *Hallelujah!* There are lots and lots of them, and they'll go crazy for you." She hugged me and laughed, and I found myself laughing with her, confused by my own reaction, a mix of feelings. As much as I was looking forward to having boys around me on a casual daily basis, I was also wary, and Jila's remark, though I understood that she meant it as a compliment, scared me.

"Stop joking me," I said.

"You mean stop 'teasing me,' not 'joking me.'" She corrected. "I'm not teasing you. They will adore you. Now we need to unpack. And we need to register for classes tomorrow."

Jila agreed to help me with registration and I resumed unpacking. I soon realized my aunt was right. I had far more clothes than space. While Jila helped me re-pack the clothing I would store at her mother's house, she scooped up a blouse Aynoor had made for me, held it against her and went to stand before the long mirror attached to my bedroom wall.

"Look at this. You have such pretty things!" she said.

"*Peesh-kesh,* take it. It's yours, Jila. It will probably fit you."

She ran to me and covered my mouth with her hand. "Sshh! Stop that *peesh-kesh* stuff right now. This minute. In America there is no such thing as *peesh-kesh*. You don't give your things away to someone just because they say they like it. I'll tell you what, though, I wouldn't mind borrowing some of these things sometime."

"Please, take the blouse as a gift."

"Layla, I just told you there's no *peesh-kesh*."

"Jila *jon*, you're my cousin. You like it, and I want you to have it. You know I've brought too much."

"No, I'm not taking your blouse. I'll borrow it. And, by the way, there's no *tarroff* here either. If you offer something to Americans, they say 'Yes' if they want it and 'No' if they don't. You have to learn that. They don't refuse something they want just to be polite so that you can talk them into it, and you shouldn't *tarroff* either."

I thought she was kidding me. "Are you pushing my leg?" I asked.

Jila broke into spasms of laughter. "I'm sorry," she managed to say. "I'm surprised you know that idiom. But you have it wrong. It's *pulling my leg*, not *pushing*. But no, I'm not pulling your leg. There's really no *taroff* here."

I had a lot of English to learn. In Farsi, the appropriate expression translates as "putting a hat on my head." Here, they pulled legs.

When we were finally finished unpacking, I called the operator and put a call through to Tehran. Though my parents were undoubtedly still sleeping, I knew they'd be glad to hear from me, to know I had landed and all was fine. It was a short call. My father answered the telephone as he always did in place of Abol when a call came at night. I told him I was with Jila and that the apartment was wonderful. I heard my mother's faint, sleepy voice in the background, thanking God that I'd arrived safely. Then I hung up and was still thousands of miles away from them.

The excitement and my long trip had taken its toll; my body clock was still on Iranian time. Definitely tired, I was too excited to rest. Jila helped me prepare a pot of the jasmine chai I'd brought from home, and I readied the shower.

Jila sang out from her room. "Dayee Hadi is wonderful. My parents could never have afforded an apartment like this. Last year, I was living with three other girls in an apartment smaller than this one. This is heaven," Jila said.

And so, I discovered that Babajon had agreed to pay the lion's share of rent to assure that I could live with Jila in a comfortable apartment she couldn't otherwise afford.

18

THE MUD THAT SAT BY THE ROSE

Jila's friends were forever stopping by.

That very night Susan and Elliot paid us a visit after dinner and my American acculturation began.

The first thing that struck me was how they sat in our living room.

Elliot claimed the club chair. I was about to move a chair from the dining table into the living room for myself and allow Susan to sit on the more comfortable small couch with Jila. That changed when Susan plopped down on the floor in front of Elliot and plugged herself in between his open legs, pinning her back against the club chair. Surprised, I sat with my cousin on the couch across from them.

Almost immediately, he began running his fingers through Susan's blonde hair as absent-mindedly as if she were a pet. I was shocked! Susan pulled has hand off and I thought, *Well done!* But then she placed his hands on her shoulders. As if on cue, Elliot began massaging her shoulders. She didn't object. Not even when he reached under the back collar of her blouse! *Oh, my God! What were these two people doing?* And in front of me and Jila! *Totally shameless!* I tore my eyes away.

Susan was speaking. "You have no idea how much we've heard about you, Layla. Jila's been so excited that you were coming."

"I'm happy to be here," I said dryly.

"Oh, Elliot, that feels wonderful."

I couldn't believe that she let him touch her like that!

"So, this is the cousin you've been hiding," Elliot said never stopping his massage. "She's beautiful."

Susan slapped Elliot's calf and I was glad. I didn't want him to get personal with me. "Leave her alone. She's barely here yet."

To me she said, "I'm sorry about my boyfriend, Layla. He's boorish but he gives a great massage. I'm on cloud nine." Susan's two hands then slipped underneath Elliot's pant cuffs and stayed there, apparently holding onto his legs.

Whatever "boorish" meant, I knew I didn't like Elliot but blamed Susan. I busied myself straightening out my skirt across my thighs, my eyes riveted on them, my face fighting to remain expressionless. Elliot removed his hands from under Susan's back collar and leaned further forward in his seat, reaching to massage her middle back. Then, as unbelievable as it was, his hands appeared at the sides of her breasts. I was stunned. This was outrageous! I'd never seen anything like it. Yet they seemed totally oblivious to any possible problem.

I looked at Jila who sat there, seemingly nonplussed even as Elliot leaned his torso all the way down, turned Susan's head around and kissed her on her mouth. I was absolutely aghast! *Why didn't Jila share my disgust?* She was actually *smiling*.

Amazing! Well, if Jila can smile, so can I. I put what must have been a stale smile on my face. A moment later, Susan got up off the floor to sit down on Elliot's lap and his hands again found their way under the back of her blouse, this time from the bottom.

I became aware of a tumbling sensation in my stomach and my smile came undone. Meanwhile, all three of them were having a conversation about registering for classes the next day, punctuated by Elliot and Susan kissing every now and then. I began to fidget in my chair. Trying to avert my gaze, I looked down at my hands, but still, the image of them burned my eyes. I was immensely affronted by his behavior, disgusted by Susan's compliance – even encouragement – and confounded by Jila's attitude of silent acceptance.

I sensed pressure building behind my eyes, and my hand went to my brows. I was desperate not to react outwardly. This was the first time I was meeting any of Jila's friends, and I very much wanted to stay in control of myself and show some poise, but I was badly shaken. I sat, faulting myself for being weak and tired, for not having taken a nap. I looked down, my eyes shielded by my hand, sure that all eyes were on me, as though I was the crazy one. All the previous emotions that had cruised through me evolved into a giant eruption of fear as I sat there silently screaming, *Stop! Please stop!*

"Is something wrong?" Jila's question got me up off my chair.

"My head hurts," I muttered, my head still down.

"Do you want an aspirin?" she asked.

"No, I'm tired ... I ... I just need to rest."

I was taught to leave a room only after going to each guest individually and saying it was good to have met them and I was looking forward to meeting again, then bid them goodbye with a kiss or a handshake along with a smile. But just then, I could barely manage a single, curt "Goodnight" as I ran to the safety of my bedroom.

Before I shut my bedroom door behind me, I heard Susan call after me, "Nice to meet you. Hope you feel better," and Elliot say, "Get a good night's rest. We'll see you soon."

I leaned against the cold wall and tried to calm down. With my heart still pounding, I stumbled onto my balcony and breathed in deeply, hungrily taking in the fresh air. I stayed out there for a long time, trying to digest what I'd just seen, unable to make any sense of it. I followed the designs made against the darkening sky by trees I'd never seen in Tehran. The moon was a silver ball wrapped in darkening clouds. I recalled the view I so often saw from my bedroom window in Tehran of this same moon seen through different trees. I came to the only conclusion possible: I'd made a huge mistake in coming to America. Maman was right. *I can't stay here. I'm going home.*

I went back inside, turned off the light, and fell on my bed. After some time, I heard a soft knock at my door and Jila's voice. Her friends had probably left by then.

"Layla, are you asleep? Are you feeling any better?"

I didn't answer. What could I say? I didn't know how I'd face Jila again. I only knew I had to go home.I couldn't stay there.

My God! *What would Ammeh Elahe and Javeed Khan do if they knew about Jila's friends? And Maman?*

How can Jila have friends like that? Has she changed so much?

I must go home immediately. Tomorrow! I'll call home and tell them I'm going back right away.

I lay there, depressed and exhausted, fully dressed, ready to leave. I was utterly disappointed and feeling tremendously isolated until sleep finally came to visit me on my first night away.

I awoke the next morning carrying the burden of the previous night.

This first day in America would be my last.

Almost as soon as I awoke, Babajon called to wish me luck in registering. The excitement in his voice was so evident that, although I had meant to, I simply couldn't bear to tell him I was already set to turn around and come home. It would have broken his heart. I knew how terribly disappointed I was, and I decided I'd spare Babajon that same disappointment – for just a short while. It was the least I could do after everything he'd done for me. So long as I didn't speak of what I'd witnessed last night, I was sure Babajon would insist that Jila stay in the apartment for as long as she wanted. Like Ferri's secret, that would remain something between Jila and me.

When our phone call ended, Jila had breakfast ready for me. I could barely meet her eyes.

"I hope you're feeling better this morning," she said. "We were worried about you last night. So, what did you think of Susan?"

"I'm not hungry."

"She really liked you. So did Elliot."

I bit my lip. "Jila, you know that Persian poem about how you're influenced by the people you surround yourself with? The one about the rose."

"You mean the mud that smells like a rose rather than mud because it was near the roses?"

"Yes. *Guillee Khosh-booee.*"

"Sure," she chuckled. "That's the only Persian poem I could recite as a child. Are you sure you don't want breakfast?"

I shook my head. "Maybe I shouldn't say – I mean, I can't tell you who have as a friend. But I think you should to be more careful in picking them." Jila was looking at me curiously, squinting her eyes as if trying to solve a puzzle. I couldn't believe I had to give her more clues. "I mean ... the way Susan and Elliot were acting!" I blurted out.

Jila actually laughed. "I appreciate your concern Layla, I really do. Honestly? I'm afraid you're in for one heck of a shock." Then she patted me on my back. "Velcome into Amreeka."

Her reaction was baffling."What–"

She shook her head dismissively. "Come on. Let's go register for classes and we'll talk on the way."

I had little choice. Babajon would expect me to register. I would say nothing to my cousin or him just yet about my decision to leave Los Angeles.

Little could I have guessed what I was about to see.

As Jila and I walked through Westwood Village on our way to the UCLA campus, I saw dozens of couples, obviously students, walking together, many holding hands, some with their arms around one another.

"See all these people?" Jila asked, pointing with her chin. "They are not engaged. They're just *with* each other ... and it's completely okay."

I'd been expecting to see boys and girls together, but now that I was actually, really seeing it, I found the phenomenon eerily threatening. They were touching ... in public!

"It's not at all like Iran," Jila said. "The sexes mingle freely here, even in public. There, a decent, *sangeen* girl would never walk down the street with a boy or sit with him at a café, right?"

"Of course not! You know that. Not unless you're in a group or engaged. You'd be crazy to".

"I know," Jila said, "trust me. Maman always tells me. Rumors spread faster than the smell of fresh kabob in the wind. Well, it's not like that here."

I looked around at the dozens of couples around us. "What about their parents?"

Jila scoffed and shrugged. "They know all about it." She smirked. "Well, except mine, of course."

We entered the UCLA campus, and I can't honestly remember if it was Jila's comment or the sight of the campus that made me gasp.

The university in Tehran was lovely, but this was huge – a good-sized city unto itself – and still there was construction going on everywhere. I held my breath as I walked alongside Jila past ivy-covered red brick English style buildings, modern glass and steel buildings, and everything in between, all in a park-like setting with grassy knolls everywhere boasting mighty oak and maple trees. I marveled at the pavilions. There was even a hospital!

Hundreds of students were everywhere. It seemed all races and nationalities were represented but, although that impressed me, what I found astonishing were the couples, hands clasped, embracing in alcoves, or laying together on the grass under the shade of a tree. I stopped to watch as middle-aged and elderly people passed by these couples without so much as a grimace or a sidelong glance.

"You're looking at Americans," Jila said in response to my comments. "They don't throw acid on your face if you go out with a boy. And these girls? Their fathers and brothers won't kill the boy they go out with to avenge their family's honor or reputation or whatever, like Iran."

"That doesn't happen in Iran."

"Oh, *really*?"

"Well, maybe in outlying, villages, but not in the city."

My cousin's chuckle told me she didn't believe that statement and to some extent, I didn't either.

The registration process was orderly. I signed up for three classes and a special English class, only so I could tell Babajon I had registered.

Walking home, Jila spotted a group of her girlfriends. Soon I was sitting at an outdoor café with Jila and three other UCLA students, ordering my first American coffee, iced. As I sat listening to the girls, I watched more couples strolling down the street, entering and leaving shops, driving by in cars, and huddled at small tables at the same café, hands clasped together, and arms linked. They were all around us, laughing easily and chatting together.

Jila's girlfriends brought my attention back to the table with their questions.

"So, what is it like in Iran?" they asked, smiling. I preferred hearing my country referred to as Persia and in any event wasn't used to hearing my country called *I-ran* the way they said it, rather that *E-run* as we *Erunians* pronounced it.

"Very different from what I see here." I winced at my own understatement.

I took my first sip of American coffee. Its bitterness made me cough. Jila passed me the sugar bowl and I began pouring spoonful after spoonful into my glass.

"Y'all sure is pretty," Jessica said. I loved the way she spoke. She had, what I learned, was a Southern accent or drawl.

"Thank you. You're pretty yourself," I said. Jessica had blue eyes and golden hair that was cut short, like the way Elizabeth Taylor had worn her hair in the photo Shireen had shown me. I thought it a shame to cut such beautiful golden hair and I knew Shireen's mother, Haideh Khanom, would share my sentiment. She wore a skirt with a red-and-white striped top that clung to her without sleeves or straps called a 'tube top.' I wore a red shirtwaist dress with three-quarter sleeves, stockings and black flats.

"You're obviously not from here. I mean, you sure don't look American." Alana said. She had long, straight brown hair that fell to her shoulders, thin lips, a large nose and very light freckles. Her pale face bore no makeup. She wore a blue-and-white checked sleeveless blouse and a white skirt with white sneakers and socks.

The girls asked the usual questions: *How I liked the city so far? How long did I plan to be at UCLA?*

Then Valerie, plump and the most animated of the three, asked, "Okay, enough small talk, now tell us, what are I-ray-nian guys like?" She wore glasses and had the habit of adjusting them on her nose though they looked fine.

What could I say? How was I to know what they were like? "Well," I started, "they're very nice." The girls snickered.

"Very nice?" Valerie repeated.

"Tell us what they're like," Jessica said.

"Are they cute? Sexy? Fun to be with?" Alana's eyebrows were raised, awaiting my answer.

"Do they know how to treat a girl?" Jessica asked in a husky voice.

They were all waiting for my answer. *How could I answer them when I didn't know?* I thought of Bahman and his friends: Jalil, Bijan, Cyrus and the others.

"Yes, they're all of those." I hoped I sounded confident. "Don't you know any Iranian boys?" Of course, that was a silly question, considering that there were almost no Iranians in the country at that time.

Yet, surprisingly, Valerie said she did. "We have an Iranian family in our building. I think they're Iranian," she said. "Anyway, they have a son around our age and he's *adorable*." She rolled her eyes. "A genuine dream." She frowned. "The only problem is that for the life of me I can't seem to make him notice me."

I was relieved when the conversation took a sudden turn … until I realized where it led. Alana took that moment to gush her news. "Okay, I'm dying to tell you. I can't wait a minute longer. Don't croak. Are you ready? Okay, here goes: I decided to go all the way with Mike."

"Oh!" Jessica screamed. "Really?"

"Yes!" Alana screeched.

Valerie gasped then uttered, "Oh, my Jingers!" and clamped her mouth shut with the palm of her hand.

"How was it?" Jila asked coolly.

I was stirring the sugar in my glass and thought I'd missed hearing the end of her sentence. "Go all the way where?" I asked.

My question was met with unexpected wails of laughter. I looked around the table, from one face to the next, wondering what the joke was. They were obviously laughing at me. I hadn't said anything funny.

"Oh, my Lord, if that is not the cutest." Jessica drawled.

"She doesn't know." My cousin explained.

"'Going all the way' is a euphemism," Jessica said. I stared at her blankly. I felt so stupid. At first, I didn't know why they were laughing at me, and now I didn't understand that word. "Euphemism?" I repeated, hoping I'd pronounced the word right.

"A nicer way of saying something," Jila explained. "Like saying someone 'passed away' instead of saying they died." I nodded my understanding as I took a sip of what was now very sweet, delicious coffee.

"'Going all the way' means sleeping with a guy – you know," Jessica winked, then "a euphemism for intercourse." She was poking her index finger in and out of a circle she'd made out of her other hand.

I felt the blush rise quickly to my face. I choked on my coffee and started to cough. My cousin slapped my back.

"Are you okay?" Alana asked.

"She will be." Jila leaned over and hugged me.In the next breath, things got worse. Jila repeated her question. "So, how was it?"

Alana shrugged. "It was ... well, it was nice, no big deal. It was okay." She grinned. "Mike liked it."

"Couldn't you have just given him a hand job?" Jessica asked.

I had no idea what a hand job was. I kept my face in my coffee and didn't dare ask. I had a strong feeling it was another euphemism.

"I've been doing that forever," Alana answered, as she squirmed in her chair for the first time. "I thought, maybe it was time, you know? We've been going steady for a year." She fingered the chain around her neck. I noticed there was a large gold ring hanging from it with a blue stone in the center.

"Well, how about–"

"No way!" Alana quickly moved one palm up like a musical

conductor signaling a pause and the other in front of her mouth. "Sshh, don't even say it. I can't!"

My face was on fire. I had no idea what they were talking about and didn't want to know. Keeping my face in my coffee, I peeked up at the others around the table. They all seemed to be at ease, as though they had conversations like this every day. Jila put her cup back down gently on the saucer and shook her head ever so slightly as if sympathizing with Alana.

I felt my heart fall into a hole. I had trouble finding my breath and it wasn't because of the coffee. There I was, sitting at a table with UCLA students on a sun-soaked day in Westwood Village, as they casually talked about having sex before marriage! I raised my head in disbelief and in the glare of the sun I saw a boy and girl leaning against a car parked in front of our table, locked in a kiss. The girls at the table never realized they'd lost me.

I came back when I heard Jila's animated voice calling out. "Oh look, there's Linda's brother." Then she stood up, waved and called out "Adam!"

The last thing I wanted at that moment was for a boy to join us at our table. Nonetheless, a tall boy walking down the street and apparently named Adam responded to Jila's call. He turned his broad shoulders around and I could see that although he wore his clothing loose, his body was solid. He was light-skinned and had blond hair, wore olive-colored shorts with a white polo shirt. He approached our table and I shyly noticed that the hair on his legs was also blond and glistened in the sun as he walked toward us. His eyes were light brown.

Though the chair next to me was available, Adam moved his tall frame into the seat across from me, dropped the notebook and textbooks he was carrying under Jessica's chair, between us, organized his long legs, and ordered an iced tea.

The other girls seemed to know Adam, too. His arrival abruptly ended the previous conversation and I felt relief as the mood shifted and the talk became light-hearted, centering on movies, both recently released and soon-to-be-released.

Adam had a lot to share with us about the private lives and personal lifestyles of famous Hollywood stars and we girls listened intently as he shared the newest Hollywood gossip: Elizabeth Taylor didn't like her soon-to-be-released movie "Butterfield 8," and Marilyn Monroe would probably soon be announcing that she and Arthur Miller were divorcing. Jila later told me that Adam's father was a top executive at American Film Studios, the largest motion picture studio in Hollywood.

Surprisingly, the entire time Adam sat at our table, I was comfortable. Yet, as grateful as I was that his arrival had aborted the girls' earlier conversation, the gist of that conversation stayed with me, only confirming my decision to leave America and return home. My mother's warnings about loose American morals floated through my mind. How wrong I had been to doubt her!

I had imagined I'd see women in the streets with necklines too low or skirts too tight, or I'd meet a troubled boy wearing a leather jacket, looking and sounding like James Dean with a cigarette poised between his lips, who would ask me for a match; I'd keep my head down, avoid eye contact, say no and run off. I hadn't counted on this!

Who were these people? The casual admissions friends gave to one another on the "who, what, when, where and how" of their sexual indiscretions – with me at the table, a girl they didn't even know! – signaled just how different the moral climate was here.

Ferri had to meet her teacher in the darkness of The Charlatan only to sit and talk with him. Here, virtually anything was okay, and young college girls like Alana "went all the way" then talked about it over coffee.

I wasn't so naïve as to think there weren't boys and girls in Tehran who had sex before marriage, albeit secretly, discretely and at great risk. I had learned to pity those girls for they would go on to live terrible lives. Their marriages – if they married – would end miserably; men could tell when their wife has been kissed or touched by another man. Yet, in the midst of these thoughts, one thought persistently nagged at me. According to all I'd been taught, all these girls who lived sinful lives had a future not worth living. Yet, when I peered into the faces of the girls I saw and looked deep into their eyes, I did not find the slightest sign of guilt, remorse, fear or damnation. On the contrary, I saw only radiance and happiness. *And didn't the parents of these girls, the parents who allowed them these freedoms, love and care about their children?*

I was most curious about Jila. She shared my Iranian Muslim roots. We shared blood. We were raised with the same values. Yet my cousin seemed very much at ease with her UCLA friends, as though she condoned their lifestyle. *How was that possible?* Maybe she had absorbed the views of these American college students by virtue of having been raised on their soil.

Was it possible that something committed by an Iranian Muslim was a sin, but wasn't a sin if committed by someone born or raised as an American or of a different religion?

Then there was Babajon. My father had gone to school in America; he must have known what Americans were like. Yet, he'd done the impossible for me to be here. He must have believed I could endure my stay here and not lose myself. *How could I tell him I couldn't do it?* He'd be so disappointed. *What would he think of me if he knew I was already about to turn around and run home?*

What was I running away from?

19
DIRECTIONS

"There is an unbroken continuum from the wisdom of the body to the wisdom of the mind, from the wisdom of the individual to the wisdom of the race."

— *Rene Jules Dubos*

Once classes began, I was in heaven.

Though UCLA's science laboratories were first rate, and the professors were all excellent, it was Professor Rene Jules Dubos who convinced me to stay and study there. He impressed me that much. I first heard him speak as a guest lecturer, then enrolled in his microbiology class. I found him totally inspiring.

Professor Dubos was then over sixty years old and, though by then he'd spent many years in America, his French accent was still strong. He had a long face and kind eyes.

He was not a big man, rather slender and not very tall, but his contributions to science and the world were monumental. As a student in Iran, I had learned it was Dubos who, almost thirty years earlier, in 1931, had given birth to antibiotics by isolating trotyricin, the enzyme that attacked pneumonia-causing germs. Later, in 1939, Dubos laid the groundwork for the field of chemotherapy when he isolated the antibiotic, gramicidin. By the time I sat listening to that first lecture, Dubos had received awards from the University of California as well as multitude of universities and major medical groups around the world.

I sat in that enormous lecture hall and listened as Dubos told us that microbiology had almost unlimited potential to improve the quality of human life. The study of microbiology had led him to conclude that people who live their lives doing what really matters to them and show resilience in the face of change will ultimately live longer, healthier lives than others, even though they may struggle, and face danger and illness.

These bold ideas shook me. Impressed as I was by Dubos' contributions to science, it was his vision of the world around him and the place of microbiology in that world that fascinated me even more. The fact that the source of Dubos' ideas about our world came from his work within my chosen field made me quiver with excitement. I wanted to know what he knew, to take in his view of life. My enthusiasm about UCLA's budding microbiology program resurfaced more fully than ever and I was ever more genuinely eager to be part of it.

The day after that first lecture, I wrote a letter addressed to both my parents, but really to Babajon. I wrote all about Professor Dubos, wondering why my words of praise sounded familiar, then realized with a start that I reminded myself of how Ferri spoke of Hamid. "*Oh, you should hear him, Layla! He makes everything come alive and puts it all together so wonderfully …*" Her words rang in my ears and echoed in my letter home.

In Babajon's letter back, I was both surprised and proud to learn my father had met and spoken with Dubos several years ago in Europe, when Babajon was invited there to receive the coveted Award of the Pharmaceutical Industries and Dubos had simultaneously received an award for his most recent work. He agreed that Dubos was an extraordinary man.

Emboldened by Babajon's response, I impulsively left a message for Dubos, asking for a meeting. He returned my call, suggesting that I visit him in his office the following day. By then, I'd regretted my call.

What could I say to a man of his stature that wouldn't sound silly? Having gotten myself into an embarrassing situation, I arrived for my appointment feeling insecure and nervous.

His office was no more than a cramped cubicle, with just a desk for himself, a small one for his secretary, two chairs and a telephone. I felt ridiculous sitting in the presence of such genius. After apologizing for taking his time, I told him how much I'd enjoyed his lecture and how taken I was with the way he had woven the lessons learned from microbiology into the bigger picture of life. I told him that my father had met and spoken with him at the award ceremony several years ago in France. Realizing as I said this that Dubois must have spoken with hundreds of people at the many awards ceremonies he'd attended through the years, I felt a new wave of foolishness. When I added that Babajon owned Saleh Pharmaceuticals in Iran, Dubos politely nodded and said it was important to manufacture quality medicine throughout the world and make them it available to local residents at a reasonable price without the added cost of importing.

Then he asked what my specific interest was. When I said it was infectious diseases, he nodded again. He took a ballpoint pen out from his jacket pocket, reached for a small pad of paper on his desk, and asked if I would be interested in taking a low-paying job as one of several UCLA students who were assisting him on a project he was currently involved in. The job would last only for as long as he remained in Los Angeles. I waited for him to say that he was only joking, but he just looked at me with his head bent to one side and played with his pen, turning it around in his hand and clicking, the point going in and out, apparently waiting for my answer.

"Really?" I was unsure if he was playing with me. After all, I was a first-year student, and my English was not very good.

He nodded, then went on to say that his time was totally taken up with the completion of his eighth book, and, as a result, he found himself needing yet another research assistant to help with the project he was working on in collaboration with others. It was an ambitious project – developing a vaccine for measles. He made sure to tell me I would not be receiving any class credits for the work and repeated that the pay was meager. I jumped at his offer. He took down my phone number and said he'd call with the particulars; I could start within the next few days.

Waves of exhilaration washed over me as I realized I would be a part of Dubos world. I couldn't wait to tell Babajon the news, so he could share my excitement. He was the only person I knew who would appreciate what an opportunity this was for me. Babajon was happy for me but reminded me that my studies came first.

My job turned out to be organizing and filing the professor's abundant correspondence and his travel itinerary, sort his bills and receipts, and other such non-scientific paperwork. That didn't make my work any less important in my eyes, for I understood that it was a necessary part of any project. I took my job as seriously as I had ever taken anything. I worked for Dubos three hours a day, three days a week. When I wasn't working, I was studying. I hurried through assignments in my general education classes, then poured over my science books, comparing my laboratory notes to those in the texts, my variables and my outcomes to theirs.

Fortunately, my English had not proven to be much of a problem, yet I felt I wasn't able to absorb the vast amount of available knowledge fast enough. When our first exam dates were announced, I hardly slept. I wanted so badly to please both Babajon and Dubos. I was a nervous wreck. Noting my stress, Jila suggested I stop working for Dubos until after the exams. I wouldn't think of it. Then the results came out. "I'm sorry. I know it's 4:00 in the morning there, Babajon. I wanted to give you the good news. I have received A's on my first set of exams!"

"*Borak'Allah,* God praise you, you did well!" he shouted. "*Ghorbonnet beram,* may I be sacrificed for you. I'm so proud of my daughter." Then, "Zahra *jon, Bee-darree,* are you awake?" The way Babajon was screaming, Maman, lying beside him, couldn't possibly be asleep. "It's your daughter. She's gotten A's on her exams! Did you hear that, Zahra Khanom? Top grades! Congratulate her."

Maman's voice came on the line. "Are you well?"

"Yes, Maman *jon,* I am. Are you?"

"Good. Thank God. Is there anything you need?"

"No, Maman *jon*. Everything is fine."

I could see her tired smirk. "Take care of yourself. Here's your father."

Babajon congratulated me again before we said goodnight. I hung up and suddenly felt strangely empty. I missed being with Babajon. I missed reviewing the day's classes with him. I longed to sit down face-to-face with him and tell him what I was learning daily. I missed Maman, too. I was homesick. Despite that, I knew I was right in choosing to stay. I wouldn't return to Iran.

I would stay and meet my changed environment with a resilience that would make Dubos proud.

20
ALONE WITH A MAN

In the weeks after my arrival, I got used to seeing boys both in and out of school and had become an expert at avoiding them.

Whenever a boy spoke to me, I kept my head down and quickened my pace. Nor was I any longer awed by the casual style of dress I saw around me, the informality that was everywhere.

I became accustomed to meeting Jila's friends for coffee between classes and came to find their conversations around the coffee table, more often than not, interesting. I came to appreciate how openly the girls shared personal information with their friends. They were as candid about all aspects of their lives as they were about their sexual activities.

From my earliest childhood, I had been taught to keep family information private; the outside world was to know only the sunniest side of the Saleh family. We never even shared news of illness in our family.When Aunt Bahia's husband died of a cancer, the "C" word wasn't spoken. "He died; may Allah preserve his soul." In contrast, it seemed there was nothing too sacred for these Americans to discuss among themselves. I found that refreshing. They talked about family issues that in my culture would be kept under lock and key in a cache inside a closet behind double steel trap doors.

Ryan, a short freckle-faced girl, told us about her fifteen-year-old brother whom she'd recently visited in a home for paranoid schizophrenics. She openly shared the angst she felt when her parents had decided to end their visits to their son. She cried as she swore she would never stop going to see him.

Whenever the topic of conversation turned to sex, my sensitivity still prickled. Yet I was becoming more and more curious to hear what they had to say about it and listened more intently than I let on. I noticed that sometimes when the girls described having sex, they seemed to be in some secret heaven; at other times, they talked about it like they'd been washing dishes in a moldy steam room. And I wondered what made the difference. It was as if these girls were specimens under my microscope. I observed that though they regularly went out with boys, they kept up with their schoolwork, and – most amazing of all – they spoke of their close relationship with their parents.

The boys they spoke of fascinated me, the boys who took such liberties with these girls, going so far as to wrap their arms around them and kiss them in public or in front of their parents; these boys that received 'hand jobs.' They certainly would have a very different fate if they were in Iran. Here, despite the fact that a future marriage was not even hinted at, Alana's boyfriend, Johnny, was invited to her parents' home regularly for barbecues and other gatherings. It was bewildering.

It was a Sunday afternoon.

I'd been in Los Angeles just over a month and it was still summer. Jila's friends and her friends were sitting at a small outdoor table, and as I pulled my chair back and and took a seat, I had a peek at six feet under the table, all covered in comfortable-looking white canvas tennis shoes, some with short white socks. I wore stockings and beige leather flats. I smiled to myself.

That August month, Hawaii had been admitted as fiftieth state, and all across Westwood Village, boys were wearing chinos or shorts with shirts covered with colorful Hawaiian prints. Girls wore skirts, summer shorts and lightweight capris that bared the ankles. That day, Alana wore a sweet, pink, short-sleeved cotton blouse. Valerie had on a cute red blouse and Jila wore a blue-and-white tube top. I was wearing a full slip under a wide, beige, cotton skirt, the most casual I'd brought, with a striped beige-and-green half-sleeve button-down blouse. In Iran, we didn't walk down public streets with too much of our arms showing or our shoulders bare; it sent the wrong message.

We girls sat across a small table, still oceans apart. Despite the gracious compliments the girls unfailingly paid me on my outfits, as the days passed, I felt ever more out of place wearing the stuffy clothes I'd brought. Finally, I asked Jila to go shopping with me so I could buy a pair of these brightly colored capris and some of these cute tops. Perhaps I'd also buy a strapless dress like the ones I was suddenly seeing everywhere. I'd at least try one on.

"Well, Jila, your cousin is quite a hit with the boys," Alana said as though I wasn't there. "They're always flirting with her." The girls had a way of talking to my cousin about me, as if I were her young child. I was still easily embarrassed and once again, busied myself drowning my coffee with sugar.

"Do you blame them?" Valerie said. "Look at her. I can see why they all like her." She turned to me. "You're different .... exotic." *Ahh, she did know I was there!* She pushed her glasses back up her nose. "You have this ... *thing* about you. It's sensual." She adjusted them again and rolled her eyes. "And then there's your accent."

"They flirt with her, and she acts like they'll bite." Alana said. Then she, too, acknowledged my presence. "Don't you like boys?" She was smiling. I felt claustrophobic and wondered if they'd been watching me.

How could I explain that although I loved boys as much as ever, they frightened me to death?

"Leave her alone, Alana," Jila said. "She's shy."

Just then, Adam appeared at our table. The boy had the strangest way of showing up at just the right time. He took an empty seat and threw his books down under a chair as he always did. "I can't stay. I've been at the library. I have an exam tomorrow. I've got to meet Linda. We're looking for apartments. She says she's found a great one. We have to be there at two o'clock." I hadn't yet met Adam's older sister.

"You think you can live with your sister?" Valerie asked. "I wouldn't want to live with mine."

"Linda's neat," Adam said.

"She's either neat or nuts if she's willing to live with her younger brother," Alana said.

Adam looked at his watch and jumped up. "I'm late. Gotta go. See you." He grabbed his books and dashed off.

When it was time for me to leave, I discovered Adam's physics book, left behind under the chair. I picked it up and took it home with me. When I took it into Jila's room, her radio was on, and she was getting ready for her date.

"Jila, we have to call Adam and let him know we have his physics book."

"Which one do you think I should wear?" Jila asked, holding up two tops.

"The red one. Jila, I found Adam's book under the table today after he left. He doesn't know we have it. Let's call him."

"I don't have his number," Jila said, putting on her stockings.

I held the book out to her. "He's written his name and telephone number inside the book."

"Then call him," Jila said.

My pulse immediately quickened. "But–" I stood there, unable to finish the sentence. *I can't call him,* I thought. *That's just not done!*

Jila busied herself putting on the red top and I realized I was about to make the first telephone call of my life to a boy.

I left Jila's room and sat on the chair by the phone.

I won't call. I'll just give it to him tomorrow.

But what if he needs the book tonight? He said he has an exam tomorrow. What if it's in physics?

I had to call.

As I picked up the phone, I couldn't ignore my thumping heart or my clammy hands and my fingers that shook as I inserted one into the holes and dialed. I heard his phone ring and prayed he wouldn't answer. It rang twice. I moistened my lips.

"Hello," Adam said. I couldn't find my voice. "Hello?" he repeated.

"Hello."

"Who's this? Hello?"

"You left your physics book under the chair."

"Well, hi, Layla! No wonder I couldn't find it."

"How do you know it is me?"

Adam laughed. "By your accent. Thanks for picking it up. Give me your address, I'll come over and get it."

"All right."

"Okay, I have a pen. Where do you live?"

I heard Jila go into the bathroom and remembered with a start that my roommate was leaving. I'd be alone in the apartment after that. I panicked.

"What's your address?" he repeated.

"A minute, please." I'd made the call and now I had bigger problems.

I put the receiver on the table and ran to Jila, who was putting on her lipstick over the bathroom sink. "When are you leaving?"

Jila looked at her watch. "I have to get going by six thirty."

That was twenty minutes away. I ran back to the telephone. "How soon will you come?"

"Tell me where you are, and I'll tell you." I gave him my address. "Oh, that's not far at all. I'll be right over."

I nodded. "Yes, yes. Please, please come as fast as you can."

On my way back to my room, I noted that Jila had closed the bathroom and so, had increased the volume of her radio. I spoke very loudly. "Jila, I put Adam's book by the front door." I went back to my studies, assuming she would answer the door when Adam arrived to retrieve his book. Distracted by the level of her radio, I closed my bedroom door.

A short time later, I thought I heard the doorbell ring. I didn't get up, knowing Jila would answer it. I thought I heard it rang again. I opened my door. Her radio was turned off. "Jila *jon*, could you open the door? It's Adam."

The doorbell rang a third time. I went to her room. "Jila? Jila *jon*?" She was gone and I hadn't heard her say goodbye.

The doorbell rang yet again. I froze. I was alone. I couldn't let Adam in. It rang again and then again. I went to the door and opened it just wide enough to look around the open door and hold the book out to him. "Here's your book."

Adam looked stressed. "I thought you'd never answer the door. I really need to use the bathroom. It'll just take a sec." He pushed the door open, passed me and hurried to the bathroom. "Sorry. I rushed to get here."

I stood immobile by the door holding the book to my chest, cursing myself for having picked it up earlier that day. I would wait by the door until he returned from the bathroom, hand him his book and lock the door behind him.

"I really appreciate your picking up my book, Layla." He was on his way back. "I hate to think what would have happened if I'd lost it." The sound of his footsteps stopped. "Is this your family?"

I turned to look into the living room. There was Adam, seeming even larger than usual in our small apartment. The framed photo of me with my parents was in his hands. He seemed to be studying it."Yes." I took it from his hands and replaced it on the coffee table.

"Neat frame. What's it made of?"

"Wood and ..." I didn't know the word.

"It looks like ivory. It's a great mosaic," he said.

"Yes," I said. I'd just learned the words 'ivory' and 'mosaic.'

He picked up the frame again and pointed at the photo. "What's that? It looks really neat. A fountain?"

I nodded. "That's mosaic too." I proudly used the new word. "Ivory and … what is the English name for that pretty blue stone?"

"Turquoise?" he asked.

"Yes, turquoise."

"Wow. I didn't think you could cut turquoise like that."

I looked at Adam. He looked big and soft and he had a warm, friendly smile. His hair was unruly and fell onto his forehead. I took the frame from his hands, noticing how different his hands and arms were from Babajon's and Bahman's and other Iranians with skin tones that were varying shades of dusk. Their arms, even the backs of Babajon's hands had black hair on them. Adam's skin was the color of noonday sun. There was blond hair on his elongated forearms and legs.

I put the photograph back on the table. I had to get Adam out of my apartment, but it didn't look like he was about to leave anytime soon. "I'd offer you some tea, but really, I have to study. I have a test tomorrow," I lied.

"Yeah, okay," he said. Then he picked the frame up yet again. "This is a recent shot, isn't it?" I nodded. He asked where it was taken.

"Tehran."

Adam laughed. "I know that. I mean where? Is this a park?"

"Oh, no," I said. "It's at home, in our gardens." I gazed at the picture longingly. "I love that fountain. There are goldfish in it. I sit by it whenever I'm sad. I like to talk to the fish."

"I can see it's really something. And these are your parents." I nodded. "You don't look very much like your mom ... not that she's not pretty too, she looks real, um ... elegant, and I can see you have a little of her face. I don't think either of them have your greenish hazel eyes, though, do they? You have your dad's great smile."

He was moving into very dangerous territory with all these compliments, and then ... "You must miss them. Is this the first time you've been away from them?"

I was completely disarmed by the question. None of the girls I'd met had yet asked me if I missed my family or shown any interest in my parents. "A little. I'll see them when I go back in the summer. I've never been away from them before, and I already do miss them. Very much."

"I'll bet. I guess I'm lucky." This time he replaced the frame. "My mom and dad live right here in Westwood. I get to see them a lot, almost too much sometimes." He laughed, put his hands in his pockets and looked around the room.

I was stumped. I hadn't known how to get him out, and now I was beginning to wonder why I had to. He was being just like he was when the others were around and, as always, I was enjoying his company.

Could I trust him alone in the apartment with me? He really wasn't being the least bit aggressive. So far, he was just being Adam. But he was a *boy! What if he did something?* I would have to be very careful.

"So, what's your favorite thing in Los Angeles?" he asked me. "The beach?"

"I haven't seen it yet," I said.

He plopped down on the couch as though my answer was too much for him to take standing up. "You haven't been to the beach yet? Malibu? Paradise Cove? Venice? Santa Monica? Redondo? Manhattan?" I shook my head at the mention of each. "Well, I'm sure you think our zoo is no big shake .... have you been to the Hollywood Bowl?"

"No and I haven't seen the zoo either." I chuckled, a little embarrassed. "I guess I haven't seen many things yet."

"Well, consider it done. As of today, you have yourself a personal tour guide, one of the best there is." He stood and bowed before me dramatically.

"Oh, no!" I was immediately sorry. By admitting that I hadn't been anywhere, I'd made Adam think I was suggesting he show me around. "That's very kind of you, Adam, but that's impossible."

"Why?"

"Because I can't – I mean, you can't – we couldn't – I mean I shouldn't – couldn't – I won't impose on you." I tried to sound final.

Adam threw his arms up. "Are you kidding?" he said. "It would be a blast." I looked at him uncomprehendingly. "I'd love it. Besides, Layla, there's more to a California education than going to classes and reading books. This is a great city, with tons to see. And trust me, I'm the only guy in the city who will take you around with no strings attached."

I was stumped. "You have no strings attached?"

"A euphemism, a way of saying something." *Was this another euphemism I'd be sorry I'd asked about?* "I mean you can trust me. I won't expect anything from you other than your undying friendship. That and a promise to keep picking up books I leave behind."

"That's really very kind of you." I left it at that. There was no need to make him go on insisting. After all, I wasn't *tarroffing* with him. It was No. Period.

"Well, I'd better get going," he said. "We both need to study for our exams. We'll make plans." I walked him to the door. "Thanks again for the book, Layla."

"You're welcome. Good luck on your exam tomorrow."

"You too. Later alligator." And with that, I showed him out and closed the door behind him.

Alone again, I fell onto the sofa and congratulated myself for having maintained my poise during Adam's visit and surviving it so well. That's what it was, really, a rather nice visit. I was sure he'd never guessed that this had been a first for me. I wondered what it would be like to go sightseeing with him. Maybe it would be what he'd called a 'blast.'

It didn't matter. I couldn't be alone with him again. It was ridiculous to even imagine such a thing. I'd be especially vulnerable because I'd be in a city that was still so unknown to me. Most importantly, I'd be encouraging Adam to think he could hold my hand or even kiss me. I'd already said No.

And yet, I felt I could trust Adam; that he was safe and wouldn't harm me. He had behaved so nicely the whole time he'd been there. Though we'd been alone, he hadn't made the slightest move towards taking advantage of the situation. Still, the idea of agreeing to spend more time alone with him was unimaginable. I would never do it. Impossible.

I got up off the couch and went back to my studies.

21
ADAM

The next weekend, wearing green capris with a sleeveless green-and-white gingham blouse and white canvas tennis shoes with short white socks, I sat in Adam's red and white Chevy convertible.

I had justified my day alone with him. We wouldn't really be alone, we'd be on public streets, surrounded by crowds in broad daylight, I'd be home well before dark, and, most importantly, there was no chance that anyone from Tehran would see us.

"First stop, Hollywood."

Adam drove away from the apartments, student housing and homes in Westwood, through Beverly Hills, where houses were just about as large as those in my own neighborhood in Niavaran. Most, like our home, had gardens flooded with flowers and vibrantly colored vines and, I immediately registered that almost all were, like our home, without walls shutting them off from the street. I saw no jasmine anywhere. The trees lining the wide streets in Westwood changed to skinny palm trees that reached to the sky. I turned my head up, glad that the car was topless, so I could enjoy the tall trees and the blue skies.

Adam turned onto Sunset Boulevard and passed the bright pink Beverly Hills Hotel. After some minutes, I saw a building with awning that read '77 Sunset Strip' alongside the parking lot where Kookie parked cars when he wasn't combing his hair. I gasped in recognition. Adam laughed when I told him that everyone in Tehran knew and loved Kookie, the star of that show. The sales of pocket combs had soared when the hit American TV show came to Iran along with the song, "Kookie, Lend Me Your Comb." My guide pointed out Dino's, then Ciro's, then Cyrano's; every few yards there was another nightspot.

"See that drugstore?" he said. "It's a legend, it's famous."

"A drugstore? Why?" "That's Schwab's. They filmed 'Sunset Boulevard' there, a famous classic movie. Lots of big stars have been in that place and some even worked there. Lana Turner was discovered there."

I froze. "Who?"

"Lana Turner, the famous movie star."

I'd heard of Lana Turner. Yet, when Adam said "Lana" the immediate connection I made was Lana Hormoz, my classmate in Iran.

Lana's mother had been branded a whore, disgraced, thrown out of her husband's house, penniless and forbidden to ever again set eyes on Lana, for having allegedly done things she shouldn't have done with the principal of our school. It was a horrible scandal! Since then, Lana has been miserable.

About a month after the rumors began, our principal was bludgeoned to death outside his house. Shireen's father, Dayee Mansoor, had been the attorney representing Lana's father in his complaint against the school for improper conduct by a principal. Dayee Mansoor had said that school authorities had opted to settle. Later, he had represented Lana's father when he had been suspected of being responsible for the principal's death. He had been freed of any wrongdoing.

There I sat, hearing Adam mention 'Lana.' *Was it an omen?*

Oh, how I hated myself for sitting in that car. I felt immensely stupid and utterly helpless. I fell silent and full of misgivings, not hearing the comments Adam continued to make as he drove.

When I again became conscious of my surroundings, the street was no longer pretty. It was dirty and crowded with shabbily dressed people. *Where was Adam taking me?*

"Okay, all out. We have arrived at our first stop. Ladies and gentlemen, I give you Hollywood Boulevard and Grauman's Chinese Theatre."

Feeling greatly relieved and chiding myself for my misgivings, I let myself out of Adam's car. We joined the many people who were out that sunny day to see the shoe prints and handprints of famous stars imprinted in cement in this tourist's Mecca. I ran from one set of prints to another, my mouth hanging open.

"Look, here's Marilyn Monroe and Jane Russell. Oh, Clark Gable!" I hopscotched merrily from one name I knew to the next, until I found myself at the same name for the third time. We went to the gift shop then, and I bought postcards. I bought five different postcards for Shireen alone and more for everyone else back home.

"I have a cousin who would kill me if she knew I'd seen this and didn't send her these postcards. She loves American movie stars. She only reads movie magazines."

"Who's her favorite?" Adam asked.

I laughed. The answer was too obvious. "Elizabeth Taylor. They both have violet eyes and Shireen – my cousin – adores her. She's always fighting with my aunt to let her cut her hair short - 'like Liz's.'"

"Wait right here," Adam said. I stood alone, feeling self-conscious, surprised that I felt more uncomfortable without Adam at my side than with him, relieved when he came back a minute later. He was carrying a camera he'd taken from his car. "Let's take a picture for your cousin."

He took a photo of Elizabeth Taylor's prints. "She'll love that," I said.

"I'll see if I can her to autograph it," he said.

"Adam, Shireen would love that." I said.

I didn't think he was serious – after all, this was Elizabeth Taylor!

He couldn't possibly get the famous actress' autograph. But I decided to play along. "Have her sign, *To my friend, Shireen,"* I said lightly.

"I'll see what I can do," he replied. I spelled her name out for him, and he took a few more photos, one of me standing by Ava Gardner's prints and one with my hands in Marilyn's prints. Afterwards, we took a walk down Hollywood Boulevard.

We passed women who'd made up their faces as though they were on their way to a masquerade, and men who eyed me as lustfully as the *alvots* of my country, the vulgar men who loiter on street corners and in the bazaars of Tehran leering at women. Like them, some of these men were unshaven and unkempt, and at least one was obviously drunk or on drugs, or just crazy, staggering and talking aloud to everyone and no one. An assortment of old, wrinkled women and many younger women were dressed in clothing I never dreamed I would see worn in public.

We passed crowded shops unabashedly aimed at the tourists. Many had someone stationed outside, coaxing people to go inside the shop, like hawkers at a circus. The boulevard was coated in grime and littered with everything from cigarette butts to discarded flyers, passed out at every corner. I saw a pair of women's panties on the ground.

At one point, I saw workers cleaning up after having completed embedding pink granite stone into the sidewalk in the shape of a star. Joanne Woodward, whose name was centered in gold above a movie camera, was given the first star created on what would eventually become the Hollywood Walk of Fame. Adam took a photo of me, posing with the workers, waving at the camera.

"Well, what do you think of all this?" He asked.

"I thought Hollywood was a little bit cleaner. And I thought it would have a lot of flushing lights."

Adam chuckled. "Flushing lights? I think you mean *flashing* lights. That's Times Square in New York. As far as Hollywood goes, my dad would probably tell you that business in Hollywood isn't any cleaner than what you're seeing here."

We had lunch further down on the Boulevard at a restaurant called Musso and Frank's Grille. I entered with a feeling of wanton abandon. I, Layla Saleh, was about to have lunch with a boy in public, *unchaper-*

oned! I felt strangely exhilarated knowing I was flaunting a great taboo. Then, as the maître d' showed us to our booth, my legs began to wobble, and I felt myself grow weak as we followed, passing other diners. I was so afraid. It took forever to get to our booth and when we finally did, I yearned to crawl under the table or run back out the door.

Driving around with Adam was one thing but sitting alone at a table with him like this trapped in a booth in plain view was something else. *I'm having lunch with a boy in public, unchaperoned!*

I felt incredibly exposed and yearned for the darkness of the Charlatan. I was perspiring, and my heart was beating as fast as a hummingbird's. If we'd been in Tehran, my reputation and my life would both be worthless as of this minute. And if an Iranian happened to see me sitting there in Hollywood, California at Musso and Frank's Grille with Adam, I may as well have been sitting at a restaurant in Tehran with him.

A waiter came by, deposited a basket of thick-crusted bread on our table and handed us long menus. I hid my face behind mine.

Adam ordered two lemonades then mentioned that the menus were changed daily. "This is the oldest restaurant in Los Angeles. It opened in 1919."

I didn't care. I couldn't relax. "What do you feel like eating?" And then it occurred to me that he would expect something of me after buying me lunch as well as having shown me Hollywood Boulevard.

I simply shook my head. "Notice most of the waiters are pretty old?" He went on unaware of my discomfort. "Charlie Chaplin used to eat here all the time. I'll bet you some of these same waiters waited on him." I had to laugh then. Chaplin was a beloved figure in Iran. Babajon used to take Maman and me to see his films whenever possible and I would laugh at Chaplin's antics as hard as my father.

Just then, my stomach growled, and I realized how hungry I was. Vulnerable or not, I had to eat. Adam ordered a hamburger and helped me decide on a salad, my first Caesar, topped with chicken. Anything would have been fine with me.

When the waiter stripped me of my menu, I turned my head down, letting my hair fall around my face like a curtain and sipped my lemonade. I didn't dare look up until time passed and no one had stopped at our table to say hello and I hadn't heard my name called out in shocked recognition.

I dared to take a peek around the restaurant. The ambience was warm, with booths of rich worn red leather like the one we sat in. The tables were taken by couples or groups of businessmen, all apparently engrossed in their own worlds. Most significantly, there were absolutely no Iranians in sight. I began to relax.

How fortunate that there were so few Iranians in Los Angeles then, and how wonderful for me that my countrymen were so incredibly easy to spot. By the time our lunch was served, I was actually able to enjoy my salad. My cool attitude had returned. "Hollywood doesn't look like I thought it would," I said.

"That's what makes it Hollywood," Adam answered. "The glitz isn't real. You liked the Grauman's Chinese, right?"

"Oh, yes. I think it was such a wonderful idea to put hands and feet in the sidewalk."

Adam set his hamburger down on his plate. "Well, your tour guide knows how that happened." He assumed correctly that I wanted him to tell me how it came to be. "The first movie theater to open in Hollywood was the Egyptian in 1922. It's down the street. We'll drive past it after lunch. It's really great looking. In 1927, the same owner built the Grauman's. While it was being built, Norma Talmadge, a famous star, accidentally walked into the wet cement. And the rest, my dear Layla, is history."

"It was an accident?"

He gave me a John Wayne look. "Yup." Then he pointed to himself with both his index fingers and said in a deep voice, "And that, little lady, as you'll come to find, is how some of the best things in life came to be."

After lunch, we continued our drive east, past the Egyptian Theater to the famous corner of Hollywood and Vine and the Capitol Records building that resembled a tall stack of white records. Adam told me it was the first round building ever built.

Then he made a U-turn and headed back east. "We'll go to Griffith Park and the observatory another time," he said. "The observatory is only open at night, anyway. I have a better idea."

I immediately tensed up. This wasn't good. *Where is he going instead? And how could he think I'll go out with him at night?*

"Right now, I'm going to take you to the homes of some of Hollywood's most famous movie stars."

My breath returned, and my body relaxed again. I realized I had nothing to fear from Adam, at least not for the moment. In fact, I was excited. I thought Adam was planning to drop in on some of the famous stars his father knew. "Won't they mind? Maybe we should call them first? And I'm not dressed very nicely. I'm not wearing a chic dress, and we're both wearing sneakers."

He howled. "*Ha-ha!* This is a classic. We're not going to see *them*. They sell maps to their homes, so anyone can just drive by and see their houses! That's all we're going to do."

"Oh! I thought because of your father, I mean –" I felt my face turn crimson as I realized what I'd blurted out. Adam had never told me what his father did; I'd learned about that from Jila. Now he'd think I'd gone searching for information about him.

"Nah, not today," was all he said, as casually as if I'd just asked if he had any gum.

I returned my head back on the car seat and thought how easy it had been to spend the day with Adam. He'd been completely proper, thoughtful and a lot of fun.

And then he shattered my thoughts again. "I had fun today. I like you, Layla. You're easy to be with."

Khodah, God, here it comes. My head straightened. I sat primly, my hands folded in my lap. "Thank you, Adam."

"We get along really well, don't you think? We have a lot in common," he said with a broad grin.

I should have known better than to think it wouldn't come to this. I feigned a yawn. "I had a lovely time, Adam. I'm tired. I think I should go home now. Please."

"Okay. We'll do the stars another day."

"You've spent the whole afternoon with me. That's more than kind."

Adam looked at me like I was crazy. "Are you kidding? I can't remember the last time I had so much fun. And, you haven't answered my question. I guess you don't know me that well, so you're going to have to take my word for it: We're a lot alike. I mean, you don't like going to parties and drinking and stuff and neither do I."

If he's waiting for me to agree and fall into his trap, let him wait.

He went on, seemingly unperturbed by my silence. "Besides that, you're easy to be with, comfortable." I still said nothing.

The more he spoke, the more certain I was that he was laying the foundation to go somewhere I didn't want to go. "Anyway, I really do like you. You're different from Linda's girlfriends and the other girls. You're not always complaining about everything like most of them. I mean, look at you. You're here, in America, alone for the first time, and you're always smiling, always happy." He was looking at the road ahead as though he saw me there.

My body tense, my shoulders tight, I spoke in a clipped tone. "Why wouldn't I be happy? I'm happy to be here. It's a wonderful thing for me to study at UCLA."

"Well yeah, that's the thing, see? You're happy. And you're friendly and sweet. Most girls who aren't even half as pretty as you are really stuck up and all they think about is dating and boyfriends. You don't."

Pretty? I must get out of here. I looked at my watch and calculated. We were passing the Beverly Hills Hotel and I guessed we'd be back at my apartment within minutes. *If his compliments are a prelude to taking liberties with me, it won't work. I can't trust him after all. "No strings attached." Hah!*

When we pulled up in front of my apartment building, my hand was poised on the door handle, ready to make a quick escape. Adam didn't make a move. He kept the engine running and turned to me. "Great time, Layla, thanks. Do you mind if I don't open the door for you? I'd rather not get out of the car." He never moved his hand off the steering wheel. He grinned. "I'm not the world's greatest gentleman. Let's do it again, okay? Next time, your tour guide will take you to the stars' homes and other great places."

I slowed down and got out of his Chevy, a quiet smile merging with a deep sigh of relief. I had nothing to fear from Adam. "Later, alligator," I said, using the cool sign-off I'd learned from him.

"See you soon, baboon."

And so, the weekends became time for Adam to show me the city that had become my new home.

We visited the L.A. Zoo, Griffith Park, Hispanic Olvera Street and Chinatown, drove up the coast to Malibu Beach and Paradise Cove and down to the southern surfer cities of Redondo, Manhattan, and Hermosa Beaches.

Sightseeing sharpened the differences between this city and Tehran. In Los Angeles, tourist sites were designed to be lighthearted and fun, part of the present culture and the technological future, like Disneyland's Future Land. In Iran, tourists came to look back into the ages at the ancient ruins of past civilizations like those of Persepolis, the gorgeous historic mosques, so quiet in their beauty, museums and palaces, jewels and other such imposing symbols of an enduring monarchy. The ancient culture of Tehran allowed visitors a peek at valuables that had withstood the test of time. The young culture of Los Angeles showed off its bright, shiny toys.

And I realized that Adam and I were as different as the cities we were born in. Every time I was with him, I felt conflicted. I stood apart from myself, watching myself allow this friendship with Adam to continue and grow, enjoying him, yet at the same time on alert to ensure that he remained harmless, and wondering what I'd be capable of doing to defend myself if he proved otherwise.

I didn't think Adam's parents were serious when they insisted that I call them by their first names instead of Mr. and Mrs. Dunn.

"Mom, this is Layla. Layla, this is my mom."

"Hi, Layla. I'm Maggie."

"I'm very pleased to meet you, Mrs. Dunn."

"No, darling. You must call me Maggie. It's short for Margaret, and this wonderful man here is my husband, Ralph." She pointed to a large, handsome man who was walking up to meet us in the front hallway.

The Dunns were the first American family I came to know. I appreciated their hospitality and soon came to admire the easy love they showed one another. Adam's elder sister, Linda, soon impressed me with her ability to tell everyone within earshot what to do and how to do it, reminiscent of Shireen though more tactful. I watched the Dunns treat their daughter and her changing boyfriends with respect. The Dunns were Catholic, but I knew no more about that religion than I knew of the Jewish religion, or even my own. As far as I could see, the family did nothing special that was religious and never spoke of it in my presence. When Christmas drew near, they spoke of gift-giving and laughed about their upcoming annual visit to church for Christmas Mass; I had no idea what that was.

Ralph Dunn enjoyed Adam's jokes, and had the habit of slapping his son on the back while he laughed a big, round laugh, bringing to mind the domed mosques of Iran.

But it was Maggie I developed a strong affection for, and when I realized how taken I was by her, I was stung by the realization of how different she was from Maman. Maggie, whom I guessed to be a year or two older than Maman, was youthful and active. She wore her shoulder-length hair, the color of warm sunlight, loose, curls bouncing when she walked, or in a ponytail. Her long lips, forever mango-orange, were most often framed in a smile or a laugh. She wore pants or shorts during the days and played tennis several times a week, listened to the same music we kids listened to, danced around the house, and spoke with her children and their friends without any formalities.

I felt lucky to have Adam and his family in my life. I had so much fun with him. I'd even come to trust him enough to venture out at night with him. Along with Pink's for hot dogs and Tommy's for hamburgers, he took me to the finer restaurants in the city, among them, Perrino's, The Brown Derby, the Polo Lounge at the Beverly Hills Hotel, Chasen's, and the Coconut Grove at the Ambassador Hotel. We attended university concerts and film screenings along with his family, or arranged by, Ralph.

Though Adam had become my closest companion and my best friend next to Jila, I never mentioned him to my parents. There was no way in the world that Maman would possibly accept any friendship I might have had with a boy. And, although Babajon's exposure to Americans may have opened him up to the view that a platonic relationship between a young woman and her male friend was possible, I wasn't at all sure that, when it came to his own daughter, Babajon's broad view wouldn't miraculously shrink. Even if such a thing had been all right with him, I would not have laden him with the burden of keeping the secret from Maman.

As midterms ended, I missed my loved ones in Iran, but I was happy to be in Los Angeles.

I enjoyed the work I did for Dubos. Though I never again had a chance to sit and speak with him as I had that first day in his office, I was proud to be part of anything he was involved with. I was doing well in my classes, and much of the material fascinated me. The laboratory work we did was the most enjoyable part of school for me. I was completely comfortable in that environment; it was no wonder when I considered how many years I'd passed inside Babajon's laboratories at Saleh. Meanwhile, my English was steadily improving. I was lucky to room with my cousin, and I enjoyed my time with Adam.

I learned the meaning of 'exponential' when we were examining the conditions that affect the growth of bacteria. Fungi and bacteria react to various conditions that affect different growth patterns, as for example, temperature.

Bacterial growth follows a curve starting from the 'lag phase' during which there is no growth as it adjusts to a new environment, then moves to the 'exponential phase' during which the bacteria grow at a rapid rate, doubling at regular intervals, and then moves into to the 'stationary phase' before entering the 'death phase.'

Analogizing my life and my maturation in the style of Dubos, I could sense that my 'lag phase' was ending as I adjusted to my new environment, and I was now in my 'exponential phase,' primed to learn from every new experience in my life. Perhaps upon graduation I'd be in my 'stationary stage.' I chuckled to myself, thinking how odd it would be if the end of my stay in America and my return to Iran would qualify as my 'death phase.'

Though I had as little in common with the girls I met in California, as with the girls at home – except for my angel, Ferri – I had come to enjoy the company of Jila's friends and our regular coffee clique. I liked listening to their slices of a life that I would never live. Of course, Maman would certainly not approve of these girls with their liberal morals any more than she would condone my friendship with Adam.

I was ever aware of how much of what I did was possible due to the absence of parental monitoring. I valued my freedom to come and go as I pleased and to spend time with whomever I liked.

As for the cultural gap I'd fallen into, I was now confident that I could live in the midst of sexual chaos and hold fast to my own beliefs.

22

THE ISLAND OF ROMANCE

The weather in Los Angeles was almost always perfect. Days passed in an ongoing summer.

Mornings, I'd look out the window, expecting some leaves on the bushy, top-heavy California trees to have fallen, or for the skies to fill up with gray clouds; after all, it was the end of October. Adam's explanation was that in Hollywood even the weather lent itself to make-believe. Then it sprinkled. People called it rain. They drove as slowly as snails with their car headlights on and talked about the bad weather. That lasted for an afternoon. Throughout the month of November, the temperatures in Los Angeles dipped no further than the high seventies.

I'd been invited to spend a clear, sunny Thanksgiving Day – my first Thanksgiving dinner – with Adam and his family. As much as I wanted to join them, I was expected to be with Jila for dinner at my Ammeh Elahe's home.

Sitting down at their dinner table, Jila snickered. "After 10 years in America, we're having *pollo keshmesh,* raisin rice, *joojeh,* chicken and *khoresh bademjon,* stewed eggplant, for dinner on Thanksgiving." I loved it all. I couldn't get enough Persian food. We ate, serenaded by my aunt's continual chatter, and I wondered if it ever stopped.

December came. Day after day, the skies were as blue as the waters of the Caspian and the temperature climbed even higher.

In Iran, skies were pale throughout December, with temperatures often below freezing. Snow transformed the interwoven branches towering high above us into intricate patterns of white lace. I had yet to see trees as tall in Los Angeles.

Cobra would prepare dinners of one or another delicious *ush*, hot, hearty combinations of vegetables and herbs, mixed with ground meats, grains, and the occasional fruits, to keep our bodies strong against the season's assault. Boots and gloves were brought out, warm underwear, winter coats, and woolen clothes were aired to rid them of the smell of mothballs. We'd turn up the heat in the house and sometimes, the fireplace would be lit.

At my grandparents' home, the house Babajon was raised in, every winter, Naneh Joon and Agha Doctor would set up their *korsi*a – a table in the small back room, a brazier filled with charcoal under it. There was a door in that room that led to the backyard, and, regardless of how cold it was outside – it could be freezing, raining, snowing, or hailing – that door remained open.

That first winter in California, I missed my time sitting at my grandparents' *korsi* as much as I missed anything.

Early every morning, their old housemaid would fill the brazier with red-hot burning charcoal and put it under the square table, then cover the table with the *korsi* quilt. As a small child, I would dare to crouch under the table for a moment or two, soaking up the heat by the brazier, before being yanked out by Maman and reprimanded; the fumes of the charcoal collected under the thick blankets could become lethal if I loitered there.

We'd gather around the *korsi* at mealtimes, Maman always wrapped tightly in her furs, the rest of us wearing warm sweaters or jackets and shawls. Our food was served from dishes on a large copper tray, and, while we ate Agha Doctor told stories of his father's adventures as *hakim,* doctor to a previous royal court. He would pause in his tales now and then to call out to the housemaid. "Affat Khanom, please bring more coals." The old woman would run into the room carrying brazier with a fresh supply of burning charcoal and exchange it for the brazier under the table.

Cold fresh air streamed into the room from the ever-open door as we luxuriated in the warmth of the *korsi*. I would lazily watch the rainfall or the white snowflakes blowing around in my grandparents' yard, the bare tree branches dancing a samba in the wind, icicles dangling from them as birds anxiously fluttered around trying in vain to warm themselves.

Though Babajon eventually installed a boiler in his parents' house and *bokharees*, radiators, in every room, my dear grandparents continued to sit at their *korsi*.

No one in Los Angeles had use for a *korsi* that year. In December, the temperature skyrocketed to the high nineties. Southern California's beaches were packed. Those lucky enough to have a swimming pool lingered in and around it.

On the first Saturday in December, Jila and I joined the Dunns for a poolside barbecue.

After lunch, Ralph Dunn went into the house and came back outside carrying a huge manila envelope and a framed photograph. Adam handed them to me. The framed photo was the one Adam had taken of me, standing inside Elizabeth Taylor's footprints at the Grauman's. The bottom of the photo bore the actress' autograph. I looked at him in surprise.

He handed me the large envelope. "Open," he said. "For your cousin." Inside was a large photo of Elizabeth Taylor wearing the white dress she'd worn in "Suddenly Last Summer." Scrawled at the bottom she'd written, *To my friend, Shireen, Love, Elizabeth.*

I was incredibly touched that Adam had remembered my request, and was thrown by the immense kindness of both him and his father in procuring the personalized autograph, exactly as Shireen dreamed. I thanked them both. "Shireen will be thrilled," I said. "You have no idea what this means to my cousin. She will cherish this." And there was no doubt in my mind she would.

I had been sending Shireen things I knew she would like and had recently sent her two records, Elvis Presley's latest hit, "A Fool Such as I" and Bobby Darrin's, "Mack the Knife." She would have them before they were available on the Iranian market. But nothing could possibly come close to a photo signed in Elizabeth's own hand addressed *To my friend, Shireen.* I would mail it to her on Monday.

The heat was the topic of discussion as we ate our hot dogs and hamburgers from the grill. Everyone agreed, it was too hot to do anything other than lay around or in the pool.

"The air man said it will be hot for at least another week," I casually noted. Laughter erupted around me.

"Aren't you adorable, Layla!" Maggie said.

"Oh, that's wonderful," Ralph said between wails of laughter. "The airman." I'd made another mistake.

"It's the weatherman," Adam said after only a short chuckle. "Weatherman, not airman."

"I am sorry," I said. I had mistakenly made a literal translation. "The weatherman said it will go on being very hot."

Adam suggested we take advantage of the warm weather to visit Catalina Island. Jila would take the boat across with Adam and me and the three of us would spend the day there. I was sorry when Jila declined, saying she'd gotten seasick the last time she went and would rather not try again.

Early the following Saturday, Adam and I drove to San Pedro where we boarded the ferry for the twenty-six-mile trip to Santa Catalina, heralded in the popular song of the 1950s as "The Island of Romance."

The small island was picturesque, with coral reefs and turquoise waters. The first thing we did was rent two bicycles. We rode down winding roads bordered by oleander bushes and other flowers, then stopped for a picnic lunch atop the green hills that looked down over the Pacific. The day was so clear we could see much of the California coastline.

After lunch we visited the island's bird sanctuary. There were birds of all kinds and colors. I told Adam about Haji Baba and how he would scream out words like *dance*, and how Shireen and I loved to dance.

Peacocks roamed the grounds, fanning their colorful tails pocked with iridescent wide-opened eyes, their crested heads bobbing as they roamed the grounds. Adam laughed when I called one a 'he.' This time I was sure I hadn't made a mistake. In fact, I was astounded that Adam didn't know that peacocks were male and that their female counterparts – I didn't know then that they were called 'peahens' – were nothing special to look at.

"That can't be. How can a man be more beautiful that a female?" he asked.

"A peacock is not a man, he's a bird," I said.

"How come you know so much about birds?" Adam asked me.

"I don't know very much about them at all. I only know Haji Baba is a male and that peacocks are male. And they're beautiful." And then I added, teasingly, "And I know about the Peacock Throne."

"What's that?"

"The shah of my country sits on the Peacock Throne." When Adam didn't pursue the subject, I asked, "do you know anything about the Peacock Throne?"

"Not a clue. What is it?"

"I can tell you what I know."

"Yeah, okay," he said.

While we continued our walk back to our starting point in the sanctuary, I related the history of the throne.

"When Nader Shah was King of Persia – around 1739 – he conquered India and carried back to Iran lots treasures and many of India's beautiful thrones. One throne sat on a platform. It was covered with pure gold and encrusted with close to thirty thousand rubies, emeralds and other precious stones. It also had one or two huge peacocks on it, but the whole thing soon fell apart. So, Nader Shah made a duplicate of it. It took seven years just to set the stones. The throne our shah sits on in the Golestan Palace in Tehran is totally different and doesn't even have a peacock, but it's still called the Peacock Throne. You see, Fath Ali Shah, who ruled Persia from 1798 to

1834 also built a platform throne. He called it 'Sunny Throne' because when he sat on it, his back was exposed to the sun. Then he married Tavous which means 'peacock' in Persian. That's when he renamed it 'The Peacock Throne' in her honor."

"I'll bet that guy took lots of great stuff back with him from India."

"He did. But when the king of India begged Nader Shah to return some, he did."

Adam seemed to be following what I was saying, so I went on. "Nader Shah had a fantastic military mind and conquered an empire; unfortunately, he soon went crazy. He became convinced that his son was going to kill him and take his place as king."

"Kill his own father? Geez!" Adam said.

I nodded. "He had his son's eyes taken out." I said.

Adam stopped in his tracks. "He blinded his own son? I don't believe it!"

"It's true. Afterwards, he realized he was wrong."

"Oh, wow, these guys were from the loony bin. He blinded his son for nothing? What did he do when he realized he'd made a mistake? Kill himself?"

I was glad that Adam was showing interest. "No. He began to kill his generals thinking they wanted to kill him."

"I guess that makes sense … if you're crazy," Adam said. "No one stopped him?"

I nodded. "The generals finally figured out that if they didn't stop him, he'd kill them all. So, one night they went into his tent and stabbed him to death."

We were back at our bicycles. "That's called a self-fulfilling prophecy," he said.

I'd never before heard that term."What's that?"

"Well, a prophecy is like a future prediction. He was afraid he'd be killed and, in the end, because of that fear, he was killed. So it was self-fulfilling."

I nodded and he went on. "That's a weird story," he said. He shook his head and his blond hair shimmered in the sunlight. "So much of your culture and history sounds like a fairytale to me. Someday, someone should make those stories into movies."

We ended our day on the island's narrow beach. We'd seen couples walking arm in arm throughout the island; here couples in dressed in swimming suits lay strewn on the sand, taking in the warmth of the late afternoon sun. Adam and I stayed in the ocean, splashing and playing like two children.

After a light dinner, we returned to the ferry.

It turned dark early, as it does in December. The day had cooled down and an ocean breeze was coming up as we boarded the ferry back to San Pedro. We stood side by side on the top front deck, looking ahead. I was overflowing with euphoria and the glow of contentment. It had been such a lovely day. Soon the San Pedro Harbor would come into full view.

Adam took my hand. It was the first time he'd ever reached for my hand like that, and part of me was immediately alert while, simultaneously, another part of me was caught up in how warm and wonderful his hand felt around mine. I looked up at him. He was smiling broadly, still looking ahead, not at me. It had been an innocent gesture. I looked away, ashamed that I again suspected him of anything. But then, in the next instant, he turned and wrapped his arms around me. I looked up at him, bewildered. That was all he needed. He saw my lips and kissed them.

In that space that comes between thoughts, for that short, delicious interval, I experienced an intoxicating mix of new sensations: the sudden warmth of Adam's arms around me sheltering me from the cool ocean breeze and a heavy scent, a male scent, up close – new to me. It filled my nostrils, and I felt his soft, full lips warm against mine, his warm breath on my face, and sensed the dormant strength of his body. I felt his warm tongue softly graze my lips. Something inside of me seemed to quiver and grow weak. Then the next thought intercepted, and I pulled away from him with all my strength.

"Let go of me!" I was screaming. I pulled back with such force that when he let go of me, I reeled back then came at him with both my fists. Adam tried to cover his face as I hit him. I was punching mindlessly and landing most.

"Layla, I'm sorry. I'm sorry. I'm so, so sorry."

I was swinging my arms, hysterical now. People standing near us on the ferry hurriedly moved away.

"Layla, please forgive me. I didn't mean to do that. I don't know what happened."

I was trying to hurt him, while at the same time brushing tears away, so I could see him clearly. In utter frustration, I threw my handbag at him. I missed him, and my bag almost fell overboard, but Adam caught it and held it out to me.

That's when I slapped his face. I saw the hurt in his eyes, a look I would never forget. I grabbed my bag and ran inside the cabin, took a seat in the corner, put my face against the window and sobbed.

Adam left me alone there until the ferry docked – whether he wanted me to cool down or because he was ashamed, I don't know, but I was glad he did. I couldn't stand to look at him.

When we went ashore, I walked without direction. He followed me. "Layla, let me take you home," he said. I continued walking, without a clue as to where I was. "I'm really sorry. I won't touch you again, I swear it." He continued repeating it, adding that we were miles away from home.

I had no choice. I finally followed him, wordlessly and reluctantly to his Chevy. For the entire time we were in the car on our way back to Westwood, I sat pushed up against my door with one hand covering my face and cried. When we got to my building, Adam turned the motor off and turned to me with his mouth was open. He wanted to say something. But I didn't let him. I was gone before he could say a word, not even bothering to close the car door behind me.

I went home to an empty apartment.

Jila was at her parents' house for the weekend and I spent what was left of it crying in bed, knowing I would never again be the same. I was doomed. I had been kissed by a man. I had trusted Adam and he had violated me.

Damn Adam! Damn all these Americans with their 'call me Maggies'! All they think about is sex! I trusted Adam. He made me think we were good friends, nothing else, and then … How could he do that? How?

I realized Maman had been right! Men would do anything to seduce a girl … take her to the beach, show her Hollywood, get a movie star to autograph a photograph, take her to his parents' house, Catalina Island, the park, movies and theatre … anywhere and everywhere, just to gain her trust. And then … and then … and then I'd picture Adam on the ferry turning to kiss my lips and I'd start sobbing anew.

On top of feeling soiled, doomed, betrayed and angry, I already felt the hole Adam's absence left in my life. I'd never see him again and worse, I was trapped.

In the solitude of my room, my sole respite from tears came when I closed my eyes and tried to recreate that incredible feeling, relive that small, delicious moment when Adam kissed me.

I was so totally and completely miserable. I couldn't deny how much I had enjoyed Adam's sinful kiss.

23
SORTING LAUNDRY

Adam's breach of trust stung my sense of self.

It completely destroyed any confidence I'd had in my ability to judge people. I shamefully recalled how I'd compared Adam's mother to mine and had found Maman to be wanting.

My blood churned with guilt for having disobeyed my mother's admonitions. She had forbidden me to play with Bahman's friends when I came into my moon. *You play, my daughter. The boys linger around you and get excited until soon they take advantage of you.*

I hadn't understood her then, but now, finally, I did.

That weekend I picked up the phone to hear my mother on the other end of the line for the first and last time during my time in Los Angeles.

She was calling to tell me that Shireen was engaged.

Too numb to react to the news, I dragged myself to the post office and mailed the autographed photo of Elizabeth Taylor with a letter to Shireen, congratulating her. It was the perfect gift and morbidly fitting.

News of my cousin's engagement was salt rubbed on the wound

inflicted by Adam's kiss. There was Shireen, engaged, with the promise of a husband, home and family, and here I was, my future doomed because of Adam, and yet, it had been Adam that had made it possible for me to send my cousin what would likely be her most cherished gift. It wasn't fair.

After that day, I kept to myself.

My first Christmas vacation in L.A. was a sad and lonely time. Invitations to Christmas parties were everywhere but I refused them all and even avoided Jila and her friends. I feigned headaches, fatigue and stomachaches to avoid accompanying Jila on trips home to Ammeh Elahe.

Unlike me, Jila was active, spending time with friends, dating and running off to parties. But though she was barely home during the pre-holiday month, she noticed that I'd become cheerless and sullen, and it must have been obvious that Adam was missing from my life.

That afternoon, Jila was busy sorting her freshly washed laundry, piled on the living room couch.

I stood by the coffee table, gazing down longingly at the photo of my parents and the life of the old me. I'd been moping around the apartment for days.

"So, tell me about Shireen's husband-to-be," Jila said.

Much as I didn't feel like talking, and particularly not about Shireen's betrothal, I felt obligated to share the news with Jila. So, I allowed myself to be drawn into a conversation I wasn't in the mood for.

I sighed. "Taymoor Moloyed. She told me about him just before I left Iran."

"Wealthy?"

"Yes."

"Very?"

"Yes.

"Very, very?"

"Yes."

"How old is he?"

I shrugged. "I don't know."

"About?" I shrugged. She persisted. "Take a guess."

"Thirty-one, thirty-two."

She stopped folding the towel in her hands and looked at me. "Thirty-one, thirty-two? Really?"

"I said I don't know, Jila."

I loathed talking about Shireen's engagement. It made me ill to think how envious Maman must be of Aunt Haideh. Her sister-in-law's daughter would soon marry and have a home and children, and here I was thousands of miles away doing what? *Being kissed! Being ruined!*

Oh, God! I could feel the hot tears just waiting to fall and I wanted to get away from Jila before they did. But Jila was in a talkative mood and kept asking questions. I turned away from her and surreptitiously wiped away the first drops.

"A bit too old for Shireen, isn't he?" she said.

I shrugged. I probably wouldn't find a "60-year-old man willing to marry me now that I was damaged goods.

"Why shouldn't Shireen marry a man over thirty?" I stormed. "Shah is forty and he's marrying Farah Diba who's twenty-one."

I'd first heard the news of the shah's engagement from Ammeh Elahe. She had come into our apartment a few days before Thanksgiving excited to share news.

"Have you heard? Shah is getting married. Aalah Hazrat, His Majesty, is marrying again." Then she added, "It's only for a son, of course. He'll never love this one the way he loved Soraya."

I had seen a photo of Farah Diba, the shah's soon-to-be third wife, on the cover of a Life magazine, a smiling girl wearing a silver evening gown and matching long silver gloves along with the simple banner, "Farah Diba, Shah's Fiancée."

She was six years younger than Soraya and seventeen years younger than Fawzia, His Majesty's first wife. Nonetheless, my countrymen had been happy when the shah re-married six months later, hopeful that he had found love again.

I wasn't sure. To me, he looked not only younger in the photos taken at his wedding to Soraya but happier as well. In photos of his wedding to Farah Diba, the bride appeared content while the shah, with lips pursed, gazes off, perhaps into some unknown, distant, and perilous future.

Fortunately, a mere 10 months into their marriage, his young wife did bear him a son, Cyrus Reza Pahlavi. And, unfortunately, in one of history's great ironies, the shah's long-sought heir was not to succeed his father to the throne after all.

Around the time of the Crown Prince's birth, a growing discontent with the monarch was taking root in the cities, a discontent that matured alongside the young boy until, by the time he'd became a young man, the monarchy toppled.

Jila was folding a pillowcase and shaking her head. "Maman feels so bad about the shah. She's totally obsessed with his love life and she's convinced he will forever be in love with Soraya. She says you just can't forget a love like they had. It stays in your heart and becomes part of it."

I had nothing to say. *What did I know about love? What would I ever know of loving or of being loved?* I'd lost both possibilities with a kiss.

Jila wasn't happy when my sole response was a grunt. Changing the subject, she asked if I was planning to join her at Alana's house for Christmas. I said I wasn't. She asked if I'd yet answered with an RSVP to Jessica's New Year's Eve party. I told her I'd already declined.

"Oh? Have you made plans with Adam for New Year's Eve?" she ventured.

I stiffened at the mention of Adam's name. He had talked about taking me to see the flowered floats at the annual Rose Parade early on the morning of January 1, then to a football game at the Rose Bowl. He'd laughed till he's cried when I called it the Rose Ball. I answered a simple, "No." Oh, how I prayed she would leave me alone.

"Then you should come with me," she said easily. "We'll go there then to John's house after midnight. It'll be fun. Your first New Year's in L.A." When she got no answer, she pushed. "Okay?"

I still didn't respond. I felt awful. I turned and was heading for my bedroom when Jila's voice stopped me.

"What's wrong, Layla?" She walked over to me. I remained mute, closed off and miserable. Jila put her arms around me. "Tell me what's wrong. Is it news from home? Are you homesick?"

I squirmed out of Jila's arms and stepped back from her. *How could I answer her without screaming? Of course, I'm homesick. Get me out of this sex-infested place! I want to go home, but I have no future in Tehran. Khodayah, God! I wish I'd never come to this country.*

I tried to sound convincing. "Nothing's wrong. I'm fine."

Jila turned abruptly and stomped back to her pile of laundry. Her next words hit me like dozens of sharp knives.

"You're really something, you know that? You really are, Layla. I invite you into my life, I introduce you to all my friends – Adam and Linda, Susan, Alana, Valerie and all the others, and then one day, you suddenly decide not to talk to me. You want nothing to do with any of us. You don't like any of us. Not me, not Adam, not even my parents.

"What am I supposed to tell them? What am I supposed to say to my parents when they keep inviting you to their house and you don't go? You're suddenly too good for any of us. You've become rude, a snob – quite honestly, Layla, you've become a bit obnoxious. Well, let me tell you something, Dear Cousin. If you have any intention of staying like this, I'm moving out."

The silence between us lasted only seconds before I broke down. She had managed to get to me. I fell onto the sofa, distraught and sobbing.

"Oh Jila, I'm sorry. You're right about everything you said," I cried.. "You've been an angel. I'm sorry. I don't know what to do."The walls around me crumbled. "I want to die."

In an instant, Jila had moved the laundry basket and was sitting next to me. She handed me a soft T-shirt to dry my tear-stained face. "What is it, Layla? What's wrong?"

"My head is pounding. I'm so miserable."

"Why? What happened?"

I shook my head. "Nothing." Then I became hysterical. "No, everything. I think I should just go back to Iran. I ... I ... I couldn't say it.

"What?" Jila said impatiently. She spoke in Farsi, perhaps believing I would be more comforted in my native tongue. "Nothing could be that bad, Layla. Stop crying just long enough to tell me what's happened."

"Something horrible." I managed to add, "very, very horrible." I turned toward her then, making sure to look at her face when I continued. I wanted to watch her expression change when she heard what I was about to tell her. "Adam kissed me," I whispered. We sat staring at one another, neither of us saying a word as I waited for my cousin to react.

Finally, she spoke. "And? I'm waiting."

I thought she hadn't heard me. "I said, Adam kissed me."

"I heard you. And what was horrible?"

"*Chetteh?* What's wrong with you, Jila? He kissed me!" I looked at her with tears. "On the ferry." I buried my face in the cushion and sobbed.

"Was that the first time?"

I looked at her, aghast. *Who or what did she think I was?* "Of course!" I said with what shred of dignity I could still muster.

"And that's it? I mean, that's all he did? Did he do anything else?"

I shook my head. "No." She had to at least believe that. "No, I promise."

Jila put her hand on my knee. "Are you sure?" She spoke so gently. "You can tell me, Layla. Did he … force you to … to do anything? Or hurt you?"

I lifted my head and shook my head again. "No, I pulled away and hit him."

Her hand came off my knee. "You're this upset because he kissed you?" I nodded and broke out sobbing anew.

Jila got up and began walking away then turned back around. "Was that the first time you'd ever been kissed?" she asked.

My eyes flooded with tears again. "Yes, of course. I swear on the holiest of Qurans, it was the first."

"Okay, calm down." She found a box of tissues and handed it to me. "I believe you … Did you like it?"

I ignored it. I looked up at her with eyes full of fire, two fists buried at my sides and asked, "Did I like what? That he grabbed me and violated me like that?"

"No," Jila said. "I'm sure you didn't like that. You obviously weren't ready for it. It was wrong. He should not have kissed you without your consent. But did you like the kiss?"

I violently shook my head, "No." Then a sob caught in my throat and I nodded, the tears pouring down my face. "Yes."

Jila sat back down next to me and I cried in her arms. "Jila, I don't belong here. I don't see how I can live here. And I can't really go home now either. I'm ... I'm ... Oh, Maman! What will become of me? What will I do? What do I tell her?"

"What do you mean? Your mother? Tell her about what?"

"What do you think? What will I say when Maman finds out I've been kissed?" I could hardly mouth the words.

She had gone back to speaking English. "It's okay, Layla. Nothing bad will happen." I looked at my cousin in misery. "How can you say that? I'm ruined." I was sobbing. "I'm not like these American friends of yours who go all the way. Oh, God, Jila, what will I do?"

Jila put her two hands on my shoulders. "Layla, Look at me. I'm your cousin. I not only love you and care about you, I am also responsible for you. If I let you go home for some reason that doesn't make sense, I'd be letting you down. I'd be letting Uncle Hadi and your mother down, too, and even my parents. Right now, I'm the only person who can help you, and by God, that's what I'm going to do."

I sniffled. "How can you even speak to me when I've been so awful to everyone?"

"You haven't been awful. I didn't mean any of what I said. You're not rude, you're not selfish and you're not obnoxious. I only said those things to get you to tell me what's been bothering you. I've been trying to find out for days and you wouldn't tell me. You wouldn't even speak to me. I didn't know how else to get it out of you. Anyway, it worked, and you told me what's bothering you. Stay, Layla, and I promise, you'll be okay." She took a tissue out of the box and handed it to me.

I wiped my face. "How can you say that? I'll never be okay again." I was exhausted from all my misery.

"We need to talk," Jila said getting up. "I'm going to make you a cup of your jasmine tea and a cup of coffee for me, and then we're going to have a good, long talk right here, right now. We probably should have done that when you first got here. My fault. I didn't realize how badly you needed it."

Thus began the conversation between Jila and me that was to be a major turning point in my life.

24
JILA'S CONTENTION

"Layla, you may not believe me, but I am telling you honestly, you're crying for no reason."

"Stop, Jila."

"Really. A kiss is nothing and no one can tell. *No one.* Rule number one: Forget everything your mother has told you. No one can tell. Not your mother or anyone else. Your body won't show it. There are no signs, no marks and no fingerprints."

She was a blur her through tears. She was trying to make me feel better with lies.

"It's not in your eyes, or in your walk. or your voice or on your lips. Believe me, men do not have super powers. They can't know what you've done, or when, with who, how many times, or if you liked it. Just like you wouldn't know by looking at him. Do you understand?"

"Jila, that's ridiculous. You don't need to lie."

"What am I lying about, Layla?"

"Everything you said. That can't be."

"Really? Why not?"

"Maman told me–"

Jila cut me off. "Rule Number One. Forget everything your mother ever told you. Let's just talk facts; nothing else."

I felt my brain react to the impact of what she'd said. Of course, it was incredible to think that everything my mother had taught me was wrong.

Jila smirked. "There's more. And I'm going to tell you all of it so listen carefully, my dearest cousin.

"We've both been raised to guard our virginity until we marry. We've been told not to let a man touch any part of your naked body as if that would de-virginize you. Well, listen up. There is one – and only one – thing that can de-virginize you. Did you get that? Only one.

"Being alone with a man won't do it. A man seeing you naked won't do it either. Kissing won't do it, having your body touched and kissed, licked, rubbed, and whatever else, won't do it, nor will anything you do to a man.

"There's *only one thing* that will, and that, cousin Layla, is having sexual intercourse ..." she chuckled then. "... fucking, going all the way, call it whatever."

She was laughing now. "You should see your face! You look like your eyes are about to pop out. I can't laugh anymore. I need to pee. Anyway, that's it. What has to happen is that your hymen – the tissue here," she pointed to her crotch, "tears when you do that. The hymen will tear from vaginal penetration. That's the proper term: vaginal penetration. And then – and only then – you're no longer a virgin." She headed to the bathroom. "Toilet break. I'll be right back."

Jila's left the room then. Her last words brought to mind the story of Nassrin, and, while I waited for her to return from the bathroom, I recalled Nassrin's story.

Nassrin did not look like the kind of girl who did the things she said she did.

She had a pretty smile – the kind that made you think she was shy. She wasn't.

It was the first day back at school following an extended winter holiday, and we girls were having lunch.

"What did you all do over the holiday?" Nassrin asked us. One by one, we related our usual family-centered activities.

"Should I tell you what I did?" She asked. We nodded. Nassrin always had a strand or two of hair that was too silky to stay in the ponytail she wore, and now she toyed with a loose strand, twirling it around her finger. "Well ..." Her stalling signaled that whatever she'd done was out of the ordinary.

"We're waiting," Afsar said.

"I went to my Amoo Som's house Friday night. He and his wife were having *pah gosha* for their son and his bride as it was their first visit to their home as a married couple. The bride's whole family was there."

"That's nice," I said.

"The new bride's brother was there, too." She was a smiling fox.

"Yes?"

"Yes. And he is really, really sexy looking. He was A-Number-One. His eyes are incredible, and his hair is one hundred percent, Elvis Presley. I wanted to walk up to him and grab him."

Some of the girls chuckled, assuming she was kidding. Not Afsar. She reprimanded her. "Nassrin!"

"Don't worry, I couldn't with my father watching me like a hawk and my mother right there, saying 'Nassrin this' and 'Nassrin that.'"

"Did he dare talk to you?" Azar asked excitedly.

"He didn't say much to anyone, he just sat there, smoking and eyeing me slyly. All I could do was pass him a smile. When the General came in and everyone was distracted, saying their Hellos, I gave him one little sexy smile. Like this." Nassrin demonstrated her seductive sidelong smirk. Then she was quiet.

"Well? Talk! There's obviously more to your story. You've made my heart stop." Afsar said.

"He grabbed me," Nassrin said.

"He grabbed you?" We were a chorus.

She nodded. "I went to the bathroom and when I came out, he was waiting for me in the hallway. He grabbed me and took me to the other end of the hallway, away from the salon where the others were."

"*Vye barr man*, oh, my God, he didn't!" Azar slapped the top of one hand with her other.

Nassrin was still playing with that loose strand, twisting it slowly round her finger, letting it fall then twisting it again. "He did," she said.

"What did he do? What did he say?"

"He held me up against the wall and pulled my hair away from my face. He put his mouth very close to my ear and he–"

"He kissed you!" Afsar interrupted. "May he die and be embalmed!"

"– whispered in my ear," Nassrin finished.

"Oh, thank God." Mahnaz sighed, relieved.

"What did he say?" Afsar asked hurriedly.

"Be quiet," Azar said. "She's telling us."

"He told me to meet him at the top of the hill by the abandoned silo at four o'clock the next day."

"May his head not remain on his body if he did," Mahnaz said. The rest of us just gasped.

Nassrin nodded and smiled again. "He did." And we knew, even before she told us, that she had met him.

"And?"

"Well," Nassrin said looking coy. "You remember how incredibly cold Saturday was? The snow on the hill had turned to ice. On my way up, I slipped and almost fell a few times, but I kept going. When I got to the top of the hill, the door to the silo was unlocked. I opened it and went inside." She paused. You could have heard a pea fall. "He was there, waiting for me."

Then Nassrin stalled yet again, teasing us as she privately relived the memory. She was twirling her hair around her finger more slowly now, then passed a strand through her lips.

"Come on girl, my heart has stopped. What happened?" Azar asked.

"He looked so damn sexy. He was all in black and his hair –"

"May his hair fall out and may the two of you die. Tell us what he did!" Afsar interrupted again.

"It was cold, and I was shivering like a rabbit's nose." We listened, all our mouths hanging open. "We sat on the floor. There was a blanket there. Actually, there were two blankets there, can you imagine that? I suppose he'd brought them."

"And?" Azar asked.

"He touched my hair and that felt really good, so I moved closer to him. Then he tucked my head into his chest," Nassrin glowed in the recollection,"and stroked my hair and my face." We were shocked into silence yet were eager to hear the rest. She was remained quiet for some time. Her face had taken on a dreamy look. "Then he told me I was beautiful."

Afsar's reaction was immediate. "*Dooroo-ghoo,* liar!"

"Excuse me?" Nassrin said, scowling at her, rudely awakened from her reverie.

"He was obviously trying to seduce you." Afsar said.

"Shh," Azar said to Afsar, waving her away, hoping to avoid an argument.

Nassrin repeated what she'd just said, her tone more forceful this time. "Like I said, he told me I was beautiful. Then he laid me down on the blanket, reached under my skirt, took my underpants off and lay on top of me. He must have taken it out then, because I felt this thing between my legs."

I was totally mortified. I didn't really believe her story, yet I couldn't believe she would make something like this up.

"*Tokhmeh sag,* son of a bitch!" Afsar screamed. "He raped you!"

My throat was closed, too tight to speak. Azar was slapping her cheeks in despair. "*Vye!* Poor Nassrin!"

"What did it look like?" Afsar asked.

"What did it feel like?" Mitra screeched.

"It was rather big and stiff but also soft and warm. It felt pleasant. He rubbed it between my legs."

Then came the part that made no sense to me then. Now, in light of what Jila had said ...

"You're no longer *baakerreh,* a virgin." Azar lamented.

"Don't be silly!" Nassrin was indignant. "He didn't rape me. And I *am* a virgin."

"No, he–"

"He was careful of my virginity."

"How can you think you're still a virgin?" Azar asked.

"He only put it *laa paee,* between my legs."

I remember thinking at the time that if Nassrin was stupid enough to believe she was still a virgin, we should be watering her daily. But now, a crack had formed in the wall of my fears and I began to wonder if Nassrin might have known more than I did.

Jila returned to the living room.

"So, Layla, what have we learned?"

She stood with her arms crossed. "We've learned that you can be kissed, touched and licked, tickled, rubbed and felt up from now till forever and still be a virgin. And no one – I repeat, *no one* – will know unless you tell them; not here and not when you go back to Tehran. What do you think of that?"

"I just can't believe it," I said.

"Believe it."

"How is it that I don't know any of this?" I asked.

"Good question, Miss Scientist. So, you're with me so far?" She asked.

"There's more?"

She nodded. "We've also learned that the only way your virginity can be lost is by vaginal penetration, which rips the tissue called the hymen. You remember that. Okay, on to the next lesson. This will really shock you."

"I don't think you can shock me anymore," I said.

"We'll see. Here goes. When you marry, your husband will never know if you're a virgin or not."

If Jila had just told me she was really a man, I couldn't have stared more wide-eyed. "You're wrong," I said shaking my head violently. "Come on, Jila! That's absolutely wrong!"

"Okay." Jila said. She sat beside me and rested her hand on my thigh. "Imagine it's your wedding night. You're in bed with your husband having intercourse at last, and you bleed a lot and he knows you've saved your virginity for him. *Alhamdo le'llah,* Allah be praised! Your mother in law will get a bright red virginity napkin in the morning to validate your worth and your mother will get a phone call from your new husband congratulating her because her daughter was a virgin. Right?"

I nodded. My cousin was continuing, as though my agreement had been a given.

"Okay, that's fine." She patted my thigh. "Now tell me, what if you don't bleed?" I stared at her. Obviously, she would go on to say it would mean I wasn't a virgin. But that's not what she said.

"Here's the thing. Not all virgins bleed. So, if you don't bleed, does it mean you weren't a virgin? Absolutely not!"

I stared at her, my disbelief apparent. *Who was she kidding?*

She went on. "The hymen – the membrane that marks our virginity can tear in lots of ways: riding a bike, horseback riding, ballet splits or whatever else."

I thought of all the things I'd done playing with the boys and how Maman had forbidden me to ride a bicycle and how she'd cringed when I climbed a tree. *Had she known all this?*

Jila took her hand off my thigh. She got up and stood in front of me. "I'm sure there are women back home who've been divorced after their wedding night, humiliated and called *jendeh,* whores, though they had been virgins when they married, only because they didn't bleed on their wedding night. But good girls don't always bleed."

That couldn't be true. I was certain that everything she'd said was crazy. In minutes she'd tried to turn fundamental truths into myths and lies.

She stood there with folded arms. "So, *begoo,* tell me, Layla Khanom: What do you think?"

"I don't know." I said, nothing more.

She knelt down in front of me then and put her hands on my two thighs. "Layla, I want you to know something. I'm going to be a virgin when I marry, because that's what I want. Not because I'm afraid that my husband would find out if I wasn't and disown me. I may bleed on my wedding night or I may not. Meanwhile, until then, you can bet that I'm not living the life of a nun."

My head snapped up to look into her eyes. She had said nothing about being a good Iranian girl or a good Muslim girl.

She slapped her thighs and stood. "I have to put away this laundry." She looked me in the eyes with a glint of mischief in hers. "Think about what I've said. Welcome to the real world, Layla."

I went to my room and stepped onto the balcony. I braced the railing and looked down onto the street. I was living on a street in Los Angeles, California, in the U.S.A. surrounded by Americans, westerners who thought like Jila. I was from Iran, where people thought very differently.

And again, I wondered, *Could the truth change from country to country?*

25
BOYS

What was the truth?

In one afternoon, Jila had presented me with a mountain of information, and all of it contradicted everything I'd been brought up to believe. I had to wonder, *Could she possibly be right?*

Two things were certain: One, my cousin believed the truth of everything she'd said. Two, Mamam and Jila couldn't both be right.

I was in a quandary, having exchanged misery for confusion. I certainly wasn't ready to throw out all my prior beliefs over a cup of tea, but neither could I completely ignore all that Jila had said, though it put a lot of what I was seeing in America into a new context.

I needed to know a truth that existed independent of one's nationality.

My God, *I was a scientist*! There on my balcony, watching passing cars travel in opposite directions with couples out to frolic, I resolved to use the scientific method. Like Dubos, I would use science to access a truth that had enormous social implications. I would conduct an experiment.

Brad was in my lab class, a senior and was taking the class to fulfill his graduation requirements.

He was always asking me for help. Within a week of my talk with Jila, as we were working on an experiment, Brad shyly asked if I'd like to join him and his friends at a beach barbecue the following Sunday, weather permitting. I was about to decline, then accepted.

As I walked down the hallway after class, I felt a soft thrill of excitement. Brad would provide me with the perfect opportunity to begin my research. I would kiss him and see if he'd be able to tell I'd been kissed before. I'd already been kissed, so what harm would it do? He would be my lab rat. I had little to lose.

Brad picked me up that clear warm Sunday afternoon.

Instead of a bathing suit, I'd opted to wear my new Bermuda shorts with a tube top. Brad's smile when he saw me was all the assurance I needed to know my outfit was a hit. He wore navy shorts with a Hawaiian shirt and had tucked his light brown hair under a baseball cap. The barbecue was at the Santa Monica beach adjacent to Venice Beach, between the area known as Muscle Beach and Pacific Ocean Park. I'd been to the rides at POP with Adam, and the memory of him made me eager to again experience the thrill of a kiss.

Sometime after dinner, when the sand around us was strewn with beer cans, Brad and I left the others to take a walk along the shore. Underfoot, the sand had cooled down and the shoreline was even cooler. The wet sand momentarily welcomed our steps with imprints that lasted until the next wave snatched them away.

At some point, Brad reached for my hand, and as I felt the warmth of his, I recalled standing on the ferry with Adam's large hand wrapped protectively around mine. That had been the first time a boy had reached out to hold my hand since the day Jalil had brought me home at the age of eleven. I bit my lip nervously, and my heart quickened.

"Isn't the ocean beautiful?" Brad asked. "It looks like we could walk on that silver path made by moonlight and lose ourselves in the horizon." His hand tightened slightly on mine, then loosened as he turned to me, his other hand resting on my shoulder. "I'd really like to kiss you, Layla." he asked. "Can I?"

I nodded. This was what I had been waiting for.

If I had been honest with myself, I would have admitted that my anticipation was not only a result of my search for the truth. It also arose from my yearning to experience the feeling I had of being lost in Adam's kiss, while wrapped in his arms.

Brad brought me close to him. His scent wasn't warm and alluring. His body didn't feel strong and protective like Adam's had. I closed my eyes and let him give me the kiss I'd been aching for and then, disappointment. His lips weren't soft and full. They felt thin, pulpless, and flaccid against mine, cool instead of warm.

I tolerated the kiss and when at last, it was over, I was ready to continue the experiment. Jila's had said a man would only know what that I chose to tell him of my past. *Could Brad tell I've been kissed before?*

"That was nice," he said.

"Yes, it was." I said. I smiled and looked at him shyly, watching him like a hawk for his reaction. "I've never been kissed before."

Brad looked so skeptical that I was sure he knew I was lying. "Come on!" He stamped his foot down onto the sand and slapped his thigh. "Are you're kidding me?"

I bit my lip. I nodded. "Really," I said. "That was my first kiss. Couldn't you tell?"

"No! I'm sorry, it's not that you'd lie, but it's just hard to believe. A girl as pretty and as sweet as you?" He chuckled. "I was really the first guy to kiss you? Ever?"

I searched his face, trying to discern his honesty. "You really couldn't tell?" When he shook his head emphatically, I was so surprised that I immediately doubted I'd made a smart decision in choosing Brad as my guinea pig. It was unlikely, but maybe Brad was as inexperienced and almost as new to all this as I was. "I'll bet you've kissed a lot of girls," I said, goading him.

"Well," Brad dug his hands into the pockets of his shorts, shrugged in modesty and nodded in pride. "I've kissed enough," he said.

"So, can't you tell if one's been kissed before or not?" I asked.

He chuckled again. "Of course not." Then he put his hands around me and brought me close to him. "But I wouldn't mind kissing you again. I really liked it."

I took hold of his hand and turned. "I think I'd like to walk for a while. I like walking with you."

"Okay." We resumed our walk, moving farther away from the others. The water was quickly darkening, an ocean of blues and greens was turning navy. "I just can't believe it, Layla. I mean, a girl like you … Wow! I can't believe I'm the first!"

I was still in awe. It was a revelation to me. Apparently, Brad honestly couldn't tell I'd been kissed before.

Okay, I thought, so much for the kiss; let's move on. In the stillness around us the ever-darkening ocean exhaled waves of white foam that flooded the shore.

"Tell me about yourself, Brad. I want to know more about you."

"Not much to tell," he said modestly. "I'm pretty boring."

"No," I said, "that's not true."

"Well, what do you want to know about me?"

The night, like the beach, stretched before us. "Everything. What will you do after college?"

"Theater. It's my passion. I want to direct one day. What else do you want to know?"

"I don't know. Let's see ... Tell me about the girls you've dated."

"What do you want to know? There's not much to tell."

"I'll bet you kiss most of them."

"Sure." He shrugged shyly.

"And … other things?"

"Some."

I tried to sound casual. "And when you do … other things with a girl … well, you can tell if she's done those other things with other boys, right?"

He stopped walking. "That's a strange question." He squatted down and ran his finger across the sand, making designs in its wetness. *Had I said too much?* "I never thought about that."

"You don't have to answer me," I hurried to say.

"No, it's okay. I supposed because they're ... you know, doing what they're doing with me ... I could think that they've done it before – but that's only because they're doing it with me. You see what I mean?" I nodded. "Like with you. I mean, my ego isn't so big that I think I'm a lady- killer. I don't think I make girls swoon and do things they wouldn't do otherwise. Otherwise, I can't tell." Then he laughed, "And I never ask."

He stood and took my hand, helping me up. He led me around a mass of kelp to higher ground where he sat down on dry sand. "I'm going to tell you something I don't think I've told anyone."

He reached for me and I sat down next to him, the sand cool against my legs. He picked up a handful, spilled it from one hand through the fingers of the other then looked at me. "Look, you told me that was your first kiss. Well, I'm going to tell you something about me. I'm a virgin."

I was confused. *How could a man be a virgin?*

"That's right. I don't do more than just play around, you know? I'm waiting for marriage. The girls I go out with? I don't really know *what* they've done or would do. I don't ask, and they don't tell. I only know what they do with me, what I do with them, and what I won't do."

If Brad was a virgin, it could only mean he hadn't had sexual intercourse. That was Jila's definition. How I wanted to believe that everything she'd told me was true! My nagging sensuality made me want to believe that I'd been taught lies, so I could share in the freedom I saw all around me. I smiled at the thought. Taking my smile as an invitation, Brad reached over and kissed me a second time.

"There," he said. "That's what a real kiss should feel like. That's your second."

It was as unsatisfying as our first. "That was nice," I said. "I'm cold, though. Can we go back?"

We returned to our group. Three of the girls were roasting marshmallows over the coals and passing them around to the others. There were so many beer cans on the sand around us that the air smelled foul. I wore my sweater and told Brad I was ready to leave. We said our goodbyes and soon were in Brad's car.

"You're great, Layla. I've told you things I've never told anyone."

"Thanks. I like you too."

"Maybe we can go out again sometime?"

"Sure. I'd like my friend Sheri to come with us next time so you two can meet. I've been thinking that you two have so much in common. She loves the theater as much as you do. That's all she talks about. I think you would like each other a lot. I know she'd really like you. You and I will be good friends."

He nodded in understanding and gave me a friendly smile. "Sure."

Things continued to going well at school.

My professors were pleased with my work. I was getting commendations in my lab class. Then Dubos left for Europe to be with his family. With his departure, the project lost its Los Angeles leg and I lost my job. As a result, I had more time for myself.

I start to take solitary walks around Westwood Village and to venture onto parts of the UCLA campus that were new to me. Westwood was always teeming with students and many couples holding hands, laughing and enjoying the day.

During one of these walks, I crossed Le Conte Avenue and continued up Westwood Boulevard. With a spring in my step, I entered the Student Union and made my way to the cafeteria, where the smell of hamburgers enticed me into ordering one, along with fries and a Coke. As I carried my tray to a table, a boy on his way out of the dining hall smiled at me. Last week, I would have turned away; I'd been raised to avoid direct eye contact with a man, told that it would be taken as a sure sign that I was a *najess,* unclean girl. But today, today I bravely smiled back.

My encounter with Brad persuaded me that Adam's kiss *hadn't* ruined my life. That tipped the balance in favor of my cousin. It therefore became probable that she was right about everything. She had most likely given me the facts, the 'real nitty-gritty' untainted by a moral or religious slant.

The old notions I'd had that had held me hostage were suddenly beginning to fall away. A feeling of relief was born, along with a new, tantalizing sense of freedom. I was already seeing the world around me differently than I had the day before. This new me condoned sexual vitality. I was happier.

I salted my fries and poured ketchup on them, then doused my hamburger with the ketchup and took a bite. It was delicious. I was in a country of choices, and I was relishing my sensate freedoms. Hamburgers were the closest things I'd found in Los Angeles to *kabob koobeedeh*, the ground meat of my country; but, of course, we didn't pour ketchup on our kabobs.

Leaving the Student Union, I headed up the stairs to Royce Hall. I resolved to ever so cautiously indulge my curiosity about boys. I would not lose myself in a pit of physical hedonism. After all, I was still Layla Saleh, an Iranian Muslim girl, and only a visitor in this land. I would be returning to Iran where I would marry and live.

But while I was in America, I had options. I was ready to stop denying myself pleasure in reverence to no more than a myth. I laughed out loud telling myself that I'd become part of the human race, albeit not the race I was born into.

I basked in the titillation that came with knowing I was embarking on the most exciting science project of them all. It would simultaneously satisfy my natural curiosity, my belief in scientific experimentation, and my personal sensuality. They were all calling out to me in one voice.

I was no longer locked inside a room with the door leading to a sensual life bolted shut. I could – and I would – be with a boy and enjoy harmless pleasure before marriage. Like Brad and Jila, I would never go all the way before marriage; but I could enjoy some of what I heard other girls talking about and I could search for a kiss that would replicate what I felt when Adam had kissed me.

Oh, how I fought with myself about Adam! I realized how unfairly harsh I'd been to him. Adam had cared about me and I supposed it was natural for him to want to kiss me. And, I missed him. Yet, as much as I wanted to call and apologize to him, I didn't. You can't turn back the water that's flowed down the river. And Jila's words filled my ear, *"I bet he'll never want to see you again."* Adding my embarrassment and my pride to the mix, Adam was off-limits. Meanwhile, the memory of his kiss was still able to thrill me.

I accepted a date with Charlie the Octopus.

Charlie was majoring in English. He planned to become a minister and he looked like a minister, tall, thin and pale, with large hands, large feet and a nose that sat prominently on his long, thin, freckled face, curly red hair and eyes that were a lackluster brown. Though he wasn't particularly handsome, he had a way about him that was appealing, a life force that emanated from him, and a friendly smile that drew me in.

After our first date, I told Jila that if Charlie approached the ministry with the same determined verve with which he approached women, Charlie would one day be Pope.

On our first date, Charlie wore a short-sleeved green shirt and drawstring pants with red socks and leather sandals, an Irish Gandhi. We had pizza for dinner and then went bowling. Charlie patiently explained the game to me and showed me how to hold and release the ball. Still, though I aimed for the center of the lane, all my balls fell into the right gutter. Charlie kept giving me lighter balls, but it was hopeless. We finally turned in our bowling shoes and went for coffee and dessert at the Apple Pan on Pico.

"I'll come up with you." Charlie said when we arrived in front of my apartment building. I shook my head. I wasn't sure Jila had returned from her date, and I didn't want to be alone with Charlie in my apartment.

"Okay," he said. "Then I'll just say goodnight." He said goodnight with a kiss. I liked Charlie's kiss, but I couldn't enjoy it because he kept going for my breasts. My heart felt thick and my body began to melt and then the pleasure faded, and I panicked as he began to unbutton my blouse. I had to stay in control; Charlie was moving far too fast for me.

"Don't, Charlie."

"Okay." Charlie's hands came away from my blouse. Just as I was relaxing into the kiss again, Charlie's hand was at the hem of my skirt stroking my thigh. It felt wonderful. Until his fingers edged their way under my skirt. I felt the delicious sensation of my insides drizzling. I had to stop him.

"Don't, Charlie."

"Okay, okay." Charlie took his hand off my thigh and took hold of my hand and moved it up *his* thigh. I pulled my hand away.

"Charlie, stop."

"Relax. Geez, it won't bite you."

He coaxed me back into his arms and into another kiss. He reached for my hand again and I began to pull away. Then, curious, I let him put my hand on his fly. With his hand atop mine, he moved my hand up and down faster and faster. His pants bulged. Suddenly, he gasped and jerked, screaming, "Oh, Christ! Oh, Lord Jesus!" He slumped over with a sigh. I was fascinated. It was like watching the final act of an opera.

"Ready to go upstairs?" he asked, moments later. I nodded. He came around the car and opened my door. "Great time," he said.

I left Charlie with questions:

Would he have reacted the same way if my hand hadn't been in his?

Could I evoke such a strong feeling in a man merely by stroking his covered crotch?

I also wondered how his penis looked inside his pants before and after the bulge.

Charlie asked me to go to Jessica's New Year's Eve party with him and silly me, I accepted. I ended up at the party without Charlie. Poor Charlie! I guess he expected a lot because it was his New Year's Eve.

When he picked me up, he came up to the apartment. Jila was running late, her hair in rollers, ironing her dress. Charlie asked for a drink. When he explained that he wanted something alcoholic, I informed him we had no alcohol in the apartment. "Holy Toledo, it's New Year's!" he said as he strode uninvited into my bedroom. I politely pushed us out of the apartment.

He drove barely two blocks away and parked on a dark residential street. "Charlie, this isn't Jessica's house."

He turned off the ignition. "I know, I know. I thought we'd have our own little celebration first." He moved to kiss me, and I let him. I don't know why I assumed he'd follow the same pattern he had last time. He didn't. He unbuckled his belt. "Let's do it. I really need to put it in you."

"You can't." I said, alarmed.

He gave me a look of utter disappointment, then sighed, as if willing to put up with my trite annoyances; he'd compromise. "Okay, then your mouth." He was pulling his shirt out from under his pants.

I covered my mouth with one hand and found the door handle with the other. "No!" I was close to retching.

"Come on, Layla, it's New Year's."

I wanted to shout at him, "And this is my New Year's treat?" I only blurted out, "No!"

"Okay, don't bust a gut. Just let me put it in you. Just for a minute." He was fiddling with his fly.

Alarms sounded. "I thought you were going to be a religious man, a priest."

"I am. Later." I gripped the door handle. Then, crazy as it was, I thought of Nassrin. I let go of the door handle, turned back to Charlie and said, haltingly, "You can put it … between my thighs."

"What?"

"*La paee.* Put it between my thighs … just don't let me see it."

"What the hell are you talking about?"

"Between my thighs."

"Okay, okay. Fine. Take off your underpants."

"No." I was a mess of emotions, foremost among them, fear and confusion. I didn't want to take my underpants off. I remembered that Nassrin had, but I was afraid to trust Charlie.

"For Chrissakes, what am I supposed to do?" Charlie asked.

This time, I spoke slowly to make sure he understood me. "Just … put it … between my thighs."

"Damn, Layla, why are you such a tease? Can't we just do it, for God's sake?"

"No!"

"Okay, okay." He moved around the confines of the front seat of his car, positioning us, bumping into the dashboard and the doors. I lay on the seat, elbows pressed into my chest, my fists clenched my body tense, my legs under the steering wheel and my head against the passenger door. My eyes were shut tightly, peeking out once, maybe twice. Charlie was too tall to lie on top of me. He couldn't find room for his long legs and large feet. He pushed me closer against my door until the metal handle pressed painfully into my head.

"Ouch! This hurts, Charlie."

"Okay, just a minute here."

"No, it hurts too much."

"Jesus Christ! Well, okay, all right, don't have a cow." He got off me – not without elbowing me – and positioned himself behind the wheel. I sat up, rubbing my sore head.

"This thigh thing isn't working," he said. He adjusted his shirt under his pants, zipped up and buckled his belt, almost in one movement. Then he looked at himself in the rear-view mirror and passed his fingers through his curly hair. He announced, "Screw this. I'm going to call Sharon."

He looked at me and asked, "Why did I ever stop seeing her? What was I thinking?" Then he turned back to the mirror as if Sharon were visible behind us, waiting for him. "I miss that girl, I really do. Damn it, we should be together on New Year's Eve. I'm going to find her. She'll know what to do."

"Could you take me to Jessica's house, please?"

"Huh? Oh yeah, sure." He dropped me off at the curb in front of Jessica's house and went in search of Sharon and, with God's help, he may have found her.

Charlie's unpredictable behavior should have alerted me to my vulnerability when alone with boys in their car. It didn't. I assumed that Charlie was simply accustomed to a more accommodating Sharon.

Meanwhile, I was pleased with the headway I was making in my physical explorations. It was unquestionably more than my scientific bent that was coaxing me out of my sexual cage. I liked the pleasurable sensations my experiments evoked. Kissing, being held, feeling hands moving up my thigh, under my skirt, and over my breasts made my body feel charged and made my skin tingle with pleasure. I felt more alive. I loved it.

Yet I began to suspect that however far I went with these boys, I'd always be expected to go further. And I wondered why American boys didn't know about *la paee*.

26
ANTHONY

Then Anthony came into my life.

I'll never forget Anthony. Never. Anthony deCordova Though I wish I could wipe him from my memory, eliminate him from my history, in the interest of complete honesty – "full disclosure," as the Americans say – I recount my encounter with him.

Anthony was handsome in that swarthy way.

He came for me in his shiny new black Corvette, wearing a soft winter-white cashmere sweater, black pants, and a black leather jacket. He smelled of expensive cologne. He did not open the car door for me.

"So, where is it you're from again?" He asked as he started up the engine.

"Iran."

"Where's that?"

I wasn't surprised that he didn't know; most people I'd met had no idea where Iran was.

"The Middle East," I said.

"Oh, right. So, you're an A-rab."

"No. I'm Persian."

"Well, Persian, A-rab, it's all the same. You all ride camels, right?"

"Yes. My father has a big one and my mother rides a smaller one."

"What about you?"

"I either sit on the other side of the hump with one of my parents or I ride alone on a smaller camel."

"Wow," he said, as he made a right turn, "all these cars and buildings, traffic lights and stuff must be really strange to you."

"Yes. I'm still getting used to it all."

"You don't even have electricity there, do you?"

"No. We recently had some oil lamps brought into the big cities. Most people still haven't gotten used to them. We laugh at my mother because she's so afraid of them." He looked at me in disbelief; not at what I'd said, but at my mother's ignorance. I couldn't resist. "She uses a candle and says that's good enough."

Anthony shook his head and sneered.

He stopped his Corvette in front of Mario's, an Italian restaurant in Westwood, not the sort of restaurant that college kids normally go to. He lectured the valet about his car before handing over the keys, then opened the door of the restaurant, and went in first. He followed the maître d' to our table leaving me to follow behind. He demanded a corner table for two. There were none available. We were shown to a table for four in the center of the restaurant. Anthony whined and was still muttering under his breath as he dropped into his chair. I took the seat to his right. He studied the wine list on the table and ordered a bottle. When the waiter politely asked to see his driver's license Anthony rolled his eyes. "You're kidding, right? No one asks for my ID. I get served everywhere. I'm known in this town. I tip big, little man."

The waiter smiled and calmly, politely apologized, explained that he was required by law to confirm Anthony's age and repeated his request to see his identification. "If you can't do your job, let me speak to the big guy," Anthony said waving the waiter away, "your boss, the owner or manager, whoever."

The manager came to our table and politely explained to Anthony that he was sorry, but it was impossible to serve him wine despite his assertions that he'd been there before and had been served without question. "Hey, relax. I'll be twenty-one the day after tomorrow. I left my ID in the car. It's the brand, new 'Vette parked right out front." The manager stood his ground. Anthony asked for the manager's card and put it in his pocket. Then, in a raised voice, he said, "We'll see about that" and that the owner of the restaurant would "soon be hearing about this fiasco." When the manager had left our table, the waiter handed us menus and almost ran away.

Anthony hadn't said a word to me since we'd entered the restaurant. I decided not to initiate conversation; I would see how long it would take him to acknowledge me. The waiter came by to take our dinner choices. Anthony ordered a pasta dish – "cooked *al dente*, with extra marina sauce on the side" – and left me to fend for myself. I ordered veal. When our salads came, Anthony complained to our waiter that the lettuce wasn't fresh. I shrunk a little, in embarrassment.

I had met Anthony at a party. He'd told me his name, followed with the name of his fraternity then asked me out, took down my address and phone number and was gone.

Jila had reacted strongly when I told her I'd made a date with him. "A very elite fraternity," she'd said. "I just don't see you with a boy like that. They all think they're gods."

Despite her comments, I had accepted the date gladly. I'd looked forward to getting to know this handsome Italian. I'd wanted to feel his full lips against mine. But before our dinner arrived, any desire I'd had to have anything at all to do with Anthony deCordova was long forgotten. I'd get through this dinner and go home.

"It's no wonder the guy's still a waiter at his age," he said, extinguishing any possibility that he may have forgotten I was there. "He's an absolute spaz. Pathetic. He's so goddamn stupid he can't even wait a table right."

He didn't seem to notice that I didn't answer him and just kept rambling on about how some men were meant to be losers their whole lives.

"Look at me," he said, pointing to himself with both hands, "a winner. I'm a college student and I've already got lots of dough. I'm a top-paid model. Cast an eye on how I'm dressed and check my wheels. Not bad, huh? Damn good, if you know what I mean."

I waited for this "winner" to ask me a question about my classes, my dinner, my life – anything. He didn't. The entire dinner came and went, and he never stopped talking about himself. He boasted about his various modeling jobs, mentioning names in men's fashion, European designers, including several names I'd heard of, and how they all loved him.

He only stopped talking about himself to complain about everything on his plate. The sauce was too salty, and the pasta was overcooked. "*Al dente,*" he said to the waiter, throwing down his fork. "This is mush. Doesn't your cook know what *al dente* means?"

When the waiter asked if we'd care for dessert and coffee, Anthony quickly said he only wanted the check. I would have liked a cup of tea. "The little lady knows about dessert," he said, patting my knee under the table. "She'll take care of that," he said, winking at me.

I'd never felt more humiliated. Anthony was rude and despicable, and I couldn't stand to be with him another minute, let alone kiss him. *Anthony,* I wanted to say, *you're wrong.* The waiter bowed slightly to Anthony in acquiescence and passed me a small smile, his eyes filled with either sympathy or pity.

Anthony was looking at the bill. He brought out his alligator wallet and dished out cash, splaying the bills on the red-and-white checkered tablecloth in front of the empty chair to his left.

"That idiot doesn't deserve a tip and he's not getting a dime from me," he muttered. There was no doubt in my mind that Anthony was a model jerk.

Between us, between my refilled glass of water and Anthony's glass of Coke, sat the dish with the extra marina sauce the waiter had brought with his pasta. I moved fast, artfully flinging my left arm out over the tabletop, knocking over both the bowl of marinara sauce and the remains of his soda. The result was far better than I could have hoped for and I squelched a smile of satisfaction as I held my hand over my mouth in mock horror. The red sauce, runnier now – thanks to the soda – spilled and splattered all over Anthony's winter-white designer cashmere sweater and dripped onto his black designer pants. He looked absolutely ridiculous. I was jubilant.

"Oh, Anthony, I'm so sorry!" I wanted the waiter, a couple of tables away, to see him. I pushed my chair back and welcomed its screech as I got up, speaking very loudly. "Look at you. Your beautiful sweater! You look so bad! And your pants. You're a mess! You look terrible. I am so sorry!"

Anthony stared down at his ruined clothing. I grabbed the dirty, wet cloth napkin from the table top, leaned over and began rubbing his sweater with it, pressing the stains in and making everything worse.

In seconds, he'd grabbed my wrist, took the napkin out of my hand and threw it on the floor. He pushed me roughly away, then pushed his chair away from the table. His cold, perfect model eyes glowered at me as he slowly rose from his chair, dripping marina sauce and Coke.

"You stupid bitch. Are you crazy? What the hell did you do that for?"

For a second, I thought he was going to hit me. Luckily, he realized that other diners were staring at him, listening to him, and he froze. Our waiter hurried to the table, picked up the cash and the bill and headed back into the kitchen.

Anthony stormed out of the restaurant without a backward glance. I followed him. The valet stared at him, then retrieved his car and opened the door for him. Anthony pushed him away and got into his shiny, new, black Corvette. I helped myself inside and sat smugly. My mistake!

As Anthony sped away from the restaurant he continued where he'd left off. "That's the dumbest thing I've ever seen anyone do. You stupid bitch. You stupid ... fucking ... A-rab bitch! I should have just left you there. If I weren't such a gentleman, such a nice guy, I would have."

Feeling extremely satisfied with myself, I said, "I'm sorry, really I am Anthony."

"I'll bet you are."

"Maybe you should just take me home."

"Are you kidding? I'm supposed to take you out, feed you, and take you home after you do this to me? You're sorry? Well, let's see how sorry you are." He looked in his rear-view mirror and made an abrupt U-turn.

I began to feel afraid. "Now you get to do your stuff," he said. He was speeding toward the UCLA campus just blocks away. I cursed myself for returning to sit in his car. I ought to have gone home from the restaurant.

"Where are you going, Anthony?"

"You'll see, bitch. Just sit there and shut your mouth. For now."

I felt the fear take me over. Anthony was making turns, then backing up, entering the campus, making more turns, then turning around, and continuing on through the grounds. I had no idea what he was looking for in the dark. Then he saw what he wanted. He drove onto the empty top floor of a deserted parking lot, stopped the car, turned off the lights, and turned the radio on.

"I don't understand." I said. "What are we doing here?"

"You're going to give me some A-rab head." Bobby Darrin's, "Mack the Knife," began to play softly on the radio. *Oh, the shark has pretty teeth babe ..."*

Anthony pushed his black leather seat all the way back then moved to unbuckle his belt. I was in major trouble. I was totally vulnerable. And Anthony wasn't Charlie; Anthony was unlike anyone I'd known, uncaring and blind to all desires save his own. I put my hand on the door handle and pushed down. It was pitch black outside. I didn't care. Nothing happened; it was locked. Anthony grabbed my arm and squeezed. "You're not going anywhere."

God, help me, I felt cold terror. I sat frozen, looking straight ahead into the darkness while Anthony unzipped his pants and settled himself in his seat. The feeling of cold helplessness that had gripped me was like nothing I'd ever felt before.

"I'm truly sorry for what happened," I said. I began to cry.

"Come here."

I didn't move. He grabbed my arm, high up by my armpit, and pulled me to him, then suddenly grabbed the back of my neck and slammed my head down to his crotch. My face hit wet marina sauce. My lips felt the jagged metal zipper of his pants, and I was hit with a foul mixture of odors – the smell of the sauce mixed with his private parts – and nausea set in. My nose, chin and lips were wet from the cold sauce. I held my breath and fought to pull my head up, but in vain; he was holding me down. He was strong and rough.

"Do it." He let go of me for an instant, just long enough to grab hold of his penis with his left hand and adjust himself again. In that instant I was able to raise my head. It hit the steering wheel before he slammed it down again with his right hand. He tried to shove himself into my mouth but couldn't; I wouldn't part my lips.

"Do it, bitch! Open your mouth." I shook my head as best as I could. The smell was horrible. I tried desperately to keep my mouth sealed but he just kept ramming himself against my mouth and slowly pushed past my lips. Then my teeth were the barricade, and I thought he might stop from pain, but he kept shoving and making noises.

This *thing* was pushing against my teeth. I tried to writhe, but he had a tight hold on me. I was struggling. I couldn't breathe through my nose – that's how foul the odor was – and I couldn't breathe through my mouth because if I'd opened it, he'd shove his penis completely in. I knew I couldn't last much longer. I grabbed at his thigh to claw him, still holding my breath. I desperately needed to raise my head and breathe. I needed air. My God, I thought I would die. Unable to help myself, to hold back another instant, I inhaled and immediately vomited. I was gasping for air now, taking in the foul odor. I couldn't stop vomiting.

When Anthony first felt my mouth open, he'd moaned. Then he realized something was wrong. "What the hell?"

I had vomited my dinner all over his private parts and his already stained pants. He yanked me up and I came up, still throwing vomiting all over him and then his car. He was screaming in disbelief. "What the fuck?" Oh, he was furious. "Jesus!" He kept yelling, "Jesus! Jesus fucking Christ! What the fuck!"

He unlocked the doors, opened his and got out. He started walking around with his hands in the air and his pants hanging down, walking around like that, with vomit and marinara sauce all over him, and he kept yelling over and over, "Jesus Christ! What the fuck!"

He didn't know what to do. He didn't want to touch himself or his clothes. I think he was in some kind of shock. I was in shock myself.

I stayed in the car for a few seconds longer till I stopped retching then I got out. I breathed in deeply, taking in fresh air, and moving as fast as my somewhat shaky legs would take me, hoping I was headed back in the direction we'd come.

When I last saw Anthony DeCordova, he was kicking the tire of his shiny, new, black Corvette, hands still up in the air, covered in my vomit screaming, "Jesus fucking Christ!"

I left the parking lot as fast as I could and fortunately found my way home.

"My god, Layla! What happened to you?"

I undressed as quickly as I could while recounting my evening with Anthony.

Jila laughed when I told her about the camels and electricity and then again when I told her how I'd spilled the sauce on him. I stopped then. I couldn't finish the story until I'd washed myself clean of him. I showered, soaping myself well and brushing my teeth then continued my miserable story to its end.

"And then I walked home."

Jila was immediately livid. "That horrible son of a bitch! Oh, Layla, what a bastard! I warned you not to go out with him! The guys in that fraternity are all nuts. I'll call the police and we'll have him arrested."

I panicked. "No, please Jila, don't! I don't want anyone to know what happened. Please don't call the police. I just want to forget it all. Please promise me. You have to promise me you won't tell anyone!"

"Layla, it's wrong not to call the police. He has to be stopped before he does that to another girl, and you know he will. You should report him Layla, it's the right thing to do."

She was absolutely right but I shook my head. I didn't tell her that I was afraid that if the police got involved my parents would be contacted.

"Well you were the victim, not me," she said at last. "You have to be the one to tell them what he did, not me. If you won't, there's nothing I can do. As for telling anyone what happened, if you don't want me to tell, I promise I won't. You have my word." She hugged me. "You must have been terrified."

"It was horrible."

"Let me make you a cup of tea. If I were a guy, I swear I'd beat the crap out of him." I'd never before heard Jila talk like that. "Thank God all boys aren't like that. He makes all boys look bad."

"Good or bad, I'm through with boys." I said. "No more for me, Jila. I've had more than enough of them," I said resolutely. I declined Jila's offer of tea. I just wanted to get into bed and end the day.

I lay in my bed and thanked God that I had escaped Anthony de Cordoba.

His words rang in my ears - *you're not going anywhere* – and I shivered.

Began to cry again, remembering the horrible feeling of having my breath robbed. The tears came easily, tears of fear, tears of self-pity, and tears of relief I could now shed freely.

I looked at the clock. When I reached over to turn it around, a fly that had settled there flew away. It was almost one o'clock in the morning. Within seconds that fly landed back on the exact same spot.

I smiled. I was suddenly at home in our kitchen unsuccessfully trying to swat a fly, when Cobra took the opportunity to demonstrate the proper way to kill one. As she moved her lumbering arms ever so slowly toward the sorry insect, she spoke softly as though the fly would escape if it heard her words.

"If you move too fast, they'll know you're coming for them and they'll fly away. You have to move so slowly that you won't be noticed until ..." By then. the napkin she held in her hand was paused just an inch or so above the unfortunate fly that had landed by the sink, clueless as to its fate, "… until you're ready to smash it."

She moved her hand ever so slowly even closer to the fly and then hammered her hand down. The juices of the squished blue-black body spilled onto the counter. Thanks to Cobra, if I'd wanted to kill the fly on the clock, it wouldn't have stood a chance.

That night I saw myself very much like that fly. I'd been gradually yet continually expanding my boundaries with boys, ever so slowly and yet persistently. I had been growing far too bold. My encounter with Anthony made me realize I'd been on dangerous ground, and his was the hand hovering over my head, just waiting for the right moment to squash me.

I was through with dating.

The paradox didn't escape me. I had cringed when I first came into my moon and my mother had announced the order to me; now I was ordering it up to myself.

No more boys!

27
DOCTOR!

Winter holidays ended and then came final exams.
I finished my first term at UCLA with a grade point average of 3.7 but with boys now out of my life, I expected to do better the following semester.

On a January morning, early in the new semester and days before my first birthday in America, I awoke with a headache and scratchy throat and by the end of the day my head was throbbing and terribly congested.

I was running a high temperature, and my throat hurt so badly I couldn't swallow without wincing; it felt like a raw wound. My lungs ached with every breath, and every breath felt like fire. I stayed in bed all day.

When Jila came home and saw me, she was concerned. My eyes were bloodshot, my nose red, and my face, pale. I was feverishly hot to the touch. Though I was wrapped in every blanket we had in the apartment, I still complained of the cold. Jila brought me a cup of tea with two aspirins and nagged me until I finally drank the tea and took the two small white pills, though they were painful to swallow.

Before she went to bed that night, Jila left me with a fresh box of tissues. "Go to sleep," she said. "The door to my room is open. If you need anything at all during the night, just holler." I peered at her through watery eyes. "Or come into my room. Or throw something against the wall and I'll hear you. I'm taking you to the med center first thing tomorrow morning."

Somehow the night passed.

I took several doses of Babajon's Galoo Cure. Even that gave me no relief. There was no question about it; I needed a doctor.

When daylight came, I got out of bed feeling even worse than the night before, and dressed in whatever was at hand, wore a warm sweater over that, and wrapped a scarf around my neck, then got back under the covers and waited for Jila to wake up. When she did, she brought me a fresh box of tissues then dressed hastily. I was too sick to even brush my hair. My throat hurt too much to brush my teeth. We hurried off to the student medical center and entered the waiting room. We went to the desk. I asked for tissues. The receptionist handed me a box of Kleenex and asked if we had an appointment. Jila said we didn't.

"I'm afraid we're very busy here today," the receptionist said. She motioned to the chairs around the room. "Please have a seat and wait." There were only two empty chairs in the crowded room.

"Look at this girl." Jila said loudly. "She's very sick. She has a very high fever. I don't think you want her around other people. She's obviously contagious." People in the waiting room looked up. "And she'll probably faint again. She hasn't eaten in over 24 hours. Maybe you should let the doctors know she's here."

The receptionist looked from Jila to me then got up and went down the hall.

"See?" Jila said with some pride. "I can be Persian when I need to be." I smiled weakly at my cousin. Even that was an effort.

The receptionist returned to her station, thumbed through some papers on her desk and found what she was looking for. She handed a sheet of paper to Jila on a clipboard. "Before a doctor will see her, she needs to complete this form."

"No problem," Jila responded. "Put us in a room and I'll fill this out for her while the doctor takes her temperature. It will be better if she faints in a room than out here."

The receptionist ambled down the corridor again. This time she returned with a woman dressed in light blue uniform who opened the door to the waiting room. "Come with me, please." She led us down the inner hallway into a small examination room and left us there to wait.

I collapsed onto a chair and closed my tired burning eyes. Jila began filling out the form.

"*Name, Date of Birth, Age, Sex, Address, Telephone number, Student ID number* – Layla, do you know your ID number by heart?" My head was so congested I could only move it slightly, slowly, from side to side.

"Okay, don't worry. *Person to contact in case of emergency*. That's me. *Name, Address, Telephone number, Relationship to patient*… Let's see: *Country of birth*, Iran. *City*, Tehran. *Mother alive or deceased*, God forbid! Alive. *Father alive or deceased*, Alive, thank God. *Brothers*, no. *Sisters*, no. *Do you have or have you ever had the following: Tonsillitis?* Layla, have you had your tonsils taken out?"

I could barely open my eyes to look at my cousin. I cautiously shook my head. It was all I could do to breathe through the congestion.

She went on. "*Appendicitis* ... have you – never mind. Let's see, *Tuberculosis, Hepatitis, Polio, Meningitis*, you haven't had any of those. *Drug or alcohol addiction, no* .... *Anemia* – I don't know if you're anemic. Are you anemic? Do you know what that is? I don't know how to say that in Farsi. Never mind. No ... no .... *Heart palpitations*, no, you've never mentioned that to me. *Heart problems, Stroke, Hemophilia*, no, no, no. Let's see, *Artificial limbs*, that's easy, no. *Gall stones, Kidney stones, Rheumatism, Arthritis*, I don't think you have any of that stuff. *Major surgery of any kind*, no; I'd know if you had major surgery, wouldn't I? *Poor vision, Poor hearing* – Can you see and hear me, Layla? Sorry, just kidding. I think I'm done. Let's see …"

The door opened.

My burning eyes were still shut, I heard the doctor had walked in. Then I heard his voice. "Hello. I understand you're not feeling well."

What was that? His voice went through me like a jolt of electricity. I opened my stinging eyes. The doctor stood with his back to me, talking to Jila.

"What exactly is the problem?" he asked. His voice was deep and smooth and resonated through my body like a loud bass. Every word seemed to drip out of his mouth effortlessly, like warm honey.

Jila laughed. "I'm not the patient, Doctor. It's my cousin. I'm just helping her fill out the form."

Be quiet, Jila! Let the man talk!

The doctor turned around and my heart bounced.

I was looking up at a man with hair the color of dark sand and the most beautiful blue eyes I've ever seen. His skin was unblemished and golden, as though he'd just come from a day at the beach. His jaw was strong, but not too strong, just strong enough. He was tall, exactly as tall as a man should be, and he was broad-shouldered, but no more broad-shouldered than a man should be. I guessed that he was in his mid-20s. All of that registered with my first look at him.

"Excuse my mistake. Of course. I can see that now." He smiled, and the world was perfect.

He's so handsome! And his voice! Say something, doctor. I felt drawn to him as if to a magnet.

"So, what can I do for you?" he asked me.

His every word was like a silken rope that tied me to him. *Anything. Everything. Look at me and speak, so I can see your face and hear your voice.*

I realized I was staring at the doctor, yet I couldn't stop myself. As sick as I felt, it was soothing to look at him and hear his voice. I wanted to watch his mouth, watch his lips move. I sat mute.

After Anthony, men had held no interest for me. I had no longer had any curiosity about their lips, their minds or their arms. This doctor smashed all that the instant he entered the room. He smiled at me. He was close enough now that I noticed that behind his velvet lips there was a slight gap between his two front teeth. I felt an urge to press my dry lips against his lips and feel that gap with my tongue and know the wetness of his mouth. I pulled my burning eyes away from him and closed them.

"What are your symptoms Layla? Am I pronouncing that right?"

His voice resonated inside my head calming the congestion. I opened my eyes and nodded, forgetting that it would hurt my head; it was so congested I couldn't move it without pain.

He took a pen out of his jacket pocket and stepped closer to me, preparing to take notes for his file. His manner was elegant, his limbs long, his movements slow and graceful. He asked me to list my symptoms.

When I opened my mouth, no sound out. *I'd lost my voice!* I looked at Jila and then the doctor in alarm. "What's wrong?" the doctor asked. I couldn't answer.

"Oh, her throat hurts an awful lot," Jila said. "It's hard for her to talk. Ask me what you need to know."

The doctor turned from me to Jila and I hated her for it. "Okay, did I pronounce the name right?"

"Yes."

"What are Layla's symptoms?"

"She has a very high temperature, or at least she did last night. Her throat hurts like it's cut, she can't eat or swallow and she's sneezing and blowing her nose a lot."

He wrote it all down. "What color is her phlegm?"

"I don't know," Jila said. "Layla, what color is your phlegm?"

I had no idea what 'phlegm' was until Jila made believe she sneezed and pointed to her nose. I understood then, but could only hold my throat and point to my mouth to signal that I had no voice.

"Is there phlegm coming up from your throat, too?" the doctor asked, misunderstanding me.

I pointed to my lips and mouthed *I can't talk*.He got it. "I think she's lost her voice," he said. "Is that right, Layla?"

I nodded and held my aching head between my hands.

"She can't move her head," Jila said. "I mean, it must be extremely congested. I think it hurts when she tries. Am I right, Layla?"

I barely nodded then tried to talk again. I couldn't. My throat felt like a deep, flaming gash. I put both my hands around my throat and frowned.

"Hmm. Your throat must really hurt," the doctor said. He seemed to carry himself so confidently, yet in place of the arrogance of a handsome Anthony, this gorgeous man was comfortable to be around.

I tried to smile. I wanted the admiration of this man and was determined to act poised. I looked at Jila and blinked deliberately, subtly forcing my eyelids down, signaling the Farsi "yes."

"Yes," Jila said.

"Okay," he said. Realizing how badly I'd dressed, I hoped that despite my poorly put-together outfit, my red swollen eyes and lack of voice, the doctor would think I was pretty and exotic, as boys in my classes did. Despite my sorry state, I very much wanted to impress him.

"Well, let's take her temperature and see what we have." The doctor put down my file and picked up a thermometer.

I panicked. *My God! I hadn't brushed my teeth!* I snatched the thermometer from the doctor's hand and put it in my own mouth with a slight, closed-lipped smile, my stinging eyes half-shut. I wanted to crawl into the medical cabinet and hide, knowing I had neither washed my face nor brushed my hair.

I was looking at a man who was a walking bit of heaven, a human candy bar, and I had never looked or felt as miserable as I did sitting there. I pulled my hair down and back with both my hands.

The doctor checked his watch and removed the thermometer. "She definitely has a fever. It's hovering just above 103."

Why are you talking to Jila about me? I understand English. I'm neither a child nor an idiot. Talk to me, Dr. Whoever-you-are. Turn around and look at me when you speak, so I can see your eyes, and watch your mouth.

The doctor came to me and examined my ears with his light then said, "I need you to open your mouth wide and say 'Ahh!'"

Oh no! This isn't happening. I inhaled deeply and opened my mouth. I said a very soft "Ahh," trying not to exhale in the doctor's face.

"Open wider, wider … now say a big 'Ahh.'" The doctor first shined his light into my mouth then took a tongue depressor into my mouth. Then he inserted a long Q-tip into my mouth and down to my throat. He was taking forever in my mouth. I constricted my hot, sore throat so as not to exhale. But I couldn't hold out forever. *Hurry, please God, please, make him hurry in there.*

He was peering into my mouth, looking down my throat when I let go of my breath in one giant "Ahh." I cringed in embarrassment. My mouth must have smelled monstrously.

"There, that's it, very good. Keep it open just another few seconds." He moved the Q-tip around, and brought it out.

Dear God, can it be that this man has no sense of smell?

I tried to give Jila as piercing a look as my burning eyes allowed, as if to say, "Do you see what's happening here? I think I'm falling in love with this man and he's talking about my phlegm and smelling my breath." Jila was looking at her nails.

Well, at least he's not asking me to take my clothes off.

Finally done examining my mouth, he made more notes in my file, then handed me a green cloth. "I'll step out of the room for a minute. I'd like you to take your blouse off and put this gown on, so I can examine you."

My eyes watered as I stared after him in disbelief. He left us, closing the door behind him. Jila came toward me. "Here, let me help you take your blouse off. Are you supposed to take your bra off, too?"

I recoiled, defending my bra with my hands. I was not taking that off. I put the soft green cotton gown on with the opening in back and had Jila tie it tightly then sat back up on the table.

The doctor knocked and re-entered. He approached me and inserted his stethoscope into his ears. "This may feel a little cold," he said standing behind me.

I found a spot on the wall and kept my eyes glued to it. He put the cold metal on the feverish skin of my back.

"Breathe in. Deeply. That's good. Again. Now out. Again? In, out. And again. Good."

I tried to keep myself from flying away on his voice, so soft, and so close to my ear. I wanted to distract myself from his nearness by focusing on the pressure of the congestion in my head. He removed the stethoscope from my back and stood straight.

"Okay, now let's try it from the front."

I tried not to move at all as the gorgeous doctor placed his stethoscope near my left breast. He seemed to be listening intently to my breathing. My heart was pounding so loudly he could have heard it without the stethoscope. I felt the warmth of his hand radiate through my already hot, sensitive skin. With every breath, every inhalation, my chest expanded, and I felt my breasts rise up to meet him.

"Breathe in, breathe in please … that's good … deeper ... okay, now exhale. Okay, again, deeper, deeper, now out. Good. One more time."

He moved the stethoscope around on my chest as if he was unsure exactly where to put it, and kept listening. I felt my nose start to run. I sniffled. It didn't help. I sniffled louder and made a horrid noise. It didn't stop my nose from running. I scanned the counters for a box of tissues. I didn't see any. I looked at Jila for help. She was staring off somewhere, so I couldn't catch her eye. Thick phlegm had escaped out of my nose. At that precise moment, the doctor raised his head and saw me, the paradigm of wretchedness, and offered me a box of tissues from behind him.

I blew my nose, while – to my utter humiliation – the doctor said to Jila, "Her phlegm is green."

He made more notes in my file. Then the gorgeous doctor with the amazing voice, who wouldn't talk to me, and whom I fervently prayed I would never see after today's humiliation, once again addressed Jila. "All right, here's my official diagnosis. Your cousin has a very bad cold and an infection. I've taken a culture of her throat for testing. Meanwhile, I'm quite certain she has strep throat, so I'm going to have her start treatment for that even before the test results are in our hands.

"She needs to be on antibiotics, which I'll prescribe, along with some medicine to loosen the phlegm in her lungs and nasal cavities, and I see there's a lot there; it will also relieve some of her discomfort. I may want her to start on some cough medicine in a day or two. I'll give you a prescription for that now as well, so you won't have to come back for it.

"Am I missing anything? I feel like I'm leaving something out."

Go ahead and ask for a sample of my stool and my urine. You may as well disgrace me totally.

"If I figure it out, I'll call you. If you have any questions, feel free to call me. You have our number."

And your name is?

The doctor was walking out of the room when, as an apparent afterthought, he turned back to me to flash a quick million-dollar smile. "Make sure to drink a lot of liquids. And try to eat something. You'll probably do best with soft foods for a while, but you do need to eat and drink a lot. And get lots of rest."

He turned to Jila. "Nice to meet you."

Then again to me, "I'll be seeing you, Layla. Pretty name. Hope you feel better."

He was gone.

Jila talked about him all the way home.

"He's so good-looking. He looked so good in that white jacket, didn't he? And don't you think he had a great personality?"

Her constant chatter reminded me of her mother. I could do nothing more than blink my itching, burning eyes and nod faintly.

She abruptly stopped walking. "We don't even know his name, Layla. What's his name?" I shrugged.

When we got home, I headed straight for a mirror and was aghast at what I saw: my eyes red and watering, face pale, hair tangled up terribly, nose a sight, and clothes obviously slept in. Miserable, I retreated to bed with my medications, a full box of tissues and a head congested with thoughts of the doctor I'd just fallen in love with.

Following instructions from Ammeh Elahe, Jila cooked me *ob goosht*, our version of chicken soup. She put some chicken into a pot of water and added chopped onion, some turmeric, garbanzo beans and two dried limes someone had sent from Iran and let it all boil. I couldn't swallow a shred of chicken, but she insisted that I drink the warm chicken broth and swallow a bit of steamed white rice soaked in the same broth.

Burying myself in bed, I wanted to forget the doctor and the entire scene that had taken place in his office. Try as I did, the doctor's face remained in my mind as if it had taken it over. Each word he said came back to me, and even as I recalled his voice and its every nuance, my body quivered under the sheets. His every move, his gestures and his appealing smile all taunted me.

He's not such a big deal. He's a gorgeous man, that's all. Gorgeous with an amazing voice! And so nice. I'm certainly not in love! I just hope that when I really do fall in love, it will be with someone like him.

I tried to fall asleep, if only to forget him. Yet, I stayed awake dwelling on him until the medicine he'd prescribed took effect and I was knocked out. I slept far better that night than the night before. The next day I remained in bed, still very sick and unable to speak, and still obsessed with the doctor. I told myself that I was being silly and over-reacting to him because I simply hadn't been myself when I saw him. Besides, I would never see him again. I would most likely be seen by another doctor on my next visit.

To my surprise, the nameless doctor called that day. I could hear only part of what Jila said from my bed. I quickly assumed that the doctor had taken a liking to my cousin and was using me as an excuse to call her, even though when Jila brought me tea, she didn't say anything other than that he'd asked how I was feeling. "He called to say that he remembered what he'd forgotten. He wants you to start on a nasal spray. I told him that your temperature was still high and that your voice hadn't come back. He said not to worry. He also wanted to remind you to bring your student ID number with you when you go in next time. What a great doctor."

He obviously likes Jila as much as she likes him. Good for them.

He called again the next day and asked Jila if my temperature was down, if the spray was helping and if my phlegm was still green. And he called the day after that to give Jila the results of my test. "He said your throat culture tested positive for strep just like he said. Anyway, he's glad you've already started the right treatment for it. He wants me and you to come to his office on Monday."

He wants to see Jila again. Why doesn't he just ask her to go out instead of using me as an excuse to see her?

"I made an appointment for us at two o'clock. I told him you're feeling better. He said to tell you he's glad."

Monday morning, I felt much better.

My temperature was down, and the congestion had subsided; the antibiotics had done their job.

As I was getting ready to return to the doctor, Jila came into my room and asked if it would be all right if she didn't go to the medical center with me. "You're okay now, aren't you?" she asked. I nodded. "So, you don't really need me to go with you; I've got some studying to do.

Perhaps Jila is pushing him away with her hand while pulling him towards her with her foot, or as the Americans say, acting hard to get. "That's all right," I said. "Go study."

"Okay, say hello to the handsome doctor for me and don't forget to take your student ID."

Maybe, I wasn't completely conscious of the extra care I took in getting ready that day. I washed my hair, paid attention to my outfit, spent extra time with what little makeup I wore, and even dabbed on a touch of perfume. It wasn't until I was entering the medical center that I realized I still didn't know the doctor's name and hadn't asked Jila. "Excuse me. I'm Layla Saleh. I have an appointment at two o'clock?"

"Your doctor?"

"I don't know his name." *I know what he looks like. He's young, tall, handsome, beautiful blue eyes and a voice I'll never forget.*

The receptionist looked up my name on the schedule. "Let's see. It's Dr. Kline. I'm afraid he's been called out to an emergency. Another doctor can see you if you can't wait."

Dr. Kline. "No, thank you. I'll wait."An hour later, I was ushered into the same room I'd been in with Jila. I waited there and continued lecturing myself, telling myself not to be surprised to see that he's not as wonderful as I'd thought. When he entered the room, I said hello first.

"Hello. I see you have your voice back. That's good."

His voice had the exact same effect on me as the first time I'd heard it. From his first hello, I was torn between succumbing to his deep, rich voice, and taking in every detail of his handsome face. His lips were perfect, and his eyes were small with startlingly blue pupils peering out in the space between his broad forehead and high cheeks. *My God, he is just the right amount of gorgeous.*

"I'm glad to see you're feeling better," he said.

I was feeling fine when I first came into the room. Now I felt a bit unsteady. "Yes, I am better. Thank you."

"That's good." Dr. Kline seemed to have filed away any awareness of his good looks. He had the air of a person concerned with being genuine and friendly, rather than finessing the aloofness that so often comes with a handsome face. "I'm glad to hear that. You should be. I'm sorry you were so uncomfortable."

His voice is a soft blanket I want to curl up under forever. "I was in a mess," I said. The doctor laughed, a perfect, movie star laugh, his mouth opening to show the endearing gap between his teeth. My heart felt stung by electrodes.

"Is something wrong?"

I must have been staring. "Oh, no, Doctor."

"Well," he said, opening my file. "You were certainly not happy the last time we met. I'm glad to see you're able to smile today. I had a suspicion your smile would be nice. It looks like you've gotten some rest, too."

I want to stay here forever. With you. Just like this.

"Your medicine was very effective, Doctor. Oh, Jila couldn't come. She said she had to study."

"Well, you seem fine. I don't see that you need her. Do you?"

"No, I don't need her. I mean I'm fine. I can speak today."

"And you speak very nicely. What kind of a name is Layla? Are you Arab?"

"No, I'm not. I'm Iranian. Persian."

"*Layla* is an Arabic name, isn't it? I think it means *dark* or *night* in Arabic."

"Yes."

"And I think Layla was the original Juliet in the story of that became Shakespeare's Romeo and Juliet?"

"Actually, that was Laylee, not Layla." I was amazed that he knew all that.

"Well Layla, of the pretty name, you have a charming accent." I smiled shyly, feeling like I'd just been awarded the world.

"Okay, let's take your temperature, make sure you've fully recovered." When he came to put the thermometer in my mouth, he hesitated for a moment. "May I?" I smiled and opened my mouth. While my temperature was registering, Dr. Kline reviewed the notes he'd made in my file on my first visit and made some brief notes alongside them. "Barely any temperature. 98.7." That meant he wouldn't be using his stethoscope again.

He broke out into a grin. "Well, Layla, it seems you are fully recovered and have no more need for a doctor." He closed my file and put it down. "I am starving. I missed lunch because of an emergency here."

"They told me you had an emergency. I could have waited while you ate. I'm so sorry you haven't eaten because of my appointment."

"Sorry? Sorry enough to join a hungry doctor for lunch in the cafeteria? My food digests better when I have company."

I nodded. "Okay."

While paying for food in the cafeteria, the petite elderly woman just ahead of us in line realized she'd forgotten a bottle of 7-Up.

Dr. Kline quickly put down his tray, darted to the cold case and returned, presenting her with a bottle. Then, realizing she carried a cane, he carried her tray to a table.

"That was nice," I said.

He shrugged. "It was nothing for me, but it helped her a little. We need to help one another."

Sitting alongside him in the cafeteria, I was oblivious to my surroundings, taking in his fluid manner, his voice, the movement of his lips, and the way his fingers moved through the air when he spoke as though dancing. His hands were perfectly proportioned, his long fingers, regular, his palm, broad, his nails, clean and well-groomed.

"Are you a Persian princess?" he asked, biting into his tuna sandwich.

"No, just an ordinary Persian girl, I'm afraid." I was turning around a cup of hot tea.

"Then Iran must be full of very pretty ordinary girls." A smile played on his lips with no thought of drinking it.

"Thank you." I was starting to dare think Dr. Kline liked me.

He was surprised to learn I was in America without my parents. "So that's why Jila plays mother hen."

"She's my cousin and she's wonderful to me. I don't know what I would do without her."Again, I noticed his eyes lingering on me a moment after I'd finished speaking.

I learned that he'd graduated from UCLA's School of Medicine and was completing his internship that year. He was twenty-five years old.

"So, Pretty Layla, what do you think of our Western way of life?" he asked.

"It's certainly different from my country," I said. "It's a difficult question to answer." I paused then looked at his tray and said, "It's like tasting a meal filled with new foods. Some I like, and it goes down easily, some taste strange and I'd rather not have them on my plate. One thing is certain: Americans are very good people."

"That's an interesting way to describe your experience," he said. He went on talking and I was happily lost in his voice until he thought to look at his watch. "Damn! I'm really running late. We've been down here close to an hour. I have to get back or I'll be here all night."

I was surprised at how the time had flown by. It seemed we'd sat down only minutes ago.

As we walked down the crowded hallway toward the elevators, Dr. Kline took me aside.

"Look, Layla, now that you're officially better and you're no longer my patient, I'd like very much to see you again. Would it be all right if I called you?" With shaking knees and a shallow breath, I nodded my head. He smiled and headed into the elevator.

"Dr. Kline," I called out. "What's your first name?" The elevator doors were closing on him.

"David," he called out as the doors shut. "David Kline."

28
HAPPY BIRTHDAY

The telephone became my Aladdin's lamp as I waited for the call that would bring me my genie.

I waited and waited … and waited.

If I had thought clearly, I'd have realized I was on dangerous ground. *After all, hadn't I just decided to stop dating?* And David was not another boy; he was a man. And, he was Temptation, custom-packaged just for me.

As it was, I waited anxiously for his telephone call. Every time the phone rang, the nest of butterflies in my stomach went berserk. When he hadn't called by January 22, my 18th birthday, I was certain he never would.

Jila treated me to a birthday breakfast at a French café in Westwood.

The mail had arrived by the time we returned to the apartment, and we went upstairs carrying it all. The top envelope bore Shireen's script. I tore it open and began to read aloud to Jila.

"First, thank you, thank you, thank you for the most wonderful gift anyone could have given me. I have framed the photo of Liz and it will always

be in a place of honor in my home. Isn't she wonderful? I'm sure you've told her all about me." Jila and I laughed at Shireen's naïveté before I continued reading.

Her parents would be hosting a formal engagement party for her that very week, and her future in-laws had promised to throw her the "biggest, most wonderful wedding Tehran has ever seen" on *Norooz,* the Iranian New Year in March.

"Ahh. *Norooz,* a lucky time to for a wedding." Jila said. "They'll probably be happy."

"It's such a short engagement," I said. "*Norooz* is less than three months away."

"Keep reading."

"I told you I would keep my vow. Remember? Although I am jubilant, I am devastated that you, of all people, will not dance at either my engagement party or my wedding. It's not fair! You, more than anyone, know what this means to me, and I absolutely hate the stupid germs that keep you away. You will be missed. Maybe you'll surprise me and be there."

"What does she mean about a vow?" Jila interrupted.

"She kept it. Remember I told you that she vowed she'd marry a very wealthy husband, have a huge wedding, and do it within the year? Well, she did it."

"Yup, she did."

I continued reading. *"Anyway, I know you'll hear about my wedding from everyone in Tehran. It will be fabulous. You'll see all the photos when you come home. Happy Birthday. Wish you were here. May I be sacrificed for you, Shireen, soon to be Khanom Moloyed."*

Jila soon left for a study group date, and I was left alone in the apartment.

I curled up on the small sofa and thought about what Jila had said about Shireen. Maybe she was right. Maybe Shireen would be happy with Taymoor. *Did it really matter that he was so much older and their engagement so short?* Maybe she really knew what it took to make her happy. She was probably ecstatic, preparing for her engagement party at that very minute.

I scrambled to open Ferri's mail next. Our last contact had been in November when I surprised my angel with a telephone call on her birthday. Reading the note that she'd written on my birthday card, I was glad to know she was, as always, fine. I smiled when I read that she was, *"enjoying the lovely watch you gave me and finding it very helpful."*

So, things remained the same with her; she was still meeting Hamid. Their meetings had been going on so long, it was almost impossible to believe their agenda was purely academic. I now suspected that Ferri was in love with Hamid, whether she realized it or not. *Why else would she willingly continue to lead a double life? And how much longer could she do it and not be discovered or go crazy?*

I held Shireen's letter together with Ferri's card against my heart. Oh, how I missed those girls! For the first time, I realized that with all their differences, they had one thing in common: they both knew what they wanted and were prepared to do what was necessary to have it.

Did I? I knew that I didn't want what either of them had. And I had taken a step most would consider as drastic as either of theirs in coming to America to study microbiology for four years.

And, I'd dated! So? I asked myself, *Was microbiology my passion? Did I have to have microbiology in my life like Shireen had to have a rich husband or like Ferri had to have Hamid in hers?*

As much as I enjoyed my classes, I was coming to see that a great deal of my excitement about science was connected with Babajon. Without him nearby to share my experiences, much of the glow had faded.

What did I want out of life? Did it even matter what I wanted?

What was the point of a degree from UCLA? Could I seriously consider continuing with a career in microbiology when I returned to Iran? Wouldn't I simply marry, be a full time wife, and bear children?

Was this all simply a way to postpone marriage by prolonging my stay in school?

What was I prepared to do to get what I wanted?

And why couldn't I be as honest with my two friends as they had both been with me?

Pondering these questions made my brain feel like a huge mess of sticky cotton.

I shared so little of myself with them. One minute I was disgusted by college kids kissing, and then I had that pivotal talk with Jila and the next minute I was chain-dating and petting, then I went through a harrowing experience with Anthony deCordova, and after that, adamantly refused to go out with boys. And yet, here I was, pining after David Kline. Yet, through it all, I had not breathed a word about any of it to either of them, had not shared an iota of who I'd become with either of my so-called 'friends.'

I sat reflecting on this when the doorbell rang. It was a delivery, a carton from Iran with gifts from home, more *gaz* candy and a tightly sealed packet of fragrant jasmine leaves to mix with tea, along with some herbs not then available in Los Angeles.

Underneath all that, lay a lovely hand-knit moss green sweater and a simple black dress. A birthday note from Maman said she'd had Aynor, our dressmaker, sew the dress to the same measurements I had before I left Iran as she didn't imagine I had changed very much. I tried on the dress. Apparently, my body had changed for the dress now hugged every curve of my body. She'd also sent a bracelet of gold filigree.

There was a beautiful copy of *The Rubayat* by Omar Khayyam, the lines of Persian poetry enhanced with lavish illustrations. It was dated and signed by Babajon, *To my darling Layla jon, To remind you of your wonderful Persian roots.* A generous check dropped out from between the pages of the book along with a photo of Babajon I'd never before seen. In the photograph, he was sitting at a Royal Underwood type-writer wearing a navy-blue cardigan sweater clearly bearing the large white "U" and smiling into the camera. His hair was short, his smile broad. He looked terribly young. On the back of the photo he'd scrawled, '1942.' The photo was taken during the time he was a student in America. I hugged the small photo to my chest. Later, I put it in the most handsome frame I could find and placed it on my desk.

At the bottom of the carton, bundled in brown paper, was a

gossamer shawl of a sheer gold fabric that shimmered in the light. I ran to the mirror to look at myself in the black dress with the gold shawl thrown over my shoulders and stood in awe. A small envelope had been wrapped inside the shawl with my name written on it in my grandmother's script. I sat down to read a letter from Naneh Joon.

Tehran, 9 January, 1960

Layla jonneh azizam, Layla my Dearest,

God willing, this letter finds you well and happy. Congratulations on your birthday. May it be Allah's wish to grant you all the results you want this year. May your father's protection always be with you. I hope you like this gift. I know you look beautiful in it and I pray to Allah that I soon see you wear it in health and that you will soon return and be fruitful.

I can't say I understand why you have removed yourself from the chance of becoming a bride before your next birthday. I trust you are learning everything you can. Your father has told me you are excelling in your classes. Do not forget why you have chosen to delay your natural destiny and go to America. You have gone there to learn and for nothing else.

My dearest child, I want you to know how precious you are to me. I would be sacrificed for you. Of my grandchildren, you have always had a special place in my heart. I love my grandchildren equally, but you, Layla, I have felt closest to from the time you were a small child. I love you very much. Your happiness is extremely important to me. Perhaps it is because you are my son's only child. You are a sweet girl with a pure and loving heart.

Your mother is sad that you are away, and I cannot blame her, particularly now that your cousin is engaged. I am sad, too, because you must soon be married to a good husband, and you must not let your chance for happiness fade. You must have your own household with children on the way. Yet your father, may Allah bless him, has allowed you to go to America to study. Why? I don't know. I only know that my son is a smart man and a good father, and you must someday compensate for what your parents have sacrificed.

Always remember, Layla dearest, what you have been taught and what you have promised your parents. Be careful in America. Do not take chances with yourself. I know you are a good girl who would never dream of doing anything to shame yourself or disgrace your family. You must be careful. Never forget who you are or where you come from. You are Layla Saleh, a good and decent Muslim Iranian girl, who has learned to abide by the lessons of the Quran.

Your dear grandfather, may God protect him, has a cold now, but he also sends his love to you and together we wish to congratulate you on your birthday. Your family never forgets you. With all my love,

Your Naneh

I put the thin sheet of paper to my nose and inhaled my Naneh Joon's fragrance. A tear rolled down my cheeks. *Was I Nana's favorite grandchild?*

I saw my grandmother clearly, her smiling face, her dancing eyes. My Naneh Joon, so good, so loving. She'd always been so kind to me. She had never said these things to me whenI was in Iran. *Why had she felt the need to now? Did she sense I'd dabbled in temptation?*

The scene in Anthony's car flashed before my eyes and I felt sick. I hurried to the kitchen and prepared myself a cup of *chai nabot* to calm my stomach and my nerves.

Clearly, my grandmother's letter was a sign, sent to me as a warning that I had been moving too far away from my roots, too close to the edge, and had been in danger of falling into the dark abyss I'd feared. I prayed Naneh Joon didn't suspect my transgressions. I doubled and tripled my resolve to have nothing further to do with boys. This birthday would mark a cleansing. On the heels of my experience with Anthony and chastened by my grandmother's letter, I would remain steadfast in my resolve like the resolve of a budding addict determined to end the addiction before it took hold of my life.

And then, when I was sure he'd forgotten all about me, David called.

I accepted his invitation to dinner Friday night with a lump in my throat.

I hung up before it hit me. *What was I thinking?* I couldn't go out with him. I would call him back and tell him I wouldn't go. I stared at the telephone. *Who am I kidding?* I couldn't wait to see him again. I justified it to myself. I told myself it wouldn't be a real date; we wouldn't be alone. He was taking me to his parents' house for dinner...how harmless. His parents' house ... how sweet.

By the time David rang my doorbell Friday night, I had emptied out my closet and all my drawers and had tried on almost everything I owned. I finally settled on a simple sweater dress, in a soft turquoise. I brushed my hair back and wore the headband of turquoise and coral stones that Shireen had given me. When I was dressed, I went to Jila.

"That's the perfect dress. Either shoe works." I looked down at my feet and was surprised to see that I was still wearing the two different shoes I'd tried on.

She pointed to my ear. "I prefer the left one, the short one." My hands went to my ears. The look on my face made my roommate laugh. "Don't be so nervous. Relax. Have a good time. He's a great guy."

When I opened the door and saw David standing before me, wearing a navy-blue suit against his sun-toned skin and met his ocean blue eyes, I almost lost my balance. I took a very deep breath.

"Hi. You look just like a Persian princess," he said.

"Have a good time," Jila called out as we left.

It was a short drive to the Holmby Hills area, where homes were large and gracious. On the way, David asked if I had sisters or brothers and our first common bond was established: neither of us did.

As we made our way up the walkway to the front door of his parents' home, David casually asked if my family was religious.

"No, not very much at all. Why?"

Before David could answer, the door opened, and his father greeted us. He handed David a dark blue velvet yarmulke braided with gold thread.

As they embraced, his father greeted him. "Good Shabbos, son."

29
FRIDAY NIGHT DINNER

"Dad, this is Layla. Layla, meet my father."

David's father was a handsome man, a weathered version of his son, tall and well-built with the same chiseled face and strong jaw, a shock of silver hair in place of David's sandy brown hair, and blue eyes a bit greyer than his son's and set among wrinkles.

"Welcome to our home, Layla. Good Shabbos to you."

I took David's lead and repeated, "Good Shabbos."

As we entered the house, I glimpsed a large living room to our right and a dining room to our left, separated by the entry hall where we stood. The tall woman descending the staircase at the far end of the entry hall caught my eye. Mrs. Kline had the air of a fastidious and competent woman. Her soft peach silk dress was a classic, her heels sensible. She wore a strand of pearls close to her neck and simple pearl earrings. She approached us and kissed David on the cheek, then greeted me with a warm smile. Her hair was dark, with scattered strands of gray, and cut short around her face. Her skin was almost my color, darker than most Americans I'd seen. Her face was angular, her dark brown eyes large and deep-set. Her complexion was flawless. Both of David's parents were older than the Dunns. They were the perfect parents for the perfect man. I presented my hostess with a gift-wrapped box of Persian *gaz*.

"Welcome, and thank you, dear. Good Shabbos. I'm Tova. It's good to have another woman here on the Shabbos. We're running a bit late, so I'd like to get started. Excuse me while I get the challah, and we can all sit at the table."

Neither of David's parents had a gap between their two front teeth.

The idea of being invited to dinner, arriving on time, and immediately sitting at the dinner table, without first making hours of conversation while filling up on more food than one could reasonably eat at a meal, was completely foreign to me.

Even Ralph and Maggie Dunn first had to have their martinis, and the family took forever to collect themselves at the dinner table.

I waited for Mrs. Kline to guide me to my chair and realized no one sat. Instead, the four of us stood at the oval dining table, David's father at one end, his mother at the other, David and I, facing each other. The table was covered with an elaborate, eggshell-colored lace tablecloth. Mrs. Kline arranged a lace shawl on her head, then struck a match and lit two white candles set into simple silver candleholders. Then she closed her eyes and put her fingers against her closed eyelids, and I witnessed my first blessing over Shabbot candles and heard my first Hebrew prayer.

She began to recite, *"Ba-ruch attah, A-dow-nai, E-low-hay-nu mellech kha-oo-lum ...."* Mr. Kline and David joined in with *Amen,* and we took our seats.

Mr. Kline reached for a crystal decanter of what I assumed to be wine as he spoke. "Layla, are you familiar with the tradition of the Shabbos evening?"

"Not really," I said. In fact, I knew nothing at all about it. More, I hadn't expected dinner with David to be a religious event. My mind raced to recall what Ferri had taught me about Judaism. I remembered the story of Passover; but this wasn't Passover. She had once mentioned that Jewish people light candles on Friday nights. This was

Friday night – *Shabbot* as Ferri called what the Klines referred to as Shabbos.

Mrs. Kline reacted sharply. "Aren't you Jewish?" she asked.

"No, I'm not. Ferreshteh, my best friend in Tehran, is."

Her hand crossed her chest to cover her heart, and with her "Oh," I felt like I'd just been dropped into the deep end of an ice-cold pool. The sneer in her tone brought to mind Ferri's loathing of religion. She used to say it made people aware of their differences and kept lovers apart.

"Layla is a Persian princess." When David said that in front of his parents, I rose out of the cold pool feeling like a queen. I breathed in deeply, taking in gratitude. Then I saw the look of utter dissatisfaction on his mother's face. It was a look I knew all too well. I had seen it often on my own mother's face. It was a fleeting look of dismissal and came with the discovery that I was not Jewish. David had been looking across the table, smiling at me and hadn't seen it.

"I'm Muslim."

David was a Jew, and I was a Muslim. Thousands of years of anger, hate, and conflict had just landed at my feet. His mother had already determined that this relationship would not survive, and anything that might be between David and me, was never going to happen.

It was all over even before it had begun.

All the while, Mr Kline continued to converse, oblivious as to what had transpired, but I knew.

He continued to speak spoke smoothly in a warm tone.

Mr. Kline nodded and spoke smoothly in a warm tone. "As most Iranians are," he said. "Your country has historically been relatively tolerant of Jews. Well, Layla, what I am about to recite is the Kiddush." He filled a beautiful glass with wine from the decanter and recited, *"Ba-ruch attah, A-dow-nai mellech kha-oo-lum, bo-ray p'ree ha-ga-fen."*

He took a sip and explained, "That was simply to thank God for the blessing of wine."

I thought, how strange that Jews thank God for the wine that we Muslims are told not to drink. When David's father passed the glass of wine around the table for everyone to sip from, I didn't hesitate. It was my first taste of wine. I raised the glass in front of me and felt comfortable despite my religious taboo; Babajon often had a glass of wine with dinner. Besides, this wine had been blessed. As I drank, I silently toasting farewell to love that David and I would never share.

"This is not a dinner wine, of course. It's meant only for the blessing. Tova and I are not wine drinkers and on Shabbos we like to drink this sweet wine with our dinner." He glanced at David and continued, "Our sophisticated son laughs at us because we cannot abide the taste of a merlot, or burgundy or any other red wine." He shuddered. "Like peasants, we prefer this sweet one." As he spoke, he poured out two glasses of wine. "Layla, perhaps you would prefer another type of wine?"

"Oh, no, no. This is wonderful. Thank you."

He smiled as he poured out a third glass, then paused, looking questioningly at David.

"You've got me tonight, Dad." David said. "Let's break out another bottle of Manischewitz."

My host turned to me again, his smile, broader. "Layla, our family is not orthodox. We celebrate our own modified version of the Shabbos on Friday nights," he said. "We enjoy it because it gives us a chance to get together for an unhurried meal, see David ... and tonight we're lucky enough to meet someone as lovely as you. I'd be glad to explain any questions you have about what you see us doing here."

"Dad, I think you're flirting with Layla," David said, in mock dismay. "What will she think of my father?"

"I think your father is. charming," I said quickly, not certain that was the word I wanted.

"Any questions yet?" David asked me.

"Yes." *Is your tongue really silken?* "I was wondering why you closed your eyes and covered them with your fingers when you lit the candles, Mrs. Kline?"

Mrs. Kline looked at David somewhat impatiently I thought but made no effort to answer me. David answered for her. "We recite every prayer before we do the act it relates to," he said, "you saw that my dad first recited the blessing of thanks for the wine before drinking it. The prayer recited over the Shabbos candles by the woman of the house is the only prayer that's recited after the act is done, after she's lit the candles. Lighting a match is considered 'work' and we are technically not supposed to work once the Shabbos begins. However, lighting the candles inaugurates the Shabbos. So, you see, we have a problem."

He gestured, flailing his beautiful hands to show chaos, and I was taken by how adorable he looked. "Besides, you can't very well light a candle with your eyes closed, can you? So, she lights the candles with her eyes open, then immediately closes them and recites the prayer. When she opens her eyes again, she is, in effect, enjoying the candlelight only *after* she's said the blessing of the light and so, in that way, it becomes like all the other prayers, said before the enjoyment of the blessing, not after."

My eyes were riveted on David. "How interesting." I wanted to ask Mr. Kline if there was a blessing of thanks for enjoying his son.

"Layla, what do Persians say when they toast?" Mr. Kline asked.

"*Salamati.* It means 'to your health.'"

"*Salamati,*" Mr. Kline said and the four of us drank to that. "Very much like the Hebrew *Shalom,* Tova," he said. Tova said nothing.

During the momentary pause in the conversation, I noticed how the faded Wedgewood blue of the dining room walls emphasized David's blue eyes and complemented his complexion. He saw me staring at him. "Do you ever light the candles?" I asked him.

Mr. Kline answered. "Men do not light the candles. The woman of the house has to light them. Women illuminate the home. They are more nurturing. The woman of the house creates the home and family and sets the spiritual tone as well."

"I see."

I also saw the sour look on Mrs. Kline's face. I was aware that she hadn't spoken a word since she discovered I wasn't Jewish. She hadn't initially struck me as the type of woman who would be quiet at her own dinner table. I wondered if David noticed his mother's coolness toward me. I took another sip of the sweet wine and tried to look calm, though my thoughts just then were neither sweet nor calm.

'The woman of the house sets the spiritual tone.' I realized that David's religion meant something to him; it meant she sets 'the *Jewish* tone.' David and I had no chance for a relationship.

Mrs. Kline passed the tray of challah, the twisted egg bread of the Shabbot, to her husband, who recited a prayer over it, then tore small pieces off the loaf and sprinkled salt on them, took a piece for himself and passed the tray around the table.

I looked at David and wondered how many other girls he had invited for Shabbos dinner with his parents. Where were they now? I knew I wouldn't see them again. *Look at him! He melts my heart.*

"Why did Mr. Kline put salt on the bread, Mrs. Kline?" I was looking at Mrs. Kline but watching David's face for a sign that he approved of my question and liked the attention I was giving to his mother, even though she was obviously ignoring me.

"There are many reasons for what we do," she said dryly. That was all she said. From what I knew of my hostess, I doubted that she would have been so cold to me if I'd been Jewish.

After a few seconds of awkward silence, Mr. Kline, kind man that he was, took over. "There are different ways to interpret many of our traditions. My own favorite interpretation is that the salt reminds us of the sadness our people have had to endure. One quirk we Jews have, Layla, is that we seem to insist on mixing even our most joyous occasions with memories of terrible times."

I nodded in understanding. I was in heaven, sitting at dinner as the guest of the most appealing man I could imagine. I was part of a ceremony touched by family love and warmth. And yet, I was miserable, for I knew this was as close to him as I would get.

I sighed. Sitting across the table from him, I knew without a doubt that his was a face I could look at forever, though I would never see it again after tonight. I hung my head. *Beh darrack, to hell with it!* He's not really all that special! I looked up at him. He's just gorgeous, and wonderful, and smart … and respectful of his parents. They're all very close and all very happy together.

"Layla came into the med center with her cousin. She's staying with her cousin while she's studying at UCLA. Was she a mess! Sorry, Layla, but you really were. Or, as she put it, she was 'in a mess.' She was so miserable, she couldn't even talk." He winked at me and I blushed. I was completely entranced by him. His mouth toyed with the words and gave them life. Every time I heard his voice a river of sensuality flowed through me, and I wondered if I could ever get used to the effect it had on me.

"Afterward, being the good doctor that I am, I worried about her, so I called to see how she was doing. When she could talk again, I asked her out, and – well, here she is."

When he said I'd come into the medical center, his mother, poised to pick up a platter from the table, had frozen, her arms in mid-air and had remained motionless. She said, "I thought you're not to socialize with patients, David."

David broke out into a smile that filled the world with sunshine. "You're right, Mom. That's why I didn't ask Layla out until she had completely recovered. She's not my patient anymore. Right, Layla?"

I smiled. I wanted the smile to be totally enchanting, despite the fact – or perhaps, because of the fact – that his mother wished we'd never met. *Well, I'm sorry Mom. Mrs. Kline. Tova.*

"David is an excellent doctor, Mrs. Kline. He knew what was wrong with me before he even took the tests, so he was able to treat me right away. Otherwise, I'd probably be at home right now, in bed and still sick." I was somewhat surprised by my aggressive reaction to my hostess' thinly disguised attack. I meant to make her even more uncomfortable with that cool remark, and I think I did. In any event, she kept quiet about David asking me to dinner after that.

Mr. Kline turned the conversation to Iran, quickly impressing me with how much he – as well as David – knew about my culture. "You come from a formidable history," the elder Kline said. "Your culture has given birth to so many things. After all, Persians invented writing, modern mathematics, and they were the first to formulate a way to keep track of time."

"That reminds me," Mrs. Kline said, rising from her seat, "the roast is ready."

"Can I help you, Mrs. Kline?"

"No," she said.

Her husband continued. "Yours is a desert country where water has always been scarce. Your people were the first to develop irrigated farming. Then, because they couldn't all live close to water, they were also the first to urbanize and have inland cities. Persians have been a great people." He took a sip of wine. "As far back as 200 AD, they had universities that taught literature, poetry, theology, philosophy, medicine, math, astronomy ... People from all parts of the world traveled to Persia to learn and carry knowledge back home with them, much like you are here, studying at UCLA."

"How do you know so much Persian culture and history, Mr. Kline?"

"I was a history buff in college. The ancient civilizations have always attracted me far more than the world we live in today."

"My father is an avid reader," David said. "While other boys were fishing and playing baseball with their fathers, my dad was reading me stories about the dynasties of China, the Japanese samurais, the Diaspora, the Persian Empire.... I just thought they were great stories. He was teaching me history." He looked up as though trying to recall something. "Let's see. If I'm not mistaken, the Persians were excellent horse breeders, right Dad? They created the cavalry and invented the game of polo." Mr. Kline nodded. I was flabbergasted. I didn't know any of that.

My hostess returned to the table carrying a platter with what, I learned, was brisket of beef. "Mom, that smells wonderful," her son said.

She took her seat and offered me the platter. As I looked at the sliced beef with bright seasonal vegetables set around it, I was thinking of how much David loved his mother. He wouldn't hurt her for the world and would stop seeing me if she asked him to; and I knew she would ask him to.

"Martin," Mrs. Kline addressed her husband. "Didn't you tell me there's some silly theory that we all came from somewhere near Iran? Or was it Iraq? Iran, Iraq, I can't tell those Arab countries apart; they're all the same to me."

"Tova, you know Iran's not an Arab country, any more than Israel is." He turned to me and informed me that his wife had lived for a short time in Israel. "Layla and her countrymen are not Arabs," he continued. "To answer your question, yes, it was northern Iran, dear. It's just a theory that we all originally came from there."

"Well, this lovely Persian princess certainly did," David said, making my heart sing.

As we ate dinner, I thought about how different David's parents were from Adam's. The Klines hadn't invited me to call them Martin and Tova. I guessed that if David had a sister, she would be very different from Linda. Most strikingly, unlike Maggie, Mrs. Kline hadn't warmed up to the Muslim girl their son had brought home to dinner. I tried to make her like me. I would have liked it if Mrs. Kline could have been just a bit warmer to me, friendlier or at least more cordial. *But could I blame her for being cold toward me?* As much as I wanted to find fault with Mrs. Kline, I couldn't really blame her, considering that my own mother would have been far colder to David if he were sitting at our dinner table in Niavaran. Mr. Kline was certainly being a warm and gracious host. *But it is the woman of the house who sets the tone.*

At dinner's end, Mr. Kline led us in a final prayer. The room had darkened by then, and I watched the shadow of the flame on the candle dance on David's face, his darkened lips capturing my heart.

"Mom, can we have dessert in the living room?" he asked his mother.

Mrs. Kline nodded, and we moved into the large living room where the furniture, like that of the dining room, was understated and comfortable. There were family photographs around the room, mostly of David at various younger ages. This was the house David grew up in.

I scanned some of the photos before taking a seat.

"Tell us about modern-day Iran," Mr. Kline said.

He asked if the people of my country liked the shah.

I answered that as far as I knew they did. "Quite honestly, those who don't are somewhat afraid to say so."

"Why?" David was missing and may be found dead, or jailed. But because the members are unknown, no one knows who works for SAVAK and who doesn't, so no one wants to criticize the king in public and take a chance. Is that right, Layla?"

"Yes."

"Well, there's rarely, if ever, a good enough excuse for torture," he continued. "On a personal level, I sympathize with the man for having had to divorce Soraya. He was apparently very much in love with her. How unfortunate that they had to divorce for matters of state and the mandate to produce an heir."

"Sometimes circumstances get in the way of love," Mrs. Kline said. "It may be unfortunate, Martin; nonetheless, that's the way it is."

Her contribution to the discussion sounded like a message to me. "Yes," I said dryly, "it is unfortunate. We all loved her. And the shah loved her very much."

"Anyway, he's married this young girl now," Mrs. Kline said. "He'll get over Soraya when this new one bears him a son."

I wondered if David's mother was as cold-hearted as all this, or if she was simply posturing to make a point to me, or more importantly, to David. Ironically, the shah's new wife gave birth to a son nine months from the night Mrs. Kline made that remark.

David then asked about the shah's drive to westernize his country. I said the His Majesty was trying to westernize the country for the benefit of the people. I was surprised to hear Mr. Kline remark under his breath that he "wasn't certain westernization was such a good thing for Iranians."

Before I could address that comment, Mrs. Kline spoke. "What are your plans for the future, Layla?" she asked. My heart jumped. "How long do you plan to stay at UCLA?" She couldn't wait for me to leave.

"I'm in my first year of a four-year program." I thought I saw David smile.

"I see." She clasped her hands on her lap. "And after you finish UCLA and you return to Iran, will you be able to pursue a career there?" If I couldn't, then I should leave right away. As if she cared about my pursuit of a career, so long as I was gone.

With hands folded on my lap, I nodded. "If that is what I want, yes, maybe. The opportunities for educated women are increasingly available." It wasn't a total lie. Opportunities for educated women *were* generally opening up, though perhaps not for me.

That led to Mrs. Kline's further questions, about the place of women in modern Iranian society and whether they are viewed as equal to men. Though I was pleased at her sudden show of interest in my country, I bit my lip in embarrassment. I guessed that her husband knew the answer to that question. "I'm sorry to say. They are not. There are areas that are, by your American standards, difficult for women."

"You mean like being stoned to death?" she asked without hesitation.

David, who had been lounging back in his seat, now sat up and edged forward in his chair. I sat up a little straighter too. "That's mostly in areas where people are uneducated; not in cities like Tehran," I said. "The shah and his father eliminated most of the bad things that used to be allowed, like girls marrying at a very young age; but it still goes on in the villages. Though women can't vote, things are improving." I looked into Mrs. Kline's eyes as I spoke.

"My family lives in Tehran," Mrs. Kline, "the capital city. My father was educated here in America – in California – and my mother is – well, very much like you, Mrs. Kline." Mrs. Kline looked down at the carpet when I said that. In fact, the two women *were frighteningly* similar. Although Maman wasn't educated and wouldn't have been either able or willing to carry on a conversation like this, both women were strong and handsome. Both had strong prejudices, were cold, distant, controlling and potentially willing to destroy any chance for happiness their child could have. Yet the power and influence in their family that each held could not be denied. And both had wonderful husbands.

"Tell us more about the women in the villages, Layla," David said. "The tribes."

"Well, they still believe that a girl is her father's to do with as he pleases, until she becomes her husband's to do with as he pleases. Girls don't have much schooling; they have little use for it. And if a girl is seen with a man outside of her family who isn't her husband, they assumed she is a ... um ... a bad girl, and they punish her very, very severely. They do terrible things to her."

Mrs. Kline's eyebrows shot up. "Even if she's blameless? Even if she's raped?" she asked.

I nodded, somewhat ashamed, imagining how aspects of my

culture appeared to these Americans. The double standard in my country was unfair. Women's reputations, homes and children – their very lives – were often unjustly taken away. I was describing barbarians! I wondered what the three Klines would think if I told them what would happen to me if it was known that I was out with David tonight. That even in families like mine, a girl's life could be ruined over a dinner date. My life would certainly have already been destroyed several times over if we were in Iran.

David broke my train of thought with another grin, and again I marveled at how the goodness in him showed through his face and made him glow. "Princess, don't tell your countrymen that we were out tonight."

He had read my mind! I put my head in my hands in mock horror and laughed. *"Vye!"* David asked what *vye* meant. "It means, wow! That would be very bad."

"Like *Oy, vay!*" He laughed. I laughed too and Mr. Kline joined us, while out of the corner of my eye I saw Mrs. Kline grimace.

"Layla, tell me," said Mr. Kline, "what is your impression of Americans? Do we seem spoiled? I'd be very interested to know what you think."

"Tell them what you told me about tasting new food," David urged.I shook my head. David repeated to his parents what I'd said to him in the cafeteria about some new foods going down easier than others.

While he spoke, all I could think of were his full lips. I so wanted him to kiss me. I longed to feel his arms around me. But it wasn't likely. I was suddenly angry, angry that I was in this incredibly frustrating situation. As we said at home, he'd kiss me and hold me when the reed blossoms – in other words, never.

As I listened to David repeat what I'd said, my anger focused on his parents for conspiring to keep David from me. *Why had they made him different than I was? Why had they taught him to celebrate wine with blessings and say blessings over bread?* And I was angry at David for bringing me into this house, knowing I would never be accepted here as his girlfriend, let alone anything more. This was like a sadistic game, the three of them watching, as I tried to keep my composure with David dangled in front of me, the prize I couldn't reach.

I needed to assert my dignity. I had to let these people know who I was. I could not let them think that I was like the other girls who had sat at their Shabbot table and floundered, never to be seen again. *I'm Layla Saleh!*

"Yes, that is interesting," Mr. Kline said. "So, you have mixed feelings about us, Layla."

I took my chance. "Americans are wonderful," I responded, smiling demurely. "They're open and friendly, warm and hospitable, like you, except that ... well, perhaps I shouldn't say."

"Oh, no, you must! Please," Mr. Kline said. "No one here will take offense."

What is it, Layla?" David's eyes sparkled. His mother's eyes were riveted on me as though my comment was extremely presumptuous.

"Let's see, how can I put it?" I looked at Mrs. Kline. When our eyes met, she looked askance as though, unlike the rest of her family, she wasn't interested in what I had to say. I turned to David and then to Mr. Kline. "Excuse me, it's only that I wasn't raised in a country with such," I searched for the right word, "such physical openness between men and women." I hurried to explain. "Of course, at home, the punishments for certain things are far too harsh, and not always fair. I think that's wrong. But I think Americans are also wrong. Here, parents don't teach their children any rules or give boys and girls ... " I searched for the way to express what I wanted to say in English. "limits ... before marriage. What they shouldn't do."

"Well, it's part of the U.S. Constitution," David said. It was as if my statement had energized him. He got up and moved to the open space in the living room and put his arms out like an politician making a speech. "It is our most basic right: freedom of sexuality. Haven't you heard?"

I looked at him closely. *Was he teasing me? Making fun of me?* I turned to his parents. "I'm sorry."

"Don't be." Mrs. Kline said. "You're making perfect sense." *Praise Allah!* "You're saying that Americans emphasize sex, and I agree with you completely. I think it's terrible. And I blame the girls. Girls of today are so different from when I was young. If they didn't let boys have their way, there wouldn't be all this promiscuity." My mind went to Anthony.

David clasped his hands. "I hate to differ with you, Mom. I have a different viewpoint. On behalf of today's younger Americans, I'd like to be heard." I was ears from head to toe. "Though it may be true that Americans are more sexually active, I don't think we exaggerate the importance of sex. Sex *is* important. It's a human need." He looked like a movie star standing there. "Princess, if you'll excuse me, I think Iranian culture exaggerates sex by repressing it. I mean, sex must be all they think about. I know it's a big reason so many there marry young, arranged or not. I don't imagine many of those marriages are all that happy. I'd also bet there's quite a bit of prostitution in the country, more than we have here."

"That, there is," Mr. Kline nodded, knowingly. Her comment could not have been more clear. I felt it was clearly intended as an attack on me. To his credit, David proved to be oblivious to the underlying message.

David went on. "It makes sense. As much as we Americans may emphasize sex, people in a sexually repressive society must be thinking about it an awful lot – and probably *do* a lot for it, including marry so they can fulfill their basic human need. It is a human need and so, while it may be 'repressed,'" he made quotation marks in the air, "it's all the more exaggerated."

The three of us were quiet, waiting for him to go on. He put one hand in his pants pocket. With his jacket pulled back, the outline of his long elegant haunches was visible. He saw the look of skepticism on his mother's face. "Mom, imagine a culture, just hypothetically, where the people are not allowed to say the word 'plant.' Wouldn't they spend a lot of time thinking about it if only how to avoid saying it? They might say lots of words that sound like it, like 'pant' or 'paint' or 'plan.' Or maybe, they hide in a closet and say it over and over."

Touché!

"So, you think our loose view of sex is better?" Mrs. Kline asked.

"No, I don't," David answered. I listened closely. "I think the answer is healthy, discriminating sex. Sex when it means something between two people, sex with someone you care about as a way of expressing your feelings, sharing love, making love, and enjoying one another as only lovers can."

I saw the passion, his belief in what he was saying. *Had he experienced this kind of love? If he had, where was the girl? What had happened? Who was she?*

Then he addressed me, and I startled. "So, I do agree with you, Layla. Americans, the college kids I see, are far too eager to have sex with partners they don't care enough about and don't even know very well. And let me tell you that, as a doctor, I've seen a lot of diseases and unfortunate pregnancies because of irresponsible and indiscriminate sex.

"Mom, I do love you. I'm just sorry that I don't agree with you. I don't think we exaggerate sex in our culture. We're just sexually irresponsible."

"I'll get dessert," Mrs. Kline said rising.

It was clear that my hostess was becoming very uncomfortable with the conversation about sexuality and was using dessert as an exit strategy.

While his wife was in the kitchen, Mr. Kline turned to me. "I must tell you how charming your English is, Layla," Mr. Kline said. "You speak fluently, yet your accent is unique."

I thanked him. He then asked about my father and I answered his questions about Saleh Pharmaceuticals. "But it was of no use to me when I was so sick. Only your son cured me."

Mrs. Kline returned to serve us coffee with apple pie a la mode and passed around the box of *gaz* I'd brought. David bit into his first piece of *gaz* and moaned in enjoyment. I was glad they all seemed to love the taste of the nougat candies, the fragrance of the rose water, and the pistachios. But it was David's pleasure that made me happiest. He ignored his apple pie and seemed determined to finish the box of candy in one sitting. He pointed to the gift box as he took yet another piece of candy. "Your calling card to our family Shabbos."

At just past nine thirty, David said it was time to leave. Mr. and Mrs. Kline hugged him tightly. Mr. Kline held my hand warmly in his, as we walked to the front door. Passing the dining room, I saw the

Shabbot candle still alive at the center of the lace-covered table and recalled that Mrs. Kline lit them with a prayer. The woman lights the Shabbat candles because she sets the spiritual tone of the house, and the tone of the Kline home had certainly been set by Mrs. Kline to my exclusion.

"It was a pleasure to meet you, Layla," he said. "We look forward to seeing you again."

"It was a pleasure to meet you both. I enjoyed the evening very much." *I'm crazy about your son.* "And thank you for a delicious dinner, Mrs. Kline." *How did you make such a fabulous son?* "Thank you for explaining everything about my first Shabbot dinner, Mr. Kline, it was lovely." *Damn your Shabbot for coming between David and me.*

"She's wonderful, isn't she Mom and Dad?"

"Goodbye," Mrs. Kline said. "Good luck with your studies."

Once in the car, David grinned widely. "Well, Layla. That was a first." I thought he meant it had been the first time he'd witnessed his mother being rude to his guest. "I've never had a girl over for Shabbos dinner before."

30
THE TIME OF MY LIFE

The time I spent with David....

After that night at his parents' home, David and I began to see each other regularly. I was head over heels in love, utterly lost in David. My awareness of all else lay atop a bed made up of thoughts of him. His voice was in my pulse, his smile was on my face and his face was before my eyes. My life was David, and my love for him, flowed from one day to the next, as easily and surely as mother's milk.

I would sit in class and think of him. My rational mind told me our relationship was a pre-determined failure. As Babajon had warned me, experiments through generations before me had determined that a long-term relationship between two people whose objective facts were as different as David's and mine wouldn't work. As a student of the sciences, I was to discard a proven failure. Yet my heart was tied to him. So, I simply drowned my head, and immersed my heart in David. I couldn't help it. Being with him was like being plugged into a high-voltage box. All my lights clicked on, and the world and everything in it, had a new brilliance. I had opened a door to a new universe of emotions that gave me contentment and a sense of belonging, even beyond what I'd known when, as a child, I'd nested in the group of

Bahman's friends. Combined that contentment there was unparalleled emotional and physical excitement. *How could I turn and walk away?*

David broke all the rules of my life, yet I loved him. He was the shining star of my American Adventure. I understood that nothing permanent could come of my love for him. I was living a fantasy. Yet, it was a fantasy that made me incredibly happy. He was the air I breathed in, and with every breath I loved him more. There may have been no future for us, but the present was definitely ours. As for the future, I told myself that I'd deal with that later. I told myself to shut up and leave me alone.

My time with David....

Every moment with him was wonderful. I couldn't deny myself a single one. The memories of my time with him carried me through the most bitter parts of my life.

On my first Valentine's Day in America, David took me to dinner at a restaurant on the beach in Malibu.

The moon was white and thin, no more than an eyelash, high in the sky that night. As we dined, we could see the waves slither toward us to caress the shore, pull back, then return for more. A flower girl passed by our table and David bought me a long-stemmed red rose. I kept that rose until it lost all its scent, turned black and disintegrated.

Early on, Jila took a picture of the two of us sitting together at a party. I first put the photo on my desk alongside the photo of Babajon. Then seeing the two photos together made me feel uncomfortable, so I moved the photo of David and me to my nightstand.

We'd spend our time together walking the streets of Westwood or watching the sunset at the beach. We'd see a movie and visit friends. No matter what we did, the air always seemed injected with an extra dose of life. It wasn't about where we went or what we did, it was being with David and that made it all so special.

We spent many evenings at his apartment. He'd cook us dinner. A few times I tried cooking Persian rice for him as best as I could, having asked for recipes from Khaleh Elahe and trying to imitate what I'd seen Cobra do, countless times in our kitchen. David seemed to like what I made. We always had things to talk about. I showed him the copy of Omar Khayyam's *Rubayat* that Babajon had sent me and translated some passages for him. I read him some poetry by Rumi, the greatest poet of love, translating the lines as well:

> *"When this love comes to rest in me, there are many people in one being.*
> *In one grain of wheat, a thousand stacks of grain, inside the needle's eye, a night filled with stars."*

Friday night was the night David spent at his parents' home and, though he'd always ask me to join them for Shabbot dinner, I consistently declined. Though I admired and liked his father, and respected his love for his mother, I was reluctant to spend time with them, unwilling to tolerate the discomfort I felt in Tova Kline's presence. More than that, they symbolized all that would ultimately keep David and me apart. Friday night was for David and his parents, and my night to stay home and study, which was a good thing, as school had taken a back seat to my interest in David.

David. David. David. Even saying his name was sensual, the way it felt on my lips to form the V hidden in the middle of the two soft Ds, the way my teeth gently tickled my lower lip as the air rushed through them: *David. His voice.* Throughout our time together, his voice never ceased to have a profound effect on me. It was a teasing pool of male tenderness. When I heard him speak, my shoulders fell, and my jaw slackened, my libido came alive and my juices started to flow. I began writing poems again, the first inspired by David's voice:

I try to breathe quietly

My heart is pounding so

My throat - this pool inside my mouth

My voice is lost somewhere below

I search. This sound is not mine

Where am I? Where have I gone?

Riding the waves of your voice

Swimming in its curves

Dancing between the walls of your mouth,

Breathing in your voice.

I watch. I want your moving lips,

Your tender tongue, behind.

Your every word, like the wings of a bird,

Begins Creation

So soft, so smooth - and I fly

I have drowned within your voice

I want to stay here forever!

Don't stop, keep on

Keep on, I say!

But where is my voice?

David, my love.

No one was like my David. David didn't try to push my sexual boundaries. He moved slowly, happy just to linger in a kiss. It was obvious he wanted more from me than a physical relationship. Yet my physical attraction to him was beyond any explanation, and as time went by, boundaries naturally expanded.

I had thought it possible that my experience with Anthony had traumatized me and that I would forevermore be horrified by the idea of sexual intimacy. But the legacy of terror ended with David. My love for him blotted out the horror Anthony had instilled in me, dissolving it away like the tide falls on the sand and washes away footprints under its weight. Never once when I was with David, did my memory of the night in the parking lot stop me from wanting the man I loved. When David touched me, an overwhelmingly delicious feeling came over me. My breasts would contract, their tips becoming taut as my body stretched out, yearning for his touch. When he touched me, his hands were warm, his touch, heaven, and his kiss, pure bliss. But it was his desire for me that came through, and hit me like an electrical charge, driving me nearly insane. I wanted to be with him all the time, to crawl under his skin and be a part of him.

Paradoxically, David was the policeman. One evening, early in our relationship, we were in his apartment. Having gotten a glass of wine for himself and a soda for me, he stood behind me as I sat on the couch sipping my drink. He began rubbing my neck and playing with my hair. I set my soda on the coffee table and sat back to relax and enjoy his hands. After a moment, his hands went down to my shoulders then came forward very slowly and began to massage my chest firmly yet lovingly until he reached my breasts. I responded by throwing my head back and allowing him freer reach. It felt so natural, so unhurried and spontaneous. I closed my eyes and strained to reach his voluptuous lips. His warm breath was on my cheeks; the smell of the wine he'd had, stimulating. In seconds, he was sitting beside me on the couch, his shirt unbuttoned. I could see the muscles of his chest come alive. I moved into his arms and we kissed. As always, when we kissed it was as though I was sipping warm nectar from a heavenly pool, sweet and soothing. His lips were soft and full, his tongue silken. I put my finger into the wetness of his mouth to feel its warmth. As he held me in his arms, he began to unbutton my blouse – slowly, from the top down. I didn't resist. I felt the ecstasy of his touch as his hands glided to my back to unhook my bra. He was looking at me, questioningly. In answer, I put my arms around him and my lips back to his. My bra fell away and when we came apart, I was, for a moment, immensely shy, not because this was the first time a man had seen my naked breasts, but because the man was David and I so wanted him to be pleased. I watched for his reaction. The flush of his face and the sparkle in his eyes was reassuring. He laid me back against the couch, told me I was beautiful and began caressing my neck and then my breasts. It was beyond incredible.

"Oh, David." I sighed.

He suddenly sat up. "Too fast, right?" I was so surprised, I couldn't answer him. He waved an arm. "Sorry. I know, I know. It's okay, Princess, you don't have to tell me, no problem." I didn't move. He reached over, picked up my bra and held it up in front of me until I took it and put it back on while he tossed his shirt back on.

My voice barely came out. "David?"

"You want to go home?" he asked.

I sat still while he hastily buttoned my blouse. "No."

"Good." We spent the remainder of that evening listening to his newest jazz records and talked about his love of medicine until it was time for him to take me home.

March heralded the coming of *Norooz,* the Persian New Year.

That entire week was eventful. Jila and I organized a *Chahar-shambeh Sooree* at the beach with a few friends. *Chahar-shambeh,* means 'Wednesday' in Farsi. The *sooree* or party, is always celebrated on the last Wednesday prior to the Persian New Year. Our group formed a line, and we took turns jumping over the four fires we'd made in the sand, each of us reciting the age-old chant over the flames, *I give you my yellow color; you give me your red and take my yellow,* discarding our worries of the old year into the fire and taking on new strength for the coming one. Jumping over fires, setting off firecrackers, and dancing are parts of a tradition borne of Iran's Zoroastrian history, meant to bring happiness, health, and prosperity throughout the New Year.

"This is the first time I'm jumping over the fires since I was a child in Iran," Jila said. "We stopped doing it when we came here. It's not the same when there's no one else around to celebrate with you. In Iran, we had the whole family and all our friends. Here, well, we know almost no Iranians and the few we do know live in Fresno or Santa Barbara."

"If I'm not mistaken," David said, enjoying a warm marshmallow, "Zoroastrians were dualists who believed in two gods, the god of good, light or fire, and the god of evil and darkness."

I couldn't take my eyes off of him that day. The golden sand and the bright blue ocean played with his face, aglow in the sun.

"I don't know how you know that," I said, marveling at his knowledge. "You're right."Then, grateful to my dear angel in Iran, I happily showed off the bit of knowledge I'd learned from her about the Zoroastrians.

"Persians were either Jewish or Zoroastrian before the Arabs invaded and brought the Muslim religion to us. When Mohammad first invited them to convert and become Muslims, their leaders declined. Had the Arabs not invaded our country seventy years later, Jila and I would still be Jewish or Zoroastrian. But they did, and this time Islam was forced on the Persians. Muslims didn't jump fires and they discouraged Persians from retaining any of the Zoroastrian ways," I went on, "yet the tradition – like many other Zoroastrian traditions – was so deeply rooted in Persian culture that it continues. You're actually supposed to burn seven thorns in the fires, one for each day of the week. It's believed that destroys all the bad news and sad times the coming year might bring." Unfortunately, there were no thorns on the beach. I ended my lecture, saying, "Zoroastrians were very advanced. All their leaders were female."

That night, suntanned, full of the day's good feelings and covered in sand, David and I returned to his place and showered.

That was when I saw David fully naked for the first time. He'd wrapped a towel at his waist and come into his bedroom where I sat on his bed awaiting my turn to shower. The towel fell. My heart raced.

I was fascinated and simultaneously petrified! Looking at him without a stitch of clothing on, I felt Maman there watching, joined by Naneh Joon, and Khanom Bozorg's piercing stare. I was caught Alone With The Naked, American, Jewish, Man Who Had Kissed Me And Seen My Naked Breasts!

I felt flashes of heat. David stood still, watching, as I bit my lip. Then he walked over to the bed and knelt in front of me. Watching him move was a lesson in grace, the way his perfectly proportioned body, his long, lean muscles worked as he walked. He held my hands and looked into my eyes. "Layla? Princess, are you okay?" I smiled. Maman and the others faded away and I was again alone with David and my longing for him – and my curiosity.

I put my head on his shoulder and rested there while he lovingly stroked my hair. After a moment, I came away and looked down at his naked maleness. Hesitating, I eventually dared to touch him there, ever so gently at first then just a bit more confidently, as I discovered how surprisingly wonderful he was to touch and to hold, full of varied sensations.

As he kissed my head and then my lips, I was mesmerized by the magic that made the warmth in my hand become fuller, longer and harder as I fondled it. I loved its velvet-like feel.

"Doesn't this get in your way when you walk?" I asked. David chuckled. He got up and walked around, sat on a chair, bent down and showed me how it all worked.

I suppose I was able to jump so many sexual hurdles with David, because I trusted him implicitly and loved him, completely. I trusted that he really loved me and cared about me. He soon saw me completely naked and as time went on, I allowed – in fact, I craved – more sexual intimacy between us.

Still, there were lines I would not cross, even for him. David said he understood that I would keep my virginity for my husband. If that's what I wanted, that's how it would be.

That's what he said. At first.

My time with David went by too fast.

31
TRANSITIONS

Norooz literally, 'new day,' was just days away, and with the Persian New Year came Shireen's wedding day.

The day after jumping over fires on *Chahar-shambeh Sooree,* I sent a telegram to Shireen and her parents in Iran congratulating them and wishing the couple a life filled with joy and dancing. I expressed my disappointment, not being present at her wedding. I pictured her in her wedding gown dancing the cha-cha, the hop and the twist, her husband trying to keep up with her and the guests looking on, some, no doubt, wondering about the strange dances.

Then, the day before *Norooz,* I was surprised by a phone call from Majid, one of the boys who'd been in Jalil's basement that day, years ago, when I'd first come into my moon. He was in Los Angeles! I couldn't wait to see him. I insisted he come to the apartment right away and gave him my address. I laughed when he awkwardly asked who else was there.

"It's okay," I said, reading his mind. "I'm not alone. Besides, Majid, this is *Amreeca.*"

I opened the door to a man who was no longer the chubby-faced youngster I had known. He was tall and well-dressed in a blue suit, a white shirt and a navy tie. His confidence was immediately apparent. I introduced him to Jila and asked him what he was doing in Los Angeles. He was in our city on vacation from his work. Over a cup of tea, he told us about his new job as a senior electrical engineer in Oklahoma City.

As the afternoon passed, he invited Jila to join us for an early dinner in Westwood Village during which we talked of Shireen's wedding. He also told us of her brother Bahman's plans to leave for London. Having finished college, Bahman would be attending the London Academy of Architecture. As we said goodnight, Jila invited Majid to join us the following evening at her parents' home to celebrate the *Norooz*. I thanked her afterwards, thinking that she'd extended him the invitation out of kindness to an old friend of mine.

She laughed. "Are you kidding?" she said, "he's adorable."

Based on our lunar calendar, the Persian New Year, *Norooz,* arrives on the first day of Spring and so it may often fall on a different day.

There was a light rain that day as Majid drove the three of us to Ammeh Elahe's house in his rented car with Jila directing. As always, Los Angeles drivers, not used to wet roads, were unusually slow. Sitting in the back seat, Jila laughed when, despite her instructions, Majid missed the freeway exit. By the time we arrived at Khaleh Elahe's home, the other guests, an elderly couple who had driven down from Fresno, were already there.

Between my time with David and my studies, I had not visited my aunt's home for several weeks. That day, I saw their house through Majid's eyes, the worn living room couch. The walls begging for a new coat of paint. I wondered if my Ammeh Elahe felt embarrassed, having Majid as well as her proud sister-in-law's daughter, witness her relative poverty. If so, she certainly didn't show any sign of it. Jila had recently told me that Uncle Javeed had finally been laid off from work. Yet despite Uncle Javeed's new unemployed status, my aunt was as cheerful and as talkative as always,

The platters of cookies, candy, nuts and fruits were set nicely around the living room in inexpensive dishes. I complimented my aunt on the *Norooz* table she'd set up in a corner of the living room with the seven items traditionally commemorating the *Norooz*, known as the *Haft Seen*, or seven items beginning with the letter *Seen. Serkeh*, vinegar, symbolizing cleanliness and hygiene; *S'eer*, garlic, symbolizing nature and natural medicine; *Sekkeh*, coins, symbolizing wealth; *Seeb*, apples, symbolizing harvest, plenty, good health and good food; *Sabzeh*, green herbs, symbolizing growth and new beginnings; *Samanoo*, cooked wheat, symbolizing our gratitude for God's grains, life's food; and *Sombol*, the hyacinth, fragrant symbol of love. A mirror meant to bring light and a goldfish in a bowl of water, the perennial Iranian symbol of good luck, were also on the table as well as a copy of the Quran.

"*Ensha'allah*, God willing, you two girls will have husbands by next year," Ammeh Elahe said to Jila and me. I was a bit embarrassed but more surprised to see Jila, who usually seemed so unaffected by her mother's words, turn crimson and then, seconds later steal a look at Majid. He was looking right at her. *My goodness, they like one another!*

We enjoyed a huge meal of various Persian dishes my aunt had prepared, including the customary New Year's meal of whitefish and rice mixed with dill and peas. We played Persian music and danced, told Persian jokes and recited the Persian poetry of the greats, Rumi, Hafez and Khayyam, until late into the night. By then, it had become clear to me that Majid had enjoyed the evening because of Jila and that Jila liked Majid. On the way home, I requested the back seat, saying I was tired.

During the remainder of Majid's stay in Los Angeles, he and Jila saw a lot of one another, always either in my company or with Jila's parents. I didn't speak of David when Majid was around – and he was always around. I knew Jila would never mention his name to anyone, certainly not an Iranian. Twice, I stole away to meet him. Otherwise, I stayed away from him and didn't even dare to speak to him on the phone in the apartment. That's how scared I was of being found out by my old friend. After all, Majid was Iranian and what's more, he knew my parents, who had given him my Los Angeles phone number. Because of that, he couldn't know about David. To me, it was that simple. And so, though I hated not seeing more of David, I couldn't take the chance.

Meanwhile, things between Jila and Majid were heating up quickly.

On the thirteenth day of the Iranian New Year, *Seenzdah-be'dar,* I picnicked in the park with Jila, her parents and Majid. Iranian families traditionally gather outdoors on that day so as not to be caught by bad luck visiting inside our homes. At some point, Ammeh Elahe directed Jila and me to knot blades of grass together, the custom for unmarried girls looking for a husband. I empathized with Jila, who flushed as she coyly held bunches of grass in her hand and knotted them under Majid's watchful eye. It was strange and wonderful to see Jila transformed into a girl in love, shy and radiant.

A few days later, Majid left the city. Jila cried. "He's coming back," she said, wiping tears. "He promised he'll be back at the end of April."

"Then why are you crying? That's only a month away."

"A month is a long time."

I was delighted to see Majid leave, for I had missed my David immensely and hungered to spend time with him. But to my shock, Majid's visit had caused a change in David's attitude toward me. He wasn't jealous; he understood that Majid was no more than a friend. Worse, he was hurt. He resented the fact that I had hidden him away while Majid was in town, stealing away to see him only twice. *Could I blame him?*

David complained that I rejected him. He started to debate my views about sex, reiterating the opinion he had aired that night at his parents' house, namely, that sex was to be celebrated between two people who truly cared about one another.

"I can't help it," he said. "You mean so much to me. I know that you love me, but only to a point – and that hurts."

"I don't mean to hurt you, David, I'd never do that. It's just who I am."

"If you won't sleep with me at this point in our relationship, Layla, you just don't love me as much as I love you."

"I do love you as much. Maybe more."

"No, you don't. If you did, you'd understand that you don't need to be afraid of me."

"I'm not afraid of you. It's just who I am."

"No, it's a vestige of who you were before you met me."

"It's how I've been raised, David."

"Well, you're hurting me." We argued back and forth as we walked together through the streets of Westwood Village.

Alongside the change in David, Jila's relationship with Majid flourished.

It was like watching a flower take root and grow. While Majid was away, at his new job in Oklahoma City, Jila was either on the phone with him or shopping for conservative, affordable suits and outfits, and clearing out her room and life of anything that might annoy him. It was incredible for me to see my American-raised cousin, so comfortable amid her Californian friends, metamorphose into a typical Iranian girl in love with a typical Iranian boy.

True to his word, Majid returned from Oklahoma City the last week of April. "He sounds so happy. He says he has a surprise for me. He's taking my parents and me to dinner tonight. Oh, Layla, what do you think it means?" I shrugged. "Do you think he might propose?" Her eyes were pleading for me to say yes.

"Would you like that?" I asked, knowing the answer.

"Oh, my God, I'd be the happiest girl in the world!"

Jila woke me up sometime in the wee hours of the morning. "Layla, I'm engaged. He proposed. I'm going to Oklahoma City with him."

"That's wonderful! I'm so happy for you."

She was so happy, there were tears in her eyes. "It's fabulous! I can't believe it! My parents are coming, too. He has it all planned. He's found a job in the company for Dad. You should see my parents. Of course, they already knew; they knew before I did. He called and asked their permission to propose to me. They're delirious."

"I'm so happy. I'm sure Majid will be a good husband."

"I have you to thank for him, Layla. I'd never have met him if it weren't for you. We're getting married this summer. I want you to be at the wedding. You'll come to Oklahoma, won't you?"

"Of course, if I'm not in Iran." In either case David would not be with me.

In less than two months I would lose my roommate and my days of living in the apartment would come to an end.

Ammeh Elahe lost no time in calling Babajon to give him the good news of Jila's engagement, and within days, I received a letter from home, Babajon urging me to contact the UCLA dormitory to register for a room for the coming year. At the bottom of Babajon's letter Maman had added a short note asking me to send my "best wishes and congratulations to Jila *jon* and her parents, whom I know are jubilant at the news of their daughter's excellent proposal of marriage." Her sarcasm didn't escape me.

I immediately investigated the possibility of taking a room in the dormitories, but they were already completely filled up for the following year and all I could do was put my name on a waiting list. Hearing my accent and my name, they suggested I try the International House.

I visited the International House and liked what I saw. In the lobby, a girl wearing a colorful sari was talking with two blond boys, both wearing simple short-sleeved white shirts. In a corner, a boy wearing a red turban played chess with his opponent, a pale, lightly freckled, redheaded boy, while a striking girl the color of night wearing lots of necklaces made of brightly colored beads watched. The International House, or the I-House as it was called, was a hotel-type residence, with maid service, and a main telephone switchboard that took messages for students. Pay phones were located in the lobby and on each one of the four floors. There was a coffee shop, a cafeteria, a library, and a lovely large room with tables and a television, as well as a lounge with a baby grand and a stage. Two rooms were still available for the coming year, and both were single occupancy. I relayed this information to Babajon. Babajon immediately urged me to reserve a room there. My housing for next year was taken care of.

David and I both loved movies, and there were some landmark

movies out that spring: Goddard's *Breathless,* Alfred Hitchcock's *Psycho* and Otto Preminger's *Exodus.*

"Let's go see *Exodus* Saturday night, okay Princess?" David asked. "Mom and Dad both loved it. People say it's going to win the Academy Award for best picture."

We did see *Exodus* that Saturday night in May. It was an unforgettable epic film, and it did go on to win that year's Best Picture Oscar. It told the story of the birth of Israel in 1948, intended as a homeland for Jews, following the atrocities committed by the Nazis. When one of the characters described the anguish he experienced in a concentration camp, I cried shamelessly. We'd recently watched "Judgment at Nuremberg" on television. That showed footage of the human ovens in concentration camps. I told David that Ferri had said Jews should celebrate the day Hitler's concentration camps were liberated as well as celebrating Passover, and that she'd compared the formation of Israel to Moses' exodus out of Egypt.

David was overly affected by the somber movie and awed by the heroism of Paul Newman's character, who challenged all obstacles to make the dream of the Jewish haven a reality. *Exodus* haunted me. Yet little did I guess what a telling part that movie would play in our future. That very night, David began talking about visiting Israel. His parents had gone there while he was still in medical school, and he regretted not having joined them. He felt that his education as a Jew was incomplete without visiting the land his people had fought for. He continued to talk about his desire to visit the country. Then, on his birthday, his parents gifted him a trip to Israel upon completion of his internship that summer. He would be gone for the same month I would be in Iran.

As the time for my return home to Iran for a summer month neared, I knew I'd miss David. But I also found myself oddly looking forward to time away from him.

Though our relationship seemed to be fine on the surface, there was an underlying tension that had developed between us as David's patience with my sexual limits and my refusal to abandon them began to wear thin. Though I stood firm in my resolve, I was distracted by my love for him and the pleasure he brought me, which joined to make me feel increasing pressured to succumb to his request. I was finally forced to admit to myself that I was glad to be going home. Perhaps, some time apart would reduce the intensity of feelings for him. And by returning to Iran, I would resurrect the Layla who left home less than a year ago, strengthening my resolve to abide by my limits and remain a virgin.

32
WHERE THE HEART IS

At the end of July, I left for Iran as planned.

David had left for Israel just days before me and would be returning to L.A. less than a week before my scheduled return.

We were both returning to our roots. David was making his first trip to Israel, to learn more about his heritage, and I, like a tree about to topple, was returning home to strengthen my roots and reaffirm the values of my heritage. Our parting was filled with mutual vows of love.

Once my airplane passed over Turkey, the terrain below began to turn greener.

As we passed over the Azerbaijan province where the weather was always cold, I could see the snow-top summit of Mount Damavand and the thick Alborz Mountain range north of Tehran.

Our plane began its descent. Soon, the mud houses on the outskirts of Tehran came into view. Slowly, those mud structures gave way to buildings of wood and brick, then to a few hotels and a scattering of office buildings perhaps as tall as twelve stories. I could see construction sites freckling the city. There was definitely building going on throughout Tehran. Dirt roads met asphalt and tar-covered highways as we approached Mehrabad Airport east of Tehran. Finally, the airplane touched ground. I was home.

I had missed Iran and my parents terribly, and I was so anxious to see my family and friends that, as I departed the airplane, I could not contain my excitement. Babajon and Maman met me. I ran to them, my father's arms already outstretched to enfold me.

Maman embraced me, repeating, "You're home. You've come home." She held me by my shoulders and searched my face anxiously. "Are you going back?" she asked. In my momentary silence, Babajon took my arm and headed toward the car, instructing Abol to carry my luggage. Maman repeated her question. But again, before I could answer, Babajon demanded that she stop bothering me with questions so soon after I'd arrived home.

Entering our house, I was met with the wonderful smell of my favorite stew, Cobra's *ghormeh sabzee*, a mix of green herbs and lamb. Too early for dinner, Fotmeh served us jasmine tea and baklava. As I enjoyed the light honeyed pastry and watched the girl's interaction with my mother, I sensed the strengthened bond that had developed between them during my absence. Fotmeh looked immaculate, in a starched pink apron over one of my hand-me-downs, a pink-flowered *roosaree* on her head. She moved like a silent gazelle, never so much as looking at Babajon or me. Maman seemed to communicate with the servant girl with no more than her eyes and the slightest movements of her head.

"How is Elahe? Tell me, what do you think of my sister?" Babajon asked jovially, obviously excited to be speaking to me in person again. Maman's eyes darted to me.

"She's been very kind to me," I answered. "I've practically lived at their home." I intentionally exaggerated, knowing Babajon would want to hear that his sister had been extremely hospitable to me. And, though I knew Maman wouldn't want to hear that I'd spent much time with Jila's parents, I felt it was important to add a veneer of family life to my parents' image of my time in Los Angeles.

"How fortunate for them all that Jila caught Majid," she said.

"She didn't *catch* him, Maman *jon*. Majid fell in love with Jila the minute he saw her and wouldn't let go of her until she agreed to marry him." She raised her brows.

"Majid is a good boy. He'll take good care of her," Babajon said.

"Yes, and with any luck, he will take good care of your sister and her husband, too." Maman answered him. My father ignored her comment, and I wondered if he knew of Majid's plans to take the entire family to Oklahoma City and give Javeed Khan a job there. If he did, he hadn't told my mother.

"I'm only sorry that their wedding won't be here. It's not possible for me to be in Oklahoma then," Babajon said. Majid had decided to have the wedding in the States as an opportunity for his parents to visit, in the hope that they would decide to stay there. "I will be in Israel finalizing some contracts at that time. Saleh Pharmaceuticals is on a tight timeline to launch an improved Galoo Cure, using ingredients indigenous to Israel. We'll begin import and production as soon as the contracts are signed."

I jolted at the mention of Israel. My father noticed and looked at me questioningly but said nothing. "Maman, will you go to the wedding?"

"No, of course not." Her answer drew Babajon's attention to her. Seeing her husband's disapproving look, Maman explained. "I won't go to America without your father's shadow."

"Tell me all about UCLA. We talked about it while you were there, but I want to hear it now that you're here." Babajon's eyes were bright with interest.

I gushed about the wonderful academic environment, my classes and my professors and made sure to mention how safe and convenient the International House was.

"It seems everyone around us is marrying off their daughter," Maman said moving us to what she believed to be a far more interesting topic. "Even your aunt Elahe. And Shireen's wedding? From another world. You've never seen anything so extravagant. It was more lavish than any queen's wedding." Although Maman knew full well that I was completely aware that Shireen's husband was a fabulously wealthy man, it was important for her to make it clear just how overboard Taymoor and his family had gone in putting on the wedding, as

Persian custom was that the bride's parents host the engagement, and the groom's side pays for the wedding.

Listening to her, I detected something in my mother's voice that I couldn't name. I only knew I didn't like it.

Before I could pinpoint what it was, Babajon interrupted her. "*Azizam*, all this talk of Shireen can wait," he said, rising from his seat at the table. "Our daughter must be tired after her trip. Would you like to rest before dinner, Layla? Your grandparents and your mother's sister and brother will all be joining us for dinner. Why don't you take a nap before they all come?" I was grateful for the reprieve he'd offered, and realized then, how tired I was. Entering my bedroom, I was overcome with the feeling that I'd never left home. It was just as it was when I'd last left it. Everything that had happened to me since I'd last walked out, could have been no more than a dream. I fell on my wonderfully comfortable bed seconds away from a deep sleep and dreamed….

"Layla, wake up!"

The voice was familiar. I opened my eyes and looked at the woman standing above my bed in the late afternoon light. In the time it took me to reorient myself to time and place, I saw her short black hair styled in a lacquered bouffant hairdo, a heavily made up face and a designer suit. As my world came into focus, I noted the lovely violet eyes.

"Shireen. Congratulations!"

"You're finally home." After kissing both my cheeks, my cousin pulled a long strand of my wayward hair away from my face. I saw her jewel-encrusted wrist and the ring that sat on a freshly manicured finger, bearing a single round diamond the size of a peacock's eye.

"I'm sorry I didn't answer your last letter," she said. "I've been in a whirlwind since the wedding. First that, then the honeymoon, then trying to re-do the house and furnish it – I swear, it never ends – in between Taymoor dragging me away again to Europe, and all these parties … what's so funny? You're laughing"

"Your hair. You've cut it like Elizabeth Taylor's."

Shireen turned for me, modeling her haircut. "You like it? It's exactly like Liz's. She's on the cover of this month's Life magazine. Oh, I'm so happy, Layla." She started jumping up and down in her designer suit and high heels just like she did when she was a little girl. "I'm married, Layla. I did it! It's heaven. He gives me a huge allowance every month for clothes and he's bought me all these things ... " she stuck her hands out to me and I saw another ring, an emerald one on her right hand. Then she dug underneath her blouse and lifted out a chain of diamonds. "... and so much more!"

I was happy for my cousin. I knew, perhaps better than anyone, how important marriage to a wealthy man was to Shireen. I got out of bed and hugged her. "How wonderful that you fell in love," I said wistfully.

"Love? Praise Allah, who said anything about love? You know I married to be free. No one can tell me what to do anymore, Layla! I do what I want. That's what I love." She looked at her gold watch then snatched her Chanel handbag off my bed and gave me a menacing look. "He doesn't *dare* say no to me."

Shireen continued talking as she made her way across my bedroom to the door. "Listen, I've really got to get going. I can't join you for dinner with the rest of the family, and I had to stop by and see you, say hello. I'm late to the dressmaker. I bought clothes in Europe and gained weight since then, so I need her to let them out a bit. You, on the other hand, are as thin as ever. How completely unfair! How do you do it? Anyway, believe it or not, the more I eat and the fatter I get, the more Taymoor likes it."

Before I could say a word, Shireen stopped and turned to me. "Oh, I almost forgot. All the girls know you're here and they're dying to see you. I've arranged for everyone to come to my house tomorrow."

"That's wonderful. Ferri too?"

Shireen frowned. "You still love that girl. Well, I haven't really talked to her much since you've been gone. I mean it's pointless. But I assumed you'd want to see her, so I made sure to invite her. Come at four, so we married women will have some time to ourselves before our husbands come home from work looking for us." In Iran, the workday ended somewhere between eight and ten pm to compensate for the long lunch break. "I have to rush. I'll see you then. Okay? Welcome home. God protect you. *Ghorbonnet beram,* may I be sacrificed for you." She blew kisses to me on her way out. As she left, I made a mental note to ask her tomorrow if she danced a lot with Taymoor.

That evening Naneh Joon and a frail looking Agha Doctor came to our home for dinner, along with Shireen's parents, and my Ammeh Bahia. Bahman had already left for England to attend architectural school. Bahia Khanom told me that my grandfather had had a cold, which had turned into a bad case of pneumonia that winter and had been admitted into the hospital for three days. No one had mentioned it to me so as not to worry me. He obviously had not yet fully regained his strength.

Naneh Joon kissed my eyes, then started to cry. "Naneh Joon, why are you crying?" I asked her.

"I missed you."

"But I'm here."

"You will leave all too soon." I hugged the woman, realizing for the first time how much taller than her I'd grown. I thanked her for her letter, assuring her that I had taken every word to heart, and for the beautiful golden shawl.

I slept like a baby that night and stayed in bed for most of the next morning, knowing Babajon had left for work and Maman would grill me the first chance she had without him to referee. I was saved, for after I had a lazy breakfast and showered, she left for appointments with her hairdresser and manicurist.

In the afternoon, Babak drove me to Shireen's new house, a mansion that sat atop a hill behind walls of stone. As we drove past the gates of the estate and up the gently sloping road, the expansive lawns, the many trees and the elaborate landscaping, I was reminded of the UCLA campus. There was a reflecting pool in the center of the sprawling grounds in front of the house, highlighted by a colossal white statue of a woman in a flowing gown. The semi-circular driveway brought us to the front steps of the enormous white house, a mix of architectural styles, with two-story beveled glass windows. Servants were stationed at the door.

Shireen greeted me inside the cavernous foyer. "Did you see the statue of me outside by the pool?" she asked. "Isn't it fabulous? Taymoor surprised me with it."

My cousin's home was a palace of white marble walls and floors interspersed with mirrors. The furniture was white gilded "esteel," the name Persians gave to furniture in the style of Louis XIV. Only the many silk rugs in muted colors here and there atop the marble floors added a hint of hue to the rooms. The only wall hanging was a large portrait-photo of Shireen and Taymoor, their smiling faces and ringed hands joined on their wedding day, encased in an enormous frame made of Venetian mirrored glass and hanging in the center of the huge living room wall. Overall, the impact was one of chilling wealth. As she moved, Shireen's bright green dress and the flashing oversized diamonds she wore on her ears, wrist and neck blazed brightly against the pale room.

As I advanced farther into the house, girls I had known from school flocked around me, asking how I was, and anxious to tell me they were now married or engaged, and happy to show me their flashy rings and perfect nails. I couldn't help but notice that their hairstyles were all similarly short, teased, and sprayed, and their makeup all similarly applied with a heavy hand. They all wore dresses of fashionable European style and their jewelry was all too visible. I searched among the guests for the one face I wanted to see. Ferri wasn't there. Disappointed, I stuck a smile on my face and spent the afternoon with one eye on the door while trying not to act bored – which wasn't easy. *Where was Ferri? Didn't she want to see me?*

A barrage of remarks bombarded me, from the silly to the inane. "Layla, forget about *meecro-whatever-you-call-it* and get married this minute. It's heaven, isn't it, Shireen *jon*?" Mojgon never stopped smiling, making her voice shrill.

"My cousin prefers germs to this," Shireen said, her outstretched arms waving as she turned her head from one end of the room to the other. "She's right. Who needs all this?" She was laughing, her gold and diamond bracelets jangling on her wrists.

"Well, maybe Layla's not so dumb. Maybe she knows what she's doing, yes, Layla *jon*?" Nassrin had remained short and wore a very tight, black, well-detailed suit. "For all we know, her American classmates are sexy boys, yes, Layla *jon*?" She winked slyly, and they all joined in the laughter. "Did you bring any of those sexy boys home with you?" she went on. "I'd take one if Ramsi wasn't constantly on my tail." The laughter continued. So did Nassrin. "Have you found a handsome American boy to marry and bring home with you? Yes? I'll be glad to teach him Farsi; private lessons, of course, when my husband is at work." Nassrin hadn't changed; she was still that girl who had trudged up the hill in the snow to the silo and knew about *llaa paee*.

Their babbling went on like that for some time. I felt as if I'd walked in on a meeting of a club I didn't belong to and couldn't leave. As they became bored with the novelty of having me there, they talked endlessly to one another about their maids, manicurists, hairdressers, dressmakers, mothers-in-law, and husbands. It seemed their lives were interchangeable. My high school classmates had all changed into the same person! I was most baffled by the snide remarks these girls made about their husbands.

Azar had been married for barely six months. "I swear to all the prophets: my husband's penis is a shriveled bean sitting atop two ugly walnuts. I cringe when he touches me."

"At least he touches you, *aziz*. My husband thinks sex is unnecessary. He hasn't touched me in months," said another.

"Touch, don't touch, what's the difference? A man needs to know how to touch a woman. My Ahmad hasn't a clue. If I don't take a lover soon, I tell you, I'll die," said Sophie.

I was aghast. *Who were these people? How could they show such little regard for their husbands?* They made fun of them the way we used to make fun of our teachers at school. *How could they have given themselves to men they feel this way about for the rest of their lives?*

There were huge crystal bowls and silver platters everywhere, all laden with food, including dried fruits, fresh fruits, nuts, pastries, cookies, and candies of all sorts. Servants constantly made the rounds, offering up trays of tea and more cookies, soft drinks and *doogh,* a bubbly yogurt soda, and I wondered what these servants thought of what they saw and heard. *Did they aspire to be like the women they served?*

Needing a break from this sort of chatter, I excused myself and headed for the dining room. As I passed across the room, I heard snatches of conversation:

"I swear on my life, it was less than ten carats … "

" … a pedicure in the morning then having my hair done and then stopping in at my dressmaker. We can shop in the afternoon."

There was no question in my mind that I didn't like what Shireen and the others had become. If I had ever understood any of these girls, it was obvious that I had absolutely no understanding of them now. Upon stepping into the dining room, my eye caught sight of the ornate silver frame on the wall facing me, holding the autographed photo of Elizabeth Taylor. I sighed, remembering the day at the Dunn home, when Adam handed me that photo by the pool. I thought of his kindness in procuring it. I wondered what he was doing just then. He'd disappeared out of my life, as though erased.

The sound of cawing distracted me from my thoughts. It was Haji Baba! His new home, a large white cage, took up a corner of the dining room and was as elaborate as everything else in the house. I happily greeted my old friend. At least, Haji hadn't changed. "*Saalom*, Haji." The parrot stared at me for the space of a second then cawed, "*Bokhorr, Bokhorr.*" I laughed in shock. The parrot had replaced his favorite command, "dance!" with the command, "eat." I enjoyed the parrot far more than the women in the other room.

"Okay, Haji, I will," I said and turned to the three tables, each set with heavy silver chafing dishes and platters that sparkled, gold serving tools at their sides. Dozens of entrees and desserts were artfully set out. I was the only guest in the dining room then, with three servants positioned at each table, one offering a plate made of the thinnest bone china edged in gold, a second to serve, and a third offering a smile and, I would imagine, whatever else was requested: nine servants in a room with only me, in addition to the others making the rounds among the guests and those standing by the door. I was overcome by the show of excess. *Surely, all this was not needed for afternoon tea with a cousin and a handful of old high school friends?* Yet before I'd left for America, I would probably have accepted all this as only a bit more than par for the course. *Would I have approved?*

I stood in Shireen's dining room with these thoughts, the first of many I'd have on my first trip home that gnawed away at old standards as I came to view things around me differently than I ever had.

Has my time in America changed my perceptions? Would these women's attitudes about their lives and their husbands seem normal to me if I'd stayed in Iran? Would I have been more like these girls if I'd stayed?

I couldn't help but compare the feelings these girls expressed about their husbands to my feelings for David. *How could they not love their husbands as much as I loved David?* And then, came the ice-cold start as I remembered that I wouldn't be marrying David.

I left the dining room, my eyes peeled to the front door. *Where was Ferri?* The elaborately flowered white Dresden clock atop the white marbled mantel in the dining room showed I had under an hour here before Babak would come for me.

I noticed Lana sitting on the chaise by the hallway leading to the foyer. She was alone, nursing a cup of tea and gazing into space. She'd been a loner in high school, stigmatized, and left almost friendless as the girl whose mother had been branded a *jendeh,* a whore, for allegedly having an affair with the school principal. Her father had divorced her mother and forevermore forbid her to set eyes on Lana. After that, girls were afraid to be seen with Lana, warned by their mothers that by associating with the girl, their own reputations would be tainted.

I was the exception. Though I didn't seek her out to spend time with her outside of school, I was always friendly to Lana in classes and when we passed in the halls. I wasn't sure if Shireen had invited her because of that or because her father, Mansoor Khan, had represented Lana's father in his lawsuit against the school for improper conduct by a principal. Uncle Mansoor had said the school authorities had opted to settle outside of court and dismiss the principal in order to prevent bad publicity. I also overheard him say that he actually had never seen a shred of evidence pointing to the alleged affair. But evidence wasn't needed; the rumors had spread and prevailed. The principal had been found bludgeoned to death and, when Lana's father was suspected of perpetrating his murder, Uncle Mansoor had represented him again, vindicating him of any criminal wrongdoing. The true killer was never caught. Yet Lana suffered.

Seeing her sitting apart from the other girls, I made the mistake of assuming that her presence at the tea meant the taint had faded and she was no longer ostracized. I made the further mistake of assuming I'd found someone to talk sensibly with. I'd tell her I thought of her while in Los Angeles, though I certainly wouldn't mention the dread I associated with her name when Adam had mentioned it as we drove by that famous drugstore in Hollywood. I went to her and sat beside her on the chaise.

"Lana, how good to see you. How are you?" She nodded. "Are you married, too?" It was my innocent attempt at sarcasm, as marriage seemed to be the order of the day, so I was utterly shocked when Lana reacted by sobbing hysterically, almost throwing her cup and saucer down, and tearing wordlessly out of Shireen's house, banging the door behind her. I felt awful, realizing I apparently hurt her.

Hearing the door slam, Shireen and the others quickly appeared to see what had happened. *Had someone entered the house without the servant there to open the door for them?* When I told them that Lana had stormed out in response to my innocent question, they explained that the owner of a small furniture business had been courting Lana for two months before recently calling the marriage off. He was unable to agree to the financial terms of the marriage contract with Lana's father.

Specifically, the man demanded that the *sheer bahar* he was to pay her family for her absence, be no more than a mere token if anything at all, arguing that the family has been disgraced. He also wanted his bride's *jehaaz,* or dowry, to include more valuable items from her parents' home than offered, and had refused to pay Lana what her father proposed as a reasonable amount of *mehree'yeh,* or spousal support in the event of divorce, arguing that marrying Lana came with a higher-than-average risk of divorce, as her family background made Lana herself prone to disgrace him – as if sexual infidelity were genetically transmitted.

In any case, agreement could not be reached, and the engagement was called off, leaving Lana in a worse situation than she'd been in before. In addition to having her heart broken, she was forced to suffer extreme embarrassment, as apparently everyone in Tehran knew the story of her humiliation. She was now even further devalued as a bride, and her prospects for marriage, dismal. Through absolutely no fault of her own, Lana's chances for finding happiness in Tehran seemed to be slim, at best.

Finally, it was time for Babak to pick me up. Shireen escorted me to her front door. As I thanked her again and said my final goodbyes to her assembled guests, with vague promises to see them again during my stay in Iran, the door opened and Ferri walked into my arms. We embraced warmly, while Shireen looked on coolly.

I was overjoyed to see my angel again, and reassured to see her looking and dressing just as she always had, in a simple black pleated skirt and a plain black sweater. Her dark curly hair still fell down her back and framed her small brown face, and she wore only a hush of color on her lips. With no time to stay and visit, we made plans to meet for lunch the next day.

Hearing us make arrangements that didn't include her, Shireen said, pointedly, "You two go ahead and catch up. I have an appointment with Taymoor at the jewelers."

33
A TELLING LUNCH

Now that I was finally to be sitting down to lunch with my best friend, I found I had mixed feelings about our meeting.

I wanted to be totally honest and open with Ferri about David. If I couldn't even be honest with her, I was lost. I needed her to listen to me and accept all my confessions without judging me too harshly, then fill my mind and my heart up with resolution, and remind me of all the reasons I shouldn't take my relationship with David to the final sexual level.

The only problem was, that I didn't know how to tell her about him. *How could I tell her what I'd never even hinted at in my letters?*

We met at an outdoor café near the University of Tehran that catered to students.

It was a scorchingly hot day and we sat at a table under the shade of a large tree. As we took our seats, Ferri asked, "So what did you think of our old friends?"

I shook my head. "I have to admit, yesterday was strange for me, seeing what Shireen has become."

"She was always like that." Ferri said.

"Yes, but Taymoor is extremely indulgent. I think she's gotten worse."

"You mean even more shallow?" Ferri said with a smirk on her face.

"Ferri *jon,* I love Shireen. But she – actually, all of the girls there – they carry on like they're crazy! You weren't there to hear them. *Khodaya, my God,* they all speak so badly of their husbands!" I laughed at the ludicrousness of it. "They're newlyweds and they made fun of their own husbands mercilessly from the moment I arrived until I left. I'm sure you heard them after I left. All they did was belittle them."

"I left immediately after you did. I never even went into the living room."

"Well, trust me. They hurled insults, one worse than the other. They weren't loving. They weren't even respectful. And between their insults, they said I should forget about my studies and marry right away – a *rich* man, of course. *So that I can have a life like theirs?"* I shook my head.

Ferri looked at me pointedly. "When you get your degree and come back, you'll be expected to marry right away – unless, of course, you're planning to stay in America forever?"

I shrugged. "So, I'll come back and marry. I'll find someone I care about though. And when I do, I hope to have more on my mind than jewelry and clothes! *Aziz,* don't look at me like that. Right now, they're all living the role of the young wife, married to the successful husband. I guess it's expected of them to flaunt their wealth. It's just that they all seem so much happier with the trappings of their marriage than with the marriage itself." I sighed. "I just don't understand."

We were both quiet as Ferri brought out her pack of Winstons and lit a cigarette. I went on. "Ferri, the girls I see in America are like… like leopards, strong, beautiful leopards moving freely through the wild, conscious of everything around them and making decisions about their lives, while these Iranian women are more like clams, closed. I suppose it's because their independence has been stifled in all areas. They're not allowed to venture out of their shells, so they know very little – if anything – about the outside world and even less about themselves. All they know is that they need to marry, and all they learn how to do is run a home, pamper themselves, and please their husbands adequately."

Ferri didn't seem surprised by my little speech. "It's all about our views on sexuality and women's supposed *lack* of sexuality," she said, continuing where I left off. "I think it's insulting to women to assume we can't be sexual without losing our minds, and our virginity," she said.

I was delighted. That last part was exactly what I'd hoped to hear from her. "And it's a bigger insult to Iranian men. I think we women are held to such a strict code of conduct, because it shields men from taking a bride with some degree of experience with other men – no matter how slight – so she can't possibly compare her husband to the men she's known and, God forbid, expect more from her husband than he chooses to give, or is even capable of giving."

Though Ferri always surprised me, her outburst floored me. It was unlike anything I'd ever heard. Yet, I couldn't disagree with the possibility that she was right. In time, I would come to believe that Iran's male-dominated society had quite a lot to gain from sexually repressing women. It worked to their benefit to convince a girl that her virginity equaled their concept of decency; that it was the mainstay of her worth as a future wife, though the same didn't hold for them. If virginity was required for a secure future, a place in society, and the promise of a home and husband, then virginity came to equal happiness. Anything that threatened virginity threatened the foundation of home and family. Consequently, our culture repressed facts about sex.

I asked Ferri, "How come you aren't married yet? Don't you want to have a husband and all the great things that go with it?"

Ferri, who had been sitting back, exhaled a stream of smoke and held up her hands shouting, "No!" She moved in closer. "And my parents are ready to kill me. They want me to marry and make them grandparents. And I have a younger sister who's angry. She wants me to marry and get out of her way, so she can marry."

"Rebecca? Why she's barely a teenager."

Ferri nodded. "Yes, Rebecca. She can't marry until her older sister does. She's deathly afraid she'll be a spinster because of me. My parents are afraid I'll become *torsheedeh,* pickled, and no one will want me, so they're really pressuring me to accept a *khostegar;* any one of them would be fine with them."

"What will you do?" I asked.

"Don't worry about me, *joonie.* You know I'm tough." It felt so good to hear her call me her dearie again. "No one will make me do anything I don't want to do. You know that." She took a final drag and extinguished the half-smoked cigarette under her shoe.

I'd put off broaching the subject of David. Though I was dying to tell her about him, I couldn't just blurt out the news. I was waiting for an opening, a cue, and hoped that our conversation would soon present me with one. Lunch came. While we ate, I told her about college life in Los Angeles and then the story of Jila and Majid. Lunch finished, and I still hadn't spoken of him. I ordered jasmine tea and Ferri ordered an espresso.

"So, your mother must be delighted with your two cousins, Shireen married and now Jila engaged," she said sarcastically.

"She's pressuring me to stay here but I'm going back to UCLA. I'll marry afterward." I laughed adding, "We'll marry together." Ferri didn't laugh with me.

"I'll probably become a spinster," she said somberly. "An old college professor who never marries."

"Don't you want to be in love, Ferri?"

Her answer was emphatic. "Yes, of course. What does marriage have to do with love?" She looked at me then and asked, "What was that look for, *joonie*? You just became so sad."

"Have you ever been in love?" I asked quietly, not looking up.

"I think I am in love." She lowered her voice and said with a twinkle in her eye, "I know I *make* love." She may as well have just said she was going into burlesque. "Don't look so shocked, *joonie,* my good little girl. I've been wanting to tell you."

"I *am* shocked. With who?"

Ferri nodded. "Hamid. I swear only after you left, Layla. I said, I swear it. He never once touched me before that, and I never lied to you."

"Oh, Ferri, he forced you?"

Ferri sputtered a laugh. "No more than I forced him. I told you I never do anything I don't want to do. Anyway, it was probably inevitable: a girl, a man, a lot of time together, as you well know, both young and healthy, sharing their thoughts."

"You willingly had –" I stopped, realized I was shouting and dropped my voice down to a whisper. "You willingly let Hamid…?" I trailed off, unable to say the words.

Ferri nodded enthusiastically. "I did. And I do. And I will, for as long as long as I can."

I squirmed in my seat. This was shocking news. I needed to sort all this out. Ferri had been physical with her Muslim teacher. Yet she had implied there was not even the smallest chance that she would marry him. Concerned for my best friend, I knew this was not good news. Yet, selfishly, this meant Ferri would far more readily accept the fact that I'd experimented with physical intimacy. I needed to know the details.

Exactly how far had she gone with Hamid? Most likely, only as much as I'd done with David. I needed to hear her confirm that she'd put off intercourse until marriage. That would validate my refusal to sleep with David. But Ferri had just said she didn't want to marry. "Okay," I said. "You're saying you've touched and kissed and well, probably done other things. But you haven't done *it*."

"*Kardeem?* Have we done it?" I nodded impatiently, so anxious to know Ferri's answer, I was oblivious to fact that she wasn't whispering now and there was a chance that people nearby could hear us. She slowly took out another cigarette, lit it, took a long leisurely puff, then sat back again, crossed her legs, dusted her skirt, checked a fingernail, looked coolly at me and then answered. "Yes."

"*What?* I don't believe you for a minute." I dropped my voice. "You've lost your virginity? You wouldn't do that. You wouldn't sleep with a man you're not married to."

"Then you don't know me, *joonie,* because I would. And I did."

I didn't know what to say. Far worse, I didn't know what to think. I just stared at her. Here was the only person in Tehran I felt I could talk to and explain my dilemma about David. This was the person who was to be my rock, who would buttress my resolve not to sleep with him, and now this. *Had everyone gone completely mad while I was away?*

"Don't look at me like that, Layla." Ferri was gazing at me steadily, and the look in her eyes bored through me. "You can stay a nice little virgin for your husband if you want to. I'm not going to play that game. And that's what it is, a game."

"Ferri, how can you say that?"

"Layla, wake up! Men hold virginity over our heads like a gun." She was holding the sugar bowl and moved it toward me as she became increasingly animated then put it down. Her dark eyes lit up with fire, as they did whenever she spoke from the heart. "Does a man stay virgin for marriage?" She lifted the sugar bowl up again and almost slammed it down. "No! Do young boys hurry to marry before they pickle? Come on! Forty-year-old men are marrying young girls. We let men control us by believing insane ideas. Think about it: Almost everything in our culture is connected to the idea of keeping a woman in her place. Well, women don't have to take that, and I'm not going to." She sat back and inhaled.

"Ferri, it was my *mother* who taught me I need to stay untouched, not a man," I said.

"Exactly. We've become so well indoctrinated that we perpetuate that garbage ourselves. And it is all garbage.

"Look at Shireen and her friends. See their lives? That's the prize that lucky virgins get. I can't stand any of it. I wouldn't have gone there yesterday for the world. Only the thought of seeing you dragged me there.

"Why do we need to wait for marriage to have sex? *Why?* Men don't. The woman trades in her virginity for a place in his home and becomes part of it, like a housekeeper or, if he's rich, a domestic coordinator." Her words were pouring out faster now, propelled by passion. "And look at them both after marriage. How many married men run around with other women, chasing after the maid, his wife's friends, or other woman like a rat after cheese? Yet if he suspects his wife so much as looks at another man, he throws her to the dogs.

How many women have you heard of that ended up like Lana's mother?

She went on, her passion unabated. "They use sex to keep us in line. And, by the way, what is that drivel we're taught, that women don't enjoy sex and that we tolerate our husband's sexual use of us only to cater to his uniquely male animal nature? How do we let them get away with that? Well, if that's true, there's no pressure on a husband to even try to sexually gratify his wife because it's impossible.

"Well, I enjoy sex. I love it, with or without marriage. Love is wonderful and if it's not love that I have for Hamid then I certainly have an enormous amount of affection for him. Anyway, *joonie,* it's totally bourgeois to demand that love or marriage be a prerequisite for having sex; men don't. If you want to enjoy sex, and you make marriage a prerequisite, you're doomed. Lots of husbands are sexually insensitive to their wives' sexual needs. They don't know or care to know how to satisfy their wives, and they have sex outside their marriage if they choose to."

The air around us was charged with the sheer intensity of Ferri's conviction. I was sucked into her energy, while struggling to pull free. "Ferri, you can't..." I stopped in mid-sentence, utterly confused. I had my elbows on the table, my cheeks cradled between my hands. Ferri was spewing crazy-talk and unfortunately, I was well aware that our history had shown it likely that I would eventually agree with her.

She threw a crumb of *nonneh barbarri* bread onto the ground. She seemed to calm down as she watched the little sparrow that had been circling by our feet picked at it.

She concluded, "We're taught to barter our virginity. What you saw yesterday at Shireen's house is the result of that. Shireen was yearning to be free of her parents' control. So, she escaped their house and flew right into her husband's cage, with her parents' blessings and without a chance to taste anything of life or any other man."

"What about *love* in all of this?"

"*Love?* You tell me, *joonie.* Is Shireen in love? Or is what she feels for Taymoor gratitude for rescuing her from her parents, and for all the goodies he buys for her in that gilded cage she lives in with her grotesque statue outside?" Shireen's own words flashed in my memory. *'Love? Praise Allah, who said anything about love? You know I married to be free.'*

"They're all exchanging one cage for another. Right now, they're newlyweds, too busy being self-indulgent and the center of attention to really care what they've gotten themselves into. And they know the faster they have a child, the more kudos they get from their rich husband and his family. Understandably, they're determined to be as selfish as possible before the baby comes. And the saddest part of all is that they're going to raise their daughters to be just like them. They'll teach them that they're nothing without a man and that happiness is keeping your virginity for him, setting up a house full of kids for him, and putting *ghormeh sabzee* on the table, like you and I have been told."

I lifted my head and looked at Ferri forlornly. My heart broke for Shireen in her loveless marriage. Ferri's view made me sad as well. Though it reeked of truth, it seemed equally depressing. "You have such a cynical view," I said.

"Just of marriage, Iranian style, which, if you're a woman, means the odds are stacked high up against you of ever having a rich or gratifying sexual life, and probably no chance to develop yourself in any way at all other than domestically. I'm certainly not cynical about sex, and I'm not cynical about love. I know sex is great, and I know love is, too."

"Love isn't just 'great,' Ferri, it's the most wonderful thing in the whole world, and I feel sorry for anyone – including my cousin – who doesn't know it," I said without hesitation.

"Listen to you, *joonie*!" She gazed at me. "How do you know what love is?" Her eyes narrowed. "Oh my God, Layla, you're blushing! You're in love!" Ferri jumped up and down in her seat and clapped her hands. "You tell me everything right now, girl. *Beh Toorah,* on the Torah! *Ha-yah kon,* be ashamed of yourself! You let me babble on like an old lady! I'm so happy for you! My Layla *joonie* is in love."

I smiled shyly. The moment to tell Ferri about David had finally arrived and I still didn't know where to begin. "*Ooeeee,* come on, tell me, *joonie,* what's his name?" Ferri reached across the table, took hold of my arm and shook it impatiently.

"His name is David and he's wonderful." I chuckled then and used the American terms. "He's totally neat and cool. He's bitchin'"

"And? Well, come on, damn it! Don't make me pull it out of you. Your face just lit up. I know he must be an American. So, tell me everything about this neat, cool, bitchin', wonderful David right now, this minute, girl, or on my soul, I'll tear you to bits."

"He's Jewish, like you." I never dreamed that would be the first thing I'd tell Ferri about David, yet there it was. And then I told her everything. I opened my heart to my dearest friend.

I shared how we met, the shock of that first date at his parents' house and his mother's coldness, how I loved him, how smart and wonderful and kind and gorgeous he was, how patient he'd been with me until now. And then I explained the impasse I presently found myself in since Majid's arrival to Los Angeles. "Now he wants me to go all the way – that's what Americans call sleeping together, doing it; anyway, I don't know how to put him off any longer and make him understand. I don't know what to do."

"Hmm," was all Ferri said.

"I can't stop from wanting him. I'm helpless when he touches me. He used to be very conscious of not going too fast. He played the part of our policeman. Now, I've become the one that has to stop myself before *it* happens."

"You, sweet friend, look and sound like a girl who is very much in love and very frustrated. Let me ask you this, Why do you say you wouldn't marry him if he asked you?"

"Ferri, I'd have to refuse! What's wrong with you? You know my parents would never let me marry an American and live in California. And he's Jewish, too. You know they would never accept that. He's in Israel this minute, learning about his history. But I'd love him to propose, just to know he wants to be with me always, even though I'd say no."

Ferri chuckled. "Funny, isn't it? You're Muslim and you're in love with Jewish man, and I'm Jewish having an affair with a Muslim man. What do you think that means?"

I sighed deeply. "It means you were right about religion. All it does is pull lovers apart. I can't believe anyone's God would want that. You should have seen how his mother treated me at their house on Shabbot when she found out I wasn't Jewish. I know I told you some of it, but you didn't see her face or hear the sarcasm and hostility in her voice."

"Let's give a big cheer for organized religion." Ferri said dryly.

"Oh, Ferri, I see Shireen and the others, I hear them belittle their husbands, and I realize I love David so very much. I thought it would help me if we were apart for a while, and here I am. I've hardly arrived, and I can't wait to see him again. And now that there's this underlying tension between us, I'm scared. I don't want to lose him."

Ferri reached across the table for my hand and held it between hers, caressing it. "Layla, I know you so well. You always want only to do what's right, right for your parents, right for his parents, right for everyone else in the world. This is the one time in your life when I wonder if you'll be able to think of yourself first.

"What's best for you, Layla? You love David? You want to be with him forever? Marry him. You want to have sex with him? Have sex with him. *Beh darrak,* the rest be damned! I don't understand why you think you can't marry the man you love. In any case, at least share the joy of making love with him. You never know, maybe you'll realize that you can be with him forever; or, perhaps, you won't, in which case, you will at least have had him when you could, and you'll have the memories."

I was so frustrated, I wanted to scream. "Ferri, you're making it even harder for me. I can't believe you'd tell me that. I know that kissing and, well, lots of other stuff is safe. But my virginity? I've been taught that's for marriage and my husband, and anything else is taboo. I was hoping my best friend would help my resolve *not* to sleep with David get stronger. Instead, you sit here and tell me to sleep with him? I'm more confused than ever."

"*Joonie,* I'm sitting here telling you that exactly *because* I'm your best friend. I love you. Didn't you hear anything I've been saying? Don't be afraid, Layla. Be strong. Be a woman who goes out into the world and experiences life." Then as an afterthought she added, "Whatever you do, just be sure to use a diaphragm so you don't wind up pregnant. That would be a complete catastrophe."

"I can't. I've told David time and time again that I must be a virgin bride. What do I do when I marry, and I'm not?"

Ferri threw her arms up. "Maybe you're not as smart as I always thought you were. Listen. You want to stay a virgin? I'll tell you how. When David enters you, hold his penis in your hand so only its top part – the 'turban' – enters you, just the topmost couple of inches, that walnut part; that way your virginity will be intact. Don't look at me like that. Lots of girls around here do that and pass themselves off as virgin brides."

"That's like *laa paee;* Americans don't understand that."

"No, it's not. I'm saying he can actually enter you, but just a little." She must have seen how completely lost I was. "Or get yourself a jar of Vaseline and offer him the back door. That'll work too." I recoiled in horror at the thought. Ferri laughed. "You're looking at me like I have open pimples oozing down my face." Ferri said. "*Joonie,* it's just a suggestion. You'd be surprised how many virgin brides swear by Vaseline. Then again, you could always have normal intercourse." I hid my face behind my hands and moaned.

"Look, Layla, if you love David, turn the world on its head and let it rot. Why give a hoot what anyone thinks? And, let me ask you this: How will anyone even know you've slept with him? You wouldn't have known I was no longer a virgin if I hadn't told you." That brought to mind my conversation with Jila. "You and David are thousands of miles away from here. Tell me, who'll know?" Just then, another little bird swooped down onto our table to pick up a crumb of bread and flew away. "You're like that bird, Layla. You have your wings. I told you when you first went to America: Spread them and fly."

"Fly? I fly, and then I come back here and marry. What happens then? What do I do when my virginity napkin has no blood on it the morning after my wedding night? What do I tell my husband and my mother in law?"

"Trust me, *joonie.* There are ways of cheating with your virginity napkin. After all, blood is blood."

I left Ferri disappointed with my friend's advice. My trip home was not turning out as I'd hoped.

34
ANOTHER WEDDING

Desperate as I was to find stability in Tehran, change seemed to be everywhere.

Stores were now deluged with American products. American music permeated the city. American businesses were setting up shop in the city at lightning speed. Ferri told me that they'd begun building an American-modeled university in the garden city of Shiraz. And she'd passed me the news that Iranian women were well on their way to being granted the right to vote.

Shireen had become a married woman, spending her days toying with the trappings of wealth. Ferri had graduated from being involved in a provocative and dangerous friendship to having illicit sex. Even Maman seemed to have changed. I knew my mother was prejudiced and class conscious, yet I didn't recall her as being quite as intolerant or quite so rude to people, nor did I recall the nagging edge in her voice when she spoke to me.

"Well, both your cousins have married and married well," she said. "And what shall I say to people now? That my own daughter has no plans to marry? She thinks she's too smart to marry?"

And I wondered if Maman had always been this edgy and sarcastic. Perhaps, I was simply seeing her through new eyes.

I was crossing the street to my house one afternoon towards the middle of my time home, when I heard a familiar voice call out from a passing car.

"Little Layla, is that you?" There was no mistaking Cyrus' nasal voice. He pulled over to the side of the road and hurried up to me. I'd heard from Maman that his already wealthy father had recently formed a lucrative partnership with the shah's relatives, and Cyrus was "doing very well in medical school." The two of us stood in front of my house and spoke for a few moments. He asked about UCLA and shared the exciting news that, come September, he would begin studies in his specialty, coronary care.

Fotmeh interrupted our conversation. She was calling out from the front door. Apparently, Maman had spotted us from the window and was calling for us to come in.

Cyrus graciously declined, saying he was already late for an appointment. We said our goodbyes and I went into the house. Maman was the foyer. "Where's Cyrus?"

"He couldn't come in. He asked me to thank you, anyway."

"You should have insisted." She looked upset. I shrugged and headed for my room. "Did you even try to make him feel welcome?" Maman asked trailing me. "Cyrus is a good *khostegar,* Layla. His family is respected and very wealthy." I turned to look at my mother, wondering what she was driving at. "He's going to be a doctor. That's a respectable profession, Layla," she said. *David. Dr. David Kline.*

She entered my bedroom and stood confronting me with her hands at her hips. "*Chet shodeh,* what's happened to you?" she asked. "Don't you see that your cousins and all your friends are marrying and settling down? What decent girl your age do you know who's still not married or engaged? Even your cousin Jila, *na ghabell,* a girl with nothing, no family, no standing, marrying a *shozdeh,* a prince, like that Majid. Are we less than Jila's parents? Are you less than her? Marry! Marry Cyrus and make a home and family for yourself. Tell your father you don't want to go back there. Stay home and make grandchildren for us. You can make Cyrus fall in love with you easily."

I knew Babajon wouldn't allow my mother to stop me from going back. When she had first tried to stop me from going to UCLA, I had wanted to go there to study. Now, David was the main reason I feel compelled to return. *She didn't understand me then; she doesn't know me now.* Maman awaited my answer; it was my silence, a continued silence that screamed out my intention to leave Iran again. She turned on her thin Italian heel and left the room.

I went to my room and looked out the window at the familiar sight of the sweet, fragrant jasmine vines growing along the trellis in our side yard and the branches of the mulberry trees laced against the turquoise sky creating a mosaic.

David. David, David.

One evening, I joined my parents at a wedding.

The bride's family, a prominent Jewish family with contacts in Israel, had been of help to my father in procuring long-term contracts for the ingredients he would soon import for use in Saleh products. Though invitations requested our arrival at five o'clock in the evening, one didn't want to be the first guest to arrive – that would make us seem too anxious, as if we were never invited anywhere. We arrived just before eight thirty. The party was barely starting.

In keeping with Persian tradition, the groom's parents were hosting the wedding, an elaborate affair held at the brand new, grand Intercontinental Hotel. Both the ceremony and reception took place outdoors, spread over the entire expanse of the hotel grounds, lush with swans adrift on ponds, colorful, fragrant flowers in bloom, and jacaranda trees everywhere. Persian rugs prevented designer high heels from sinking into the grass, and, on that beautiful summer night, there were enough lit torches on the grounds to mask the deepening shadows of nightfall. Soon after our arrival, I was wonderfully surprised to run into Jalil. He was apparently a close friend of the groom and had come alone. His parents knew no one in the bridal party and were not invited. He was clearly delighted to see me back in Tehran and sat with us during the ceremony.

I'd been to an Iranian Jewish wedding before, and I knew their rituals differed from those of a Muslim ceremony. The Jewish wedding I had been to, invited by one of Babajon's associates, had an indoor ceremony. There, the guests had taken seats, and the rabbi had taken his place in front of the room. Musicians began to play music as the bride and groom entered the room, followed by their entire families – parents, sisters and brothers, uncles and aunts, grandparents – all dancing and, as the onlookers sang *"Congratulations, Let it be, Congratulations, Let it be,"* their two families escorted the bridal couple to the rabbi. The entourage took their seats only when the rabbi began to recite the blessings. It had seemed a joyous, family affair.

Nothing had prepared me for the lavish fanfare of this wedding. Perhaps it was a function of the changing times in Iran; whatever the reason, extravagant was the single word that described this event.

Adam would have said this wedding was worthy of a Hollywood production.

Act One was The Ceremony.

Close to eleven o'clock, what sounded like hundreds of chimes signaled it was time for the guests to take their seats. Red and white satin ropes hung on either side if the aisle, lined with gilded torches. A red velvet runner had been laid over the Persian rugs that covered the grass. When the live mini-orchestra began to play soft, sedate music, the guests quieted down; the ceremony was to unfold. The bride's parents came down the aisle first, she in a deep Russian-red silk ball-gown, sparkling with diamonds at her ears and throat.

"Her parents look elegant, don't they?" I whispered to Jalil. "Her mother doesn't look old enough to be marrying off a daughter."

"The bride's barely seventeen," he whispered back.

The groom's parents followed. His short, overweight mother waddled down the aisle, holding onto her husband's arm. Her husband was neither taller nor thinner than his wife. "God, would you look at those jewels!" Jalil screamed under his breath.

As the guests applauded their hosts, I wondered how the woman managed to walk at all with the combined weight of her body fat and all that jewelry. She wore a red gown of taffeta with white piping. Her tiara, placed atop her somewhat balding head, was designed of graduated marquis-shaped diamonds and rubies. She wore matching drop earrings and two necklaces – one strand of diamonds, the other of rubies.

"My friend comes from wealthy stock," Jalil remarked.

"How can you say that?" I shot back. "Just look at that poor woman! She has to wear two necklaces because she can't afford one with both diamonds and rubies." We giggled like two kids.

Next came a stream of bridesmaids, each on the arm of a male. I had no idea how my mother knew so much about these people. As each girl walked by, Maman would whisper to me, "She just got married," or "She's engaged to a wonderful boy." I passed the information along to Jalil, sitting on my other side.

Then came girls without escorts. "Ah, this year's crop," Jalil snickered. We stifled our laughter, while Maman eyed us in silence.

Meanwhile, the girls on the never-ending line continued to get shorter and younger until three toddlers, wearing elaborate dresses of red net over white silk, scattered flower petals as they bounced merrily down the aisle. Midway, one of the toddlers decided to sit down and was soon joined by the other two. The guests, of course, loved this. Laughter filled the room. Finally, an older bridesmaid appeared and coaxed them down the remainder of the aisle. One of the toddlers, probably startled by the sudden commotion, began to cry and ran into the arms of her mother.

The crowd fell into an excited hush. Certainly, the groom and his bride would be next. But no. Down the aisle came two boys, no more than three or four years old, wearing red tuxedos and pulling an ornate wagon cloaked with silver-trimmed red velvet carrying a sleeping infant dressed in a tiny red and white gown and propped on a slanted board. Again, there was a wave of comments from the guests. "That must be their baby." Jalil joked. I slapped his arm.

At last came the groom, short like his parents, wearing a white tuxedo with red bow tie, red cummerbund and poplin, his head held high. That left the bride.

An expectant hush fell over the murmuring crowd. The sound of chimes rang out; the sound of violins came from the orchestra, and the bride appeared, prepared to advance down the aisle to her future. Guests stood and applauded both out of respect and awe as she passed. Obviously young, she was a swan with luxurious white feathers framing her long neck and again trailing the hem of her structured white satin gown. Her headpiece had a white net that covered her face, enmeshed with tiny rhinestones – or perhaps, diamonds – glittering brilliantly. Drop diamond earrings adorned her ears and around her neck was a delicate chain from which hung a single diamond. She was a vision of beauty, absolutely lovely to look at as she walked down the runway with grace and poise.

The rabbi began his part. I closed my eyes and imagined it was David and I being blessed at our wedding, and that the rabbi was addressing the two of us as he spoke of the sanctity of marriage, announcing to the world that two were now one.

"Do you take this woman to have and to hold for the rest of your life in sickness and in health…" David had already cared for me in sickness. "And do you take this man…" *Yes, yes, yes! I do!* We were pronounced 'man and wife.'

Seeing me wipe away tears, Jalil asked, "Why do women always cry at weddings?"

We four joined the other guests on line waiting our turn to congratulate the new couple. As we filed down the reception line, Maman whispered, "Definitely Jewish. These people don't show any of the restraint we do." I was grinding my teeth. I itched to tell my mother how restrained David and his parents were compared to us.

Act Two was The Bounteous Feast.

During the ceremony, the staff had replenished the endless tables of hors d'oeuvres we'd snacked on since arriving and added enormous amounts of food. Jalil and I counted seven large pits roasting whole lambs and long tables piled high with the requisite sweet rice, green rice and several other rice dishes, a variety of stews, salmon, fillet mignon, chicken and white fish kabob, as well as various salads, fresh fruits, Persian and French cheeses of all kinds, and of course huge platters filled with iced beluga caviar accompanied with all the trimmings imaginable.

"I'm looking for one hard-boiled egg but can't find any, and all the eggs are chopped up in that dish alongside the caviar," Jalil joked.

The four of us took our dinner plates to one of the many tables on the hotel grounds. There were eight settings at each table, each with a white tulle handkerchief tied with a red velvet ribbon holding *noghl,* sweet candies made of slivers of almonds covered with sugar and rose water, plentiful at weddings, births and other joyous occasions.

Maman and Babajon were soon engrossed in a conversation with another couple also seated at the table. Jalil and I were free to exchange our news. "So, tell me, Layla," Jalil asked. "Do you like America?"

"Yes, but it's good to be home. I ran into Cyrus the other day, and now you. What have you been up to? Staying out of trouble?"

"Ah, I must confess, I am the most terrible boy in Tehran. I make trouble wherever I go. I crashed this party. I wasn't really invited; I'm never invited anywhere anymore." I enjoyed the absurdity of his humor. "And are you enjoying the attention of American men swooning before your feet?"

If I blushed, I hoped it didn't show in the evening's hues. "Silly!" I said. "Please, tell about yourself. What are you doing?"

"Changing the subject, I see. You don't want to talk about it. Okay. Well, let's see. I graduated, the youngest in my class, and I've been working. It's not a bad job at all. It's interesting, actually. I work for the Pahlavi Foundation. His Majesty is planning to put well over one hundred million dollars of his personal fortune into it. I'm involved with the land reform programs of what has been called, the shah's White Revolution."

"Land reform?"

He nodded. "Aala Hazrat, His Majesty, believes that land reform will help to improve economic and social conditions. Large estates will be subdivided and sold. Estates belonging to the Crown will be sold at reasonable prices to first-time landowners who couldn't otherwise afford to buy land. He intends to sell about a thousand Crown-owned villages. The profits from the sales will go into the Pahlavi Foundation to be used for charitable purposes."

"That's interesting. The shah's White Revolution must have great support."

"Not from the clergy," Jalil said. "The clergy has historically been the largest of all landowners. They're definitely not happy about any part of their land being taken. They also don't want to see women able to vote anytime soon, which is also included in the shah's program along with free, compulsory education, and setting up arbitrators in each locality to decide on disputes. All of these will naturally decrease the power that the clergy will exert over people's lives." Jalil moved his chair closer to mine then and slung one arm casually across the back of my chair. The gesture was not lost on me. I noticed my mother give us a sidelong glance and smile.

"And you decide the what price to ask for the land?" I asked.

Jalil leaned back and laughed. Maman was still looking in our direction. "No, *azizam,* my dear, you give me far too much credit. I'm just one of several people on a team that gathers information and gives it to the higher-ups. They decide those things. They're also thinking about selling several government-owned factories to private parties." His arm returned to the back of my chair.

"You're excited about it," I said.

"It's a good program; all of it. More people will have land, more people will own businesses, there will be more money going around, and people will have more power."

"Excuse me, Jalil *jon*." Babajon appeared and bowed before me ceremoniously. "May I have the pleasure of a dance?"

I rose, curtsied, and took my father's extended hand. "I'd be delighted."

Babajon and I stepped onto the dance floor. The traditional Iranian music had given way to ballroom dancing, and the band was playing my father's favorite, a tango. Babajon led me through the intricate steps he'd taught me from the time I was a young girl. Soon other dancers had stopped to watch us as he expertly led me, slithering across the dance floor, doing the conversation step, kicking our heels, our faces turning this way and that, our arms joined and pointed now straight up, now down and at my back, Babajon in his black tuxedo and me in a bright pink ball gown. I knew Babajon was enjoying the attention as much as I was. We relished sharing the moment.

I noted that Jalil had left his seat and was watching from the edge of the dance floor. When the music ended, he applauded. Maman, eyeing Jalil while conversing with the woman sitting next to her, had a tight smile on her face.

"Thanks for the dance." Babajon kissed me on my forehead. "I'm going to insist your mother come dance with me."

As he walked me off the dance floor back to our table, we heard a boisterous voice. "Hadi, you son of a bitch, is that you dancing with this gorgeous young girl? Shame on you! I'm going to tell your wife."

It was Hooshmand Karaji, an old friend of my father's, looking jovial as always. Cigar in hand, he embraced my father with a bear hug then embraced me. "Ah, you've come home, Layla."

I saw my mother being ushered away by a couple who had just found her, while Jalil made his way to us. Babajon introduced him to Hooshmand Khan who then turned to me. "You don't know how sick and tired I am of hearing this poor old bastard talking about you all the time. I know you're doing well in America; I know all about you. Your father won't shut up about how smart you are. He's very proud of you. Well, I don't blame him. It's good to see you. Come, let's sit down." He took a seat at our table, empty now except for we four. Hooshmand Khan took a puff from his cigar and asked, "Your flight to Tehran from California, Layla, how long did it take?"

"Too long," I answered.

"Hah! That's what you think." He rocked back and forth in his chair. "Jalil, I want you to hear this, too." He turned to my father. "Hadi, has your memory left you in your old age or do you remember that first time I went to America?" Babbajon nodded. Hooshmand Khan pointed his cigar at me. "It took me 10 days to get there! *Ten days!* I had to fly from Tehran to three other cities to get a flight to Europe. Each flight was separate; on a different plane, a plane you wouldn't put your mother's enemy on today. There were no regularly scheduled daily flights; not many people flew and those who did not generally have ambitious destinations. Some flights were scheduled every few days, maybe weekly; many weren't scheduled at all. Am I right, Hadi? We'd all had to wait until there were enough people wanting to go. Then they'd organize a flight." He patted Babajon's shoulder. "Right, Hadi?" Babajon nodded. Hooshmand Khan's arms went up. "And mailing letters? *Vye!* Don't even ask. It took weeks – sometimes a goddamned month or more – for a letter or postcard to arrive."

"It's a different world today," Babajon said. "Everything is faster."

"Progress is a wonderful thing," my father's friend offered. "We old men have seen great progress. We've seen this city change from donkey carts to cars, electricity, telephones, radios, phonographs and televisions. You're going back?" he asked me. I nodded. "When you get on your flight to Los Angeles, think of what your father and I had to go through to get there and back."

"I will."

"Good. There's no room for much more change, huh, old friend? We've seen it all." He nudged Babajon's arm and Babajon smiled. "Your father is a good man," he said to me. "I've put up with the son of a bitch for many years. I love the old bastard." He sighed and turned his attention to Jalil with the next puff of his cigar. "What do you do?"

When Hooshmand Khan heard Jalil was involved with land reform, he chuckled and slapped Jalil's shoulder. "So, now he's giving it away. You know how our dear shah came to own so much land, my boy?"

Jalil shook his head. "I assume he bought it?"

"Hah. Not quite, huh, Hadi? Shah's father was a soldier, and most likely quite poor before he staged the coup that eventually led him to the throne. Then, when he was shah, he'd say to a landowner, 'What a nice piece of land you have here,' and of course, the poor sucker was obliged to offer it to him, maybe *tarroff*. 'Your Majesty, *peesh-kesh,* please, accept it as yours.' What choice did he have? This was the shah! And His Majesty invariably accepted." Hooshmand Khan let out a walloping laugh. "He took title to parcel after parcel after parcel like that. It's nice that his son sees fit to return some of it to the people, albeit not the poor bastards it was taken from."

Hooshmand Khan interlocked his fingers on the tabletop, and a sort of sadness passed over his face for a moment, then was gone as quickly as the flutter of a bird. He leaned into Jalil and me. "You two are young. Life is interesting, and things change. Your own lives will change, huh, Hadi, my friend? Change in ways you wouldn't guess in a million years."

He stood. "I'm leaving you. I will now wander the grounds and see if there's anyone who's not here tonight. It's good to see you, Layla, keep up the good work. I wish you good luck with your work, Jalil. Hadi, you swine, join me and we'll have a drink on the way."

Babajon got to his feet. "I was going to find my wife and ask her to dance before we ran into you." He kissed my forehead before walking off with his friend. "You enjoy yourself tonight," he said to me, "I'll come find you."

As they walked away, Hooshmand Khan said to my father, "If your wife is still as stunning as always, I might run off with her tonight."

Act Three was The Cake Cutting.

This was my personal favorite act for its wonderful special effects. It must have past two am when an announcement was made over the loudspeaker requesting that guests gather at the table facing the hotel's southern broadside. All the music stopped. The bride and groom had positioned themselves on a platform facing the many guests, with their backs to the two- hundred-room hotel. With both hands on the oversized cake cutter, they sliced into their multi-tiered cake. Toasts were made, and applause was heard. Suddenly, every one of the lights facing that side of the ten-story hotel turned on-off-on-off repeatedly in total synchrony for about fifteen seconds as a white dove was released from each of the balconies and flew into the evening sky, carrying either a red or white balloon, eliciting loud gasps from the guests.

Then there came the Coda.

The remainder of the evening was left for more socializing and dancing. I danced with Jalil, sensing in his embrace a desire to move closer to me, hold me tighter. But there were watchful eyes all around us, and Maman seemed to be everywhere.

I'd always had a great affection for Jalil. As a young child, I'd preferred him to the other boys and loved it when he paid extra attention to me, perhaps helping me climb a tree. When I'd been scared of the mysterious blood on my shorts, it was Jalil who cared for me, escorting me home and informing Maman of my condition. Now it became clear that the feelings I'd held for him had been mutual.

At twenty-one, he was no longer the young boy I knew. Dancing in his arms, I wondered what life would be like with him. My reverie was broken when I felt his lips close to my neck and felt his hot breath on me as he breathed in deeply, taking in my scent before he turned his head away. It was a fleeting gesture, so quick it almost didn't happen. But it did, and in that instant, I knew his heart.

"So, I guess you're going to marry a king now," he suddenly said.

"Where did that come from?" I asked.

"Well, that's what happens to gorgeous girls who come home after going to college abroad."

I was touched. There was a time I would have been euphoric to hear Jalil say I was pretty. That was before David. "Thank you for the compliment, but I don't understand."

"Ah, my dear, beautiful Layla *jon*, is it possible that you don't know that our own Empress Farah met our shah as a college student studying in France?"

"I didn't know that." I said.

"When she was a student in France, she complained to Zahedi, the Iranian ambassador to France at the time, that she was having a hell of a hard time living there because of the Iranian restrictions on taking money out of the country. He invited her to meet with His Majesty and tell him herself."

"Zahadi married to the shah's daughter." I said, "Shahnaz. Her mother was his first wife, Fawzia. And after she complained, the shah married her?"

Jalil nodded. "He was impressed. He invited her to tea and the rest, my dear, beautiful girl, is history."

The story lifted my spirits and made me feel hopeful, though I didn't know exactly why. Perhaps it was because things had turned out surprisingly well for the college student. She took her problem to the shah and he married her.

Jalil pulled me away from my thoughts. "Maybe I shouldn't have told you the story," he said. "It might make you expect to marry royalty."

I had no interest in marrying a king.

35
PARVEEN KHANOM'S DILEMMA

As my month in Iran went by, the days moved ever slower, like a toy truck with a dying battery.

Ferri's time was taken up with a summer classes at the University, and I'd seen the entire family numerous times. The novelty of being back in Niavaran had worn off. In its place, was a lack of interest, born of my dissatisfaction and frustration at not having found the moral adhesion I had looked for at home.

Meanwhile, my yearning to see David seemed to grow. I had been trying to keep myself occupied during my trip home and to spend as little time alone as possible to lessen the chance of dwelling on David. I'd even welcomed an inane lunch with Shireen at the Club. Nonetheless, I'd become anxious to return to him. I even came to fear he would forget me. Perhaps, he'd meet and fall in love with a Jewish girl in Israel.

One day, during the final phase of my trip, I found myself at home alone.

I spent the morning wandering around the house, then went out into the gardens I so loved and sat on the edge of the mosaic fountain that was captured in the photograph Adam had remarked on that first time he'd come to the apartment … the first time I had been alone with a man. So much had passed since then ….

I looked down at the water, at the goldfish that were thought to bring good luck, and I prayed they would bring me good luck. The lump in my throat as I thought of my dilemma with David made swallowing, hard. I returned inside the lonely house and the comfort of my father's study.

My trip had been a disappointment. Even my father was unavailable. I had expected to return to Tehran and bathe again in his love. But he was occupied, working on contracts that would secure delivery from Israel of the key ingredients Saleh Pharmaceuticals needed, and faced government deadlines for tariffs to be imposed. He was also working on a new look – new packaging – for Saleh products. I sat in the study at Babajon's large Spanish desk, found a sheet of paper and wrote mindlessly

David David David

You are all there is.
You are all there.
You are all.
You are.
You.
David.

I sat daydreaming, seeing David there in Babajon's study with me. With a start, I tore up the page and distributed its pieces among three different trashcans in the house.

I went back to the books on the shelves in Babajon's study. I rummaged through them, stopping at a compilation of poems by Molana Rumi. Conventionally, Persians consider the works of Hafez to reveal the unknown and they consult them when needing counsel. A question is asked, and then a book of Hafez's is opened to a random page. A finger falls on a random line, and the line is thought to divine the requested answer.

My father thought differently. Babajon venerated Rumi's works over those of Hafez and turned to Rumi for the answers he sought, believing that Rumi held the answers to all the questions of life. Holding Rumi's book, I formulated my question: *What should I do with David?*

I held the book loosely open, allowing it to fall to a random page then put my index finger blindly down on the page and read the poet's answer:

Drunken with love, I sail like a boat,
Anchored to mind, I fail to float.

I slammed the book shut and almost threw it across the room. Even Rumi was part of the conspiracy, describing me as stopping myself from feeling the bliss of floating, of sailing in love. I angrily replaced the book and stormed out of the house, violently slamming the door shut behind me.

As the anger and frustration bottled up inside me began to pour out, I smacked one foot down in front of the other. Gradually, I couldn't help but notice my surroundings, and as I did, I eventually gained some comfort seeing the sights I'd grown up with. In the midst of so much change, I was finally reassured. My pace slowed down as I focused outward on my surroundings.

At least my street looked exactly the same as I'd remembered it. I crossed the street to the flourish of bushes in the field I'd romped in with the boys as a child. Memories of Bahman and his friends came back to me, and I recalled playing hide-and-seek in those bushes. I had a flash of memory: Jalil once finding me in the thick bushes and smiling at me, touching my cheek before calling out to the others. I saw myself on countless occasions, sitting on the long, low branch of the old tree with the boys as they shared their stories. I remembered the day I came into my moon and my mother found me playing with the boys there. I breathed in deeply, as if I could smell the fresh fragrance of my memories and take in those simpler days.

I continued my walk, passing familiar houses. I came to the house owned by Ali Hussein. Ali Hussein was an aide to the shah and, though I never understood exactly what his job was, I understood it was important, and, that he socialized with His Majesty and Farah Diba. Ali Hussein's home behind me, I turned back towards home.

At some point, I stopped for a moment on a crack in the sidewalk, perched on a gap, a space between two worlds. The thought came to me that at that very moment in my life, I stood on such a space, and that my decision regarding David would propel me into one of two worlds, forever closing off my access to the other.

How was I to choose between them? How could I even know how to choose? I put one foot on either side of the crack, both worlds now joined at my heart. I was standing like that when I heard someone call my name.

"Layla *jon,* is that you?

"Come closer, let me see you!" It was Parveen Shirazi. As always, when outside her house, she was covered from head to toe in her black chador. Her warm voice melted my paralysis, and I hurried to meet her. "*Alhamdo le'llah,* praise Allah, it *is* you," she smiled her lovely smile.

"*Saalom,* Parveen Khanom." We exchanged the traditional greeting. She tightened her grip on the chador at her chin and we kissed one another on both cheeks.

"When did you return home, Layla?"

"I've been back for a while. I'm leaving to go back soon."

I saw a flicker of disappointment in her face. She took a gentle hold of my arm. "And I haven't seen you?"

"I came to your door. You weren't home," I said.

She scoffed. "I've been with my parents in Shiraz quite a bit this month. I came home this morning. Come inside with me."

"Oh, I can't impose on you now," I said. "You've just returned from your trip. I'll come later."

"Please honor me by coming now and joining me in a cup of tea," she persisted.

I politely declined. "You're very kind. I just had tea at home a moment ago. You're tired and you'll want to see to the children. Don't let me disturb you. How are the boys?"

"They're fine. They're still in Shiraz at their cousin's house. So, you see, you're not keeping me from them. *Beh jonneh man,* on my soul, Layla, you cannot refuse to have a cup of tea with me right now and tell me about your time in America."

Having completed the requisite rounds of the *tarroff* ritual expected of a genteel guest, I was happy to follow Parveen Khanom to her courtyard entry, where we again went through the ritual of *tarroff.*

"*Befarmayeed.* Please, Layla *jon,* enter," Parveen Khanom said.

"Oh, no, *bee zahmat,* please, after you, Parveen Khanom."

"You are kind. *Bee zahmat,* please, do me the honor of entering my home," she repeated.

"No, no, I must insist you enter first," I replied.

"On my soul, please, enter and indulge yourself as my honored guest," she insisted.

I graciously ceded victory to my hostess and entered first. "Thank you. You are too kind."

A similar exchange took place when her maid opened the front door and again, I relented, entering first, in deference to my status as a guest.

Once inside the house, Parveen Khanom took off her black chador, exposing a white top tucked under a dark blue skirt. I looked around. Nothing seemed to have changed since I'd last been there. As usual, Parveen Khanom called for her maid to serve us tea and escorted me down the steps that led into the gracious living room. We sat in the same chairs we'd taken on my last visit, just before I'd left for California. It felt good to be there again.

"How are you, Parveen Khanom? How are the boys and Parviz Khan?" The servant served us jasmine tea and hardened *halvah.*

"*Allah akbar,* God is great. The boys are fine. They are two handfuls, *Khodara shokr,* thank God, as two healthy boys should be. I thank Allah for the great blessing of having two male children. May God be with her, it is my mother who is in my thoughts."

Her gaze traveled to the black-and-white photo of her mother on a nearby table wearing a black chador identical to her daughter's. It was a small photograph, and her face was the size of a riyal, the small Persian coin. I could barely make out the unsmiling face in the photo.

I'd never met any of Parveen Shirazi's family. I knew she'd had five siblings. When one of her three sisters, the second eldest of the four children, had died while delivering her second baby, the widower had married her eldest sister. Parveen Khanom's two boys were now staying visiting that sister in Shiraz. Parveen Khanom was very proud of her two brothers, both *mullahs,* clergymen and teachers of religious law, and of her father, a most revered *ayatollah,* a Shiite Muslim religious teacher and clergyman of the highest rank in the city of Shiraz. I knew nothing at all of her mother.

"Is she ill?" I asked.

Parveen Khanom nodded. "She has a very bad heart. Her condition is only worsening. My dear father is so saddened, it has been almost impossible for him to perform his daily religious duties. Yet, though as an *ayatollah* he's certainly not required to lead services, he does. I don't know how it would be for him if, may God forbid it, something happens to my mother."

I surmised that her mother was as devoted to her husband as Parveen Khanom was to hers. "They have been together since my mother was a child," she continued. "Of course, God is great, and He will provide for us all." Parveen Khanom smiled then, erasing all traces of sadness and changing the subject. Seeing how I hungrily ate the delicious, sweet *halva,* she ordered her servant to bring me more, along with some *sohan,* the Persian circular pastry of fried flour doused in honey.

"We brought *gaz* back with us from Shiraz and I bought this *sohan* from Qom on the way home. We visited the holy mosque there." Qom was the holiest city in our country.

"I hope your mother's health will improve," I said.

"God willing," Parveen Khanom said. She thanked me then said, "Tell me about America. Do you like it?"

"Yes." I said.

"Thank God. I knew you would. What's it like? How do you spend your time?"

I tried not to blush at the question and thought to stall. "It's good.

People are friendly. It's very pretty where I live, and the university is huge and very beautiful. I study, and I see friends … girlfriends ... actually, my roommate's friends, mostly ..." I looked up and saw the five individually framed pages of the Quran on the wall in front of me. "I also read the Quran you gave me. Mostly, I study."

"And are you doing well at school?" She asked.

"Yes." I took another bite of the pastry. "This is delicious, thank you. It's better than the *sohan* here in Tehran." Then I asked, "How is your cherished husband? He's such a wonderful man." I was pleased with the way I'd moved the topic away from my activities in America.

"Yes, thank God, Allah has smiled on me. I am a lucky woman. I try, with Allah's grace, to be a deserving wife. Yet Parveez Khan," here she let out a short musical laugh, "– may God always bless him and hold him in His hand – has complaints."

Her comment surprised me no end. I couldn't imagine what her husband would possible have to complain about. It also raised alarms and made me uncomfortable. I remained silent. Under absolutely no circumstance would I encourage Parveen Khanom to confide her marital problems to me. I was not about to watch her transform from my pious neighbor into one of Shireen's friends, complaining about her husband. I wouldn't have been able to endure a change like that in this wonderful woman.

Parveen Khanom continued. "My dearest husband – may he live forever – has asked me to appear without my chador when we entertain his business associates here in our home. He says it would help business greatly if we appear to be more *westernized*." She emphasized the word whether by way of sarcasm or explanation.

I was stunned to hear that her husband would ask her to make such a huge concession. Though I wanted to remain uninvolved, I knew how humongous a thing it was to ask Parveen Khanom, the daughter of an ayatollah, to remove her chador in the presence of any man outside her immediate family. "What will you do?"

"May his protective shade above the heads of my esteemed children and me never lessen, Parviz Khan is my husband and I will do whatever he asks of me with honor. I am only his wife, and I will serve him, do as he asks. I have told him only one thing: he must understand that if I remove my chador in the presence of other men even once, *Allah akbar*, God is great, may Allah forgive me, it will stay off forever, and God is my witness, I will never wear it again. I cannot appear to be something I am not. I will either be westernized, or I will not be. I cannot be covered in the presence of only some men. Parveez Khan, my esteemed husband for whom I will forever do anything he asks – may I be sacrificed for him, may he live for another hundred years – can have two wives if he pleases, but he cannot have two wives in one. He must choose which way he wants me." She spoke with neither rancor nor anger, only conviction.

"What do *you* want?" I realized what a silly question I'd asked. She wanted to wear her chador. But would she say that?

"I want only what Allah wants and what my revered husband wants for me. When Parveez Khan decides, I will obey that decision. I will either continue as I am, or I will throw the chador away forever."

"Parveen Khanom, you've worn it your whole life." I said.

"Yes. May God protect my beloved mother and father and guard their dear souls forever, I only dread what discarding it would do to them."

We talked a while longer. I told her I'd heard the news that Iranian women would soon be given the vote.

"Yes, I have heard it is likely to happen," she replied. "God willing, if it is what Allah wants, it will happen."

When Iranian women are permitted to vote, how will a woman like Parveen Khanom decide her vote?

I rose to leave. We exchanged embraces. I returned home with the knowledge that there was the possibility that in my absence, a life-changing drama would soon unfold within my neighbor's home. Like the drama unfolding in my own life with David, I could only wonder how it would end.

Never in a million years would I have guessed that her decision would change the course of my life.

The day finally came when I was to leave Iran.

Ferri came by our house to kiss me goodbye. "My heart is pounding David's name," I confided in her. "I miss him so much, I can't stand it."

"I'll be thinking of you, *joonie.* Just remember, in California, away from everyone and everything here, you have the chance to see who you really are. Come to know yourself. Follow your heart and do what's best for *you,* Layla. I love you and my thoughts are with you. I know that whatever you decide to do will be right and I'll be rooting for you whatever you do. May God watch over you."

This time, when my parents drove me to the airport, no one sprinkled water after our departing car for good luck. At the airport, I showed the immigration officials my renewed exit visa evidence of my father's permission to leave Iran. When the time came to board the plane, Maman held me and kissed my head, whispering one last frantic warning in my ear. "If you must go back, God be with you. Be careful with yourself."

"I will," I said and turned to Babajon. "Take care of yourself and Maman *jon*. I love you both very much." Then I turned and walked away.

This time, as I boarded the plane, I knew David awaited me.

36
OH, DAVID!

August 31, 1960, Los Angeles

I barely slept on the long flight back to Los Angeles. I was too excited.

I reviewed my month at home. I thought of Shireen's life in that huge house of ice, and I wondered how long she would enjoy that loveless life. I thought of Maman. She seemed bitter, envious and small-minded. And there was Parveen Khanom, completely willing to leave her fate in her husband's hands, even if it meant discarding her chador and all it signified. Finally, I replayed my lunch with Ferri and wondered if the only thing that stopped me from sleeping with David was a lack of courage.

Most of my time in the air was spent anticipating a delicious reunion with David. Within hours, I would see him, hear his voice and be in his arms. And, though I had not found the moral grounding I'd hoped to find in Iran, I was certain I could hold onto my resolve and remain a virgin.

My plane landed at LAX late at night.

David was there to meet me, glowing with happiness. I ran into his arms and inhaled deeply, filling myself back up with his scent, realizing anew how hungry I'd been for him.

As we drove away from the airport, I asked how his trip to Israel had been. He answered with a nod of his head and a short, "Great." Then he asked about my trip, my family and friends, and my answers took us the rest of the way home.

I told him about my parents, without voicing the negative view I now had of my mother. I told him about Shireen and her new life, her new house, and her statue on the lawn, and the other girls who'd come to see me, but I said nothing of what they'd said about their lives and their husbands. I told him how good it was to see Ferri again, omitting my discovery that she'd been intimate with Hamid. I described the three-act hotel wedding and my run-in with Jalil, without mentioning his feelings for me.

David was quiet the whole time. I assumed it was because he found my stories interesting. He didn't stop for coffee before taking me home. I assumed that was because it was late and he was anxious to be alone with me.

My apartment looked odd, stripped of all my roommate's belongings, her bedroom empty. Jila and her parents had packed and left for Oklahoma while I'd been away. I would be leaving the apartment as well, moving into the International House in a matter of days.

As soon as he deposited the luggage in my bedroom, David surprised me. "Goodnight, Princess. Welcome home. Get some sleep. Tomorrow night I'm cooking a special dinner. I have something to tell you, something – something important. I'll pick you up at seven, okay?"

Before I could respond, he gave me a light kiss on my forehead… a quick kiss, hardly a kiss at all… and headed for door. I thought he was teasing me. *He couldn't be leaving already!* Then he was gone, the door shut behind him. I stood, struck by his strange behavior. He'd left in a hurry and hadn't even properly kissed me. And what did he want to tell me? There was no doubt, something was odd.

I fell on my bed and replayed the night. He'd looked happy to see me. But he hadn't talked about his trip to Israel at all, except to say it was 'great. He had let me do all the talking. Though he hadn't seen me for a month, he'd left without a single kiss.

Why? What happened? Could it be he didn't love me anymore? My body temperature suddenly soared, and I sprang up from my bed in the midst of a panic attack.

I tried to calm myself. Pacing, I told myself I was being silly and insecure. Of course, nothing had changed. David loved me. He was there waiting for me at the airport and he was happy to see me. He hadn't talked about his trip because I had been talking my silly head off the entire time. And he assumed that I was just tired and wanted to sleep, so he left. With that, I changed for bed and, deciding I would get a good night's sleep and unpack the next day, I climbed in between the sheets.

My mind immediately resumed its nagging.

What could possibly be so important that he had to tell me over a dinner? That's when my insecurity intensified, this time, conquering my exhaustion and leaving my imagination to roam freely, and I imagined the worst.

He'd met me at the airport only because he had no choice! I was expecting him. He must have met lots of pretty girls on his trip, Israeli girls, Jewish girls.

That's it! He's met someone! After a month in Israel, he now sees me as a Muslim girl who doesn't belong in his life. Oh, my God! No wonder Israel was great. He's met a Jewish girl … a girl his mother would approve of who doesn't obsess about remaining a virgin. *Khodaya!*

I felt like I'd been thrown out of an airplane. I shot out of bed, my stomach falling, my heart, beating wildly, my temperature, soaring. My mind flooded with images of David holding someone who wasn't me, kissing and caressing a faceless girl. The taste of bile filled my mouth.

I saw David running his hand up and down a thigh that wasn't mine. I ran into the bathroom and slumped down onto the cold tiles of the bathroom floor, my head over the toilet, my heart plummeting into my guts.

While I was in Tehran, figuring out how to keep him away from intercourse, he was in Israel, making love to someone else. *Oh my God, I've lost David!* He's going to tell me it's over tomorrow night. He's going to cook me dinner then break up with me in some wonderful Jewish way, trying hard not to hurt me. I sobbed into the empty room, helpless, as waves of self-pity crashed down on me. *"Oh David! Oh God!"*

I couldn't rid my stomach of the rising bile. Then my blood pressure suddenly dropped. I was cold, and weak, and felt faint. I needed fresh air. I pulled myself up with every ounce of energy I had and went to my balcony. Neither the darkness nor the night air obliterated thoughts of David leaving me for another girl. Visions of him, happy with this phantom girl clung to me, and I recoiled, infuriated.

My hand went to my aching heart. He can't love her. *How could he?* I wouldn't let him! There's no way I could let him go. Anger pumped my blood pressure back up. I could feel the surge of energy. I went inside and began furiously throwing clothes out of my luggage. *I won't give you up, David. I love you too much. Oh, no! You'll see, it's me you love. I'll change your mind. I'll make you love me again. You'll break up with her, not me.*

By the time I'd emptied my luggage, clothes strewn all over the room, I came to the naked realization that David had tired of arguing with me, tired of trying to wear down my resistance and my insistence on remaining a virgin for marriage. He had apparently decided I was longer worth the battle or the abstinence. He had fallen for another girl. If I expected my relationship with David to resume, I would have to compete with the faceless girl.

It was crystal clear: the time had come for me to decide whether I would sleep with David or lose him. And so, I sat down amid the contents of my baggage, to confront the most difficult question of my life.

In the end, it had come to this.

My fear of losing David held me hostage through the night.

When I thought of sleeping with him, my heart tried to take over my whole being, beating wildly from anxiety, guilt, and fear. It went against everything I'd been taught. It also beat with anticipation and yearning. I loved David and longed to be locked in his arms without limits imposed on our intimacy. If I didn't sleep with him, I'd lose him … tomorrow night. *How had I arrived at such an impossible dilemma?*

The moon began to yield to the light of the rising sun, and still I meditated in my room. I recalled my mother's words of warning and remembered the bitterness I felt when Adam had betrayed my trust, how I felt he'd proven my mother to be right.

I remembered my misgivings when I read Naneh Joon's letter on my birthday after my horrible sexual encunter with Anthony. I connected to my family and to my childhood, my culture and my Iranian roots with incredible love and attachment. David didn't share any of these. They took me down a path that led away from him.

Against these I put my love for David.

I recalled the words my father had used the day he told me I would be deciding my future. They rang out. "Be true to your heart," he'd said. "Make sure you are not sorry for what you haven't done." *Oh Babajon, if you only knew what is in my heart!*

His words were so much like Ferri's. "Go out into the world and find yourself. Do what's best for Layla." How ironic that the two people I love the most in Tehran said the same thing. Still, their words didn't help me decide what I should do.

In David's arms, I felt completely safe and totally content. But I wouldn't marry David. My husband would be an Iranian man who would expect a virgin bride. I tried to imagine something more of the man who would be my husband; anything. But my mind was a blank. *Could he possibly be as wonderful as David? Would I love him as much?*

A vision of Shireen flashed in my mind, laden down with jewels. "Love? Who said anything about love?" Even my angel had separated love from sex, and both from marriage. My heart started to pound again. I felt light-headed, dizzy. I was coming close to uncovering the truth I'd always known about myself.

I wouldn't be with David forever. Yet, I was not willing to lose him a minute before I had to. *Beh darrack!* Everything be damned! I will sleep with David! If virginity is the greatest gift I can give my beloved, then truly, I would give it to David whom I loved with all my heart. I would sleep with him and he would be mine for as long as I could possibly have him.

I'd tell my future husband I rode a lot of horses in America.

My decision made, I fell into a deep sleep and awoke with a start. I had a lot to do.

37

SEDUCTION

I awoke and began to prepare myself for David.

I followed the rituals performed by brides of my heritage as best as I could. I bathed and scrubbed my skin, exfoliating until my entire body was as pink as a baby's, then removed all my body hair and washed my hair with perfumed shampoo and, when it dried, I brushed it till it shone. I rubbed perfumed oils assiduously all over myself until my skin became as smooth as ivory and as lustrous as the finest silk. I tweezed my eyebrows for the first time. I groomed my nails and feet, rubbing them first with pumice then with oils until they, too, were soft and pink.

I turned my attention to my wardrobe. Eyeing my chosen dress, I was aware of the irony. Rather than selecting something white and virginal, I reached for my most seductive dress, the short black crepe dress Maman had set for my birthday that clung to the curves of my changed body like cooked rice clung to the bottom of the pot. I wore nothing underneath. I reached in my drawer for the sheer gold shawl Naneh Joon had sent me, pushing aside thoughts of the letter she'd sent along with it.

With another girl waiting in the wings for the man I loved, I would leave nothing to chance. I had to show David that I was his, his without reservation to take and to have, completely.

The look on David's face when I opened the front door was gratifying.

"Princess, you look sensational!" I took his hand and led him inside toward my bedroom. He followed the sensual scent of my fragrant oils. "Where are we going? I thought we'd leave."

"I have something to show you," I said.

At the threshold to my bedroom, David's eyes widened. My room was aglow in the soft light of dozens of candles I'd placed around the room. The air was alive with the sweet, heady scent of fresh gardenias. Persian music played so softly, it almost wasn't there, a man and a woman singing to one another. Even without understanding their words, the message of love's yearning was clear. David reached for my lips. I turned away. He spoke, his throat thick. "Princess, this is amazing. But we should leave-"

I murmured, "We will." I led him to my bed and he sat down. I stood between his legs and kissed him so that he had to lay back, and when my lips left his mouth, it was only to cast a line of kisses to his ear and his closed eyelids. I could feel his hot breath. Maintaining the initiative, I reached a hand down under his belt and began to feel my way around his groin.

"Layla, I have something to tell you."

"Not now, David," I whispered.

"Layla, I want to-"

I pressed a finger against his lips. "Sshh. It can wait." I undressed him, undoing his belt, then unbuttoning his shirt and easing him out of it before returning to his pants, drawing them down slowly, deliciously, running my fingers on his skin and landing kisses everywhere. He succumbed to my hands and gentle kisses moving along his bare skin. Tonight, nothing and no one would stop us from finally consummating our love.

When he reached for my face and lips once more, I stood and began to strip in the flickering candlelight. I looked directly into his eyes as he watched me peel my dress slowly off my shoulders. He gasped when it fell to the floor. I removed the pins that held my long hair up and shook my lightly scented hair loose. Then I lay beside him, my head resting against his strong arm, feeling the warmth of his body and inhaling his masculinity. I was fully content and completely serene, at the same time wholly alive, aware and excited. I'd made the right decision. Now I would reap the glory of that choice.

David held me and smelled my hair, smelled my neck, stroked me, then strangely, groaned as if in anguish. I had barely brushed my lips against his cheek before he found my lips. We kissed forever, our lips fitting together in infinite ways, our bare bodies pressed against one another. I braced myself above him, my breasts brushing against his chest. "I want you, David. Take me."

"Layla don't tease me. Please."

"I want you to take me. Please." I didn't wait for him then. I guided what I wanted of him to me, unfolded myself and led him inside me. The immediate shock of sensation was immense. My innermost muscles went into spasms, flooding us both with the juices of my pleasure.

David's instincts took over from there. He gently turned me on my side and then on my back so that we'd exchanged places. Moving his pelvis away from me, he put his chest close to mine and looked down at me. "Layla, are you sure you want to do this? I can stop now." At the open door of desire, David's love for me was so genuine, he would have stopped, even then.

In answer, I enveloped him into my arms and pressed his pelvis down toward mine. "I love you, David."

He moved slowly at first, moving ever so gently, every millimeter of movement, an ocean of sexual pleasure unlike anything I had ever dreamed I would experience. I wrapped myself around him as he unwrapped layers of wonder in a hundred ways. I felt my body responding to him and to his yearning: insatiable, unstoppable, incredible. The gentle movements led to a pinch, became more frantic, then again mellowed as together, we discovered a rainbow of sensuality.

I was lost somewhere within David's movements – or had *I*

moved? I was lost within his breath at my ear – or was that my own breath? I heard his cries of joy – or was it my voice I heard?

I was unaware of myself moving, speaking, or crying out, so enmeshed in bliss was I, I was not fully conscious. The circle of our sensuality brought response to response with no distinction between giving and receiving joy.

We went on and on like that for hours, bonded together like sunlight and air, bathing in the realm of pure sexual pleasure. Our love making, like a piece of great music, passed through various tempos. David rang out my name or whispered, "I love you," for the umpteenth time, and each time, I was carried into a new dimension. We knew neither time nor space, locked together, through that wondrous night and finally spent, we fell asleep as one.

38
SHIPS

When I awoke the next morning, I had a smile on my face. I'd dared to answer my heart and I had David lying beside me to show for it.

This man I love, this is what he looks like in the morning light after making love; this is what he smells like.

Curious, I got out of bed and pulled back the light blanket. There was no more than a faint pinkness on the sheet, barely visible. *This is what all the fuss was about?*

David awoke to my laughter. "Come here, Princess. I want to breathe you in and feel your velvet skin." He took me to him and our bodies joined once again. "Last night, I knew I was born to make love to you, Princess," he said.

I teased him. "You were supposed to feed me dinner and you didn't. You'll have to stop this at some point, so we can eat. I'm so hungry I could eat a house."

"You mean horse. You're so hungry you could eat a horse. Me too. Let's go eat."

Seated at a table at Ships, I thought David seemed distracted.

I told myself I was imagining things. There was absolutely no question in my mind that he loved me. *But what had he wanted to tell me?* I felt secure enough now to ask. After we ordered, I did.

David reached across the table for my hand. "I've been wanting to tell you," he said. The look that came over his face scared me. It was that distracted look, the look I thought last night would forever obliterate; it was back. I tensed up, waiting. The waiter came back, served us coffee and gave us bread David set into the toaster at our table. He was waiting for our waiter to leave before he continued. I prayed he'd never go.

"Layla, it's about Israel." My insides reacted hysterically. *Israel!* He had met another girl on his trip after all. I waited. I knew that whatever he said next was my enemy and I didn't want to hear it. I swallowed hard. "It's an amazing place, Layla. What's happening there is unbelievable."

"Is it?" My breathing had become shallow as if I was afraid to disrupt the air between us.

"Yes. The people live in *kibbutzim* – collective farms or group homes where everyone lives and works together. It's a small country, smaller than Southern California, and it must defend itself from the many powerful countries that surround it. All young Israelis go to the army, male and female."

As I listened, I tried to guess where this was leading. I wondered if this girl lived on one of those. No doubt she was in the army. I took my hand away from his. "I know all that. Do you think we don't learn about Israel in Iran?"

David was becoming increasingly excited. "Bear with me," he said. "Remember *Exodus?* Well, that same spirit is still everywhere. These kids don't *have* to go into the army, they *want* to go. That's the thing that's so hard to believe unless you've been there, seen it, and heard it yourself. They want to spend two or more years defending their country. Think about that."

The toast popped. A tentative relief was making its way through me, and I began to relax in the thought that David, extremely impressed by Israel and its people, had simply wanted to share his perceptions with me. Wherever David was going with this would not be that serious after all. The waiter brought our orders, and we began to eat hungrily.

"Would you willingly spend your life from ages eighteen to twenty in the army?" he asked. I shook my head. "Would any of your friends in Iran? Or your friends in the U.S.?"

"I hope not," I answered. "I wouldn't be willing to have anyone I love do that. I'd worry about them all the time. Why do they?"

"Because, Princess, the Israelis want to be a part of building their country. Israel was born in 1948. It's barely a teenager; it's younger than you are! There's even a special name for a person born there after Israel became a state; they're called *sabras*. Israelis build a road or a house or a vegetable garden and they feel they're building a country. It's a fantastic thing, and it's everywhere you look."

He was obviously extremely excited about the place. He took another forkful of his omelet before going on. I could smell the mix of vegetables and turkey sausage.

"Of course, it's young, it's poor and so vulnerable to attack, it's busy just trying to survive." He stopped abruptly then, put his fork down onto his plate and looked at me meaningfully. My dread returned. "They need people there, Layla. They need people on the *kibbutzim*. Young, healthy people who'll make Israel their home and help build the country. And they need doctors desperately." I saw the bomb falling, but it was too late to take shelter. "I'm going back to Israel to stay, Layla." I sat there numb. "That's what I wanted to tell you last night. Before we got … sidetracked."

I felt sick. David was leaving me. I struggled to keep a clear head. *Do not cry. Do not lose your mind. Stay calm.* My temples throbbed, and it felt like my skull trembled. I felt the blood drain from my body. I could hardly speak. I put my fork down and sat back."Israel? When?" I felt a sudden wave of anger wash over me realizing he knew he was going to Israel last night.

"Very soon. I'm ready to go. I've been waiting for you to come back."

I was destroyed. I looked up at him, my eyes overflowing with tears. I'd given him my virginity because I'd thought he loved another girl and lost him anyway – to another country. "Why? To say goodbye?" I managed to say as the first hot tears fell.

He laughed and shook his head. He held my hand tighter. "No, Princess. I want you to come with me. Marry me. Come to Israel with me, as my wife. You know how much I love you. You're everything to me. Marry me, Princess. We'll go together."

I was dumbstruck. My head was spinning. Too much was happening, too fast. David did love me! He'd just asked me to marry him! My heart soared. Then, before it beat again, it crashed. He was leaving. Our relationship was over and dead. His marriage proposal sealed the death certificate of our life together.

He mistook my tears as a sign of happiness and went on, excitedly. "We'll live on a *kibbutz* called Na'an near the Lebanese and Syrian borders."

Then I was sobbing, and he jumped out of his chair, came around the table to sit next to me and wiped my tears with his hand. My crying didn't stop. He held me. "What's the matter? I'm asking you to marry me, Princess." I could only pull away and shake my head. Tears fell onto my lap. "You can't say no. You love me. That's obvious. Even if I didn't know that before last night, I know it today. You can go to school in Israel. They're building universities, the likes of which you've never seen. Say yes, and we'll leave as soon as you're ready."

I cried into my hands. "I can't marry you, David. Don't go." I took his hand and held it in mine. "Oh, please, please don't go."

"Why can't you?" he asked deadpan.

I looked at him as if he'd just asked a very, very stupid question. "Why?" I laughed the, the hollow laugh of a ghoul. "Why? You're asking me why I can't marry you and go live with you in Israel?" He was a blur through my tears. "Because I'm Iranian and you're not? Because we're from two different worlds, two different ends of the earth? David, what are you saying?"

David took a napkin off the table and wiped my tears. "Layla, what difference does any of that make? We're in love," my love said.

"It makes all the difference in the world! I can't call my parents and say, 'Hi, Babajon, hi, Maman. I'm calling to say I'm in love with an American named David. You've never met him. You see, I gave him my virginity last night and we're getting married because I love him. Oh, did I tell you he's Jewish? And by the way, I'm not going to be coming home. I won't be finishing UCLA either – which was why I came here in the first place. No, you see, David has decided that we will live in Israel on a lovely *kibbutz* in poverty, under the constant threat of war, because, you must understand, they need doctors like my Jewish David.'"

"They sent you to America, why not to Israel with your husband?" he asked.

I could only stare at him with burning eyes. Finally, I said, "They've sent me to America to go to school, then return home to marry a Persian man. Not to marry and leave them forever. Would you come and live with me in Iran?"

David's eyebrows joined. "I can't, Layla. They need me in Israel."

I nodded miserably. "I know you can't. That's the point. You couldn't even if you didn't go to Israel. I'm just telling you how impossible it all is. And what about *your* parents? They'd never let you marry a Muslim Iranian girl like me."

David took my hands in his and kissed them. "Layla, I hope my parents will be happy to welcome you into the family. If not, I'll marry you anyway, and I wouldn't care if I never see them again. They won't stop me from having you beside me for the rest of my life."

"Don't David!" I cried out, pulling my hands away. "Please, please don't do this. Stay! Maybe your parents are more tolerant than mine, I don't know, and you don't know. I won't let you take that chance. I won't let you break their hearts. They're your parents and they love you. You love them. I won't stand between you."

David put his head in his hands and looked as distraught as I felt. "My relationship with my parents is not your concern," he said gently. "If they can't accept my decision to marry you, I'd rather break their hearts than have mine broken without you." After a moment of silence between us, he said, "Princess, if you won't marry me, why did you sleep with me? Was that all just talk when you said you were saving all that for your husband?"

I shook my head. "I love you, David, and I thought … I thought …" I turned away then, not able to look him in the face. "I wanted to,

David. And I thought you wanted me to." I was totally miserable, and ashamed to boot. I couldn't tell him the truth; the truth was that I'd been wrong about him. A new panic hit. "You're not joining the army, are you? It's not even your country. David, you might die!"

He shrugged. "I'm hoping they'll take me into the medical corps," he said. "They need doctors desperately."

"I need you more." I said.

"And I need you, Princess. Marry me! Marry me and come with me." He stretched his hand out to me. I turned away from him. He leaned forward. "Please understand. I became a doctor to help people in need, and I am needed there. There are plenty of doctors here, but not in Israel. They need doctors badly, Layla, desperately." I kept silent. Sitting there, waving his arms as he spoke, that look of passion on his face, he looked irresistible even through my desolation. "I went to Israel to learn about my heritage and found my future there." I didn't respond. He tried again. "Layla, please! Come with me."

"I can't, David. Life isn't as easy as that. I can't just get up and marry you, leave everything, *my* heritage and who *I* am, my family, my studies, marry you and go off to Israel. There are people around us who love us. We have obligations to them."

"What about me? You're willing to let me go? What about obligations to yourself and to us?"

I leaned towards him and lay my hands on his. The pain in my heart took over my whole being. "You're the one going, not me. You're taking my love with you." When I kissed his forehead tenderly, David didn't wipe away the tears I'd left there.

His bags packed, David postponed his departure, begging me to go with him, hoping I'd change my mind. It was hopeless.

When his calls stopped, I understood. He was gone

39
THE END OF A FAIRYTALE

My dream had been too sweet.

David was gone, gone without a trace. In his absence, I replayed my recollections of him and treasured my memories of our time together, every moment with him, culminating in that single night we spent together.

I had absorbed those seconds of pleasure into my very being, and now, with him gone, I lived to relive them. I dwelled in the memory of that bliss. Every second we'd been joined, those were the seconds that made up my life. The rest was empty.

Never once did I regret having given myself to him. The truth was, I'd always known our relationship would end. I'd just never imagined how terribly I would miss him when it did.

I quietly moved my things into the International House and left the next day for Oklahoma to attend Jila's wedding at their apartment.

The bride was radiant with happiness. Majid's family had travelled from Iran to be there, and it was heartwarming to see how well they treated my cousin and her parents. My aunt and uncle were in an excellent mood. Ammeh Elahe's affection for me was comforting. For once, I found her constant conversation to be a welcome distraction. Majid's parents made a fuss over me. I only wished Maman could hear how profusely they thanked me for introducing their son to Jila.

Theirs was an abbreviated Muslim wedding ceremony. When I approached the seated bride to present her with the gold bracelets my father had sent as a wedding gift, she hugged me tightly. "Layla, I pray you find this same happiness."

When we were alone for a moment, she asked me about David. I didn't tell her I'd slept with him, or that he had asked me to marry him and that I had refused, broken-hearted. I didn't want her pity. I only told her that he'd decided to live in Israel. Her look lingered on me for a moment then looked down. She said nothing.

I returned to UCLA and my new loneliness, everyone I'd cared for gone. Everything reminded me of David. I tried to be realistic and face facts. I'd lost both my virginity and my heart to him; I resolved not to lose my mind as well. I needed distractions and was glad that fall classes were starting. I poured myself into my studies.

During the day, I functioned as required. I was happy Jila's friends still included me in their circle.

"Oh, I'm not seeing David anymore," I said to them as nonchalantly as I could. "I'm tired of men."

"I know *exactly* what you mean," the girls said. "They're hardly worth it."

I was determined not to share my depression or repeat the sulking I'd done when Adam had kissed me and Jila had accused me of being obnoxious. I went to the movies and out shopping and sat drinking coffee with the girls with a smile on my face. And that was that.

Alone in my room at the I-House, I cried. I'd lost so much. I missed my life with Jila in our apartment. I missed going to Ammeh Elahe's house and the occasional home-cooked Persian meal. I missed Adam's friendship even more now that I had no one around me I truly cared for. I had thought that sleeping with David would give me more time with him, but I'd lost him anyway. There was a huge gaping hole in both my life and my heart where David had been ... and so I cried.

Strangely, I missed David and even Jila and Adam, more than I had ever missed my family and friends in Iran ... and so I cried. When I wasn't crying, I was praying for David's safety. And life went on.

I watched the first presidential debate between Richard Nixon and John F. Kennedy in the lounge downstairs at the I-House, the first presidential debate ever televised.

When the camera met Kennedy's face, his resemblance to David was obvious. I'd always thought David resembled Paul Newman, and now I saw that bits of his face resembled the young Democratic presidential hopeful as well.

I was glued to the set. There were more debates in October, and during each, I sat pinned to the sofa in the television room at the I-House. I'm sure I wasn't the only one in the roomful of foreign students fascinated by the mechanism of the American political system that allowed me and another seventy million viewers to watch as these two men spoke directly to the voters, sharing their vision of the future for their country and their ideas on how to make that vision a reality.

Then October neared its end. The girls discussed costumes for the upcoming Halloween party Jessica was having at her parents' house.

"Chuck and I are going as Romeo and Juliet," Sheri said, bringing to mind how surprised I had been to discover David knew that the story of Romeo and Juliet had been taken from the Persian story of Laylee and Majnoon. *Would everything always remind me of him?* "We're studying it in History of Theater," she continued. "You know why Romeo and Juliet is considered classic tragedy?"

"Duh, cause they both die?" Jessica asked, trying to sound stupid.

"No, smarty, that's not why. You can have people die and still have a comedy, make people laugh. It's a tragedy because there's no hope. Though Romeo and Juliet are in deeply in love, they can't marry. No hope."

No hope. That was as good a definition of tragedy as I'd ever heard. My abysmal wound bore witness.

Jessica's question brought me back. "Y'all have Halloween in Iran, Layla?"

"No, not really. But around the time of our New Year, in March, men and women go from house to house banging a cup with a spoon. They wear a *chador* that totally covers them. And the men speak in girlie voices."

"Men wear the *chadors*, too?"

"Yes. They try to show only one eye from beneath their *chador* and act like women, but you can usually see their mustaches and beards peeking out."

"How funny." Sheri said. "So, is that what you're going to wear to the costume party? A *chador* and mustache?"

I hadn't given it a thought. Though the furthest thing from my mind was dressing up and going to a party, the idea of becoming someone else sounded inviting.

I shrugged. "Either that or Scheherazad" I said.

"Who's that?" the girls asked.

"Never mind," I said. "If no one knows who she was, it doesn't make sense to go as her, does it?"

"Who was she? Tell us." Sheri said.

I obliged them. "Scheherazad was a Persian woman who saved her life a long time ago by telling the shah a different story every night." Intrigued, the girls wanted to know more.

"The Persian king – Shahryar – learned that his wife was unfaithful to him with one of her slaves. He killed her and all her slaves. Then he went on a trip with his brother, who was also a king, and his wife had also been unfaithful. On their way they came across a *jen*–"

"Y'all mean a genie?" Jessica asked.

I didn't know what a genie was. "Something very bad."

"Oh," Jessica said. "Genies are good; they grant your wishes."

"Go on with your story," Sheri said.

I continued. "The *jen* was asleep in the arms of a beautiful woman he had kidnapped. The two brother-kings were afraid that if the *jen* saw them, he'd kill them, so they climbed a tree. While the *jen* slept, the woman he'd kidnapped ordered them to come down off the tree and make love to her. They refused, knowing that if they did, the *jen* would surely kill them. The woman, the most beautiful either of them had ever seen, convinced them that if they didn't do as she ordered, she would immediately wake the *jen* who would kill them on the spot. So, they came down the tree and had turns making love to her,"

"And the *jen* killed them?" Jessica asked.

I shook my head. "He slept soundly, snoring through the entire thing. When they finished, she ordered them to run away as fast as they could because the *jen* was about to wake up. One of the kings asked how she could dare to be so bold. The woman laughed and told them that the *jen* thought he was the only one to make love to her but, as he slept, she had been made love to by no less than eight hundred forty-eight men." The girls gasped. "That convinced the kings that all women are untrue and can't be changed, that it's in their nature to be that unfaithful and untrustworthy."

"Like a leopard's spots," Sheri offered.

"Or a zebra's stripes," Jessica chimed in, "or a tiger's stripes."

"Okay, shush up and let her finish," Sheri said. "Go on, Layla."

"When Shahryar, the older shah, arrived back at the palace, he ordered his *vizier* – that's like a Minister or Secretary of something – to bring him a virgin every night. The king would sleep with each virgin and then, believing she would not be true to him, he had her killed in the morning."

"Eww, how awful!" Jessica said.

"No one did anything to stop him?" Sheri asked. I said no one had. "They must have known what he was doing up there in the palace."

"He did it for many years," I said.

The girls looked at one another, their mouths agape. Sheri gasped. "Years?" she asked.

"That's a lot of women," Sheri said.

"That's a lot of virgins," Jessica countered. "I'd sleep with someone so fast you wouldn'tbelieve it, lose my virginity at eight or nine so that crazy king would have no interest in me."

"So, what happened with Shehzad?" Sheri asked, nudging Jessica to stop talking.

"Sheherazad," I corrected her. "At last, he had killed every virgin in the country except for Scheherazade and Doniazad, the vizier's own two daughters."

The girls had their eyes glued on me. "Oh, geez, every virgin!" Jessica was duly horrified.

"What did the two poor girls do?" asked Sheri. "Run for their lives?"

I sighed and continued, as if I cared. "No, they knew that the king loved stories. They came up with a plan. Their father presented Scheherazade to the king. That evening, before bed, Scheherazade asked the shah to allow her to see her sister one last time. He could hardly refuse, so he allowed it. Doniazad arrived and asked Scheherazad to tell her a story. Scheherazad asked the shah's permission. "Why not?' he said. "Sure. Go ahead. Tell me a story." She did. And he loved it. It was a very long story and lasted all through the night. When morning came, she still hadn't finished it. The shah's men came to kill Scheherazad, but he told them to wait. He wanted her to first finish her story. But she never finished it. The story just went on and on, night after night, as she tied one story to another and her life continued."

"What a smart girl." Sheri said.

"Great plan!" Jessica smiled.

"What if he hadn't liked the story?" Sheri asked.

"Ah, but he did. He was entranced by what he heard. In fact, Scheherazad continued her story for a thousand nights."

"That long? She must have been an amazing storyteller!" Sheri said.

"What happened then?" Jessica asked.

"The king married her." I said.

The girls were duly impressed. "Then again," said a thoughtful Sheri, "What else could he do? I mean there was no TV. He didn't even have a radio and all the other virgins were dead."

"There was still her sister," Jessica reminded her. "I'll bet she was glad their plan worked."

"What kind of a story could she have made up to last a thousand nights?" Sheri wondered.

"She told him the stories of Ali Baba, and Sinbad and Aladdin –"

Jessica interrupted me, crying out. "I know those stories!"

"I know them too!" Sheri said. "You're talking about the Arabian Nights! Scheherazad told king what's-his-name stories from Tales of the 1,001 Nights for three years!"

"I love Scheherazad," Jessica said. "I wish I had met her. She was neat. Smart. And the woman could obviously tell a great story. Too bad she's not teaching story structure at UCLA."

They wanted to know how I planned to dress as Scheherazad. I shrugged. "I thought I'd dress the way Americans would picture her to have dressed, you know, my hair down, a coin belt and bracelets, lots of scarves and things, like a belly dancer."

"That would be neat." Sheri said.

"I agree," Jessica said.

"It's unanimous then, motion carried," Sheri said.

The Halloween party that Sunday night was little more than a chore for me, and I was glad when it was over. I came home and lay in bed thinking, as usual, about David, missing him, wondering where he was and what he was doing, and whether or not he was thinking of me. The I-House had a switchboard, so he couldn't reach me through my old telephone number, but I had all my mail forwarded to the I-House. David hadn't once written to me since he'd left for Israel. I supposed he felt that there was no point in contacting me. I guessed he was trying to spare us both the pain, hoping we could both get on with our lives. I wondered how he was getting on with his.

Monday morning, with costumes off, reality reared its head.

I awoke with slight discomfort in my stomach. Hungry, I opted against the cafeteria and went down to the coffee shop to have some hot tea and toast before classes. Upon entering, the smell of food made me feel nauseated and I barely made it to the ladies' room before I vomited. I sought out fresh air and felt better.

My first class that day was lab. As I entered the room, my stomach turned over from the smell and I ran to the ladies' room. *Stomach flu!*

I missed lab and went to the student medical center for a prescription. I entered, announced myself and took a seat. I was filled with powerful nostalgia. I brushed away the tears that came to my eyes as I remembered the first time I'd been there with Jila, so sick, never dreaming I was about to meet the love of my life. David had cured my strep throat and ended up breaking my heart.

Trying not to think of him, I picked up the first magazine I saw and blindly turned the pages until I heard my name called. "Layla Saleh? Follow me please." I followed the red-haired woman down the hall and past the room I'd been in twice with David. My heart bled. "Wait in here," she said, guiding me into an examination room. "The doctor will be right in."

A moment later, a young woman knocked and entered. She took my temperature and blood pressure, smiled and left, closing the door behind her. I waited, occupying my mind by counting the small rectangular tiles on the floor. I lost count twice and was up to fifty-six on my third try when the door opened and a tall, slender doctor came in, older that Babajon, likely in his fifties. He removed his thick glasses, put them in the pocket of his white jacket and smiled. He had small, deep set eyes. He introduced himself as Dr. Ribcot.

"Good morning, Layla. Now, what seems to be the trouble?"

"Hello, doctor. I have the stomach flu. I need a prescription for something please."

"Stomach flu," he repeated. "Okay. What are your symptoms?" he asked. I described my bouts of nausea and my vomiting. "I see. Any other symptoms?" He checked the file he was holding. "You have no fever and your blood pressure is fine. Do you have a headache? Dizziness? Fatigue? Congestion?"

"No, nothing except some fatigue."

"I see." Dr. Ribcot closed my file. I noticed the wedding band on his hand and idly wondered if he had children. I'd have guessed he was the sort of father who took an interest in his children's lives. He looked at me and frowned, then asked, "I see you're eighteen. Tell me, did your boyfriend bring you here?" he asked.

What a peculiar question. "No. I don't have a boyfriend." It was none of his business anyway.

Dr. Ribcot opened my file again and flipped over to another page. "It says here you were seen here last year for strep throat and laryngitis. You were seen by Dr. Kline."

I hoped the doctor's eyes were still on my file as I felt myself blush and said, "Yes."

"Well, Dr. Kline is no longer here." I nodded. Dr. Ribcot closed my file then and took off his glasses and rubbed his forehead. "Before I can prescribe anything, I'll need to take a blood test and a urine test."

"Tests?" I was surprised. Though I was okay with the idea of a blood test, I didn't think a urine test was needed to diagnose stomach flu. "Do you there might be something else wrong with me, doctor? Could it be something serious?"

Dr. Ribcot rubbed the bridge of his nose. "I doubt that," he said, looking at me. "Nonetheless, unfortunately, I can't treat you or give you any medicine for your nausea until we rule out certain things. It's standard practice in a case like this." There was a pause. He re-opened my file then, put his glasses back on and studied it. "Now, it says here you last menstruated in mid-August?"

True, he was a doctor. Still, I felt uncomfortable talking about my moon to a man I didn't know. I was embarrassed. "I've always been irregular. And I travelled. I went home during the summer, so that's why."

"I see. So that's been, let's see now – just over two months now, is that right?" I nodded. He nodded in turn. "Tell me Layla, are you sexually active?"

What a question! "No, Doctor, I'm not." The question made me realize he thought I may have been pregnant, which was ridiculous. I'd given him my answers and wanted no more prying questions. In fact, I'd been feeling fine since my last episode, almost two hours ago, and was now pretty sure it had all been due to something I'd eaten at the Halloween gathering last night. I was fine and just wanted to leave.

"When will I have the results back?" The doctor was holding my file, looking lost in thought. "Dr. Ribcot?"

"Hmm? Oh, yes, we'll let you know as soon as we're certain. It shouldn't take too long. I'll rush it." He put my file in the pocket by the door and offered me his hand. "Good to meet you, Layla. Take care of yourself. Try to eat. I'll be talking with you again soon. Meanwhile, the nurse will be here to draw some blood and help you with the other things we need."

"Thank you, Doctor."

I left blood and urine behind with the same young woman who'd taken my temperature and blood pressure, then walked back to the International House. The thought that the doctor had believed pregnancy was even a remote possibility made my knees shake. After just one night with David, it was impossible, I knew, yet the more I thought about it, the more frightened I became. I stopped thinking about it.

There was a crowd in the lobby of the I-House huddled around the television. I was curious to know what they were watching, but I was taken by a sudden retching and headed for the nearest ladies' room. I heaved, then went to my room and lay down on my bed, feeling weak, hungry, and scared.

I replayed my meeting with the doctor, his questions about my sexuality tugging at me, giving way to feelings of guilt and self-reproach. The thought of using protection that night with David had never even occurred to me. The sorry truth was that, if I had thought of it, I wouldn't have known what to do. I'd simply been intent on seducing David, and he certainly hadn't come prepared. And though he did try to stop at every critical point, I didn't allow it. I'd stayed in total control and insisted that everything be done my way from beginning to end ... and my way had not included protection.

Darkness came, and I fell into a nightmare. I dreamed I was lost in a desert on a starless night, merciless winds blowing dry dust into my eyes. Finding shelter in a cave, I was grateful that I'd been saved from a likely death in the desert. The belly of the cave was cold and even darker than it had been outside. I reached out for the wall to guide me through the cave and felt a sharp sting and then a burning sensation as something scurried across my hand. A scorpion! I awoke, shivering. The rest of the night passed with little sleep.

The next morning, I awoke with a huge headache and an appetite to match. I needed sustenance. I hurried to the coffee shop downstairs, grabbed two plain doughnuts and a cup of tea, and ate them outside in the fresh air away from the odor of food. I couldn't get the food down fast enough. When I was done eating, I felt better. My headache was gone, and I felt like myself again.

Incredibly relieved that I was able to keep the food down, I was convinced I was not pregnant. Then as I entered my first class, I was again overwhelmed by the odor in the lab and had to rush to the ladies' room where I every bit of the doughnuts and tea found their way into the toilet.

Far too upset to go back to class, I returned to the I-House. I couldn't tolerate the suspense; I had to know that I had the stomach flu and not the beginnings of a new life within me. I would call Dr. Ribcot's office if I hadn't heard from him by one o'clock that afternoon. Surely, he'd have some results for me by then.

Entering the I-House, I checked my mailbox in the lobby and found a pink slip with a telephone message from Dr. Ribcot's office asking me to call. I hurried to the payphone in the hall and dialed the telephone number on the slip of paper. A woman answered.

"This is Layla Saleh. I have a message from Dr. Ribcot."

"Yes. The doctor would like you to come in, Miss Saleh. Let's see, can you be here tomorrow at three?" she asked.

"Oh, no. I have to come in right away."

"Well," a pause. "As a matter of fact, I see there's been a cancellation. Can you be here by one thirty? That's less than a half hour from now."

"Yes, I'll be there. Could you please give me the result of my tests?" I asked, heart thumping.

"I'm sorry. Only the doctor can do that."

"I see. Then can I talk to Dr. Ribcot please?" I asked.

"I'm sorry, he's with a patient."

"I'll hold on." I said.

"I'm afraid it may be quite a while," the woman said."Can you ask him what the results of my test are?" I asked.

The woman's voice took on a nasty edge. "No, I'm sorry, I can't do that. I have other phone calls to take care of."

"Can someone else help me?" I probed.

"Miss, we're all very busy here. Dr. Ribcot will see you at 1:30 today. If he has anything to tell you he'll tell you then."

"Why-"

"Please make sure you're on time." I heard the click as she hung up.

I looked at my watch. It was just past one o'clock. I hurried out, heading for the med center. I walked as fast as I could, anxiety and a swarm of questions following me. *Why couldn't I get results on the telephone?* I didn't bother to cross at the corner and dodged passing cars in the street. *Was I pregnant?* Impossible. *Did I have a serious illness? Would I have to go to the hospital? Back home?* I passed green lawns and stately buildings. *What's wrong with me?*

At last I was at the medical center. I yanked the door open and made such an awkward entry into the reception area that all eyes were on me as I made my way to the desk. I checked in and checked my watch; it was exactly eighteen minutes past one. I sat, biting my lip. It was twenty minutes past one.

Why did the receptionist keep looking at me like that? It was twenty-two minutes past one. I told myself to calm down. Everything is fine. I pictured Dr. Ribcot confirming that it was the flu. I closed my eyes and prayed fervently to Allah – to all the prophets, and powers that be, to my god and to David's god – *please, Allah, Khodah, Jehovah and Adonai, please let it be the flu.* It was twenty-five minutes past one.

At one thirty on the dot they called my name. Now that the doctor was about to give me the results of my tests, I followed the woman who led to his private office with great reluctance.

"Ah, hello again, Layla. Have a seat." Dr. Ribcot greeted me, looking up from behind his cluttered desk. I sat in one of the two chairs facing him. "How are you feeling today?"

"I'm okay. I'm still throwing up, though. Do I have a stomach virus?"

Dr. Ribcot took his glasses off and put them on his desk. "No," he said. "You don't."

"Then, what's wrong with me?"

"Well, you're not sick," he said. "Nothing is really wrong with you. You're a healthy girl, Layla. All your tests show that."

"Then what is it?" I felt my skin begin to crawl off my body and my heart cringe as the blood rushed downward through me like a waterfall, and I knew. I knew without even hearing the doctor's words, words that slammed into my brain like a pendulum.

"You're pregnant."

Then there was nothing.

40
FALLING

When I heard the word *pregnant,* I wanted to die.

"Take a sip of water, Layla.

"You're okay. You just fainted." I opened my eyes to see Dr. Ribcot standing above me. I was still sitting in the same chair in his office.

My brain was twisted. *Pregnant?* The doctor was wrong. The tests were wrong! "Please, Doctor. Tell me I'm not pregnant. I can't be," I pleaded.

"I wish I could tell you that, Layla. The fact is you are."

"No, it's a mistake. It's impossible." I was crying.

"I'm afraid there's no question about it." He put the glass of water down and handed me a box of tissues. "Are you saying you used precautions?"

I shook my head, "We were together only one night."

Dr. Ribcot shrugged and shook his head. "I'm sorry."

I was filled with resentment and hurt. "Why don't the other girls get pregnant?"

"They do," said the doctor. "Unfortunately, it happens all too often.

It's always difficult to give a girl the news, tell her she's pregnant. Still, you're going to have to accept the fact that you *are,* so you can begin to take care of yourself and your baby and make plans for the future." His voice softened. "You did consent to intercourse with the father? I mean, it was someone you know? Or... was it nonconsensual?"

"Nonconsensual?"

"Without your consent."

Scenes from the night I seduced David played before my eyes. "No. I consented."

Dr. Ribcot's face relaxed a little. "Well then, is there a chance you'll marry the father? Under the circumstances?" I could only shake my head.

"Will you at least tell him?" I continued shaking my head. The doctor reached for my hand and looked into my eyes. "This is his child too. Don't you think he should share the news and the responsibility?"

Tell David? David was someplace in Israel, there by his own choice. I wouldn't pull him back. "He's no longer in the country. I have no way of finding him."

Dr. Ribcot returned to his chair on the other side of the desk and picked up my file. "Well, it says here you're living with your cousin." I explained that Jila had married and moved out of state. Afraid he might try to contact her, I told him I'd lost touch with her as well, though I hadn't. I could never let Jila know of my shame. I shivered at the thought. I could never let anyone know. "Some other family member then? Anyone from home?" I shook my head violently. "Layla, you need to be around people who'll support you through the coming months."

"I'm not having this baby, Doctor. It's impossible. Make it go."

Dr. Ribcot sighed, took his glasses off and rubbed his eyes. "I can't do that."

"Who can?"

"No one. It's against the law for any doctor to abort this pregnancy."

I was stunned. "I don't believe you! Please! You must tell me where to go."

"There's nowhere you can go, Layla. Listen to me; abortion is against the law."

"Against the law?" How could that be? "In America?" Impossible! In my own country, abortions were legally possible and commonplace, performed every day. My own aunt, Khaleh Bahia had recently had one. *Was he saying that the laws of America where people had all sorts of choices would not allow a woman to abort?* "Please, Doctor." He just nodded. I shook my head defiantly. "That's absolutely impossible. I won't have this baby. I can't!"

Dr. Ribcot leaned forward in his chair. "Now look, Layla, I'm sorry. I find myself telling this to far more of you young girls than I'd like. I don't like telling you you're pregnant, a young girl like you, with no plans to marry. Nor do I want to tell you that it's illegal to have an abortion. It's the law." A sympathetic smile sat on his face. "Please, whatever you do, don't go looking for someone who will abort your pregnancy. Illegal abortions are extremely dangerous. You could be very badly hurt. You might hemorrhage and die without proper care or be left unable to have children."

I took yet another tissue out of the box. "What if I'd said I had been raped?"

"I'm afraid even if you'd said that, it would have been illegal to offer you an abortion. In the present state of the law, no doctor can abort or legally induce a medical miscarriage even if this child were the product of a rape or an incestuous relationship.

"Even a young, unmarried student, a visitor to our country like you, coming from a country where abortion might be legal, cannot abort here. Even if the pregnancy endangered your own life, which I have no reason to believe is the case, even in that case, it would be illegal to bring about a premature end to your pregnancy."

This was unbelievable! My life would be ruined, but American law didn't care about protecting my life. I'd fly to Iran, abort and return to Los Angeles. No, not possible. Iranian law required that my parents be notified of my request for an abortion. *My parents!* I wanted to lie down right there and die.

Just then, Dr. Ribcot asked. "Will you be telling your parents?

Perhaps you'll want to return home and be with them until you have the baby?"

I jumped, hysterical. "My god, doctor, my parents can't know! Please, please don't tell them. They can't ever know. Dr. Ribcot, please! Don't tell them!"

The doctor stood and came to me. He held my shoulders. "Layla, you must get a hold of yourself. Under California law I'm under no obligation to notify your parents."

I was surprised again. My parents would not have to be told. What a strange country! In Iran, I could easily get a legal abortion, but the doctors would consider my pregnancy to be very much my parents' business.

"Now, let's talk about your next seven months or so," Doctor Ribcot said and launched into a lecture on the responsibility I had to make sure my baby stayed healthy until birth.

I suppose he gave the same lecture to other young pregnant girls who'd sat there, soaked in their desperation and begged him, as I had, to change their fate. Lost in my thoughts, his voice sounded far away like the distant voices that came through my open bedroom window early mornings during my childhood, calls of vendors spreading word of their produce or wares.

As he spoke, the doctor took some pamphlets from a shelf behind him and handed them to me. "These will explain how to eat healthfully and how to take care of yourself and of the baby growing inside you. At some point you'll be contacted by the prenatal division here. You'll also be assigned to a gynecologist for the duration of your pregnancy, who'll examine you regularly and answer all of your questions."

I had only one question to ask: *How can I kill myself?*

The doctor made a notation in my file and replaced his pen in his pocket. "You can deliver your baby here," he said. "UCLA has fine obstetricians. If you choose not to raise the baby, you'll have options. You'll have access to counselors who'll help place your baby with a family." He walked me to the door. "The nausea will probably disappear soon - as suddenly as it came on. It usually does after the first trimester. Have faith, Layla," he said. "Have faith and pray for your child."

Just then a woman came into the room to tell the doctor he had an important phone call on hold. Explaining that he'd been waiting for that call all day, he walked me to the door, then returned to his desk.

With every step I took, my future ebbed further away. The woman who had interrupted us, ushered me out of the office and into the hallway. Somehow, I got myself out of the building just in time to vomit on the grass outside the UCLA student medical center.

I sat on a nearby cement bench under a weeping willow and sobbed pathetically.

My life was over. I don't know how long I sat sobbing. Time was not my friend, for its passing would bring me nothing but more anguish and tears. Eventually, the grass turned a darker green as the late autumn sun faded, leaving my misery undiminished.

"Layla?" Amid the haze of my misery, a familiar voice, male and warm, called my name, then someone sat down beside me and held my down-turned head in the warmth of a broad chest.

I knew this scent. "Layla, what's wrong?" Adam spoke in a voice so full of affection and concern that I only buried my head in the caring warmth and wailed, streams of tears pouring from my eyes. "Layla, talk to me. What's happened? I tried to tell him but couldn't speak through my convulsions.

"Oh, my god, Layla!" Adam was holding one of the pamphlets Dr. Ribcot had given me. The realization that Adam actually knew the reason for my tears fanned the devastating fire of humiliation and fear within me.

He said nothing more, just held me close to him in an embrace filled with tenderness. As he rocked me, ever so gently, I could feel his desire to protect me from my fate. We sat, me slumped, with my head on his chest, and his arms around me, the last of my pride, vanquished. He spoke softly.

"*Sshh,* it's okay. I'm here. You'll be okay." After some time, he helped me to my feet as if I were made of a delicate glass. "Layla, you're shivering. Come on, it's getting late. Let me take you home." He almost carried me to his red and white Chevy. The top was down, and the evening chill froze the tears on my face. He reached over to hold my hand as he drove.

"You'll be okay, Layla."

In the recesses of my muddled mind, I heard a younger voice say those words to me in Persian years ago, trying to reassure me and ease my fears. *You'll be fine. We just need to get you home to your mother.*

Maman! The thought of my mother brought a fresh ocean of tears. Years ago, I'd been afraid because I didn't know that the blood on my shorts was a normal and healthy thing. Now, I was gripped by a horror not born of ignorance, but from of a clear understanding of my dire position. And this time, Maman was the last person I could go to.

My parents had sent me to America trusting that I would steer clear of temptation. To my eternal shame, I'd failed miserably. I could hear my mother's voice, filled with pride as she spoke of her lineage, a lineage I'd brought shame to. Nana Joon's letter had been a warning to me to back down. Yet, with the first ring of David's phone call, I'd forgotten her words.

Adam had parked and was looking all over his car for a tissue. Finding none, he held my face and wiped my tears away as best as he could with his broad hands. "Does Jila know?" he asked.

I shook my head. "No one does."

"Okay," he said. He opened his door and swung out of his car with such forcefulness, as though he was ready and willing to go out there and take on the world. When he opened my door and I saw where we were, I realized he'd driven to my old apartment on Weyburn Avenue. Adam hadn't known Jila was gone or that I'd moved. I told him Jila had married and moved away; I was now living at the International House.

"Well, if you don't want her to know, then that's a good thing." He got back into the car and started the ignition. "I'm taking you to my apartment."

"No, you can't. Please!" I was adamant. "Take me to the I-House. Please, Adam, I don't want Linda to know."

"Layla, if there's anyone you'd want to know about this, it's my sister. Trust me. Linda will know exactly what to do."

Humiliation exploded in every cell of my being. I had no idea which way to turn. So, I let Adam drive me to his apartment and his sister, hoping she would know how I could end either one of two lives.

Adam and Linda lived in a small building off Pico Boulevard.

Their two-bedroom apartment was large, with a spacious den. It was furnished comfortably, a mix of typical student decor, some pieces, no doubt taken from their parents' home, alongside the most up-to-date television and stereo equipment on the market. When we entered, Linda was sitting on the thick cushioned, well-worn L-shaped couch in the living room, her feet up on the glass-topped coffee table, listening to music and giving herself a pedicure. Adam turned the stereo off, fell into a padded chair and told Linda about my condition while I died and died again.

I'd been standing. Linda directed me to sit down. I gingerly sat, trying to ignore the smell of her nail polish."Who's the father, and where is he?" She asked the question so matter-of-factly, I wondered how often she'd heard girlfriends tell her they were pregnant.

"He's gone," I whispered. My sweet David had no idea I was carrying his child. "Far away."

"Jila is gone too," Adam said. He pointed at me. "She's living alone in some room at the I-House."

Linda reacted like Adam had just told her I was living with squirrels up in a tree. "The I-House? That's ridiculous! You can't be pregnant and live alone at the I-House."

She'd finished applying her polish and closed the bottle. After the briefest pause, she said, "You'll live here, with me and Adam. Don't look at me like that. We have more than enough room and we both insist. That's that." That's how Linda spoke, as if she was already tired of arguing with you, impatient and final from the start.

Adam clapped his hands together. "Yes. Yes, we insist."

"I have a place to live." I said. I couldn't stand their kindness and didn't want their charity.

"You need more than a place to live," Linda said. "You need someone to make sure you're taking care of yourself. And you need someone to talk to."

"She's absolutely right, Layla. You need to be around people who know you and care about you. The father's gone and Jila's gone. You have no family here. There is no one else. You're moving in with us."

I looked at him baffled by his offer of kindness. He looked down, then back at me and spoke earnestly. "Don't worry. I promise I won't bother you again," he said. After what I'd done to him, his generosity was too much to bear. What was more, alluding to his kiss as "bothering me" sounded absurd in my present condition.

Finally presented with the opportunity to apologize to him, any attempt seemed feeble. "I'm sorry, Adam. I'm so sorry."

"You'll get through this, Layla," he said, as though I had apologized for my condition and not for my unfair treatment of him. "We'll make sure you do."

I put my head in my hands. "I just want to die," I muttered.

Adam came to kneel beside me hold my hands. "*Sshh,* everything will turn out fine. You'll see. You'll be okay, Layla. I promise you'll get through this." I looked at him in disbelief. "Let's go get your things." I had no intention of invading Adam and Linda's lives with my misery. I simply didn't have the energy to argue.

"Excuse me, no men allowed in the ladies' wing," the woman at the desk called out when she saw Adam start up the stairs of the I-House with me.

Adam didn't want to let me go on alone. "I'll wait here for you," he said at the foot of the stairs. Get your toothbrush and whatever else you need. We'll come back for more things later."

I went to my room, closed the door and fell on my bed. I wasn't going anywhere. All I could think was, *Dear God, what have I done? How could I have been so stupid? What was I thinking?* Even Ferri had warned me to use protection. "It would be a complete catastrophe if you get pregnant," she'd said. I hadn't even *thought* about protection! God, how I hated myself! I deserved no sympathy. I didn't deserve Adam kindness or his sister's. I deserved to live what life I had left in isolation and misery until I died.

There was a soft knock on my door. I ignored it. It became louder, insistent. I got myself up and opened the door. It was Adam. "That's what I thought," he said, slipping into the room. "You're just lying here crying, forcing me to break all the rules to come save the princess in the tower. Well, Princess, I'm here."

I almost broke apart then. Adam had unwittingly called me by David's pet name. "I appreciate your kindness. I really do, Adam." I tried to stop crying. "I know you want to help me. Thank you. Really. But I really don't need to live with you. I can stay here. See?" I motioned to my bed then went and sat on it, grabbing a tissue from the box on my dresser on my way.

"Not good enough," he said. "I know how you are, Layla, you'd never ask anything from anyone. I'm insisting. I let you down once. I'm not going to let you down again. You need me now. You do. And, believe me, you need Linda." He sat on the edge of the bed. "Look, I know it was meant to be. Otherwise, I wouldn't have even seen you today. You know, I've seen you on campus a few times. I don't think you saw me. I've always left you alone. Then today, I was reading under those trees – I go there to read sometimes – and I couldn't focus. My mind kept wandering, and I was just people-watching and I saw you. I wasn't going to say anything to you today either, though I wondered what you were doing by the med center. But then I realized you were crying. I couldn't stay away. I had to know what was wrong." He put his two hands on my shoulders. "See? It was meant to be."

"What will I tell my parents? How can I tell them I'm living with you and Linda when I have this room? It's impossible."

"Your parents don't need to know. As far as they're concerned you're living here. How will they know you're not? No one will know that you're not here. We'll come by every day, get your mail and messages at the desk. You just won't be here." He stood. "I'm not leaving without you, Layla, so get your stuff and let's go. Now. We've got to skedaddle out of here before the evil witch finds I've invaded the castle and made it to the Princess' room." He looked around the small room. "Where's your toothbrush? You get that and your pajamas; and some clothing. I'll take all your books." He began piling my books on the desk.

I looked at my old friend and nodded in acquiescence. I couldn't deny the truth. Without him, I would be totally alone. Maybe he *was* meant to be there for me. And maybe Linda knew how I could end this pregnancy. If not, I thought I could eventually persuade one of them to help me end my life. I didn't even have the courage to do that myself.

I put a few things together and with the verve of a director ordering curtains to rise up on opening night, Adam said, "Let's go!" Off we went, the heavy-hearted princess in distress and her knight, to the refuge in Adam and Linda's den.

41
WAITING

On the day John F. Kennedy's triumph over Nixon made headlines and the good-looking young politician officially became the President-elect of the United States of America, I tried to abort myself with a douche of herbs mixed with vinegar.

I'd hoped their combined acidity would cause a chemical imbalance and result in a miscarriage. With my knowledge of science, I should have known that was utter nonsense. I'd have had more luck poking around inside me with a wire hanger. Yet, I chose the douche, not because I was afraid that I might die, but because I just lacked the guts to withstand the pain.

I hated myself for that, too.

Though I tried to keep out of their way, Linda and Adam poured their attention on me.

Adam drove me to the I-House every day to check my messages, get a change of clothes and, as Adam instructed, lay my head on my pillow and rumple my bedding so as not to arouse any suspicion among the I-House staff that would lead them to tell my father I was missing.

I dreaded the sight of mail awaiting me at the I-House. Letters received from Iran spoke to a shadow of the girl I'd been, and I read each, with heartbreaking nostalgia for the irretrievable past and the old me. It was torture. Before picking up my pen to answer letters from home, I struggled, like an actress preparing for a role, to put myself into the mindset of the earlier Layla.

Then I received an elaborately printed card from Shireen announcing proudly to the whole world that she and Taymoor were expecting their first child. I sent her a congratulatory greeting and tried to sound lighthearted, though I ached to simply write, "Is it fair now?"

Linda accompanied me – actually dragged me – to my prenatal exams. There was no question regarding the date of conception and based on that, I was told I would deliver in mid-May. My doctor's office contacted an adoption agency on my behalf. They told me we would meet before the baby was born to complete the necessary paperwork that would legally put my baby in their hands at birth, thus simultaneously expelling it from my body and extricating it from my life.

I actually came to hope that my parents would never learn of this pregnancy. If I delivered before June and the baby disappeared before my expected return to Iran for the summer month, it was conceivable that my parents would never discover that I'd given birth. And so, I prayed to a God I was no longer sure I believed in that, at least for that, luck would be on my side.

I continued to attend classes, but it was a challenge to concentrate on my studies. I couldn't harness my mind. It wandered off after my heart in a million different directions. I'd stare at other girls in the class, so carefree, so serene ... so *not* pregnant. I used to be one of them. Now I was riddled with a mass of questions about my future, painful questions that bore into my being like so many bullet wounds.

How could I possibly hide my condition from my parents? What would David do if he knew I was pregnant with his child? Where was he? Had he fallen in love with someone new? Did he still love me? What would happen to me?

I spent that Thanksgiving at the Dunn home. I remembered sitting at my Ammeh Elahe's table eating Persian food at my first Thanksgiving, a year ago. I was teary-eyed, thinking of Jila wrapped in Majid's love with her parents' blessing, the four of them sharing a loving, carefree meal together, and my envy of her tore at me like nothing I had ever experienced. Though neither Maggie nor Ralph acknowledged my pregnancy, they knew I was living with Adam and Linda, and I was ashamed, knowing that even if they didn't yet knew, they would eventually learn of my shameful condition.

The weeks went by.

November passed, and with it, my nausea as predicted by Dr. Ribcot. Adam and Linda would accept no money from me toward rent, saying that I was already paying rent at the I-House, so, I insisted on paying for groceries and began to cook dinner as often as possible. I'd never been much of a cook, and in my emotional state, the food I prepared was often sorely under or overcooked or too salty, as if soaked in tears.

In December, Los Angeles began preparing for another sun-drenched Christmas. My waistline disappeared, and my stomach began to take the shape of a balloon being blown up. Though I tried to hide my swollen stomach as best as I could, classmates eventually began to notice my state. Looks lingered and eyes held questions. Though I searched, I didn't see one other pregnant girl on campus, and, despite what Dr. Ribcot had said, I was sure I was the only pregnant girl at UCLA.

Christmas Day, I was caught off guard by the first flutter of life within me and from then on, Adam and Linda were forever putting their hands on my stomach, trying to catch the waves caused by the tiny body moving within me. Seeing the expression of wonder on their faces brought home to me how deeply and desperately I wanted David to be there, both for him, as well as for me. I longed for him to feel his baby move, validating the life inside me. Without him there, it meant nothing to me.

I spent New Year's Eve alone in the apartment. Linda and Adam celebrated separately. I'd declined both their invitations. I had absolutely no reason to celebrate either the passing of one year or the start of the coming year.

In January, John F. Kennedy was inaugurated as President and I had another birthday. I was nineteen. Adam and Linda insisted on taking me out to dinner. I complied. I was no more fun to be with that night than I'd been on any other night. And still they tolerated me.

Throughout those months I spent with Adam and Linda, I was a complete mess, living a total disaster. My pregnancy affected my hormones, heightening an emotional state that was already out of control. My mind whirled with both real misgivings and fantasies. Nights were cold. Thoughts of the future made me shiver with dread. *What would tomorrow bring? What could it bring other than sorrow, shame and more tears*?

I lay in the dark, quietly crying for the innocent child that would be born, unwanted. My whole world had turned into a story full of pain and unhappy endings. When news of my pregnancy reached home, I would forever be known as *kesafat,* indecent, and a *jendeh,* a whore. My life and the lives of those dearest to me would be ruined. I would be disowned and left homeless. I thought of never returning home.

I cried for the lies. I'd lied to David, afraid to admit the true reason I'd seduced him. And I cried for all the lies I would yet have to tell in the hope they would buy me a life which, truly, was no longer worth living. Alone with my terror and loneliness throughout those long, cold nights, I feared the vulnerable little life within me might freeze and perish.

And I cried because I'd lost David. Asleep, I dreamed of him, of being locked in his arms, our bodies one. Or I'd have nightmares, David badly injured, bleeding and unable to move, or Khanom Bozorg's photo in my mother's room coming to life only to scream insults at me as well as the ever-recurrent dream of scorpions.

During the day, I was jumpy and walked the streets like a criminal in hiding, so afraid that the improbable would happen and a Persian would spot me, sending the news to Tehran, despite the fact that there were hardly any Persians in the streets of Los Angeles in those days. At some point, I no longer went to the market. I cut out all contact with the outside world except for my classes, the prenatal doctor visits

Linda dragged me to, and trips to the I-House with Adam, my large coat hiding my ever-enlarging belly. The specter of Maman lurked around every corner.

Adam was my protector and Linda was my bedrock of emotional support. She was far more than magnanimous, and exceedingly level-headed. When, in my fifth month, Adam offered to drive me to a doctor he'd found who performed late-term abortions out of Mexico, it was Linda who talked me out of going. In addition to harping on the danger I would be putting myself in, she insisted that I look past myself and realize that the life inside me was comprised of the love that was between David and me. After that, there was a huge change in the way I related to the baby growing inside me. I no longer resented it for having ruined my life; after all, the baby wasn't to blame. In place of that resentment came feelings of sorrow and pity for the child that would know neither mother nor father, and for David who would never know he had fathered a child. Neither he nor I could provide for our child. And David's child deserved to have the best.

In March, I received *Norooz* greetings from Iran. The Persian New Year was far more meaningful to me than the one Americans celebrate. I held the cards and letters I received, recalling the day at the beach last year when Jila, David and I had jumped over the fires to bring good luck. A year later, Jila was married and gone, David was missing, and I was pregnant.

The three of us were sitting at the table having breakfast on a Thursday morning in April.

"You have to let David know," Linda said.

This was the first time she'd said that, and the statement shocked me. On one hand, I hungered for David, while on the other, I didn't want him to know he'd unwittingly left me alone to deal with this situation.

"That's ridiculous. There's no point," Adam said. As I no longer trusted my own judgment, I sat silently while Adam debated the idea his sister. "Besides, even if she wanted to let him know, she couldn't."

"Of course, she could!" Linda said.

"How?" Adam asked.

Linda gave him a droll look. "Duh. His parents."

I pictured the look on Mrs. Kline's face when she heard I was carrying her son's baby in my womb. "Never!" I said. "I would never want that woman to ever have anything at all to do with my baby!"

Adam and Linda looked at me wide-eyed, surprised at my sudden outburst. I stood and folded my arms and looked back at them. "You don't know how David's mother hated me for being Muslim. How cold she was to me. She would rather I died than to give birth to her grandchild." Linda was about to say something, but I cut her off. "Trust me. I know what I'm saying. She'd never admit to having a grandchild that's half Muslim. Anyway, no matter what, I would never allow that woman to have anything to do with my child."

"Okay, Layla. I got that. But don't you think David has a right to know he's a father?"

The thought of David almost made me swoon and I sat back down, silent again. I had made my point. What happened next was up to my friends.

"What's the point, Linda?" Adam asked. "You expect David to come home and take care of the baby?"

"Maybe he will, maybe he won't. That's his choice. In any event he has a right to know."

They argued like this, back and forth. Linda said, "Damn it, Adam, it's David's baby too, and he has a right to know. Layla owes it to him to let him know."

"Why?"

"It's his baby for God's sakes, his child! Wouldn't you want to know if it was yours?"

That was the clincher. Adam turned to me. They'd decided that I would pay a visit to the Klines.

Knowing my baby would be safe from Mrs. Kline, I was looking forward to the visit for my own reasons. I thought there might be a chance in a million that I'd find David there, that I'd see him again and hear his voice, even in disappointment, despair, or anger and rejection. I didn't care. I missed him that much.

On the first Saturday in April, Adam, Linda and I drove through Holmby Hills. I located the Kline house. Adam parked on the street in front of the stately home. Perhaps it was because he saw the many steps leading up to the front door, or perhaps he feared I had trepidations.

"I'll come with you," he said, "Linda, you wait here."

As we silently climbed the path of stone steps to the Kline's front door, I was excited just to be near something so dear to David. Perhaps, if my love learned of his child, we would, one day, walk hand in hand on this path Then Adam rang the doorbell, and I simultaneously noticed the mezuzah nailed to the doorframe. I jolted with the realization that I had no idea what to say in this version of reality. When Martin Kline opened the door, I couldn't speak. He looked so very much older.

"Who's there, Martin?" It was David's mother calling from somewhere inside the house.

"It's David's Persian friend, darling. Remember Layla?" As he spoke, he noted my condition and glanced at Adam. "Layla and her gentleman friend."

I heard Mrs. Kline come to her husband's side, though she didn't appear at the open door. Adam extended his hand and introduced himself. "Hello, Sir. We'd like to get in touch with David," he said. "We've come to get his address."

I still couldn't manage to say a word. Mr. Kline's face fell. From somewhere just behind him, Mrs. Kline spoke. "David is dead," she said softly.

I almost fell over. Adam caught me in his arms and moved to enter the house with me. Mr. Kline put his arm up, effectively blocking our way. When he spoke again, his head hung down and he sounded far away. "My wife is assuming the worst. We only know David is missing ... " He sighed. "He's possibly perished." He raised his head and looked past Adam and me toward the horizon. "We're still hopeful." He paused. We waited. "The Israeli government and the U.S. State Department are still trying to determine just what may have happened to him." He looked at me then, and I recognized the enormous pain in his eyes. "There were shells thrown from across the Lebanese border into Israel a few days ago. His *kibbutz* was hit." He shook his head. "There was a huge explosion. Everything was so badly burned … a positive ID has not yet been made."

"My son is dead." Mrs. Kline repeated from behind her husband. As she moved away from her place behind Mr. Kline, I saw her for an instant. She was wearing black.

Mr. Kline looked haggard. "Tova is devastated. She refuses to have any hope. But David was planning to visit the *kibbutz* at Tavi around that time, so it's possible that he wasn't at Na'an when it was hit. That's my hope. Or, he may have been taken hostage … " His shoulders slumped, and he shook his head. He neither looked nor sounded hopeful.

Adam was watching me as he listened to David's father. "When did you last hear from your son, sir?" Adam asked.

"We received a letter from him a week ago." He took a folded sheet of paper from the inside pocket of his jacket and held it gingerly. He sighed and held it out. "He'd just returned from his shift." He held David's letter out to me. I was trembling so, I couldn't move to take it; Adam did. He unfolded it as gingerly as Mr. Kline had held it and read to me, his voice so soft that only I could hear.

Dear Mom and Dad,

It's Friday and as I write, our kibbutz is preparing for the Shabbos. I'm happy to say that our kibbutz population increased by three in the last two weeks. But this has been a grueling week.

I've put off my visit to the kibbutz at Tavi where I am needed for the last week because I've been needed here. A spray of gunfire injured more than a dozen people at a kibbutz not far from mine, including 3 children, all under the age of 7. The children wrench your heart. Their days are uncertain. I can't help comparing their lives with my life at their age. The security I grew up with is something they don't know.

When I got here, I thought I would get used to the seemingly perpetual sound of gunfire and the young soldiers forever drilling, patrolling, and guarding Israeli lives and what little they have, but it hasn't happened yet. There's so much needless bloodshed.

The hardest thing for me as a doctor is that I most often have to do my work in the field rather than in a medical facility. I laugh to think how I took the luxury of a sterile environment for granted. I hope to make it to Tavi with my assistant very soon. Maybe we can swap some supplies.

Let's pray this bloodshed will end. I love you and wish you shalom.

Your loving son, David

Although Adam read the letter, it was David's words and David's voice I heard. I didn't want it to end, didn't want Adam to stop reading.

When he finished, he returned the letter to Mr. Kline's outstretched hand. He tenderly folded it and replaced it inside his jacket, then looked at me. "Were you two keeping in touch?" *Was he simply curious or was he hoping I'd heard from him more recently?* I moved my head.

"Martin?" Mrs. Kline beckoned.

He looked back, presumably at his wife, before continuing. "I'm sorry to give you the news Layla. I know you two were good friends. I'd ask you and your friend inside, but this is not a good time. You'll have to excuse me. My wife is calling me, and I don't want to leave her alone. She's not taking this news well at all. Maybe you should come back another time?" He nodded toward my inflated belly and added, "Congratulations to you both and good luck." With that he closed the door. I stood, dizzy from the news.

Adam moved to ring the doorbell again. Pointing to my stomach, he said, "He thinks that's my child. We need to tell him it's David's."

I blocked his arm, stopping him. "Don't. I don't want to see their faces again." They had cut the last thread of hope connecting me back to David.

"Okay," Adam said. "Let's just go home." We turned away from the Kline's front door. "I'm so sorry," Adam said. "Are you okay? This was a really bad idea."

As he led me down the stone steps. I spoke, as much to myself as to Adam. "They're going through enough without knowing that their grandchild has a Muslim mother and that the father is missing." I couldn't bring myself say *"or dead."* It was impossible. *That beautiful man, those blue eyes and gorgeous body gone?* His laugh, those lips ... they may have been gone from my life. *But for his life to have ended?* It wasn't possible!

I looked up at the thin white clouds above us and that's when I misstepped, stumbling on a stone, and fell. Though I didn't roll down, it was a sudden fall, and if I hadn't intuitively protected my stomach as I suddenly went down, my oversized belly could easily have hit a jagged stone.

Poor Adam and Linda! They were both so frightened. Linda dashed out of the Chevy and came running up the stairs to help Adam take me back down to the car. As they rushed me to UCLA's emergency room, I sat in the car, rubbing my belly the whole time. After a complete checkup, I was told the damage was no more than a twisted ankle and scraped hands. I was enormously relieved. I'd been scared for my baby.

That our baby was unharmed was a sign to me that David was still alive. I was certain that I'd have sensed David's death. He was alive and would eventually be found. Moreover, I felt I was meant to hear his letter for his baby's benefit. I was to ensure that his child would have the safe and secure future he'd spoken of. I would not let him down.

I resolved then to actively participate in placing our baby in the best home possible. I couldn't leave our child's fate to the decision of an adoption agency or to chance. David's child – our child – would have a secure life in a happy home with loving parents. Our child would live a peaceful life. Our child must never know the sad consequences of its birth. I'd make certain our child would be placed in the bosom of a couple able to provide all the coddling David and I weren't able to provide. I'd also make sure that whomever parented our child would believe in a god that didn't exclude other religions. After all, religion had separated me from David. Beyond that, even the fact that he was missing and might yet die was the direct result of religious differences.

I was increasingly exhausted both physically and emotionally.

The baby was growing, its kicks, more aggressive. My back often ached, and it was almost impossible to sit through classes. The debacle that was my pregnancy was nearing its end, leading to the next phase of my shame.

One day in early May, I was sitting on the couch in the living room with my feet up on the coffee table writing a letter home, a cup of *chai nabot* beside me, when Adam came home with a strange look on his face. He stood before me. "Layla, put your book down. I need to talk to you." He sat down in front of me and scratched his chin. "Now listen, I've given this a hell of a lot of thought, so please, don't say no."

"What?"

He took a deep breath. "I don't know how to say this ... I guess I've never been so sure of anything." As resolute as his words may have been, he sounded full of uncertainty.

"What are you so sure of?"

"I want you to marry me."

"What?"

"Will you marry me, Layla?"

Maybe he'd been drinking. "Adam, that's not funny." I reopened my book.

"I'm serious, Layla." He knelt beside me and I instinctively took my feet off the coffee table. He took the book out of my hands laid it on the coffee table. "Layla, will you marry me?" I looked at him in disbelief. He repositioned himself then, sitting next to me on the couch. I leaned away. "I'm serious," he said. "I've thought the whole thing out."

"Adam, stop. Be serious."

"I am serious. You know how I feel about you. I've always loved you."

"We're like sister and brother," I said.

He shook his head. "You're more than a sister to me, Layla. You're the only girl I've ever loved."

"I don't love you like that, Adam, and I wouldn't let you marry me even if I wanted to marry you."

"Hey! Hear me out. Please! I do love you. You're so wonderful, I'd marry you even if I didn't love you that way – I mean, like a lover."

"Adam, this is crazy." I reached for my book on the coffee table, but he took my outstretched hand and held it in his.

"No, it's not. You deserve better than to have your baby come into the world without a father. If we're married, your baby will have the name Dunn on the birth certificate."

I looked at my knight in shining armor. My friend was giving me a chance to legitimize my child, a chance to prevent my baby from being born a bastard. He was ready to declare to the world that David's child, the seed of a man he'd never even met, a man I loved and had made love with, was his. I put my hand on his knee. "Adam, I really appreciate this. You're kind, loving, and wonderful, and it's so much more than generous of you to offer. The answer is, no."

"I'm not being generous. Goddamn it, Layla!" Still holding my hand, he lifted it slowly to his lips, those lips that started it all. "I love you. Please say yes."

I had love for Adam. *How could I not love this selfless man who was willing to make such a sacrifice to help me, despite what I'd done to him?* It was beyond remarkable. But I would never love him the way I loved David.

"Let me be the father," he implored.

I leaned in to him and kissed his cheek. I looked into his eyes, pleading kindness. "You're not the father, Adam."

He became agitated then and stood up. "No, I'm not. The wonderful Dr. David Kline is the father." He lifted his arms and looked around. "Do you see him here? No! The guy is thousands of miles away – if he's even alive. I'm here, Layla, and I want you to know I would do anything for you. Look, it's not like I want to get married. But I'll marry you in a second. Don't be stubborn. Think of your baby. Marry me, Layla! Please!"

I gave him my final answer. "Adam, even though David's not here, I think I'll always be in love with him. I'll always dream of him. As for marrying you, neither of us is ready or able to take care of this child for a lifetime. I can't marry you for the same reasons I couldn't marry David. My parents would feel as betrayed by my marriage to an American Catholic they've never met as they would have felt if I had married an American Jew they'd never met."

"Think of your baby! Let's marry. Then after it's born, we can divorce if you want to."

"No, Adam."

"Why?"

"Because I love you, and I couldn't do that to you. I've ruined enough lives. You want me to ruin yours too?"

"You won't be ruining it. I want to be there for you. And the baby … your baby ... it could be ours."

"Adam you've always been there for me. I'm the one that let you down. I hurt you. But I won't hurt you again. Marrying you – whether I divorce you or not – will only compound the problem. Let it be. Please, don't ask me again. My life is miserable enough for the two of us."

"It can-"

"No!"

Adam shook his head in wild frustration. "Okay, Layla, you'll always have your way with me. I'll do what you want even though it's a mistake. Let me know if you change your mind. I'll always be here for you."

The following week, one of the worst rainstorms in the history of Los Angeles began. It poured every day for over a week.

When the Los Angeles River was in danger of flooding, my water broke. Adam drove me to the hospital to give birth.

42
JASMINE

Westwood, California — May 16, 1961

I dug my fingernails into the thin mattress and clenched my parched lower lip.

Sweat laced between my breasts. I felt the veins of my neck swell and my facial muscles tighten as I choked down my screams.

The wiry nurse with the short red hair came to check on me at regular intervals. Seemingly unaware of my agony, she approached my bed and adjusted her black-rimmed glasses. "Would you listen to that downpour! How are we doing, Sweetie?" I gasped. "Don't be afraid to scream if you have pain, sweetheart. The pain is a natural part of the process. Here, hold my hand."

I looked at the nurse's extended hand, the skin so thin and white – the skin of a stranger, not a hand I wanted to reach for. Never loosening my grip on the bed, I turned my head away. I writhed in anguish. This pain was not a natural part of the process. No, so much of it came from my heart. Another contraction.

The nurse timed this one, then reached over to pull away some hair from the side of my face. "Just hold on, now, sweetie. The contractions are coming really close together now. Your baby will be coming soon."

There was a flash of lightening, then a burst of thunder. The nurse went to the window and pulled the shades up to look outside, letting in the gray. "Lord, look at that rain! Looks like it might never stop." She moved back toward my bed.

"You went through the first stages of labor pretty fast," she said. "But this last stage is taking its pretty time." She played at arranging the sheets I'd been scratching at and lifted her eyebrows. "I'd have thought a girl like you, so young, and this being your first time and all, you'd be spared a lengthy labor. Just goes to show, you never can tell. You've been in labor for almost twenty-five hours. Anyway, there's nothing we can do now. Just have to wait."

Wait. I'd waited and dreaded this day for months! The contractions continued, cramping my insides until I thought they'd turn me inside out. I'd been in the hospital for over a day. I couldn't blame my baby for not rushing to come into this world. Perhaps it knew there would be no father, misty-eyed with happiness, arms outstretched to hold it, no announcement of its arrival, made to the world with pride or joy. This baby was conceived because of my jealousy of a woman who didn't exist for a man I knew could never be mine. This baby would be born of anxious lies and deceit, a closely guarded secret, and soon after birth, it would be given up to strangers.

With the next contraction I shuddered, sick with helplessness. *God, help me,* as one contraction ended and another began, I was caught under the spikes of a never-ending wheel of torture from an emotional pain that was far more excruciating than anything physical.

"Hang on, Dearie, you're doing just fine," the nurse said.

I lay with my knees bent, clutching the sheets at my sides with whitened knuckles, victim to the terror that my parents might one day find out where I was at that moment. *What if they've been trying to reach me in the hours I'd been there?*

The nurse stroked my forehead, then took a wet towel, and patted down my neck and chest. She wiped my lips. "I'm going to call for the doctor, Dearie; I think you might be ready." She left the room. There was another clap of thunder. My sole comfort as I lay in bed, was the bellowing sound of the rain pounding against the windows, punctuated by bursts of crashing thunder.

The doctor came in and bent to examine me, his bald head shining between my open legs. He spoke to the nurse. "Okay, she's ready. Let's move her into delivery."

I was put on a gurney and wheeled out. As I passed under the overhead lights, painful pictures flashed through my mind: my beloved Babajon's face etched in disappointment; Maman grieving the ruination of her family reputation; Khanom Bozorg sneering at me in disgust; Naneh Joon, crying is disappointment; my cousins, Bahman and Shireen, eyes wide in disbelief; Ferri, distraught. And all of them mouthing the same vindictive curses: "*Bemeer,* die! *Harrom-zadeh da-ree,* you have a bastard! *Jendeh,* you whore! How could you do this? *Sharrm, Sharrm,* shame, shame! You've blackened your future!

I thrashed my head from side to side. *Stop! You don't understand! I didn't mean for this to happen!*

Just before my gurney turned a corner, I saw David's face, bewilderment and confusion filling his lovely eyes. Poor David! He never even knew I was pregnant.

Then the voices came back, louder this time, screaming in disgust. "*Jendeh,* whore! *Batchehet harrom-zadeh ast,* your baby is a bastard!" "*Jendeh!*" the chorus screamed again. "How could you do this to us?"

I was lifted and set down on the delivery bed, my heart and my body ripping apart. A harsh light glared its brightness in my eyes and bounced off the white walls. I was in Maman's bathroom. Strangers had gathered around me, wearing blue, with masks of white that showed only their eyes. Then there was an undertone of incomprehensible conversation. I was certain I saw Parveen Khanom peeking out at me from her chador. And then I couldn't breathe. I clamped my eyes shut and my breath became even more of a struggle. I was suffocating.

Saved at last! I was dying. In one primal, ear-splitting scream that arose from the depths of my soul I vented my emotional pain. My final utterance rang out in a single word, shattering and explosive. "*David!*"

The obstetrician fell back, startled by my scream. The nurse by my side whispered, "That's it, dear, let it out."

The obstetrician recovered and stood ready to grab the baby's crowning head. "One more push," he urged. "The baby's coming. You must push once more. Push as hard as you can."

As my baby emerged, it felt like my heart was being pulled out of me. Silent tears accompanied the sudden innocent wail.

The nurse put my baby in my arms. "Congratulations, Dearie. You have a beautiful baby girl," she said.

I turned my head away. I didn't want to look at the newborn child. I couldn't face my baby.

The nurse put her ear close to my lips. "What did you say? Speak louder, Dearie. I can't hear you."

"Shame." I whispered. "Nothing but shame."

PART III: GOING HOME

PROLOGUE TO PART III

THE RETURN

I was a mother.

I named my daughter Jasmine after the sweet, beautiful, white flower that grows on the vine, thriving wherever it's planted.

She was the tiniest thing I'd ever seen. She had my tawny skin and David's facial features. I smiled in awe of nature when I noticed David's crescent-shaped beauty mark on her tiny left calf and wondered if she would have a gap between her top front teeth and his blue eyes. Our little girl was beautiful.

The UCLA Hospital and Maggie Dunn had already gifted me everything I'd need for Jasmine's short stay at the apartment, including a small used crib, baby blankets, cloth diapers, some tiny, soft Tees, and warm sleepers. I would pass all of them along with her to her new parents. Linda found a doll wearing a pair of satin slippers and put them on Jasmine's tiny feet.

Agency people had approached me in my ninth month and hovered around me at the hospital expecting me to sign papers giving up Jasmine for adoption from the moment of her birth. But I couldn't give her up like an unwanted sweater and told them as much.

I'd been told that under American law, I would not have her adoptive parents' contact information. I couldn't know anything at all that might lead me to my daughter should I change my mind in the future. They would know nothing about me as I would know nothing about them. Yet, I demanded to have a say in deciding where she went.

I didn't want names or addresses, but I needed to know facts about her new parents to make sure she was put in the best possible home environment, so she could have the sort of life I'd envisioned for her. I was adamant in my desires for Jasmine, and I let the agency know that I was determined to remain fully focused on her placement.

My parents expected me to arrive in Iran to spend a month or so there as classes (I was no longer attending any) ended. That was just a few days away. I told the adoption agency that I would meet with them to go over their candidates on my return from Iran in a month.

Adam and Linda were wonderful. They agreed to care for Jasmine for the entire month I'd be away. I prepared everything I thought they would need for the four weeks they would have with her: a mountain of diapers, baby bottles and formula, and all the cash I had. They couldn't call me, of course. They'd have to write to me at Ferri's home address.

I was a mess. I wondered how I'd explain my condition to Maman and Babajon. I decided to take Linda's suggestion and attribute my physical weakness, my pallor and exhaustion to a recent bout of bronchitis, saying I'd kept it from them to alleviate their worry.

I'd capitalize on that lie by explaining that I would have to return to school no later than the first of August first to sit for two final exams that I'd missed due to my illness. I packed my suitcase, mindful to leave behind all my American-bought clothing and photos of David, kissed my roommates and Jasmine goodbye, prayed to a God that either didn't exist or was, at best, callous and uncaring, that all would go well, and boarded the plane for home.

43
JENDEH

I was home.

As I walked off the plane at Mehrabad Airport, my parents spotted me and hurried my way. It felt good to be embraced by them. I put on the mask of the girl I used to be and fell back into being my parents' daughter without a care in the world.

"Layla, *chet shodeh,* what's happened to you? You've become so thin, so drawn. And you have no color."

Maman pulled back, shook her head in disdain and slapped her hand.

"I was sick," I said. "I'm completely fine now."

"*Amreeka*!" Maman said. "Look at her, Hadi." She turned back to me. "That's the second time you've gotten sick there. You call it a fine, good, healthy country, yet you come home pale and withered. I'll tell Cobra to make some *ush* with meat. We need to make you look like yourself again."

The second day home, I headed to Ferri's house. When I told my friend I'd taken her advice, followed my heart and slept with David, she was ecstatic. I told her that David had asked me to marry him, and that I'd refused, and that he'd left for some unknown *kibbutz* in Israel. "Oh, Layla!" she frowned. Then I told her about Jasmine. I could barely stand to look at her as she listened, her face crumbling and, when she cried, I cried with her. "What will you do?" She asked.

"What can I do? I have no choice. I'll have to give her up for adoption when I get back. The people from the adoption agencies were all over me. As soon as I get back to Los Angeles, I'm going to make sure she gets the very best; that's the least I can do for our daughter."

"And then what? Will you see her after that?"

"I don't know. I'm confused. I don't think I can, and I don't know if I should. It's probably better if she never finds out I'm her real mother. I want her new parents to love her so much she'll never know she was adopted, never know her pathetic mother abandoned her."

"Oh, Layla *joonie*, my Layla dearest, don't blame yourself for having to give her up. It should have ended up differently. You deserve so much happiness."

Though Ferri's statement was meant to be kind, it pierced my heart like an iron skewer. My tongue moved to moisten my dry lips. My teeth bit down. "For the month that I'm here, my two friends, Adam and Linda, are taking care of Jasmine. They'll be writing me. I've given them your address."

"No! They can't send letters here! My parents will be suspicious if I get letters from America that are not from you. They'll ask questions and might even open the letter."

"But they-"

"Give them Hamid's address at the University. That's much safer, and I'll be sure to get them from him."

"Are you sure?"

"Absolutely."

"Won't he wonder?"

"Don't worry," Ferri said, "He has no curiosity about things like that. I promise, *beh Toorah*, to the Torah. It's our secret."

"Okay. Give me his address and I'll tell them to send letters to him. How is Hamid?"

"Fine." The simple answer spoke volumes.

I allowed myself a tired smile. I couldn't bring myself to try to coax her into not seeing Hamid anymore; that would have been ludicrous. Yet I was more concerned for her than ever before. "Be careful," I whispered without emotion.

My days at home were spent primarily resting and eating, and whomever I visited was as determined to fatten me up as my mother and father. It was good to see my beloved grandparents. Agha Doctor had become weaker. He needed a cane to walk and help sitting and standing. Naneh Joon also looked frail. She hugged me. "I've cooked your favorite lamb dish," she said. "Did you get my gift on your birthday?"

"You mean the beautiful shawl, Nana?" Along with the letter reminding me to be a good girl.

"Yes, yes, that one."

"Thank you so much," I said. "It's very beautiful." I didn't remind her that I'd thanked her for it on my trip home the previous summer.

She kissed my eyes. When she let go of me, she patted my head and wiped a tear from her cheek. "Why are you crying, Naneh Joon?"

"You are my only son's only child." Her voice cracked. "Wait until you have your own child. With Allah's blessing it will be soon. You will see how much you will love that child. Then when that child has a child, you will understand how I love you."

What a cruel, cruel world.

"It's not fair!

"I've gained every kilo you've lost. How do you do it? Don't you eat in America? Thank God, Taymoor doesn't seem to mind my weight. He says a woman should have some meat on her. Look what he bought me." With that, my cousin showed off her new jewels, almost the size of the new-born girl she introduced to me then, seemingly as an afterthought. Shireen had named her daughter Tallah, Farsi for 'gold.' Her middle name was Elizabeth. It was perfect!

"How do you like being a mother?" I asked my cousin, trying to sound casual.

"*Vye Khodah,* oh, God. I'll tell you. First, the pregnancy, that was dreadful! My back hurt constantly. I had to have my feet up all the time and my feet and back massaged constantly. The poor masseuse hardly rested. And, trust me, I rubbed my stomach with three oils every single day, and still I have stretch marks.

"Then labor. I never dreamed anything could be so painful! I begged the doctors to medicate me. They refused. Can you believe that? Finally, after two hours of screaming, those sons of bitches gave me something."

I looked at her in awe. She took a breath and continued, "And now the baby is, well, you know, she's a baby. She cries. And I have to put up with this donkey of a nurse who thinks she knows everything better than I do. I fight with her constantly and she's never there when I need her."

"That's too bad."

"Hah! You haven't heard the worst! Taymoor wants *three* children. And he wants them right away, back to back. He says he's getting old. Is that my fault? Tell me how I'm supposed to be able to travel to Europe every few months, pregnant or with two or three children."

She sighed dramatically and shook her head along with her hands, her gold bracelets jangling. "Layla, could you ever have imagined me as a mother?"

I said nothing.

On my eighth day back in Tehran, Ferri slipped me a letter from Los Angeles.

I led her to our back garden and tore the envelope open. I was delighted to see a photo of little Jasmine included, a close-up of her asleep on the sofa in the den. I read Adam's note.

Just to say hi.

Everything here is fine except that we miss you already. As you can see, Jasmine is dreaming of you. Have a good time and hurry home. Love, Us.

I took the letter with me later that day when I left the house and threw it away in a public trashcan. I couldn't discard the photo of

Jasmine. Knowing it was one of the few photos I'd have of my daughter, I hid it in the back of a frame with a picture of me holding my high school diploma. I would look at it at night, alone in my room. I could smell my baby's warm head and almost feel her silken hair.

Babajon didn't seem as busy as he'd been the previous summer.

He spent more time at home. I assumed Saleh's new products were coming along well. One Friday, we drove to our villa in Vallian for the weekend. Fotmeh hadn't wanted to go. In fact, she begged my mother to let her stay behind in Tehran. I watched my mother's thin, tight smile.

"Don't you want to see your village? Your sisters and your new little brother?" I asked.

Fotmeh had no use for her parents. "This is my home," she answered emotionally. "By Allah's grace, and by His goodness, Zahra Khanom and your esteemed father are better parents to me than any family I ever had."

Her mother and father had given Fotmeh away as I would be giving Jasmine away.

Fotmeh had changed. She no longer wore a *roosaree*. She'd given it up sometime after my last visit home. She wore her raven black hair firmly braided and tied behind her head with a small ribbon, the same shade of pink as her starched apron. She'd also become far more verbal, stronger somehow, even assertive.

"You cannot stay here alone," Babajan said, as much to Maman as to Fotmeh. "You will come to Vallian with us."

Maman interjected, "You needn't visit your family if you don't want to."

I hadn't visited Vallian since high school. We four drove northwest to the village, heading toward Ghazvin on roads that hadn't been there on my last trip. As we approached the village, our road followed the path of the river that ran through the vast plain like a thick snake, leading us to rows of clay houses rising from the ground.

For two days, I worked alongside Babajon in his gardens there, turning over the soil and planting new herbs and flowers. It was immensely comforting to be with him – so long as I didn't think about how much my life had changed since the last time we'd been there together.

On our last evening at Vallian, Maman asked if I was determined to return to Los Angeles. "Yes, Maman."

My mother and father shared a lingering glance. My father nodded before he spoke. "You're studying very hard," he said. "Perhaps you are driving yourself a bit too hard, not taking the proper care of yourself. You've been sick. You're not strong. Your mother and I are both concerned about your health."

"I'm fine. Really."

"Well, there's no reason for you to rush back. You seemed exhausted when you arrived," he said. "Perhaps you should prolong your stay here another month before you return? There's no reason to stress yourself."

I hurried to kill that option. "Oh, no, Babajon, I can't do that. I *must* be back by the first of August to take my exams or I'll fail. Besides, I really am fine." I smiled as radiantly as I could. "I promise I'll take it easier. It was a difficult semester."

Babajan nodded again. He seemed satisfied.

Not so, Maman. I sensed her coldness. "Think about it," she said.

The last days at home went by, each hotter and longer than the one before and my anticipation to go back to Los Angeles grew daily.

On my final Tuesday in Iran, Maman hosted her weekly afternoon ladies' card game. I watched as her guests arrived and helped themselves to the spread of food set out on our dining room table – cold chicken, a whole cooked salmon, kookoo sabzee, a potato dish, yogurt and cucumbers, fruits, nuts, a mountain of pastries, tea and coffee – then took their seats.Four women at a small round table would play rummy, and another six at a larger round table would play poker, Iranian-style, twos through sixes removed from the deck.

As they started their games, I left home to visit Ferri who had called to tell me that Hamid had received another letter from Los Angeles. This second letter again assured me that all was well and ended, *Can't wait to see you soon!* It was signed *Jasmine.*

"You miss her," Ferri said.

"Yes, I do." I missed her immensely. I missed the feel of her skin and her scent, I missed holding her against me. Now that I was rested and felt better than I'd felt in almost a year, I was anxious to return to Los Angeles and see my baby. I'd been home for a month, and my secret was safe. Soon I'd be returning to her.

"She's so cute, Ferri. She looks like David. She has his dimple and the same forehead. She even has an adorable rose-colored crescent-shaped birthmark on her calf just like his."

"If she's lucky, she'll look like her mother," Ferri said.

"She has my skin color ... and maybe her eyes are shaped like mine because they are larger than David's, but I hope she doesn't have my stupidity."

"You're not at all stupid, Layla. You've just been unlucky."

When I arrived back to my parents' house from visiting Ferri, all Maman's guests had left except for her sister, Bahia.

The two women were in the kitchen. I said hello to them on my way to my room. There was no sign of Cobra, and I guessed she'd left for home. I felt so carefree that I was whistling as I went to my room. Minutes later, I returned to the kitchen to pour myself a cup of tea.

When entered, I overheard my mother and my aunt in the midst of a heated conversation.

"It serves her right," Maman was saying.

"Zahra, those poor children will be without a mother," Khaleh Bahia said.

"Better to be without a mother than to have a mother that's a *jendeh,* a whore," Maman replied.

"Whom are you talking about?" I asked nonchalantly, taking out a cup from the cabinet. *Curiosity be damned, damned, damned!*

"It's heartbreaking. It's unbelievable," my aunt continued.

"It's filthy," said Maman.

"What's heartbreaking and filthy, Khaleh?" Khaleh Bahia didn't answer me.

Maman went on. "And she can't go home to her parents. They'll shred her to pieces and feed her to the dogs."

I poured some of the strong brewed tea into my cup and followed it with boiling water. "*Jendeh,* whore!" Maman repeated under her breath.

I froze. Those were the very words I feared would one day be directed at me. yet it was obviously not me that Maman and Khaleh Bahia were talking about. "*Kee,* who?"

"Remember Katia, my good friend? Her brother went to school with her husband," Khaleh said to my mother. "Her brother says he's a fine man. She didn't deserve the life he'd given her. The poor man trusted her."

My curiosity increased along with my frustration at not being answered. I put down my cup of tea and nearly screamed to get their attention. "*Kee,* whom are you two talking about?"

They looked at me as though they'd just become aware that I was there. My Khaleh Bahia opened her mouth to say something, looked at my mother, then closed it.

"Maman, who are you talking about?"

"Nobody worth your while," she said as she prepared a fresh cup of tea for herself. "Just a piece of filthy trash."

"Please tell me."

She said the name as though it dirtied her mouth. "Parveen."

"Parveen Khanom? Parveen Shirazi?" *It couldn't be!* "Our neighbor?"

My mother stirred her cup, nodding just barely, as though "the whore" didn't merit more of her energy. Then she suddenly spit her name out like she was spitting out venom. "Parveen! Your *Parveen Khanom,* may her name be erased from the living," she mocked the title of respect, injecting sarcasm into the her name. Then she continued in a normal tone. "Parveen Khanom, *jendeh* Parveen Khanom, who has brought poison and shame on her entire clan." She went to the platter of cookies sitting on the counter. "Our *najess,* filthy neighbor, daughter of a revered *ayatollah*. She's made a mockery of the chador she used to wear."

My mind reeled. *What could have happened to that pious, good-hearted woman?* I flashed back to the scene in her salon, recalling the future she'd left for her husband to decide for her: continue wearing her chador, or throw it away forever.

"What did she do?"

Maman looked at me. "Your Parveen Khanom was seen having tea ..." she paused before adding, eyebrows stretched to meet her hairline, "... with a man." I waited for Maman to go on, but that was all she said before turning her attention back to the cookies. She put one on her saucer.

I was so stunned that I forgot everything in that moment. "That's it? Having tea?"

Those were the exact words I blurted out. Oh, God, how many times I wished I had kept my mouth shut! It was too late. The words were out.

My mother and my aunt both turned, looking at me in shock. I saw the cookie my mother held drop onto the counter and her teacup rattle, the tea inside spilling out, as she practically dropped it on the countertop and stormed over to me, her arm poised to swing. She swung a stinging blow to the side of my face that left me reeling. The room spun around me. Then everything went red and my head was pounding.

"Tea with a man is nothing to you?" she screamed. "You've gone to America to have tea with men?" In seconds Maman had shifted from normalcy to madness. Khaleh Bahia was up, running to stop Maman from striking me again. Before she could reach us, my mother had hit me again, this time smacking me on the other side of my face by my ear. Terrified, my hands went to my hot, stinging cheeks. Maman was about to strike me yet again. I cowered and tried to cover my face with both my arms. Her arm stopped in mid-air. She just stood there staring at me. Then, worse than hitting me, she began to beat herself, hammering her chest with her two fists. I was mortified to see my mother like this. She rolled her eyes up to the ceiling and grabbed her silk blouse, ripping it, pulling it down and apart as she spoke to the ceiling. I was far too stunned by her blows and her vehemence to utter a sound.

"Allah, what have you done to me? What have you done? My daughter is ruined! My daughter is spoiled! I've lost my child, the daughter I raised. Poor me, poor, poor unfortunate me!"

I stood frozen in fear, my ears ringing, both my head and heart throbbing. I'd never seen my mother out of control. She was hysterical. I think I was more frightened for her wellbeing than I was for my own. She began pulling at her blouse again, howling like a badly wounded animal.

"*Ayondeh-moono seeya kardee,* you've ruined our future!" she wailed as another button popped.

Though I yearned to reach out and comfort her, I couldn't. I was paralyzed by fear. Suddenly, she reverted from sorrow back to fury, shaking her finger at my absent father as though he was standing alongside me, screaming at him. "You foolish man! You stupid man! I told you not to send our daughter to that hell hole of dogs and cats." Now she was angry with Babajon as well.

I was absolutely petrified. She grabbed Khaleh Bahia, who'd been trying to hold her away from me, and clutched her close as she sobbed. "I begged him not to send her there! I did! I told him not to do it!" I could hear her rapid breathing. "He promised me she'd be okay. 'She's different than other girls,' he said. Now what will I do?" She began to shake Khaleh Bahia. "What will I do now that my innocent daughter has been corrupted?" Then she let go of Khaleh Bahia and turned to me with hatred in her eyes and unleashed a torrid temper.

"*Amreeka!*" She spat, barely missing my face. "Let it rot in hell, six feet under the ground. *Amreeka!*" She spat again. "*Khok be sarrash* dirt on its head! *Berreh, bemeereh* may it go and die!" Her fists were clenched at her sides, her arms rigid, blood vessels rising above her skin like so many thick lines on a map. She took a few steps away from me and I thought she might begin to calm down. But no, she suddenly turned and came back to me, grabbed me by my shoulders and began shaking me violently as if trying to shake the effects of America out of me. "You have tea with men? You won't go back. Do you hear? Oh, no!

You are not going back to that disgusting place. UCLA? May it be bombed!"

Jasmine! "Maman –"

"*Khafeh shoh,* choke on your words and die! *Kooft,* shut up!" She let go of me then and pointed a single commanding finger so close to my face I pulled my head back. "You will tell your father you are *not* going back. Do you hear me?" I nodded. She put her hands at her hips and began to walk away then changed her mind and turned back to me.

"You will tell him nothing of this. Do you understand?" she screamed. I nodded again. Her eyes were enlarged and fiery. I turned away from her, unable to see her like that. She took a firm hold of my chin and turned my face back to face her. "Not a word!" she continued. "You will tell him you do not *want* to go back. There is no point in telling your deluded father what you have become. I don't know what it would do to him in his condition."

His condition? "What –"

"*Khafeh shoh,* shut up, *Jendeh Khanom! Bemeer,* die! Don't *Maman* me. I am not the mother of a girl like you. Get out of my sight."

I couldn't move. My feet were lead, my knees cotton.

Khaleh Bahia took me by my arm, holding me up as I made my way to my room and away from my mother's wrath.

44
THE DRIVE

The following morning, my mother awoke me from a poor sleep.

Though it was still very early, she was fully dressed. "Get up! Be outside and ready to go in five minutes."

"Maman-"

She was gone. I hurriedly dressed and went outside to find my mother seated in the back seat of a strange black car. I didn't recognize the driver who opened the back door for me. I slid in and sat by my mother's side. I'd had no dinner the night before and nothing yet to eat that morning. I was hungry, very tired and extremely afraid. I spoke softly, almost in a whisper, afraid to set her off again. "Good morning, Maman. I'm sorry about yesterday."

She didn't respond. I reached over to kiss her cheek. She evaded me, stretching forward to give the driver what looked to be a business card.

"This is the address," she said to him as the car took off. I noted the clock on the dashboard; it was not quite eight o'clock. I waited until Maman was sitting back again. "

I'm sorry about yesterday," I repeated. Maman didn't answer. I tried again. "I don't know why I said what I did. It was silly. Of course, Parveen Khanom was wrong to be with a man who was not her husband in a public place – or any place." I wiped my clammy hands on my skirt.

If my mother responded in any way at all, I wasn't aware of it. She simply sat looking straight ahead. I began chewing my lip. I was to leave for Los Angeles in two days.

I tried a different approach, taking it for granted that it had all blown over. I tried to sound light. "Where are we going so early?" It didn't work; she didn't answer. My anxiety increased. "I never spend time with boys in California," I said, matter-of-factly. "I mean, not unless they're in my class. Of course, if they are in my class, I spend time with them in class but that's all. I don't talk to them and would never dare be alone with one, let alone have tea with one …" Nothing.

I began to panic. "Maman, I can go back to Los Angeles, can't I? Please say I can. My return ticket is in two days. Maman … ?"Silence. Silence and stillness.

Is it possible? Could she really stop me from going back?

"Maman, where are we going? Please talk to me. Maman, please say I can go back to UCLA ... back to my studies. I have exams. May I, please? I'm so sorry. I said I'm sorry, Maman. Maman *jon*, please! Say I can go back!"

She didn't even look at me. She just sat there perfectly still, clutching her handbag on her lap, looking at the road ahead, barely blinking, as lifeless as those life-sized cutout celebrity posters I'd seen in stores and movie theaters in Los Angeles. She wouldn't talk to me, and I knew she wasn't going to let me leave and go back to my waiting baby.

It was too much to bear. I totally broke down.

– Zahra –

She definitely has a boy waiting for her there.

As I heard my daughter's persistent pleas to return to America, I grew steadily more certain that Layla was living a life in Los Angeles that had to be aborted. Immediately.

I didn't answer my daughter because I'd said all I needed to say the day before. Let the girl tire herself out. She'll stay here and marry, forget about the boy soon enough. God only knows who or what he is. She'll stay and do things my way from now on.

The entire time we were in the car, my daughter sobbed, her arms flailing at her sides as she whimpered, "I have to go back," tears falling down her contorted face.

Some 40 minutes later, we were on the outskirts of the city. Our driver stopped in back of a small wooden V-framed house, its white paint far from fresh in the midst of an open field, just as it had been described to me. The driver opened my car door, tipping his hat, then ran to the other side of the car and opened Layla's door.

Layla, sobbing incoherently, was too far-gone to notice. The driver removed his hat, scratched his head and looked at me for instructions. I addressed my daughter. "Get out of the car!"

"I have to go back," she whimpered repeatedly, head between her hand that rested on her thighs. "Please!"

I spoke to the driver. "Don't just stand there, man, help her out of the car."

"But Khanom, the girl is–"

"*Khafeh shoh!* Choke! *Loll shoh!* Become mute! Don't you dare have the impunity to talk to me about my daughter! Do as I say!"

The impudent driver finally saw fit to help Layla out of the car. Once out, she broke lamely away from him then began running wildly in a sudden burst of movement, wailing and kicking up dirt, with obviously with no idea where she was headed. I motioned the stupid driver to go after her and watched with some concern as the burly man grabbed my daughter by her slim arms and grappled her to the ground. When the driver hauled her back to me, she seemed oblivious to the blood trickling down her left leg, probably from a stone she'd hit on her fall.

"Wait for me here," I commanded the driver.

I took hold of Layla and led her to the back porch of the house a few steps away. She followed in complete submission, her head bent, through the unlocked door and then into a room immediately to the right that bore a white sign reading, "Patients –Enter."

There was no waiting room, only an examination table and a couple of chairs. I took out my handkerchief and dusted off a blue leather chair and deposited Layla there. The girl slumped down, weeping. I could see she was very weak. I dusted off the only other chair there, a dark wooden one, and sat down to look across the small square room at Layla.

What a pathetic sight my daughter was! *Delam sookht barrosh,* My heart burned for her! I pitied her, seeing her in such sadness.

Alhamdo le'ellah, Allah be praised, it was a good thing I found out about the boy. Apparently, *kesee cheshm-zadan,* someone had given us the evil eye. No matter, I would see to it that she never laid eyes on him again. *Ensha'Allah,* God willing, it was not too late and, *ensha'Allah,* the doctor's unique services wouldn't be needed. And if they were? I'd wait until he examined her. I would know what to do then.

I sighed and looked around the room. Our appointment time had passed minutes ago and I anxious for the doctor to arrive. There was not much to look at; the examination table, of course, in the center of the room with metal stirrups, glass cabinets on two walls shelving medical supplies and countertops holding a stock of smaller medical staples as band-aids and gauze.

The doctor's several medical licenses hung on one wall. The one that caught my eye was the center one, the largest, framed in black, declaring Doctor Yadollah Baharati, a Diplomat of the University of Medicine in Geneva, Switzerland, an M.D. specializing in Gynecology and Obstetrics. I had been advised that the doctor had studied in Switzerland and I believe, as most intelligent Iranians do, that a European education adds an extra something to his medical training.

I consulted my watch and frowned. I hated waiting for doctors, especially when I was paying exorbitantly for their services, and this doctor was quite expensive. Whatever else he had learned in Switzerland, he certainly had not learned the Swiss trait of punctuality.

Just then the doctor entered. I was relieved to see that, contrary to our worn surroundings, he looked fresh and well-groomed, wearing an immaculate white jacket over fine, lightweight, beige linen trousers and well-made, clean, white leather shoes. He wore his thick, straight salt-and-pepper hair back, off his forehead; I could see the teeth marks left behind by his comb. He smiled.

"*Saalom,* Khanom. I'm Doctor Baharati."

45
THE EXAMINATION

– The Doctor –

I didn't ask the woman's name and she never gave it to me.

She greeted me dryly. "I've been waiting for you, Doctor." I hadn't been more than five minutes late.

"*Bebakhsheed,* forgive me, I'm sorry to have kept you." My attention was immediately drawn to the girl slouched in the other chair, her head in her hands, whimpering and mumbling. I noted a small amount of fresh blood on her left knee. "She knows why she's here?" I asked, assuming the girl's tears were attributed to her visit.

"No."

"What's wrong with her then? Is she ill?"

"No, she's not ill. She's … upset. Perhaps you should sedate her."

"I can't do that if I'm to examine her."

"Why not?"

"Khanom, I am not in the habit of examining unconscious women," I said.

"And I am not in the habit of letting people waste my time,

Doctor. Things will be much easier for my daughter if she is sedated. You can see she is not well. I'm certain you will not allow yourself to make a habit of it."

While she spoke, the woman opened her purse and counted out some bills, which she put into a thin envelope she'd brought. She leaned over and put the envelope on the nearby countertop. Rather than acknowledge it, I asked the cause of the cut on the girl's knee. Her mother explained that the girl had fallen outside on their way up the stairs.

I didn't like the woman, yet she was right about the sedation. The girl was obviously quite upset and somewhat incoherent, rendering her unpredictable. Under the circumstances, it would be easier to examine her sedated. Furthermore, if this woman was indeed her mother, she had the right to request sedation. Nonetheless, it went against my professional integrity, and I resented the woman's condescending attitude. The fact that she didn't try to comfort her obviously miserable daughter didn't sit well with me. I didn't like her at all.

I went to the counter where the envelope lay, picked it up and looked inside, all the while eyeing the woman. There was a lot of money inside, far more than necessary for an examination. I replaced the envelope on the counter and looked again at the girl who still sat limply. I wasn't at all certain she was aware of my existence even now.

I prepared an ampule of fast-acting medication, took some alcohol, and cleansed a viable spot on her arm before injecting the solution into her slack muscle, then I helped her up. She responded submissively and complied as though already sedated. I sat her down on a large white towel spread out on the examination table as gently as I could and laid her head back, her legs straight. As she fell into semi-consciousness, I stood looking down at her. I had seen many other girls like her, young, perhaps not as pretty, but none as miserable as this one.

"Well, what are you waiting for now, Doctor?"

"Hmm?"

"Continue! Examine your patient."

I hesitated one brief second before forging ahead. I first cleaned the wound on her leg and placed a bandage over the cut. I removed her shoes. I lifted her skirt, removed her pink cotton underpants, pulling them over her buttocks, down her thighs, knees and legs, and placed them on the chair she had sat on. I stood at the foot of the table and pulled the towel toward me, bringing the patient closer. I placed the heel of each shoe into the metal stirrups on either side of the table, then pulled her a bit closer yet, so that her bent knees collapsed outwardly. Finally, I put on a pair of rubber gloves, lubricated my finger and inserted it into the girl's vagina, careful so as not to disturb her hymen if she was a virgin.

I immediately discerned from her internal condition that the girl had recently delivered a child. Moreover, I realized that as the purpose of her mother's visit was to determine whether or not her daughter was a virgin, the woman was obviously unaware of that fact. Undoubtedly, she had a right to know. *Ha!* I would enjoy shocking the condescending woman with the news that she had a grandchild. I would enjoy seeing her face change at the news.

Then again, something gnawed at me and I thought further, ostensibly prolonging the examination for some seconds as the thought struck me that perhaps I shouldn't tell her.

What about this young girl's tears and utter despondency? I guessed that the girl didn't want her mother to know of the child. Perhaps the baby had died; what would be the point then? And, if the baby were alive, I was certain neither this girl nor her baby would receive much solace from the woman who now sat like a stone statue in my office.

She was obviously not married. If she were, the beautiful daughter of this wealthy woman would most certainly be wearing an impressive ring. And, if she were, would the point of the visit to my office be to determine if her conjugal state had been consummated? I didn't think so. Besides, the woman had been most abrasive to me. Why should I give her any unsolicited information?

No, I decided I would say nothing about the baby. I would only provide her with the information she'd sought and paid for.

I took off the gloves, disposed of them and turned to her. "The patient is not a virgin," I said.

The woman didn't flinch. She simply rose, as though expecting the news, and opened her handbag. She brought out a second envelope already bulging with cash and held it out to me.

"There's one thousand U.S. dollars in here, Doctor. Sew her back up. I'll be waiting in the car."

– Layla –

I awoke to pain in my vagina.

I was in bed at home, a curl under my sheet. It was dark outside my bedroom window. Babajon was sitting on the edge of my bed, caressing my face. "Ah, my golden girl, I missed you at dinner last night and again tonight. It is sometimes hard to be a woman, no?"

The last thing I remembered was the drive, walking up some stairs with Maman and sitting down. I was a blank after that.

Now Maman approached my bed holding a glass of water and a bottle of pills. She held out the vial of medicine to my father. "The doctor has given her these to help with the pain. She's to take two every few hours and should be fine soon."

Then she spoke to me. "I told your father that the doctor said you're just having an unusually difficult moon, probably because you are in such bad health from your stay in Amreeka."

Why was Maman is talking to me? And why had she said I was in my moon? I wasn't.

Babajon took the vial from my mother and gave me two pills, small and blue. As I took the glass of water from my mother's hand, I understood in my grogginess that something had happened to me and whatever it was, it was my mother's doing.

Babajon said something to Maman and she answered him. I was preoccupied trying to figure out what was wrong with me. I moved and immediately felt thick pads between my legs and the belt that held them. There was cramping and a sharp biting pain, definitely within my vagina. *What had Maman done to me?*

With a start, it came to me that she must have found out about

Jasmine! In that case my life was no longer worth the sheet I was laying on. Yet, as Babajon caressed me, Maman smiled. She was talking to me, so she couldn't possibly have known I'd had a baby. *What in the world could she have done to me?*

"Your mother tells me you don't want to go back to UCLA," Babajon said. I remained silent. "I can't believe it's true, Layla," he said.

I felt like I'd been cut, as though I'd had surgery. *Had she had me sewn back up? Was it possible?* I looked at my mother through eyes heavy with disbelief.

Her eyes met mine defiantly. "Layla, answer your father," she said calmly.

That was it. She had me sewn up! I looked into my father's trusting brown eyes. "You don't want to return to Los Angeles?" he asked.

"Yes, I do," I said weakly. Babajon shifted on my bed and looked up at my mother, puzzled.

Maman was looking down at me with eyes that spoke of secrets and laughed airily. "Whatever for?"

"I need to say goodbye to everyone," I said. That was no challenge for her wits.

Her response was flip. "Silly girl," she said, "what's the point of going all the way back just to say goodbye? That's pointless, isn't it?"

"I need to take my exams."

She mimicked a laugh. "It must be these pills. You don't need to take exams if you're not continuing on with school."

Babajon shrugged. "Your mother is right, Layla. It doesn't make sense if you're no longer continuing your studies.

"I have to tell you; your decision surprises me. One minute you won't take a semester off and the next minute, you decide not to go back. I know you can do it. You just need to slow down." A look of disappointment fell off his face as he put his hands on his knees and stood up. "But, if this is what you want, this is what shall be. I can't say I'm sorry to hear you'll be back here with us." He smiled down at me. "I've missed you. It'll be good to have you home."

"I need to get my things," I said looking up at Babajon. *Please! Say, "Yes!"*

Maman was quick to answer. "I'm sure there's nothing there of too much importance, a few books … Your father will contact the manager there and ask that your things be packed and sent home. It's nothing for you to worry about. I'm certain that for a generous fee, the Americans will oblige."

She drew my curtains then gestured to Babajon. Taking him by the arm she led him away from my bed.

"You just rest now. Don't think about anything." Though her tone was level, her face bore a mixed expression of concern and resentment.

I tried to sort out my thoughts. *What had she said?* Ahh. *There is no point in telling your deluded father what you have become. I'm not sure he can take it in his condition."*

His condition! No doubt that the concern in Maman's face was for him. "Fotmeh will bring you some hot *chai nabot* with *nonne barbarri* and cheese," she said looking back at me. "The bread will do you good." Then she disappeared with Babajon.

Though I was filled with questions, the pills had made me groggy. I'd fallen asleep before Fotmeh came to the room with food. It was just as well, for I was far from hungry.

The next morning, Babajon woke me early to see how I was feeling and kiss me goodbye.

Sometime afterward, Maman came to my bedroom. She pulled my curtains apart and opened the window, then, with her arms folded across her chest, barely looking at me, she spoke. As she did, she kept looking around my bedroom, as if looking for something I'd hidden from her that might suddenly show itself.

When her eyes landed on me, she looked at me as though I were rotting fish. "You have disgraced your family. You have given yourself to dogs without giving a thought to your parents or to our impeccable reputation. You were raised to be a decent girl. Yet you've given your virginity – the only thing you had of real value – to infidels. Though you dare to come home and act like an innocent girl, behind that veil of lies you are nothing more than a *jendeh,* a whore, and you deserve to be thrown into the streets like the dog that you are.

"I have removed the signs of your past whoring only out of mercy for your poor father and for the rest of my family whose name you bear. My dear mother deserves far better than a slut like you for a granddaughter. Forevermore, you and I will share the secret of your infernal past and of my bravery in rectifying the evidence.

"But be warned, Layla: from this day on, you will live your life as the good, decent Muslim girl I raised you to be. You will forget everything you ever did in that foreign hell they call Amreeka and everyone you knew there – that includes your American boyfriend. You will bury him. You will marry immediately, and you will be the perfect wife, loyal, faithful and obedient. And you will go to the mosque and beg Allah to forgive you."

She said what she had to say and left me, but not before turning to me at my bedroom door. "And by the way, I have your passport. You won't be needing it."

My mind raced to Jasmine. Adam and Linda were expecting me home! I tried to get out of bed, but groggy and in pain, I fell back against the pillows. I would not take any more of the blue pills. I needed to stay awake.

When Fotmeh came to my room with breakfast, I idly asked her where my mother was. She said Maman was preparing to go out. I told Fotmeh I wanted to rest and that she was to return with the breakfast tray in an hour. I waited. When Fotmeh returned, I requested she summon Maman to my room.

As I'd hoped, she said, "Zahra Khanom has gone out."

Only then, when I was sure Maman wouldn't listen on the extension, I pulled myself out of bed and slowly made my way to Babajon's study. I called the post office and sent a telegram to Los Angeles: ARRIVAL DELAYED – STOP – RETURNING HOME SOON – STOP – MISS YOU ALL – STOP – LAYLA

46
ON THE MARKET

In my mother's attempt to repair a torn woman, she'd had a doctor sew my vaginal tissues together to reconstruct virginity.

Though the stitches healed, and my physical pain soon subsided, I was emotionally butchered. My heart, already in shreds from the trauma of losing David and then a secret pregnancy, was slashed anew.

The "American boy I was to bury" as Maman had so delicately phrased it, was already buried, embedded deeply within me.

There were those who, unlike me, believed that David was had died, but not one hair on his head, not one moment I had spent with him, not one word I heard him speak, would ever be erased from my memory. No surgery could sever David from my heart or lessen my love for him.

After what Maman had done, I could no longer deny that her love for me was conditioned on being the daughter she wanted. A mother's love wasn't meant to girdle. Her actions helped me confirm the resolve that had budded in me through my time that last month at home, my meeting with Shireen and her newborn daughter and my longing for Jasmine. Now it blossomed into a promise: I would never give Jasmine away.

I resolved that I would keep her close to me as my own meat and bone and the seed and blood of my beloved. I would mother her.

And, by all that was holy, I swore that I would be a very different kind of mother to her than Maman had been to me. Yes, I would keep my child at my side and, somehow, I would make it work – *if* I could get back to her.

I'd telegrammed Adam and Linda to let them know that although my return home had been delayed, they could expect me back shortly. They had their own lives to live and had done far too much for me already. I couldn't expect their kindness and generosity to be limitless and I was plagued by thoughts of what might happen to my daughter if I didn't return to her soon.

Ironically, I'd planned to abandon her to strangers because I was so certain I was unable to keep her. Now, determined to keep her yet unable to get to her, I was in danger of abandoning her nonetheless. I had to return to her.

In addition to thoughts about Jasmine, I was concerned for my beloved Babajon. Maman had said he was ill, but I had no idea what was wrong with him. Maman had been vague.

I turned to Cobra for information about his health. When she categorically denied knowing of any problem with him, I turned to Khaleh Bahia.

"*Beh Khodah*, I swear to God, your mother hasn't breathed a word of it to me. That day in the kitchen was the first I'd heard of it and she will say nothing more to me. I swear to all the prophets that's the truth."

Why wouldn't Maman tell me what was wrong with my father? Then again, Babajon hadn't the slightest clue that I had been subjected to surgery. Or why. He knew so little of who I was, or rather, who I'd become. Maman had hoarded both our secrets, holding hostage the intimacy I'd shared with him in the past.

I watched my father like a hawk but could detect nothing different. I didn't see him take any medication, change his diet, tire easier, lose weight, gain weight or complain of pain. If there was something wrong with him, it was well hidden.

"Babajon, I want you to tell me honestly, how do you feel?"

"Excellent. With my golden girl back home, better than I deserve."

"Do you have regular checkups?"

He patted my back and smiled, looking into my eyes with curiosity. "Yes, I do. As a matter of fact, I've seen my doctor recently and I'm healthier than he is. Who has told you to worry about your father? Think of more important things."

Yet Maman had alluded to his "condition." *Had she lied?*

Living under the same roof as my mother was uncomfortable to say the least. Her chilly attitude towards me took on a veneer of light cordiality when my father was present.

I had to live with the knowledge that in her eyes I was a *jendeh,* a whore, whom she would tolerate only for as long as our secret remained safely hidden from the world. Babajon's discovery of our destination the day we rode in the back of that strange black car would be the final blow to a relationship between Maman and me; I would be kicked out of the house – perhaps trailing after Parveen Khanom.

Maman immediately began to spread the word that I had decided college was not for me after all.

I would be staying in Tehran. As soon as she decided I looked well enough, we three went to the Club, an announcement of my availability in the marriage market.

No one seemed to notice that I was miserable. Everyone remarked on how well I looked, and how wonderful it was that I'd regained my sanity and returned home to stay. Even Shireen didn't find my sudden turnaround confusing or worth noting. Only Ferri knew the truth.

From that night on, my life changed. I was no longer the schoolgirl I'd been before I left for America. I was now the marriageable daughter of Zahra and Hadi Saleh, and my life was a blur of fittings and social affairs that consumed me full-time.

As I assembled a trousseau, Maman set about selecting a son-in-law. She approached the job of finding me a husband with unrelenting vigor, harnessing and focusing all her manipulative talents to the task. It became her passion, and she worked me with the savvy of a seasoned Hollywood publicity agent, choosing which parties I attended, deciding whose home I would and wouldn't be seen at and outfitting me in expensive dresses for each event with jewels that were expensive, yet modest enough for an unmarried girl to wear.

It seemed Tehran had become a minefield; there was a new *khostegar* at every turn. Suitors began to appear as plentifully as if we had put a sign up in front of our house, "Anxious, wealthy mother has sole, virgin daughter, available for immediate marriage." And, though it was assumed that because of our rank in the community, "only the very best need to make offers," I could detect that under the circumstances, my mother would have willingly married me off to any reputable male. It was my father who became the more discriminating parent. She discussed little other than potential male callers with Babajon during breakfast and at our dinner table, pointedly excluding me from the conversation.

"Hadi *jon,* did you see how Dariush was courting you last night?" Maman said at breakfast the morning after a soiree. "I thought he would never let you go."

"He wants his youngest brother to call on Layla."

She nodded. "You said yes, of course." Though it could have been interpreted as a question, Maman meant it as a statement.

"No, of course not. Don't you recall? His mother's side? Her brother is an alcoholic."

I sat and listened to this sort of talk and thought about Linda Dunn, Susan, Jessica and the other Californian girls I knew, and I wondered how it came to be that I was sitting at this table and they were not. Had I kept my mouth shut about Parveen Khanom, I would have been in Westwood at that very moment.

But, even then, wouldn't I have ended up at this table in a year or two? It seemed this was the result of choices I'd made. *But when had I sealed my fate? When I refused David's marriage proposal? When I agreed to go to UCLA? When I fell in love with science? When I accompanied Babajon to work? When I was born?*

I'd spoken to David of obligations I had to other people. I was speaking of these two people sitting at the table with me. *Had I actually refused a life with David, so they could choose my husband? And what about Jasmine?* I'd left my daughter behind with the intention of giving her up, my own flesh and blood, my beloved's child. *Why?* To save the reputations of these two people. A woman who treated me with such disregard. In any event, I'd allowed David to leave me behind and relocate a *kibbutz* in Israel, and I'd left Jasmine behind in Los Angeles. I was trapped in Iran.

"Apparently, many eligible men have taken note of our daughter," Babajon said, smiling at me proudly across the table. "She was always beautiful and now she is even considerably more valuable as a wife because of her stay in America."

He spoke directly to me and the pride he felt showed on his face. "Now that you've lived in the United States for two years, you are an important asset to any up-and-coming young businessman, particularly since our country is so intent on becoming westernized." I smiled at his goodness and his naiveté.

He reached for a platter of food and spoke to Maman. Though his tone was light-hearted, no doubt he meant what he said. "On top of that, our daughter has lived among the beasts and survived; she's returned from a place of a different culture with her decency intact. That also is a credit to her." He tipped his head to Maman. "As well as to your impeccable upbringing of her, Zahra Khanom."

I thought Maman might choke on her food.

In the weeks following that first evening at the Club, we sometimes received two *khostegars* a day, one arriving for afternoon tea and another for tea after dinner.

An intermediary acting on behalf of the gentleman caller seeking a wife – his parents, his uncle, or perhaps his married older brother – would mention to my father that the boy's family was interested in visiting me. If my parents approved of the boy, he'd make an appointment to visit, along with his parents, of course. I sat quietly during these visits, while our respective parents directed the conversation. Through their visit, I remained quiet, the deafening sound of my broken heart filling my ears, completely miserable, wishing I could disappear. I spoke only when addressed. As tradition required, I circled the room serving our guests *chai* on the tray Cobra had set out, then took my seat again, sullen and mute.

Each word these *khostegars* spoke was like a scratch on the blackboard that was my heart. Every hungry glance they stole at me churned my stomach. Their very presence challenged my ability to return to Jasmine, and I hated them for that. I would wait some decent amount of time before making eye contact with Babajon, requesting silent permission to leave, which he always allowed. Excusing myself, I would return to the sanctum of my room, Maman's look cold as ice, my head splitting, my life in shambles. There, in my solitude, I would uncover my little girl's photo from its hiding place and gaze at it, while I tried to figure out a solution to my problem.

I couldn't run away and didn't even try. My Iranian passport was still valid as were both the student visa stamped inside and the exit visa allowing me to leave Iran. But both were useless to me. Maman had them all along with my plane ticket back to Los Angeles, and I had no idea where she had put them. Besides, I had no money. I was helpless. There was nothing I could do to extricate myself from Iran.

I found reasons to reject every *khastegar* that called on me. Yet, they continued to line up at our door like ants to water. While my rejections amused Babajon, Maman became increasingly angry.

Alone with me, she remonstrated. "Layla, don't you try to play your smart games with me. If you think you can keep refusing every *khostegar* that comes to us, you're wrong. I will not stand for it. And don't think you're too good for them, because you are not. You should be happy that any of these men even look at you with the thought of marriage. And you can thank me that they do!"

Shireen misunderstood. "Holding out for the top of the heap? *Vye!* You always were clever, Layla. Every time you reject a *khostegar*, you add another pearl to that strand of pearls you so proudly wear around your neck. With each fine prospect you reject, it grows longer, and you become even more desirable to the next man. Just be careful you don't say no to the top of the heap."

Ferri was my safe haven, the only person with whom I could be myself. How many tears I shared with my angel! I confessed how sorry I was that I'd left Jasmine behind and told her of my decision to raise her myself on my return to the States.

Yet even Ferri didn't comfort me, but instead, fought with me constantly. She loathed Maman for what she had done to me and called her barbaric. "Find your passport, Layla! Where could it be? Think! It must be somewhere in the house. Keep looking! You must find it! Find it, and leave! I'll get you the money for a ticket. Hamid will help. You have to weigh the love for your father and your horrible mother against your love for your child and her need for you. For once and for all, get out and live your life!"

During those first weeks stuck in Iran, all I could do was send Adam and Linda quickly scribbled postcards saying I was "coming home very soon." I could barely face the truth of the situation myself, and I was frantically trying to keep my ex-roommates from realizing how bad my situation was in Iran, fearing what would happen to Jasmine if they realized I was stuck, unable to return to my baby.

One morning, after I'd overstayed my time in Tehran for almost a month, Ferri suggested I telephone Adam and Linda. "Layla, call them so they can hear your voice. Don't just write. Call and tell them you'll be home soon. You're bound to find your passport. You're over three weeks overdue now. You can't just keep sending postcards. They'll want to hear your voice."

I agreed. As Ferri didn't want her parents to see the long-distance call on their phone bill, we went to the post office to make the call. Ferri stood by me as I placed the call to the apartment through the operator. Adam answered after two rings. "Adam, it's Layla."

"Layla! Thank God you're home at last! My God, we were afraid you'd never come back! Are you at the airport? I'll come pick you up. What terminal?"

I'd made a mistake. I shouldn't have called. I began to cry. Ferri moved closer to me, as though to shield me from my tears.

"Layla?" I waited, hoping my weeping would subside before

speaking. I had intended to present a happy voice to my friends, to sound carefree and reassure them that I'd be home within a week, two at the most. Instead, I became hysterical, realizing all over again how desperately I yearned to be in Los Angeles – where both my child and my home were and where I belonged – and how futile my situation was. It seemed impossible to leave Iran. "Layla, are you there? What's wrong? Where are you?" Adam's concern was evident.

I tried to speak coherently through my tears. "I'm okay. I'm still in Iran. Jasmine. How's Jasmine?"

There was a pause before Adam responded and when he did, his disappointment screamed out over the wire. "She's fine." Another pause. "She's getting to be a handful though. I sure wish you'd get back here. We could use you around here. How soon will you be back?"

I wanted to say "soon" but the lie wouldn't come out. "I miss you all so much."

"We miss you, too. What's the matter, Layla? You sound like you're crying. Tell me what's wrong."

"My mother won't let me come back," I blurted out between sobs.

"What?" Adam shouted in disbelief. "You're not coming back? Is that what you just said? Your mother won't let you come back?"

I couldn't find my voice. Ferri held me in her arms and tissues appeared in her hand. When she tried to wipe my tears, I pushed her hand away and stiffened my shoulders. I had to sound resolute, make it clear that I'd be back in Los Angeles in the very near future. "I am coming back soon, Adam. I promise. I'll make her change her mind. You just expect me. I'll be there, I promise."

There was a moment of horrible silence on Adam's end before he said, "What's the problem?" When I didn't answer, he said, "Layla, we really need to know when you'll be back. This is terrible. I'm sorry. I mean, you know, school will be starting soon and Jasmine's a handful for me and Linda and … well, things are happening here, things that I haven't written you about but they're happening. Jasmine–"

"What's happened to Jasmine? Is she sick? Has something happened to her?"

"No, no, Jasmine is fine. You just really need to get back here fast. Does your mother know about her?"

"Adam, I know what a strain it must be for you and Linda to take care of Jasmine. I'll never be able to thank you enough. I promise I'll be back before classes start."

"Layla, you've really got to get back sooner than that! This baby thing is way too much for us. There's cleaning and feeding and she's up at night and, well, it's all just exhausting. We need you here!"

I took a deep breath and sounded as calm as possible through my panic. "I'm trying Adam. Believe me, I'm trying."

I needed a miracle.

47
MOBARAK! (CONGRATULATIONS!)

That evening, yet another *khostegar,* Rostam Shamshiri appeared at our door with his parents, the sort of people who have wealth written all over them, and the type of family Maman had always dreamed of marrying me into.

As usual, I didn't pay much attention to the *khostegar* or his parents.

I would follow my usual routine, greet our guests, serve them tea, then sit and ignore them until I could leave for the solitude of my room.

After the initial formalities, Rostam's father, Majid Shamshiri, spoke to Babajon. "Hadi Khan. I've been meaning to contact you. We may be able to help one another. I may be of some help in arranging for Saleh products to infiltrate other countries and you, my friend, may have some valuable contacts for me as well. And here we are." Mr. Shamshiri had the exclusive rights of distribution in Iran, Saudi Arabia, Lebanon and Kuwait for a popular American soft drink.

Babajon smiled. "Of course. I will invite you to lunch as my guest at the Club. I'd be happy to discuss all this."

I lost interest in the conversation at that point. After several minutes, Maman suggested I serve our guests tea. Although they all refused as expected by the ritual of *tarroff,* that was my cue. I took the tray of tea Cobra had set out on the table and made the rounds, offering our guests tea, serving first my potential mother-in-law, Azar Khanom, then my mother, then Rostam's father, Babajon and finally Rostam.

As I circled the room, tray in hand, my parents were conversing with Rostam. I learned that he was an only child and that he was engaged in business with the United States as the distributor of several American record labels in Iran.

As I was serving my father tea, I heard Rostam say that he was very pleased with his business and that the future looked even brighter. He had no real love of music, he said, and in fact had no appreciation of music at all. I stood before him, holding the tray out to him, two cups of tea remaining on it, one for him and one for me. As I bent slightly so that he might take his cup, he said, "My business will be requiring me to go to America more often in the future." The tray tilted in my hand and I almost dropped it. The tea splashed over the rim of the cups.

"Layla!" my mother said, trying not to sound sharp. "You've spilled tea on our guest."

"*Bebakhsheed,* excuse me," I said. "I don't know what happened."

Rostam put his cigarette down in the ashtray beside him (the second since they'd arrived) and smiled up at me. He said the first words that were directed solely to me, spoken with a heavy Persian accent, pronouncing all the i's like long e's, rolling the r's and emphasizing every syllable equally. "*No perrr-oblem,*" he said. "*Eet ees no perrr-oblem.*" I smiled.

He took a cup of tea off the tray, dropped three sugar cubes into it and began stirring his cup with the teaspoon I quickly offered him along with another smile and several napkins.

My heart was racing. *He goes to America!* I sat down and smiled at him. "You go to America." I said in English. That's why you speak English so well." I felt the rush of adrenalin.

He put out the cigarette he'd left burning in the ashtray, then answered me in Persian. "You are kind. I don't speak English very well. I am sure you speak far more fluently after living there. Did you like it?"

Be smart, Layla. "Not really. UCLA had good teachers, but I didn't like the people there or the lifestyle very much. After all, I am an Iranian."

I knew my mother was intent on listening to our conversation, and I could see her face, seemingly calm, except for eyes that were glowing. All I wanted to do was grill Rostam about his trips to America. Yet I couldn't appear forward and had to be careful not to dwell on that topic in front of Maman.

My father was unable to totally hide his surprise at the fact that I was actually speaking with one of these *khostegars*. Out of the corner of my eye, I saw him looking at me with wonder in his eyes then look at my mother, slightly baffled. I spent the duration of the visit smiling at Rostam, as much as decorum allowed, hoping to encourage him.

When the Shamshiris left, Babajon addressed me. He was more than mildly curious. "Is it my imagination, or do you like this boy?" Maman, who had held off smoking while in the presence of unknown men, now lit a cigarette and inhaled deeply. That she chose to smoke in my father's presence was evidence of her excitement.

"It's not your imagination, Babajon. I do like him."

My father knew me well. "Somehow, I didn't think he would be your type," he said. He was wrong. Rostam was my type, the type that traveled to America.

"You mean broad-shouldered?" Maman asked. "He's quite tall and broad-shouldered."

Babajon shrugged. "He smokes a lot."

"He seems very nice," I said, "and I find him interesting." I hadn't really noticed much about the way he looked except that – as Maman had said – he was well over 6 feet tall, and his overall stature was rather large, making him, I suppose, a bit of a giant. Beyond that he struck me as a larger-than-average typical Iranian man.

"I like his mother," Maman said. That was excellent for it meant Rostam had met with her approval.

That night, with my head on my pillow, I felt hopeful for the first time since Maman had taken me hostage. It seemed there was a chance that God had not totally forsaken me after all. If I were to marry Rostam, he could take me back to America and my Jasmine!

The following evening, Rostam's father telephoned Babajon to ask if Rostam could call on me again and Babajon consented.

Rostam returned to our house that Thursday afternoon, while Babajon was still at work. He sat in the living room and talked with me and Maman. This time, Fotmeh served us tea. Of course, he smoked. I found it odd that Maman joined him, for she'd only just met him.

After an hour or so of general conversation, Maman asked Rostam if he liked flowers.

"Flowers?" The question seemed to take him by surprise. "Yes, I suppose I like flowers."

Maman looked pleased. "My gardener took the liberty of planting some new bulbs and they've just came into bloom, actually, quite late in the season," she said. "I'm afraid I don't recall their name. They are quite pretty." She put out her cigarette and stood as if our meeting was over. "I think you'd like them. Layla *jon,* it's a lovely afternoon. Why don't you take Rostam to our gardens and show our guest the flowers that have recently bloomed?"

It was my turn to be surprised. Maman was hurling us together, inviting us to be alone without her as an escort – on Rostam's very first visit! Once again, my mother's unpredictability stunned me. The sheer force of her will astounded me. But I was all too happy to lead Rostam through the French doors off the living room to one of the side gardens to further probe his statement about traveling to America without my mother present.

In the summer temperatures, the fragrance of blossoming grapefruit and orange trees hung in the air. When we passed the swimming pool their sweet aromas mingled with the distinct odor of chlorine. Walking ahead of Rostam, I had the strange sense that his eyes were glued to my derrière. I was glad I'd chosen to wear a somewhat telling skirt. "Your mother likes Rostam," he said. "I can see that."

"Does she?" I asked, acting the coquette. "How can you tell?"

"Why else would she want us to spend time alone like this? And, though I'm happy she does, it would make Rostam far happier to know her daughter likes me."

Some part of me noted how he sometimes referred to himself by his name, but, in the big picture, it seemed unimportant to me. "Why else would I be here?" I asked.

"Because your mother asked you to show me the flowers and you are a good daughter."

I laughed. "You know that's not what I mean."

We passed the Japanese peach tree flaunting its summer fruit. I picked a ripe peach off the tree and handed it to Rostam. He insisted I enjoy it. I held it, toying with it, turning it around in my hand, feeling its odd flat shape then bit in. It was sweet, and its juice filled my mouth.

We approached the rose garden where dozens of roses in an array of colors shot out on branches in all directions like so many exploding firecrackers, lighting up the garden with brilliant hues. "Do you like roses?" I asked.

"Why not? Do you?"

"Yes. I like their scent and I like all the colors," I said.

"Your favorite being?"

"Oh, I couldn't say. There are so many pretty ones to choose from; scarlet, pink, white..."

He was looking me up and down. "Rostam very much likes the color you're wearing, Layla. It becomes you. What do you call that color?"

"Thank you. I'm not really sure. It's a rust, or burnt pumpkin, orange," I chuckled. "Call it what you like. Do you travel often to America?"

"As I need to. Do you enjoy traveling?" he asked.

"Yes, very much."

"And how do you like being home?" He brought out a pack of cigarettes, took one out and lit it with the gold Dunhill lighter he took out of his pocket.

"It's wonderful. Have you been to Los Angeles?"

"Yes," he said as he pulled on the fresh cigarette.

"Have you seen Disneyland?" I asked casually.

"No, I'm afraid I haven't."

"No doubt you've seen the round Capitol Records building. You probably go there since you work with music." I wondered how Rostam would react if he found out I'd seen it with a boy… alone … a boy who later kissed me, and that I – I stopped myself. I knew the answer.

"I only go to Los Angeles for business and hasn't seen much of it. I spend my free time in Las Vegas. Rostam likes to gamble." My heart sank; quite possibly, my face reflected my disappointment. "I think there's quite a lot I haven't seen in Los Angeles. Perhaps I just need to know where to look," he said. "or someone to show Rostam the city." He smiled broadly then, and I noted that his teeth were amber from cigarette stains. But I didn't care. He was willing to go to Los Angeles and that's all I cared about. I breathed in deeply, filling my lungs with renewed hope. I spoke more enthusiastically than I meant to, anxious to encourage his last thought.

"Yes! Los Angeles is a wonderful city. There's the beach, and the mountains, and the theaters, Hollywood Boulevard, and – just so much to see!"

Right then and there I was sure. I knew that if Rostam would guaranty me a ticket back to Jasmine, I'd gladly marry him. I'd never feel as good about any *khostegar* as I did about Rostam at that very moment.

Rostam looked at me through squinting eyes. "What do you want out of life, Layla? May I ask you that? What is your dream?"

"My dream? To marry and travel."

"And children?"

"Children?"

"Yes, do you like children? Do you want children?"

"Oh, yes. Yes, of course. Still, if I marry a man who doesn't want children, that would be fine too, because my priority would always be my husband."

He looked thoughtful. "You will make a fine mother," he said, smiling again.

"And you, Rostam? What do you want out of life?"

He took a long drag of his cigarette then looked up at the horizon and waved the cigarette across the sky. "I want it all. Know this, Layla: Rostam is a greedy man who wants it all, and wants only the best of everything." He looked at me. "And Rostam will have it all."

He passed his arm across the gardens in a sweeping gesture. "My business is excellent, and it has made me very rich. I have everything money can buy. It is not for nothing that I was named after the greatest hero Persia has ever known." He took a hurried drag off his cigarette and patted his heart. "That Rostam was a myth; this Rostam is real." I again noticed that he spoke of himself in third person and found it odd, but again, I didn't care.

He took a step back and spoke forcefully, counting on his fingers as he enumerated, "Rostam has the best house, the best furniture, the best suits, the best car … Rostam never settles for second best. And I shall have only the best there is for my wife." He took a step towards me.

"There's no need to play games or draw this out. I saw you at the Club before you left for America and wanted you then. I made inquiries and was certain I did. But then, I was told you had left. Since your return, I've been abroad on business, in Italy and elsewhere. No matter, we are now face to face.

"You are the best there is, Layla, and Rostam must have you. You are the most desirable girl in Tehran. I see your beauty; I am physically attracted to you. I know who you are, I know your background, and I've seen how you carry yourself. On top of that, you are highly educated.

"You are as pure and sweet as any of these flowers your mother wants you to show me. You are the one Rostam chooses to be his wife."

He extended his arm. "May I hold your hand?" he asked. I nodded shyly, so happy I thought I would burst. "I intend to ask your father for your hand immediately. Rostam will arrange an excellent marriage contract, most beneficial to you. We will marry and go to America for our honeymoon, New York for one week and then Las Vegas before going to Los Angeles for a week and you will show me the beach and Disneyland and these places you speak of."

I was breathless. "Can we go straight to Los Angeles and then Las Vegas? Let's not stay in New York at all. Is that all right?"

He bowed. "As you wish."

It was that simple, that fast. *My baby was safe!* I would marry him, this angel who would take me to Jasmine and I would be with her at last to love her and take care of her at last and forever. I'd never leave her again. I was ecstatic.

"Now, where are these nameless flowers your mother wants Rostam to see?" he asked, smiling widely.

"I have no idea."

We shared a good laugh, then returned inside the house. Rostam told Maman he would like permission to return that evening when Babajon was home.

When he left, Maman showered me with questions.

I told her nothing of his proposal. Then I secluded myself with my thoughts and my photo of Jasmine until he returned that evening and told Babajon of his desire to marry me.

"Although my wife and I are certainly honored, this is most unusual," Babajon said. "I'm sure you are aware that it is the place of your esteemed father to ask for our daughter's hand in marriage." My father looked at me, wide-eyed. "And my daughter should not be present for these discussions."

"Please don't misunderstand me, *Aghayeh* Saleh," Rostam said. "Rostam intends no disrespect to our traditions, to my parents, to Khanom Saleh and yourself, or to your lovely daughter. I simply must first speak for myself and tell you that it is I, Rostam, who has decided to marry your daughter and it is I, Rostam, who will be setting the wheels in motion and negotiating the marriage contract through my father.

Ask for whatever you want and Rostam will direct his father to accept your terms, so long as you give me your word tonight that you will allow me to marry your daughter before the onset of *Muharram*."

This was wonderful news or, as Rebecca would have put it, "the nuts on the banana split with a cherry on top!"

As Shiite Muslims, we were not to wed during the three-month period of *Muharram,* a time of grief, fasting, and mourning, commemorating the death of Mohammad's son-in-law and successors and had not realized that the start of *Muharram* was just ahead of us.

I could not guess what Rostam's reasons were for wanting an expedited marriage, and I asked no questions. I was in a major rush myself, so his request suited me perfectly. Babajon, however, hadn't taken to this novel style of proposing, nor did he care for the idea of a hurried marriage. He looked at me questioningly; I nodded, enthusiastically. Then he looked at his wife. Sitting regally on the couch, Maman met my father's eyes calmly, merely holding her eyelid down a mili-second longer than needed. Babajon turned back to Rostam, who'd just put his cigarette out while waiting for Babajon's answer and extended his hand.

"You have my word," Babajon said. They embraced. "*Mobarak!* Congratulations! My daughter is what I prize most. I wish her and you, both health and happiness."

My mother rose to meet Rostam's outstretched arms. "*Mobarak!* Congratulations! Allah willing, may you live long happy lives together and have many sons." Arrangements were made for Rostam's father to meet with Babajon to confirm the marriage contract, Rostam kissed me chastely on both cheeks and left. No sooner had the door been shut behind him then my father eyed me sharply. "Are you certain you want to do this?" he asked, skeptically.

"Yes." I know I sounded enthusiastic.

"You're sure you want to marry this man?"

"Yes, Babajon. I'm sure."

"You'll be happy as his wife?"

"Yes." My heart was aching, for I understood he had stopped himself from adding, "and nothing more?" Ever since Maman had ordered me to convince him that I no longer desired to return to UCLA, I think my father came to believe he didn't know me all that well after all. He put his hands in his pockets and his shoulders twitched into a shrug.

"All right then, Layla, if it will make you happy, it's fine with me." He wrapped his arms around me tightly.

"Thank you, Babajon."

He embraced me, holding me tightly to him. *"Mobarak!* Congratulations!"

Maman held my shoulders and kissed my forehead, her lips barely grazing my skin. Beneath her smile was a world of relief. *"Mobarak!"*

The following morning, I ran to Ferri's house to give her the news.

"*Joonie*! What are you doing? You can't marry this man! You don't love him. You don't even know him!"

"None of that is important and I couldn't care less," I said. "I only know that marrying him is the only way I'll get to Jasmine."

"Don't do this!" she begged. "There must be another way."

"There isn't," I said calmly. "Besides, aren't you the one who always says love and marriage are two different things? I'm not marrying him for love."

Ferri wasn't persuaded. "You're not me, Layla," she sulked. "And you're definitely not Shireen. I'm sorry you're doing this. I wish you'd reconsider. Please!"

"Ferri, Rostam is the miracle I asked God for. He even has the name of a great hero! Let's go to the post office. I want to call Adam and Linda and tell them I'm coming home." I practically dragged her back to the post office pay phone I'd used to call Adam before.

"Linda? Hi! It's Layla."

"Hold on," she said dryly, "let me get Adam."

"Wait–" She was gone. She hadn't sounded happy to hear my voice.

"Layla! Are you still in Iran?" At least Adam was glad to hear from me.

"Yes, I'm coming back soon though. That's why I'm calling. How's Jasmine?"

"Bigger. When will you be here?"

"I'm getting married. I'll coming to Los Angeles on my honeymoon. I don't know the exact date. It'll be within the month."

"Wait. You're getting *married*? Who to? Does he know about Jas?"

My Jasmine was now Jas? "No, of course he doesn't know about her and he can't. It doesn't matter who he is. I'll be there to take care of her. Okay? Tell Linda, too."

"Uh, okay. So, you're getting married and the guy doesn't know about Jas." Adam's voice had changed. Now he sounded put-off and distant. "Well, okay, congratulations on your marriage. So, what's the exact date you're arriving?"

"I don't know. Please. Tell me how Jasmine is doing?"

"I told you, she's big." He took a deep breath. "And she's getting bigger." A pit fell in my stomach.

"Layla... Linda and I are really having a hard time here with your baby. Our lives are pretty messed up. We expected you back over two months ago, and now you're saying ... what the hell? You're getting married? I'm thrilled for you, really. But the guy doesn't even know about Jas? And you're coming here on your honeymoon? And you don't know when you'll be here ... " His voice trailed off. "This is messed up."

Now my stomach was drawing knots around itself. I tried to think clearly. I didn't know how much of the truth I could share with Adam.

He went on, sounding angrier now, impatient with me. "Look Layla, this is really hard for us. No, it's not hard, it's impossible! We can't keep this up. Linda and I have classes ... and there's other stuff going on that's, well ... it's really, really frustrating."

My eyes were shut. I didn't know what to say but it didn't matter. Adam didn't give me a chance to say anything. "Jas still wakes up a few times during the night and cries until we pick her up and walk her around, sometimes for hours. I mean, hell, Layla, she's a full-time thing and she's *your* baby!"

Adam's anger was so hard to accept. My heart was racing, and I felt my jaw freeze. I couldn't respond. Adam composed himself and went on, forcibly calmer. "Look, Linda and I have talked about this. When we said we'd take care of Jas, we didn't think you'd just take off like this and not come back. We never figured that your mom wouldn't let you come back, and we'd have to do all this for too long. Now you're getting married and going off on a honeymoon somewhere and–"

"I'm sorry. I didn't know either! And it's not somewhere, it's L.A."

"Yeah, well, you were going to place her with an adoption agency when you get back anyway, so – well, we've talked to UCLA, and they've put us in touch with a few agencies."

"Adam, No, you can't do that! I'm coming! I told you. Adam don't do that. Please! I'll be there! I promise, I swear! I'm getting married soon. I'm coming right after the wedding."

"Okay, okay. Calm down, I haven't done anything yet. But Linda has definitely had it. So, all I can tell you is to just hurry home. Okay?"

"I'm coming. Tell Linda. I'll give you the exact date as soon as I know. I promise I will. Please promise me you'll wait. Tell Linda not to do anything."

"Get back here."

After Adam hung up, I stood holding the receiver until Ferri took it from my hand and replaced it on the hook. I spoke to my friend as if recounting a bad dream. "They talked to UCLA about giving up Jasmine! They're calling my baby 'Jas'! Ferri, they're going to give her away. Oh, my God, I have to marry him."

"Did you tell them that you want to keep her?" Tears in my eyes, I hung my head. Ferri had heard every word I'd said. She knew I hadn't told him of my changed intention not to put Jasmine up for adoption. I'd been too nervous, too thrown by his anger. But I did tell him I was coming soon and begged him not to do anything.

"Layla, to hell with Rostam and the wedding. Don't marry him. Don't wait. Go home right now and tell your mother that Rostam needs your passport and Iranian identity card and he needs them *now*. Take them. Get yourself to Los Angeles. I told you, I'll get you the money."

That's exactly what I planned to do. When Adam said they'd talked about adoption agencies, I felt like they'd talked about ending my life. That's when I was absolutely positive that I'd never let anyone take my child. I was her home and she was mine.

I would have left Rostam in the lurch in a second and would have left my parents humiliated, left them to deal with the mess after I'd gone. All I wanted was my precious baby, to see her, smell her, touch her, wrap my arms around her and hold her close to my heart. I wanted to smile at her and call her name, hold David's child in my arms and tell her about her father. I wanted to mother her and be there for her in ways my mother had never been there for me. I wanted my child and to hell with everyone else.

"Maman *jon*, Rostam has asked that I give him my passport and my identity card."

"Why?"

"He wants to take it to the passport office and get a new one."

"He doesn't need the old one to do that."

"He says I should give them to him now."

"I won't give them to you. I'll give them to him myself tonight."

That night, Maman wordlessly handed an envelope to Rostam with my passport and identity card in it. On it, she'd written the word *Layla*. The keys to my freedom had been passed from my old warden to my new one.

That very night, we set our wedding date for September 4. The following morning, I telegrammed Adam and Linda: ARRIVING BY SEPTEMBER 7 – STOP – POSITIVE – STOP – I TOLD YOU – STOP – PROMISE – STOP – LOVE LAYLA

48
VOWS

The day before my wedding, Ferri came to my house.

As soon as we were alone, she dug into her handbag and gave me an envelope from Adam sent air mail. I tore it open, wary because of the anger in his voice when we'd last spoken and his mention of the adoption agency. Inside were three handwritten pages. He'd enclosed no photos.

Dear Layla,

We got your telegram. We were really upset with you for leaving us in the lurch like that with Jas. Thank God you're coming home!

Now that you're sure you'll be home by the 7th, I'm going to tell you what I meant when I said there were things going on. I couldn't tell you on the telephone because Linda was there, and I didn't want her to hear me.

I don't know how to tell you this, except to just say it. I want you to know before you come home. I met someone last month and I think I'm in love. The thing is, he's a boy. His name is Levi, and he's wonderful. We're moving in together this weekend. We found an apartment yesterday, so by the time you get here, I will have moved out.

Linda doesn't know how I feel about Levi. She thinks we're just friends. I'm not sure how to tell her or anyone, except you. I haven't been able to move in with him until now because I couldn't leave Linda alone with Jas. So, you see, Jas has also been in the way of Levi and me. Now that I know you're finally coming home, I can leave.

I've never kept a secret from Linda. I'm not at all sure how to tell her this. She doesn't know any other guys who like guys and I'm afraid of how she'll react. Even though people may not think that this is a natural preference, it is with me, and I can't let it stop me from letting love into my life if that's what this is. I'll wait and see how things work out between Levi and me before I say anything to anyone else. Maybe I'm wrong about myself. In any case, I just have to tell someone how excited and scared I am, and you're the one person I know will be supportive and happy for me. You've had your secrets, too. I know I can tell you anything. I guess I always sensed I was different from other guys and just didn't want to face it.

Surprised, huh? Kind of ironic, I know. Life is funny. You slapped me that day for kissing you on the way back from Catalina – and look at us now. You have a baby, and I'd rather kiss a guy.

I think I tried to kiss you that day because I figured if it would work at all for me with a girl, it would be with you since I liked you so much. No, I loved you. I did, Layla. I think I still do. You are so beautiful and sweet, so different from other girls. Any man would be lucky to have you. And I meant every word I said about marrying you.

Anyway, I think it may be tough for Linda to accept or even understand what's going on with me, and I'll wait, at least wait until you get back before I tell her, so she'll have you to talk to. I'm not telling Mom and Dad, at least not for now, and Levi hasn't told his parents either, though he's known for a lot longer than I have and he's had other boyfriends. I just wanted to tell you. I think you have a right to know after all we've been through together.

Don't worry that I'm moving out. When you get back, I'll always be there for you and I'll be Uncle Adam to Jas. Glad you're coming home at last! You were gone way too long, and it's been really hard without you. We all miss you. Hurry home. Make sure you're here by the 7th. We're all counting on it.

Congratulations on your wedding. He's a lucky man.

Love,

Adam

Adam liked men! *The man in whose arms I'd melted and whose lips I'd so enjoyed, preferred kissing men?* Yes, life was funny. I wondered what else was going on in Los Angeles.

I realized that without Adam there to support her, Linda would have an incredibly hard time dealing with Jasmine. I couldn't blame her. She'd never expected me to be gone so long and she'd done far more than anyone had the right to expect. One month had become more than three.

Now, at last, thanks to Rostam, I'd be back there within days. Our wedding was set for the following evening. The morning after, Rostam had a short meeting scheduled with his office staff and after that we'd head for the airport. I'd be back in Los Angeles not a moment too soon – just in time to snatch my baby out of harm's way. Though I'd told Adam and Linda that I would see them on the seventh, Rostam and I would be arriving in Los Angeles on the sixth, so I would be surprising them, showing up at their apartment a day earlier than expected.

I would simply figure out how to get away from Rostam once we were in Los Angeles.

The day of the wedding, women of our two families prepared me for the auspicious occasion of sleeping with a man that night. With the exception of Maman, they all assumed it would be a first for me.

My eyebrows were plucked, my pubic hair and the hair under my arms was removed with a depilatory and a female *band andoz* pulled the rest of my body hair off from the roots with a simple line of thread, leaving only my eyelashes and the hair on my scalp intact. The women sang ancient songs while they rubbed my body with oils until it glistened, then rubbed henna on the bottoms of my feet and my palms for good luck. I was well aware of the fact that Rostam was also being groomed for our wedding night, his body hair removed as well, and his feet and palms also rubbed with henna. I imagined, ancient songs and jokes were being shared among the men.

Throughout my preparations, I was dreaming happily of David, remembering the afternoon I'd readied myself for him.

Aynor and her two assistants had worked like donkeys to have my wedding dress ready in time, a white silk gown and train embellished with French lace. A long white veil fell from my crown to the floor, covering me like a sheer shroud.

We were married at my parents' home. In addition to the customary official from the Tehran registry office, there to mark the occasion into the city's public records and to record the event onto our identity cards, the only people present were our closest family members. The ceremony, held in our living room, was a traditional Muslim religious affair presided over by a *mullah aghd*, a clergyman. Rostam and I sat cross-legged on the floor facing the mullah on the *sofreh aghd*, a large silk cloth with paisley designs of white with deep burgundy and gold. Various items had been assembled on the *sofreh* along with a Quran: sweets, flowers, silver and gold covered hazelnuts and a decanter of water. There were items of symbolic value: apples symbolizing plenty, honey to ensure a sweet life, gold coins for prosperity, bread to signify God's blessings and a bowl containing goldfish for good luck. There was also a gift from Rostam's to me, a pair of large ornate stand-up mirrors framed in silver and gold with matching candleholders. Shireen, along with Rostam's sole female cousin, Mojgon, stood over our heads, each rubbing a large solid piece of sugar, sending powdered sugar around us like a haze.

The *mullah aghd* recited prayers, then asked, "Rostam Shamshiri, are you ready and prepared to be good to this woman who is to be your wife, and take care of her, love her always and be faithful to her?"

Rostam answered solemnly "Yes."

"Layla Saleh, are you ready and prepared to obey this man who is to be your husband, honor him and be faithful to him?" By tradition, the bride's silence indicated shyness borne of her virgin innocence. The guests chuckled and chanted on cue. *The bride has left to cut flowers.*

The *mullah* repeated, "Layla Saleh, will you obey this man who is to be your husband, honor him and be faithful to him?" I remained mum and again our audience, responded, *The bride has left to gather honey.*

The *mullah* adjusted his turban and reset his glasses on his nose, signaling mock impatience. "I will ask you one more time. Layla Saleh, are you ready to obey this man who is to be your husband, honor him and be faithful to him?"

I was to answer now. "With my father and mother's permission, yes." I heard the applause of the onlookers. The men whistled, the women chanted a high-pitched, pulsating *'Lee-lee-lee,'* their tongues clicking off the backs of their palates, as their voices undulated with the mantra for blessings. Rostam lifted my veil and we spooned honey into one another's mouth.

The mullah's job done, he left, along with the registrar who had entered the information of our wedding onto our two identity cards. We were officially man and wife.

It was time to receive our wedding gifts. The guests approached us in turn and presented their gifts to the *shah damaad,* the groom, and his *aroos,* his bride, after first kissing us both, pressing their cheek to each of ours, and officially congratulating us.

It went on and on, family members alternating between my family and Rostam's, each paying their respects with a gift to the newlyweds, the new *Agha va Khanomeh Shamshiri,* Mr. and Mrs. Shamshiri, as we sat on the floor around our *sofreh.* Throughout, the high-pitched women's voices singing, *'Lee-lee-lee'* filled the air and gold coins, rose petals, and white sugar *noghl,* rained over our heads.

I knew I had made all these people happy by marrying Rostam.

I saw my mother's smile. She'd managed to fool the world and save her family's name. I'd married into a family that was almost as wealthy as Shireen's in-laws, though Rostam was still a working man. Babajon was happy to think that I truly was happy. I'd even thrilled the guests by wearing an expensive and elaborate wedding gown, then playing the traditional prank when asked by the mullah if I'd be faithful and obedient before answering, "yes."

None of it meant anything to me. I simply did what I had to do to get to Jasmine, much like applying for the new exit visa I'd need, packing my suitcase, consummating my marriage that night with Rostam, and boarding the plane for Los Angeles.

Though we'd rushed the marriage ceremony, it was impossible to rush the wedding reception with all the preparations required for a large and opulent event. It was agreed that the formal reception would be held after our honeymoon and after *Muharram* had passed. Of course, I had no plans to be present in Iran to attend that reception. Following the ceremony, there was only an abbreviated reception for the families. Then it was time for me to leave my father's home for my husband's. Rostam and I said our goodbyes . My parents and in-laws kissed the Quran and held it above our heads to bless our journey as we passed under their arms and across the threshold on our way to our new lives.

I entered Rostam's house as his bride. The house was palatial, each room larger than the next, with ceilings so high I thought I'd shrunk, intricate moldings and imported doors. The rooms were furnished ostentatiously with silk Persian rugs everywhere that shimmered in the light. Shireen's house was not far away. This was to be *my* gilded cage.

Hah!

49
VIRGIN BRIDE

– Rostam –

Rostam is pleased.

I look at my new bride. I gaze at her ripe body as she stands naked at the foot of our marriage bed. I see she is more beautiful than I'd imagined. Her skin is the color of dusk. Her eyes, like topaz, are cast down, too demure to look at me. Her long hair, earlier combed into an elegant up-do, now falls gracefully to her shoulders in soft, rich waves. Her breasts are full and as luminous as lotus blossoms. I follow her body down to a slim, tapered waist then to gently flared hips and proportioned thighs, her legs as long and lean as a gazelle's. She is at once exquisite and erotic.

Rostam is proud for he has done very well. I have looked forward to this night. Forevermore, this beautiful woman belongs to me. She has it all. She is not only beautiful, she is a woman of upbringing. Rostam has tested her. She did not succumb to my advances, which most women find irresistible, and had allowed me no more than a kiss. Once, I offered her my tongue and she had pulled back in utter confusion. She has proven herself to be a good Muslim girl, a woman Rostam can trust. Yes, she will make an ideal wife and a good mother.

Fortunately, though her parents took an unnecessary risk in sending her to UCLA, she did not fall prey to Western views of a woman's independence, or to crazy American ideas that teach girls to treat their sexuality as though they are men. They raised their daughter well.

She was smart enough to realize her mistake, put silly ideas of college behind her, and return home to fulfill her life as a dedicated wife and mother. She will give Rostam strong sons. Should we have a daughter, Layla will ensure she, too, remains a virgin until marriage. She will never be allowed to live away from this house before marriage as her mother had allowed her daughter.

Layla will cater to Rostam, my home, and my children. She will be a valuable asset to my business interests as well. American music – like everything from that country – continues to climb in popularity. Though I know some English, an English-speaking wife will only add to my strengths as my business continues to flourish. Her exposure to the West has also given her a sense of style that combines the chic flair of the new American president's wife everyone speaks of – that Kennedy woman – with the conservative decorum that befits the wife of such a rich and important man as Rostam. Yes, Layla will benefit me greatly.

What a wonderful night this is! Just looking at Layla's naked body arouses my desire as it has rarely been stirred before. I will be gentle with my new wife. Rostam's vast sexual prowess will serve her well in helping her get through this night as painlessly as possible. Women have always liked my large stature and my ample size. I have sampled a multitude of them in bed: women of all ages, the youngest, a schoolgirl of thirteen, and the oldest, I later discovered, was my father's cousin, over seventy. I have bedded women of all sizes and shapes, poor women who gave themselves to me for the price of a beggar's meal, and women with family's wealth that came close to my own – well, perhaps I exaggerate; but they were very rich. Rostam enjoyed the company of some more than others, yet never thought for a second of making even the most beautiful of them his wife. A woman who would sleep with a man outside of marriage is not worth serious consideration, for such a woman is no more than a whore.

Yes, I resolve to be gentle with Layla. Of course, a woman of her class will never enjoy sex very much. So, I will complement my marriage bed with other sexual liaisons, to suit my fancy and satiate my substantial sexual needs. That is any man's prerogative and will lessen her wifely obligation. When I do choose to be physical with her, I know I will please her.

I notice that Layla holds a white square cloth in her slender hand. "What's that?" I ask. "Why are you bringing a handkerchief to our marriage bed?"

Layla speaks without looking up. Her voice is soft. "My mother has told me to do this."

Of course! Lost in thought, Rostam had forgotten the significance of the virginity napkin, as much a part of the wedding night as the marriage vow we took earlier, as much a tradition as marriage itself.

No doubt, Zahra Khanom has given her daughter proper instructions as to what to do with it and Layla will comply. I will say no more. I shall not allow it to distract me.

I'm anxious now, and full of anticipation. I reach for Layla and bring her down on the bed to me, then press my body to hers.

– Layla –

I try to suppress the surprising surge of passion I feel when Rostam presses against me.

When, during the last week he kissed me and I'd felt his tongue escape his mouth, I pulled away feigning puzzlement and indignation. Rostam had apologized. Now, as I feel his tongue press against my closed lips, I allow it to seduce my mouth and finally open and accept it as my body begins to accept his.

This is the first time I am experiencing arousal since the night with

David just over a year ago when Jasmine was conceived. David is my love; Rostam is my survival.

Rostam's desire for me is palpable, it's heat, contagious and, I suppose, all the various pent-up emotions in me that have been straining to burst, are now being given this physical, sexual outlet. Yet, I am determined to leash my passion for I must keep my head about me. I pray I will not appear experienced. And I fervently pray I will not conceive tonight, for I have proven to be fertile, and Rostam has thus far shown no intention of taking precautions.

And there is the napkin Maman has given me to be mindful of. My blood on the napkin will be Maman's reward for the doctor's handiwork. It will ease any fear that Rostam might discover the girl he's married is a fraud. As Rostam prepares to consummate our marriage, I ensure that the piece of white cloth is positioned properly underneath my pelvis.

I had expected intercourse with Rostam to somewhat resemble what I'd experienced with David, but it does not. My body naturally accepted David from the start, taken to him as if he were a part of me, craving his re-entry deeper inside me between every thrust. As Rostam enters me, my feeling of anticipation turns to physical anguish. I feel only pain, and more pain, as he forces his way past tissues sewn together.

My body tightens, and I claw his back, clench my fists, catch my breath and bite my lip, but refuse to utter a single cry. Then, even more horribly, I find that my body begins to respond. This pleasure is torture. I don't want to enjoy sex with this man. Yet, though I try not to move in rhythm with him, or rise up to meet him, I find the pleasure unavoidable, and again, find it difficult to restrain from crying out.

Upon awakening, I recall the day I'd awakened to David lying beside me.

I remember David's smell as Rostam rolls over and wishes me a good morning, smiles, and reaches for a cigarette. When he gets out of bed, he picks up the bloodied cloth, evidence that my maidenhead had been intact. Sometime this morning, he will call his mother and then one of them will call my parents to congratulate them on my proven virginity. Looking at the red-blotched cloth brings recollections of that wonderful morning with David when I'd found no more than a pink spot on my sheets. How I laughed, thinking what a fuss was made for a shade of pink. This blood is red. I will give the bloodied cloth not to my mother-in-law, but to Maman, who will safe keep it and show it to his mother should they ever accuse me of having been an unchaste bride.

My night of anguish has passed. I am almost with Jasmine.

50
ESCAPE

Early on the morning of the first day as man and wife, I cleansed myself with a douche consisting of cider, dill, vinegar and the essence of evergreen.

The mixture, which I'd obtained several days before, was believed to prevent conception or cause an early miscarriage if pregnant. I knew it was foolish, yet I performed the ritual.

After breakfast, I was introduced to our driver and Rostam's butler, Hassan, who drove us to the visa office.

Now a married woman, I could only leave Iran after receiving an exit visa upon presentation of a letter of permission signed by my husband. Rostam decided that I would travel with my old passport; we would apply for a joint passport as husband and wife after our honeymoon.

When we returned home from the visa office, Rostam instructed Hassan on what he was to pack for his trip, then went to his study for a few minutes before he left again with Hassan for his scheduled meeting with his office staff.

When Hassan returned home to finish packing for his master, I was in the midst of sorting through the clothes that had arrived from my parents' home to pack for Los Angeles. Hassan was to gather our luggage and some paperwork from Rostam's study, and together we would drive to Rostam's office, pick him up and continue on to Mehrabad Airport, well before our flight to Los Angeles was scheduled to depart. Once in Los Angeles, I'd find some excuse to leave Rostam. I'd flee to my child. *How could Rostam find me when he realized I was gone?* No one had the address to Adam and Linda's apartment. *What could he do?* Nothing.

I was finally packing to go home to Jasmine! All the while my heart was racing. I was going to start a new life for us in Los Angeles. The valuable gifts of jewelry I had received as wedding gifts would bring enough cash to take care of my baby and myself until I could settle and find a job. I would make sure Jasmine had everything she needed. I now understood that what she needed most was her mother. As for my parents, I thought I might lie and tell them that I'd escaped Rostam because he had abused me. Babajon would understand that. No matter, I would think about that once I was in Los Angeles, had secured Jasmine, and the secrecy of my location was ensured.

That morning was the first time I'd been alone with Hassan. The man made me uncomfortable. He was short and stout with beady eyes and a jaw line that seemed to reach up to meet his nose in the way a rodent's does. And he was continually scurrying quietly around the house and hovering underfoot like the rat he resembled. I came to think of him as The Rat. His voice was gruff, and he was, like his master, a chain-smoker. As I moved around the house, the man was everywhere I turned, making me feel as though he was watching to make sure I didn't steal anything from his master's house. I was moved to lock our bedroom door to ensure my privacy.

In my excitement, I packed very little clothing inside a small suitcase, opting to forego the larger one. Then I searched for my identity card, which I'd need at the airport. I thought Rostam had given it to me when he'd handed me my passport that morning stamped with the new exit visa. I couldn't find it. It was not in my handbag nor in my pockets. Rostam had handed both our identity cards to the registrar who had officially recorded the fact of our marriage along with the date and city of our wedding on them. Yet somehow, I'd misplaced my identity card. Then, as I thought back, I remembered that the registrar had returned them both to Rostam. I had to make certain and know that it wasn't lost. I went looking for it in Rostam's study, my heels scratching on cold marble between silk rugs.

There were two envelopes on his large, otherwise empty mahogany desktop. I recognized the envelope that held our identity cards.

"Does Khanom require something?" The valet's sudden presence at the door startled me, his constant shadowing, unnerving.

"No, Hassan," I said. He stood stationary, guarding his master's space. "Actually, yes, I would like something to drink, please. Something cool I think, a ginger ale." He bowed and was gone.

I opened the envelope. Inside were our two identity cards. I took mine out and started to back away from the desk, when I noticed that the second envelope on the desktop bore the name and mark of the travel agency.

Thrilled at the idea of holding my ticket back to L.A., I turned the envelope upside down. Two tickets fell out onto the desk. I picked one up. I felt glorious. I'd done it! I'd cleverly maneuvered my way back to Jasmine.

I held it to my heart, then read the printer destination, wanting to bathe in the wonderful reality of what I held. For a second, I thought I'd read it wrong. I re-read the destination. I dropped the ticket that I held and picked up the second one. It said the same thing. *Round trip: Tehran to Rome, Rome to Tehran. Rome?*

I looked for the departure date: September 5. I read them both again. The third time I read them, the destination line still said Rome without any further destination stated. I read the passengers' names: One read "Shamshiri, Rostam," the other read "Saleh-Shamshiri, Layla." *I was horrified!*

Feeling suddenly light-headed and dizzy, I grabbed the desk rim to keep losing my balance. Hassan entered the room.

"*Befarmayeed,* here you are, Khanom; your ginger ale."

As Hassan placed the tray carrying my glass on the desk, I turned and walked out of the study, instinctively trying to hide the envelope

I'd swooped up holding the two airplane tickets along with my identity card. I ran into my bedroom and locked the door behind me.

I was beside myself.

Rostam had lied to me! I didn't know what to do. I first thought to call him, then thought to call and tell my parents, then quickly realized both were absurd. I dialed Ferri's number. There was no answer. I had to think fast and act faster. I realized I had to leave that house, leave as fast as I could, with no time to lose.

I stuffed the two tickets to Rome along with my passport and my identity card and exit letter into my handbag, and jammed some of the valuable jewelry that I'd put in the larger suitcase inside the smaller suitcase and grabbed it along with my handbag. I opened my bedroom door, and made for the front door as quickly and quietly as I could. On the way to the front door I passed Rostam's study, the door ajar. I hadn't heard the telephone ring, yet there was Hassan standing at Rostam's desk speaking into the telephone. "Yes, Agha, I am sure. I will do as you say."

Hassan had called Rostam to report me! I had to hurry. There was no doubt that Rostam would order his driver to come get him from his office immediately. I hailed a cab. When I was seated and on my way to the airport with instructions to my driver to hurry, I reviewed my situation. I had a perfectly good passport with a valid exit permit stamped into it. I had my exit letter. I had my Iranian identification card. I had some jewelry of value. I could do this! I could escape at last!

"Hurry, please. You must hurry!" I nagged the cab driver all the way to the terminal. Disembarking from the cab, I paid the fare and realized with a start that I had very little cash. I ran inside the terminal and made a mad dash to the counter. "I have two round trip tickets to Rome," I said.

"Khanom, are you checking in?"

"No. I … there's been a change in plans. I'd like to return these two round trips to Rome and purchase a single one-way ticket to Los Angeles. When is the next flight?"

The attendant took his time consulting the fight schedule. "There's a flight that stops in Beirut and Paris before landing in New York and then connects to a flight to Los Angeles. I doubt you can make it. You'd have to hurry. It leaves in 20 minutes."

I estimated it would take me roughly 15 minutes to get through passport control. I'd have 5 minutes left to get to the gate. "It's very important that I make it. Please hurry."

"All right," he said, then, "Just a minute, I'm sorry, I see we have only one seat available on this flight."

"That's fine. That's all I need."

He took the tickets to Rome from me and while I waited, I tapped my fingers on the countertop and nervously bit my lip. Once or twice, I looked around me, not sure whom I expected to see. Finally, the transaction was complete, and he handed me my ticket to Los Angeles along with cash for the difference due from the two refunded tickets, solving my cash problem.

"Would you like to check your bag?"

"No." I grabbed my bag, thankful it was small, and made a dash toward the passport control table. I handed the official my identity card and my passport stamped with the exit visa. I was beyond excited! I was actually standing there with everything I needed for a seat on a flight to Los Angeles. After about fifteen minutes, I finished with passport control and was making my way to the gate. *I would make it!*

"Layla Shamshiri, please report to Security."

I was stunned! My name was being called out on the loud speaker. I turned, and I saw six policemen starting to walk in various directions in pairs, two heading towards the passport control table I had just left. They seemed to have something in their hands. I hurried.

The loudspeaker called out. "Khanom Shamshiri, Layla Saleh Shamshiri to Security, please." Immediately following that came another announcement. "This is the last call for Flight 1587 to Beirut, Paris, New York and Los Angeles."

When I turned around again, one of the policemen spotted me and nudged the other. "Khanom Shamshiri!" they called out. They quickened their pace.

This can't be, I thought; it wasn't possible. They moved rapidly, advancing in my direction. I ran toward the gate.

"Stop, Layla Saleh Shamshiri!" My knees shook but I kept going. "Khanom Shamshiri, stop! You are ordered to stop!"

I was now only steps away from the departure gate, but I felt like I was barely advancing, as though my body had become too heavy to move. The same message blared on the loud speaker again, calling for me to report to Security. I continued on with wobbling knees.

I made it to the gate and was about to hand the airline employee my boarding pass when the two policemen called out, "Stop!" I didn't. They grabbed me then and held me fast. One was holding a photograph of me and Rostam. "Please, Khanom. May we see your passport?"

I smiled as sweetly as I could as fear overtook me. "I'm sorry, I'm about to board my plane."

"Your passport and identity card please."

"I can't. My plane is leaving."

They held on to me."Please, Khanom. Your papers please."

I had no choice; they had me. I dropped my suitcase and handed one my opened handbag, my papers inside, obvious to see. He extracted them and they inspected them, then looked at each other and nodded.

The taller of the two smiled. "I don't think you'll be on that plane," he said.

In desperation, I pushed one of the officers aside as hard as I could with my suitcase, but the other grabbed for me. Of course, it was futile. In no time, they had me once again. They stood on either side of me, holding me tightly.

"No!" I screamed as they turned me around and led me away from the gate, "You can't do this!" I still held my handbag in one hand, my suitcase in the other. My head was turned, looking behind us, watching with sick despair as the airline employee closed the door behind the last passenger that was to board my plane and closed the door on my last tiny parcel of hope.

The two policemen led me away from my flight, from my life, away from my baby, and away from any chance at happiness. They led me away like I was a criminal.

We walked toward the security guards' station close to the terminal's front doors.

And then I saw him.

Rostam was just entering the terminal with a dark urgency, his head towering above all others. He spotted me and moved his large body like a huge stalking panther about to attack. When he reached me, his demeanor was not at all what I would have expected.

"Layla, *azizam*, my darling. *Alhamdo le'llah,* praise Allah, they found you." His anger showed only in the furious way he smoked the cigarette he held. He spoke to my two captors behind a wall of smoke with a smile on his face, not unlike an embarrassed schoolboy's grin.

"Thank you," he said. "Thank you for finding my lovely bride. You know how shy a new bride can be." He winked at my two captors. "I'm afraid I've been insensitive. I'll make it up to her."

He sounded so sickeningly sweet, I wanted to throw up on him. Then he brought out his wallet and offered each of the two policemen some amount of cash.

"Oh, no, we cannot accept that, Agha," the short one said. "It is enough to know that we've reunited the two of you."

"Thank you, but I insist. Buy your wives or your girlfriends some flowers," Rostam said, jamming two folded wads of money into each man's breast pocket, like a man who had paid double duty often.

"Thank you, Agha, you are a generous man. May God hold you to his bosom and protect you," said the shorter one.

"May the two of you have many happy years together, and live to see your sons marry," said the other.

Rostam turned to me, took his handkerchief out and wiped my tears with it, not too gently. "Come, *azizam*. Let's go home."

Still smiling, he put his arm out for me to give him my bag. I didn't. The policemen gave him sympathetic faces, shook their heads, said goodbye and went inside the security office, chuckling and whispering to one another.

As soon as the officers were gone from view, Rostam transformed. He grabbed my bag and my purse and held them both in one hand and wrapped his other large hand around my arm so tightly, it felt like a tourniquet. He yanked me close to his side and dragged me out of the terminal and to his car parked at the curb where Hassan awaited us. He gave both my bag and purse to Hassan and pointed to the open back door.

"Get in."

"No."

"What? Get inside, you insolent bitch. I'll see what to do with you." I didn't move. "Get in the car this very second." I held my ground. He forced me in, pushing my head down and forcing my body inside. Hassan opened the other back door, and Rostam entered the car as well. Hassan slammed both of our doors before speedily starting the car. I looked over at Rostam. His eyes bled with anger. With his hand extended only inches away from my face, his palm stiff, he screamed, "Why did you do this to Rostam? Why did you try to run away?"

"You know why."

He looked like he might not be able to contain himself. I was too angry to care. "I know why? I *know* why? I know why my wife of barely a day tries to run away from me?"

"You shouldn't have stopped me. You had no right."

"By all the prophets! *Deevoneh shodee?* Have you gone mad? What do you mean I have no right? I am your husband! Don't you know we're married? *Zanamee,* you're my wife! You belong to me!"

I looked away from him. The idea of *belonging* to this man nauseated me. He took hold of my chin and turned my head around to face him. "What the hell are you running away from? If you're running away from me, why the hell did you bother to marry me? How dare you do this to Rostam? How *dare* you!"

I ignored his question. I saw his face turn purple, but my own fury made it impossible for me to be intimidated by his wrath or by his booming voice. I wanted to kill the lying scum. All my hopes of returning to my child had just come crashing down on me. His promise to take me to Los Angeles proved to be nothing more than an empty lie. I'd married a fraud, nothing more.

"I marry you, bring you into my house, give you Rostam's name... What girl wouldn't give her right leg to be in your place? I could have married any one of a dozen beautiful girls with more wealth and power than your father has with his silly little factory. Yet you treat Rostam like dirt?"

I wanted to choke him for speaking of Babajon like that. My head was blasting, with the blood rushing out of my screaming heart. "You should have let me go," I said through clenched teeth.

Rostam lit another cigarette with a snap of his Dunhill lighter and spoke through a Marlboro veil. The lighter's click seemed to punctuate a sudden change in his tone. He sounded genuinely curious now, finally even more curious than angry.

"Did you really think you could do it? Didn't you know Hassan would call to tell me you'd left with the tickets? He called before you were out the front door!

"I thought you were smarter than that, College Girl. Apparently, you're a donkey. It just took one call to Feraydoon Seyah. The Captain of Police is my friend. Didn't I mention that to you? We play poker together every week. He had all the policemen in Tehran looking for you, though, of course, with the tickets in your hand, the airport was the logical place to find you, so that's where I went.

"I would have easily found you even if I hadn't known you were headed for the airport. I told him we'd had a lover's spat." Then his curiosity took over again. "Why Layla? What has Rostam done to deserve this?"

"Rostam is a liar."

"How dare you call Rostam a liar!" he said angrily, not realizing the ridiculous fact that we were both speaking about him in third person. "What did Rostam lie about? I demand to know."

"What did Rostam lie about?" I spat at him. "You mean you don't know? The tickets! You lied about the tickets for our honeymoon."

He turned away from me then and looked out his window at the people in other cars having an easier time than us. He calmly removed some tobacco off his tongue. "You snuck around, went snooping in my things."

"I was looking for my identity card. I went into your study and saw the envelope with the two tickets. I didn't snoop. It was lying right there on the desk."

"And what did I lie to you about?" He faced me again, his large body turning and adjusting and spoke smugly.

"Why don't you just admit it?" I said. "*Beh jonneh khodet,* on your own soul, and for God's sake, at least admit it. We weren't going to Los Angeles. The two tickets were for Rome."

His eyes took on a dangerous look as if the curtain had lifted and he suddenly understood the big picture. He looked at me in disbelief mixed with a certain awe and venom. "I see. So, you were running to California."

His voice was so quiet, the look in his eyes so filled with wonder, that I had every reason to be even more scared of him now than I'd been, for this was, most likely, the calm before the bigger storm. But I didn't fear his rage. I'd welcome it. I wanted him to feel what I was feeling.

He sat back in his seat looking thoughtful, as though trying to work something out, and smoked. "So, your plan was to marry Rostam, take advantage of my generosity and run away back to California?" He toyed with his cigarette in the ashtray.

That's when I realized that Rostam hadn't known where I was hoping to go until I'd just told him, though he would have found out soon enough when he saw my boarding pass.

"Tell me: Why do you need Rostam's generosity? No, tell me what is in Los Angeles – *who* is in Los Angeles that you are so anxious to get to, so anxious that you would dare pry into my papers and then do this – this *thing* – that you have done?"

I looked at my lap. "Nobody."

He looked at me as if he wasn't sure he'd heard me. "Nobody?"

I sat silently until I realized I would have to take the offensive or chance the possibility of saying too much. "I wanted to go there when I realized you'd lied to me about it. You never intended to go there. You lied. I wanted to get away from you and your lies."

"How dare you? You pry into my papers. You dare call Rostam a liar. What right do you have to begin to question what Rostam intends to do? How dare you question what Rostam does? Nobody does that. *Heech kassee,* nobody!" As his voice hit a crescendo, the car stopped. We'd arrived at the house.

The three of us got out of the car.

Rostam headed for the front door. I stood in the street not knowing where to go, then remembered my purse and suitcase were in the front seat of the car. Wherever I went, I would need the papers that were in my purse and the suitcase with the few pieces of jewelry inside. I looked but they weren't there. I saw Hassan walking through the front door holding both. I followed the two men into the house. Rostam was in the dining room. Hassan had just put my suitcase on the dining table and Rostam was dumping out the contents of my purse. I made a quick mental inventory of what I had inside. There were no letters, no hidden photos of Jasmine and no Los Angeles telephone numbers.

"I see I will have to teach you how to be Rostam's wife." He took the time to light another cigarette and inhaled deeply, then put one hand into his pants pocket and played with something there while he spoke, looking above my head.

"You may have gone to some fancy American college, but you don't know the first thing about how to be a wife. You will never again question Rostam. You will not be impudent. You have only those rights Rostam gives you, and you ask no questions unless Rostam allows it."

He was obviously relishing this moment of reasserting his manhood. I'd never loathed anyone more.

"Hassan told me you made a call before you left. Tell me, did your little Jewish friend plan this fiasco for you?" His reference to Ferri provoked further hatred of him.

"So, you are a bigot as well as a liar." I said.

Deeming my comment too unimportant to merit a response, he simply turned his attention away from me and back to the items spread out on the table, his fingers turning each object over.

"You will never again leave the house without first telling me or Hassan where you are going and with whom." He emptied my lipstick and powder out of my small makeup kit and turned back to me, tapping the table forcefully with his fingers. "You will most often be escorted by Hassan when you go out. And we will not be taking a honeymoon. You obviously have no desire to travel with me, so I will travel alone while you, my little donkey wife, will stay right here." He picked up my passport and identity card. "You won't be needing these." I lunged at him, trying to wrest the two documents out of his hand. He pushed me away as easily as one might push a kitten out of the way.

"I don't want to be your wife. I want a divorce."

For a moment, he turned crimson again, and his jaw pulsated below his ears. Then he laughed. I saw my passport and identity card disappear inside his jacket pocket. Then he said, *"Talogh,* divorce? Rostam, divorce? You must be crazy or even more of a donkey than I thought. I will never divorce you, Layla. Never."

I dealt a battery of punches against his chest. "I won't stay with you, you pig." That was the first time he slapped me. Only once. A slap across my face. The shock was blinding.

"I will repeat myself just this once. There will be no divorce. I was far too generous with our marriage contract. Which brings us to your allowance."

He opened my suitcase and began fumbling through it. My high school photo was there among my clothes, the one with Jasmine's picture hidden in the frame. When he saw it, I thought to anger him so as to distract him from paying attention to it, then decided to stay quiet and still, not to react at all. When he saw the wedding jewelry I'd put into the suitcase, the photo was forgotten. He fingered some of the pieces and put them all in a pile on the table. I didn't move.

"You will receive money on a regular basis as you require. You won't need much cash. Hassan and the other servants will see to the household necessities. You will open accounts with your hairdresser, dressmaker and the like, and I will see that they are paid. You will require only pocket money … not very much as you will never go far from home." He smiled triumphantly like a winner, leering at me, the pathetic loser, and began to separate out the jewelry, fingering, weighing and eyeing each piece before dropping it into his pockets. "I will put these in my safe. You may have them when you wear them the evenings you go out with Rostam."

He went back to the contents of my purse. He looked through my wallet and took out the cash from the tickets I'd returned, leaving only a pittance. When he was finished examining everything, he called for Hassan, who came running. "Hassan, I will be going to Italy alone. I'll arrange for my tickets. I will leave now and will have to take a later plane.

"I will be gone for ten days. Khanom will be staying at home. She is not feeling well. See to it that she does not leave the house until I return. She will have no callers, as everyone believes she is on her honeymoon. Should anyone call for her, keep a list for me and inform them that she is unavailable. She is permitted no visitors. Take the telephone out of our bedroom so it does not disturb her."

"I understand." Hassan bowed with his fist at his heart, a gesture of his allegiance. "I will obey you, Agha, *roo sheshm,* on my eyes." Hassan left the room.

"My parents will know what you are doing to me."

Rostam looked truly unconcerned. "Your parents? Hah!" He blew smoke rings to the ceiling. "Tell me, do your parents know that you would attempt to run away from Rostam to return to Los Angeles? I don't think so, Layla. Do they know you would run away from me to get to someone there?

"Believe me, if you dare complain to your parents, I will drag your name and their names through the dirtiest joobs of Tehran with the help of Captain Seyah, until not even the wildest of dogs will go near any of you." With that, he walked out of the dining room.

I sat on a dining room chair and tried to think. My mind couldn't function. Everything I'd married Rostam to get was gone.

I looked at my belongings on the table. Then I remembered the jewels that I hadn't put into the suitcase. I probably had only minutes to act. I went into our bedroom hoping that Rostam wasn't there. I locked the door and hurriedly swooped up the gifts of jewelry still there and tossed them into the back of a drawer and threw some clothes on them. I would find a better place for them after Rostam left.

Then I ran to the phone and called Ferri. I thanked God she was home at last and poured out my message of distress as fast as I could. "I can't talk. Rostam lied. I found the tickets. They were for Rome not LA. I took them to the airport. I was steps away from a plane for L.A. He'd called the police Captain and they got me just as I was boarding."

"My God!"

"Be quiet! Listen! There's no time. He's taking the telephone away and won't let me out of the house. Don't tell anyone; don't tell my parents whatever you do. And don't call me. He hates you and his servant is keeping a list of all my callers. I'll call you or come to you as soon as I can. Call Linda!" There was a knock on the bedroom door. "Call Adam!" The knock had become a loud banging. The door began to shake.

"Layla-"

"I have to go. Call them!"

"I don't have their nu-" The lock broke and Rostam came bursting through the door, pulled the receiver out of my hand and put it to his ear. Ferri had apparently hung up.

"Who did you call?" His arm was poised to hit me. My lips were sealed. "*Ma-darr-sag!* Bitch! *Ma-darr-jendeh!* Daughter of a whore! You dirty-ass bitch!" Then he slapped my face again. This time I screamed out in pain as I fell back on the bed. He picked up the phone and yanked it so that the wire easily disconnected from the wall and handed it to Hassan. He looked around the room. His eyes lingered on the windows. He went to one and looked down. I guessed he was thinking about the feasibility of an escape.

"The airport police are on alert," he said. "You can't go far without a passport. And remember, bitch, if you try anything stupid again, the police will be all over you. The Chief won't let me down."

He tried the lock on the bedroom door. Satisfied that it was broken, he looked around the room once more. Then he said his parting words to me before leaving for his honeymoon. "You call me a liar. You are the liar and the cheat, you, *jendeh,* whore, and *ma-darr-jendeh,* daughter of a whore. I thought I was marrying a sweet, simple, honest, decent girl." He shook his head and walked out of the room.

A minute later, Hassan came into the bedroom to pick up Rostam's two fully-packed suitcases.

As he walked out of the room, The Rat winked at me.

51
PROLOGUE TO PURGATORY

When I awoke the next morning and realized yesterday's reality had followed me into the new day, warm tears of the deepest sorrow rolled down my face.

With no reason to get up, I spent two entire days in bed, lost in a sea of despair and depression.

I was still in Rostam's house in Tehran, captured and imprisoned in Iran and tied to a man I'd never loved, on a shorter leash than ever. I couldn't believe that God had forsaken me like this, and I resented Him as much as I did Rostam; more, for He was all-powerful and had brought me to this wretched state.

How I wished I had never left my baby!

I was in terrible danger of losing Jasmine, the dearest thing in the world to me. I would have given anything to see Jasmine's lovely little face, her little thighs, her tiny fingers and toes and the incredible birthmark of a crescent moon on her calf that was proof she was her father's child.

After stalling Adam and Linda for so long, I had finally given them a deadline promising I'd be back by the seventh of September. *What will they think when I don't show up? How can they ever guess how hard I've tried to get home? How much longer can I expect them to hold out?*

I had to talk to them, to persuade them to take care of my baby until I was able to get back – and I would get back, no matter what. I tried to think of a way to contact them with no access to a telephone. There was only Ferri, and I realized with a flash of burning heat that she had neither Linda's telephone number nor her address and I could neither call man angel nor go to her. I definitely could not leave the house. Hassan took his job as warden very seriously. Several times a day he would knock on my bedroom door with the broken lock to ask if I wanted anything. No doubt he was checking up on me to confirm that I'd not yet jumped out the window. Each time he asked, I told him to go away. I tensed up every time I heard his footsteps, for I was afraid he might enter my room and, God help me, I didn't know what to expect if he did.

After two days in bed, I moved the remaining jewelry from the drawer to find a better hiding place. I put a chair behind the door and scoped the bedroom. I looked through Rostam's meticulously organized drawers then opened his closets. With both, the unwelcome odor of stale cigarette smoke greeted me. The man had more clothes and shoes than anyone I'd ever seen, including Shireen. I finally decided to hide my loot under the bottom pads of a box of Kotex. I put the box in the furthest back corner of the bathroom cabinet.

Eventually, I ventured out of the bedroom and began to examine the house more completely than I'd yet done. The only other telephone was in Rostam's study, but there was never a time that I could have used it to call Ferri without Hassan knowing. Perhaps there was another way to escape. I passed around the entire house several times on each of those ten days. Once I overheard Hassan on the telephone. "Yes, Master … No, no one …Yes, I give you my word, *roo sheshm,* on my eyes, I am and I will, Master … Yes, Master ... *Ghorbonneh shomah,* I would sacrifice myself for you."

There were doors leading out to the gardens on all sides. All were locked. And what could I do in the gardens? They were all enclosed with walls. I eyed the front door and thought about making a run for it. Where would I go? Home to my parents? No doubt Feraydoon Seyah, Tehran's Chief of Police, Rostam's poker buddy, would quickly inform them of my attempted escape and recapture at the airport. How would I explain an attempted escape to my parents so soon after my marriage to the man I had wanted to wed? My father's heart would break; my mother would immediately know my motive in marrying Rostam. More importantly, and without a doubt, I'd be extricated from my parents' house and sent back to my husband's as required by law, a law that would give me no refuge. Rostam was correct: As long as he was my husband, I was his property.

According to my understanding of Iranian law, Rostam could effectuate a religious divorce simply by saying, "I divorce you," three times in the presence of two male witnesses; females were considered half-witnesses. I could initiate divorce only with proof that our marriage had not and could not be consummated, or that Rostam had abandoned me, or that he had leprosy. And even then, it was in the judge's discretion to grant or deny a request for divorce. In a country that allowed polygamy and looked the other way when hordes of girls were married below the legal age of fifteen, the awful reality was that I could only divorce Rostam with his consent, and he had made it plain that I would never have that.

How could I have not seen what an egotistical and cruel person Rostam was before this? Had the pointless hope I'd clung to in the face of utter desperation make me that blind?

During those ten days, I received no phone calls. Ferri was the only person outside that house who knew the truth.

One afternoon, while I was in my bedroom, my angel came to our door. I heard the doorbell ring and made the mistake of assuming the caller had no business with me. It was only when the housekeeper entered my room to clean, that I walked went into the living room. Hassan had just closed the front door. "May I get you something Khanom?" he asked. He had a way of saying *Khanom* that reeked of sarcasm.

"No." The Rat's face bore a peculiar expression, his grin cagier than usual. "Who was at the door?" I asked.

Hassan shrugged and his face contorted into an ugly sneer. "No one important, just a nothing girl who'd come for you. I told her you were unavailable."

Ferri had come! I sprinted to the door and tried to open it, but Hassan was right there leaning up against it. "What did you tell her?" I screamed at him, pulling hopelessly at the door handle.

"I told her you weren't home." He said calmly and shrugged. "She's gone." Though he remained leaning against the door, I didn't let up. I would show this disgusting man that I could beat him. I had told Ferri not to come; if she had ventured here anyway, it must have been for good reason. "Why trouble yourself so, Khanom? She's nothing more than a *najess* Jew girl," he said.

I stopped pulling at the door then and looked at this piece of garbage, this man who taunted me, daring to call my angel *najess*. "How dare you call her *najess*?"

He shrugged his rotund shoulders again and the corners of his thin lips turned down. "She said her name was Ferreshteh Kohan. Kohan is a Jewish name, no?"

I moved away from the door dejectedly, in apparent surrender. Hassan started to cross the foyer as well. Maybe I could still catch her. I turned and made a mad dash back to the door and managed to open it a few inches before Hassan was back to slam it shut. "Please, Khanom. Rostam Khan will be very mad at me if you open that door. Anyway, the Jew is long gone by now." He swung the front door wide open then, blocking the entrance with his body. "See? There's no one there. Your Jewish friend is long gone." He quickly shut the door. "She's far away by now and she's not coming back."

I returned to my bedroom, my bed, and my tears. I was encased once again in the all-too- familiar feelings of self-pity and helplessness.

And so, each day started out with a gnawing emptiness in my heart that was quickly filled with such intense feelings of remorse, sorrow, self-loathing, and fear, that I quickly wished it were empty again.

I thought to write to Linda and Adam, but it would have been utterly pointless. I couldn't get to the post office, and my letter would only be telling my old roommates what they would already know by the time the mail arrived: I hadn't been back by the seventh of September.

As bad as the days were, the nights, oh, the nights were worse. By daylight I was a captive of Rostam's cruelty and lies. By moonlight I lay in bed, a captive of my body.

My night with Rostam had reawakened my sensuality with a vengeance. I'd close my eyes and imagine David, remember his scent, the feel of his skin, his eyes and his face. I would sink into that blissful night we'd made love, locked inside a world that knew no ego, no right or wrong, no religion, no country, no war, no pain. Then, God help me, David's light clean scent would become the smell of stale cigarette smoke mixed with a stronge cologne, his beautiful hands would become larger and clumsier, and his body, darker, hairier, heavier and stronger. I'd open my eyes in horror, not wanting to see what lay before my closed lids. A million humiliating thoughts would pass through my mind.

I thought of David again. His slow pace when we made love was incredibly sensual, every fraction of movement, every slight slice of friction. I'd felt loved and worshipped David. Then my mind would trick me and in my imagination, lovemaking would take on a far less fluid pace and become more erratic, definitely uncompromising, as Rostam bludgeoned his way into my thoughts, making me feel desired in a far more primal, carnal, lustful way. And, though I completely detested my jailer, I found my body responding to unstoppable mental replays of sensations that I'd experienced with him on our wedding night.

The hateful flashbacks interfered with my beloved David. I hated myself for it.

Rostam returned home late one night, entered the bedroom and turned on the lights.

I'd awakened when I heard his voice. "Ah, there's my new wife. How good to come home after a wonderful vacation to find her in my bed." I opened my eyes to the glare of the light and the smell of smoke. He stood, with a cigarette lodged between his lips, looking rested and pleased. He put his sweater down on the chair, took his cigarette away from his mouth and exhaled a stream of smoke, which curled, languishing in the air between us. "Did you have an agreeable time while I was away?" he asked.

"Go to hell."

He looked at me with the glint of malice in his eyes. "Ah, I assume your honeymoon was a disappointment for you, and for that I forgive your disrespect."

I turned onto my other side so as not to look at him. "I missed you," he said, as though the thought surprised him. My heart began to thump. I closed my eyes. "Italy was very beautiful. It's a romantic place. I lay on the beach on the Riviera all day and at night roamed the casinos, the nightclubs, seeing beautiful women everywhere. I wanted you to see it all. There was so much to share."

I heard him walk around the room and listened as he undressed. I heard his shoes falling off, his belt being undone. Then he went into the bathroom. I willed myself to fall asleep before he came out but couldn't. I was filled with anxiety.

He returned to the bedroom and then he was beside me in bed. He made himself comfortable under the blanket and turned to me, naked and erect. His hands molded my breasts. Feigning sleep, I didn't move. I felt his aroused state and felt my breasts respond to his touch, my nipples hardening. I cursed myself. I tried to turn onto my stomach. He grabbed me. I wanted to fight him, but it was impossible to move.

"Tell me what you like," he sneered into my ear. "Is this what he did?" He went at my ear, licking it softly at first, then ferociously. Though it was nearly impossible, I remained still, just long enough for him to relax and loosen his grip on me. Then I came at him, twisting his ear and yanking it as hard as I could while simultaneously propelling myself out of bed as his body jerked up in surprise. He'd been thrown for just seconds, but it had been enough time for me to be on my feet. He got onto his knees and crawled toward me on the bed. "What do you like? Huh? Tell me how you played in California." He was smiling as if ready to play a game with me. I couldn't have dreaded him more if he were an approaching rattlesnake, head up and hissing. "Your American boyfriend played rough?"

I backed away. "I didn't have an American boyfriend."

He laughed. He got up off the bed and walked slowly toward me. He looked huge as he loomed naked before me like this and carried his erection, which I had not seen before, like an oversized weapon between his legs. He came and stood so close to me that I felt his penis push against my abdomen. I could see the beginning of hairs that had been removed for our wedding night erupting on his chest. He towered over me and looked down into my eyes. "Rostam was never fooled," he said, "not for a second." Suddenly, his large hand gripped my mouth and squeezed my lips into a kiss. I gasped. "Do you think I believed that mine was the first tongue to enter this mouth? Though only Allah and you know who else these lips have welcomed, don't think Rostam is a fool." He released my face with such force that I fell back. He whispered gruffly. "Come here." I didn't move except to instinctively protect myself with my arms crossed at my chest. He repeated himself. "Come and kiss your husband."

I shook my head. "You are not my husband. You are my jailer."

"I am your husband; and you are my wife, my prisoner, my whore, whatever I want you to be. Come here, whore."

"I'm not a whore."

Again, that loud laugh. He was enjoying this!

"You tell me why you or anyone would want to escape a fine marriage to Rostam? Of course, you have a *boy ferr-rend* in California!" He emphasized his use of the English word. "In Italy, I thought to myself, 'So! She had a boy ferr-rend! But after one night with Rostam, why would she want to return to him?' And then I knew."

He reached for me. I turned to run. My foot caught on a leg of the small, narrow stand where the maid kept a vase with fresh flowers. I knocked it down and the table fell to the floor along with the crashing vase as water sprayed and crystal shattered. Rostam squatted down beside me and pinned me down with his knee at my groin. I lay with my heart convulsing. He ran his index finger from the top of my head, down my face, to my throat, down to my silk nightshirt, circling around one breast inward toward the nipple then slowly across to the other breast.

"I know. My pretty little wife had many lovers." He was toying with me. "My lovely Layla Khanom was a sex freak. Yet, you were a virgin, were you not?"

The question scared me. *What did he know?* He bent his head and I could smell his breath again, hot and dry. He took his index finger from my nipple to the space between my breasts then down my stomach to my silk pajama pants and to my pubic area, where it rested for a moment before playfully slapping me there. "God only knows what sexual acts you've performed. What did you enjoy the most, Layla? Huh? Tell me."

I was so scared I couldn't have spoken my own name. He was spewing insanity. "Did you eat cocks? Did you lick black American cocks? Did you swallow their juices? Don't look at me like that. Did you take it in the ass to remain a little virgin for me? We can do that." As he said this, his hand moved to my backside. I went cold.

"Or do you like women? Is that it? You have a gurl ferr-rend? You don't have to go to California for that. I can arrange to have a woman with us. Tell me what you like, my pretty little whore wife."

He adjusted himself, so that he now lay on his side on the floor alongside me with one elbow bent and his head propped up on that hand, looking down at me. I would have tried to squirm away but I was too scared, too shocked by his words to move.

He tapped at his temple with the fingers of his other hand. "But I said to myself, whatever she did was before Rostam. Now that Rostam has taken her virginity, now that she has experienced Rostam, why does the pretty wife want to go back to her old friends?" Now he started tapping my forehead instead of his own, nodding and peering at me slyly. "Then it comes to me." I waited.

He just kept nodding and tapping. *God! Tell me, what came to you!* He ran his finger ever so softly down my nose. "I was very gentle that night. Foolish me. Perhaps my little wife doesn't like things so gentle." My heart was pounding. "I think perhaps my beautiful Layla Khanom likes to play rough."

I shook my head, terrified. My hands were shaking, my breath, fickle, my mouth dry, and my throat so closed up, I couldn't speak. Rostam grabbed my top with both hands and ripped it. He put his mouth to one nipple, biting hard. I cried out in pain. "You like that?" He went to the other. As he bit down, he pinched the other, already sore, painful nipple. Then he entered me. He took hold of my legs, forcing them high up, and rocked me furiously against the carpet. He resumed pinching and biting my nipples as he rammed himself into me as hard as he could, as though I were nothing more than a hole to receive him. As his thrusts moved me along the floor, shards of crystal bit my skin off and water stung the wounds. I felt the skin on my back turn raw. Rostam was euphoric in a realm where nothing other than his supremacy mattered, riding me like one of us was an animal. Yet, I thanked God he had forgotten all thoughts of sodomizing me.

When he finished with me, he simply dropped my legs and lay atop me, spent. I lay silent and immobile beneath his weight, my body one continuous path of pain from my twisted neck down to my breasts and back, my insides, and down the length of my thighs and legs. At some point he decided to get off me, opting for the comfort of bed. I stayed where I was, having neither the energy to move nor the desire to lie near him. As he moved away, he said, "By the way, whore, I spent the whole time in Italy. Without you, and for only ten days, there was no point in going on to your godforsaken, goddamned California."

Bastard! The man was a demon bent on ravaging my mind as he had ravaged my body.

Was he telling me he'd planned for us to go on to Los Angeles from Rome? Did he have tickets from Rome to L.A. that I hadn't known about? He was an absolute monster! He knew I'd never be certain of his true intentions now, and that I'd always hate myself for what might have been as much as I hated him for what was.

I cried there on the floor, muffling my sobs throughout the night. I suppose I fell asleep, for when I next opened my eyes it was morning. Rostam had left. He'd simply walked over me and left me lying naked on the floor, just as he'd left me. I looked at the clock. It was still early. With any luck, The Rat was still out of the house, not yet back from driving his master to work.

I got up and forced myself put some clothes on quickly, despite my wounds and my soreness. I didn't even bother to douche. I was racing to get to Ferri's house; I had to find out why she'd come to the door. *Had there been mail from California? Was that why she'd come?* If so, I'd go to the post office and call Linda then come home and douche. The hell with whatever punishment Rostam would have for me when I returned.

When Ferri saw me at her door, she ran to embrace me.

My back hurt so badly that I had to pull away from her comforting arms. "*Khodayah,* God, I've been so worried about you. You look awful! I came to your house. That ugly little man wouldn't let me in. I told him I knew you were in there, but he blocked my way. Thank God you're all right."

As much as I may have wanted to share my ordeal with Ferri and be comforted by her, every minute counted. I was far more eager to get word to Los Angeles of my change of plans and explain yet another delayed arrival.

"There's another letter for you," she said.

"Did you call Linda?"

Ferri shook her head. "How could I? I don't have their number. I never called you there and you never gave me the number. You hung up right before I could get it from you. And their letter had no return address. Wait. Let me get it."

I waited breathlessly for her return. As soon as I saw the letter, I recognized Linda's handwriting on the envelope and ripped it open. I didn't expect any photos; none were enclosed.

Dear Layla,

Wherever you are, I hope you get this letter. I'm sending it to the only address I have for you. I don't know where you are right now, and I really don't care. I only know you're not here.

I'm really sorry. Adam moved out a while ago, and I just can't do this anymore. You were supposed to be gone for one month and be back here by the end of June and then by the middle of July and now it's September and you're still not home. Adam said you swore you'd be here September 7th. That was yesterday. I never heard from you. I honestly don't think you're ever coming back. I don't know why you just didn't tell us that.

Adam told me you got married. Well, good for you. I guess now that you're married, you don't think it's important that you come back. I don't blame you. Adam told me your husband doesn't even know you have a baby, so I can understand that you want to start your new life with your husband without dealing with "The Problem." That's fine. Except that I have a life, too! At least I did before you left me with your baby and went off.

I looked at Ferri. "My God! What is she saying? I didn't want to get married!"

"She doesn't know that," Ferri said. "Go on."

I never even go out anymore. I can't date and I don't even see friends. Now that Adam has moved out, I'm alone with Jas most of the time. I'm not saying he doesn't still help out. Even with his help, it's just too much for me. I can't do it anymore.

The letter trembled in my cold hands.

School has started. My mom has to watch your baby so I can go to my classes. And I want to go out. It's not right. I'm sorry. Jasmine isn't my baby and you were intending to find another home for her anyway.

I was feeling faint. Nausea was overtaking me. I had to read slower.

If I knew when you were coming back or if even knew for sure that you were coming back, I would maybe do this a little longer with help from my mother and Adam. The thing is, Layla, I don't think you are ever coming back.

I was too scared, too weak to go on reading. I lost my grip and Ferri caught the letter as it floated towards the floor. She continued reading.

I think you should have let the adoption agency take Jas when she was born. Every baby needs a mother and by now she would have hers. You should see her. She's so pretty. Her eyes are shaped like yours and her skin is your color. I'm guessing that the bottom part of her face looks like David's, though I've never seen him. And she's so sweet. Sometimes, she looks around like she's looking for you and then starts to whimper, like she's sad because she can't find you.

I'm sure she recognizes Adam and me. She smiles and laughs when she sees us. She probably thinks we're her parents. It's really sad, because she needs parents who are there, a mom who'll be there, and that's not me, and certainly not you!

Ferri's eyes left the page to gaze up at me with sadness and pity. Neither of us said anything. She resumed reading.

Now that Adam is gone, I'm moving out of the apartment, too, on September 15th to a one-bedroom. Please understand, Layla. I can't take Jas with me and I don't know what else to do with her. If you're not back in L.A. by then I'm giving Jas up for adoption.

"No!" I screamed. *"You can't do that!"* I grabbed Linda's letter and read the remainder myself, not wanting to believe my own voice or the words I read.

It's the best thing we can do for her. I think you know that. It's the only thing we can do with her. Jas needs a home. You promised you'd be back by the 7th. If you don't want her to be adopted, you absolutely have to let me know by September 15th. Otherwise, that's what Adam and I agreed we would do. We know you will understand.

I looked at Ferri and read the last line, holding the letter in one hand, ready to fall.

I hope you are happy back in Iran with your husband and your new life.

Linda

My hand went to my forehead. Suddenly, my brain switched back on. I grabbed Ferri's hand and pulled her from her seat. "We have to call her. Rostam came home on the 15th. That was yesterday. We have to call. Hurry!"

Ferri hesitated. "From my house?"

"I can't waste a second!"

"I–"

"Ferri, I have to call now!"

She nodded and we ran to her telephone. I prayed that Linda hadn't yet moved. True, her letter had said she'd be gone after the 15th but I was well aware of how plans could change. What was one day?

I envisioned Linda still packing what Adam hadn't taken: kitchen things like the dishes her mother had given her, white with pink flowers on their borders, in one box, her albums we'd play on the stereo set in another box or two, her clothes and books. Then Jasmine's things in a separate box to go elsewhere, and I said to myself that if I was able to picture her packing, it was a sign that she hadn't yet left the apartment.

With Ferri by my side, I called the long-distance operator and asked her to connect me to the apartment in Los Angeles, station to station.

I gave her the telephone number and waited to hear the phone ring and Linda's voice answer. Though I was prepared for a difficult conversation, I'd make her understand my situation. The operator put through the call. Instead of the sound of a telephone ringing, I heard this horrible noise in my ear, like a busy signal played in double time. The operator came back on the line. "Miss, would you repeat the number you requested?" I did, this time speaking very slowly and clearly. Silence. A pause. A lifetime. The operator. "I'm sorry, Miss. That number has been disconnected."My chest emptied my heart out. I couldn't breathe; my lungs had no room to expand. I could feel my pulse throughout my entire body. "Operator, that's impossible. It can't be."

"Miss, I'm certain the number you gave me is disconnected. Is there another number I can connect you with?"

I was in a daze. "She's gone." Ferri took the phone from my hand and replaced it in the cradle.

"Call Adam," Ferri said.

I rubbed my eyes. "I don't know where he is."

Ferri pressed my hand within hers and spoke softly. "Call someone."

Ralph and Maggie Dunn. I was back on the telephone with the operator again, renewed energy with renewed hope. "I need a phone number in California, Ralph and Maggie Dunn … Comstock Avenue in Westwood or Los Angeles, California. What? … D-U-N-N… D like David. It may be under Margaret if not Ralph." Ferri scrambled to find pen and paper. She wrote down the number the operator gave me before connecting me to the Dunn house. I grabbed Ferri's hand and squeezed it so hard that she yelped. My heart was in my throat. This time I heard the phone ring. Twice. I heard a woman's voice. Hope had resurrected itself. I spoke. "Hello, Mrs. Dunn? Maggie?"

"Mrs. Dunn ain't at home." It was Buelah, the Dunns' housekeeper.

"Buelah? It's me; it's Layla."

"Miss Layla. How you been, child?"

"Oh, Buelah, I need to talk to Mr. or Mrs. Dunn."

"Theys ain't neither of them here."

"Will they be home soon?"

"No, theys out of town, gone on a trip."

The life force was leaving me like air seeping out of a hole. I slid down the wall onto the floor, oblivious to the pain all along my back, and, still holding Ferri's hand, I pulled her down with me. "When will they be back?"

"I don't rightly know. Theys put the key down for me like theys do."

"Do you know where they are?"

"Let me see. I's thinkin' I heard Mrs. Dunn say she was goin' to Texas? I don't rightly recall."

"Do you know how I can reach them?"

"Can't say I's do."

"Do you know when they'll be back? It's important, Buelah."

"Don't rightly know, child. I'll be fixin' to lock up and leave as soon as I's done with this here ironing."

"Buelah, do you know how I can find Linda or Adam?"

"Uh-uh. Ain't theys at home?"

"No. They've both moved. Do you know how I can get their new phone numbers?"

"Honey child, those kids theys don't tell me nothing." I was crying. "Miss Layla? You there, honey? When theys come back, I's gonna tell 'em you called. Now, child, you take care'a yourself. You hear?"

I don't know if she heard my muffled "Goodbye." I hung up the phone and sat against the wall curled in with my head between my hands as Ferri tried to console me. I'd never felt so forlorn.

"Layla, maybe this is the best thing for Jasmine." She spoke to me in the soft voice of condolence.

My heart felt like an empty cavity, deep and painful. "I want my daughter."

"But you're not there."

"I should be."

"You couldn't be. You tried everything. *Beh Toorah,* on the Torah, you did everything you could do. You even got married just to get to her! And then you tried to run away from your husband. What else could you do?"

"I should never have left her. She's my child! She's David's child. She deserves so much more than ... than to be given away when someone moves like – like a sofa that doesn't fit anymore."

"If you were there, you might have given her up for adoption yourself."

"No! I'd have kept her," I said.

"That's not what you said when you first came back. Maybe you were right."

"I was wrong. Oh, Ferri, I was so wrong! When I saw what my mother did to me, and when I couldn't get back to my own daughter, I would have done anything to keep her. I'd have gotten a job and made us a life. Oh, God! All I've done is turn my back on her."

I pushed harder against the wall; I deserved the pain from the cuts and bruises I'd gotten the night before. "God cut my tongue off for saying this: *Did I tell you I tried to abort her when I found out I was pregnant?* I didn't want her to be born!

Oh, Jasmine, I'm so sorry! God, forgive me. Oh, David, I'm so sorry!" I sat sobbing. I yearned for the second chance no one could give me. *"Khoda, God, what kind of a person am I?"* I wailed.

Ferri wiped away her own tears, held me in her arms and rocked me like a baby. "You'll find her," she whispered. "One day you'll find her."

"Where? How? What have they done with her?" *Oh God, where's my baby?*

52
ALLAH AKBAR! (GOD IS GREAT)

Once I knew I'd lost Jasmine, my spirit broke.

I returned to my husband and home from Ferri's house with the heart of a dead animal. With nothing left for me in Tehran and no one to return to in Los Angeles, I had no future. And Rostam had made it resoundingly clear that he would never divorce me.

I no longer cared.

First, I'd lost David and now Jasmine had been cut away from me forever, sent to strangers, and there wasn't a single thing I could do about it.

I would remain where I was forever, wither away and die right here, haunted by the man I'd loved and lost, by our beautiful little girl, Jasmine and by thoughts of the life we could have created and the happiness ripped from me forever.

My life became a muddy ocean of days, meaningless waves of questions tumbling at me, a jumble of unknowns:

Is David alive?

Why did I let me leave me?

Where is Jasmine?

Is my baby all right? Will she be well taken care of?

Why did I leave my child?

Could I have refused to return home without her?

Should I have told David's parents the truth about the baby I was carrying? Of course, I should have! What a fool I was! I'd not only succeeded in denying the Klines their grandchild, I'd also denied my daughter the only family that might have been accessible to her now. *Why hadn't Adam or Linda suggested it?*

Why had I been so stupid?

Would Mrs. Kline have rejected her son's only child?

Who had adopted Jasmine? Being raised in America meant she would almost certainly *not* be raised as a Muslim.

Did the agency even ask about religious preferences? Did I care? Not in the least. I only wanted my daughter to be happy and healthy.

Was it wrong to love David? Absolutely not! His face would take shape in my memory, his smile would become mine and his voice would fill my head.

What a fool I was not to have married him! We could have been a family in Israel.

Was I kidding myself to think he was still alive?

What kind of a woman would Jasmine grow up to be? I prayed that she would be nothing like me. Perhaps she'd be like Ferri.

When will I see Ferri again? As the empty days went by, I longed to see my angel. I hadn't seen her since that day at her house when I'd cried in her arms after losing Jasmine. Rostam had forbidden me to have anything to do with her and I didn't see how I could get away from Hassan. And so, I'd lost my best friend as well. Now there was no one in my life who knew about my baby, no one who really knew me, no one who knew what my marriage was really like. With Ferri gone, I had no one to comfort me, no shoulder to cry on. Not a single friend.

Was there anyone who cared about me? Maman wouldn't listen or care if she knew how miserable I was. She would have no sympathy for me at all, not a hair. She was finished with me. And, quite frankly, I was not eager to let her know how unhappy my life was.

Babajon was a different story, the only person left in my life I cared about and the only person I was certain loved me – him and Naneh Joon.

What is wrong with Babajon? I was still trying to figure that out.

"Khaleh Bahia, please! He's my father! You have to tell me what's wrong with him."

"*Beh Quran*, I swear on the Quran. *Beh jonneh Layla*, I swear on your own soul, Layla, I don't know."

Despite the hideous things Maman did to me, I couldn't believe she'd lie about her husband's health; she was too superstitious. So, I assumed he was afflicted with some disease and I lived in anxiety about his health. I would never – not in a million years – dream of upsetting him with the knowledge that my husband had turned out to be a violent, horrible, narcissistic bastard. So, I stood by and watched him pat Rostam on the back, hug him and treat the monster like the son he'd never had.

Hassan accompanied me everywhere I went and waited for me outside like a rat lurking near its hole.

He really wasn't necessary. Without Jasmine waiting for me in Los Angeles, any pathetic attempt to elude my fate would be pointless. I would not try to escape again.

I tried to keep myself occupied as best I could. Though Shireen and her posse were always available, I preferred to spend my time in solitude. I wrote. I didn't want my writing shared by my husband or the prying eyes of his rat, so I wrote in English. Still, afraid to document my history or set my true feelings on paper, my writing took the form of poems reflecting my angst.

Lime-colored lights shadowing scenes
With nothing left but long-past dreams
Dreams of long ago that lingered for a while
Lingered and left, laughing at the child
The child who dreamt and died in the night
And left nothing.

Nothing but a dream
A dream in the lime-colored scene of life's act.

I wrote limericks and a lot of silly poems, too. At moments, I saw life as a joke, and I told myself that nothing should be taken too seriously. Passing through Maidoneh Shemiran one afternoon, I saw a middle-aged woman in a flowered *chador* walking swiftly across the square with her head down. As she walked by me, her *chador* flew open for a brief moment and I was inspired.

I asked a chadoree whom I met on the street.
"How can you wear that sheet in this heat?"
She nodded and said, "It is hot, I agree,"
And then she wickedly smiled and said me,
"Allah be blessed. Don't tell. I fake it.
Underneath this chador, I'm totally naked."

For the hundredth time, I wondered what became of our neighbor, Parveen Shirazi, that dignified and devoutly religious woman, devoted wife and mother, whose fate was sealed with a cup of tea, and came to seal my own fate, as well.

With thoughts dwelling on my old neighbor, I decided to visit the mosque. I hadn't been since Maman had ordered me to go after my hymenoplasty. This time I went voluntarily, daring to take the chance that my prayers might be answered. Nothing else had been of help.

Hassan lit a cigarette and waited outside near the stall where I obtained the requisite *chador*. The outside, the exquisite dome and tile work, had always left me breathless. Completely covered with the cloth, I entered the cavernous mosque. There were other people there, mostly males on their prayer rugs, knees down, feet turned under, heads bowed toward Mecca.

I quietly joined a group of women near the rear of the mosque, being careful not to walk in front of anyone. I assumed the position and waited. At first, I was nervous. I felt guilty and uneasy. I wasn't able to recite a single prayer. I closed my eyes, took several deep breaths and calmed down, then prayed for Jasmine. I prayed she be blessed with all the things I didn't provide for her, all the things I wanted for her. I prayed David was alive and well.

I opened my eyes. The mosque was emptying. At my side, an elderly woman sat staring at me. Five women surrounded her, like flower petals.

"Do you know me?" I asked. She didn't answer me. "Who are you?" Still, she didn't answer and only continued to look into my eyes. Eventually, she shook her head knowingly, her lower lip lost behind the few upper teeth she had. She rubbed her hands together. I turned to the women surrounding her. "Who is she? Why doesn't she speak? Why is she looking at me that way? What does she want of me?"

"She is Setarreh," one of the petals volunteered.

"Setarreh prays here all the time," said another.

"That is all she does," the third said.

"She is a most religious woman," said the fourth.

"God listens to her because her heart is clean, very clean, very pure," said the fifth woman.

Setarreh finally spoke in a voice, too young for her apparent years.

"*Bebakhsheed,* excuse me," she said. "You are so very sad. I felt your tears and sorrow when you first entered the holy mosque. Now that I look into your eyes, I see a deep unhappiness there. I feel it. I can touch it. Can you tell me why you are so troubled?"

"I recently had a disagreement with my husband," I said.

She eyed me carefully and, with a shake of her head, said, "No, there is more."

"My husband abuses me," I said.

Still gazing into my in my eyes, she shook her head again. "No, there is more."

And then, I broke down and found myself telling this stranger my deepest secret, admitting to her what I would never admit to anyone. I told her I was praying for the infant daughter I had lost track of in America.

"Do you want me to pray for you?" she asked.

The women around us murmured, "oohs," and, "ahhs."

"Say yes, and she will do it," urged one petal.

"She is very powerful," said another.

"She is pure. She has Allah's ear," repeated another.

"Her prayers are answered," said the fourth as the fifth nodded, wisely.

"You will pray, and I will pray with you," Setareh said. "Allah will hear, and perhaps your child will come back into your life."

"When?" I asked.

She shrugged and said, "That is up to Allah,"

"But I cannot leave Iran, and she is in America. Besides, she is only a baby. She will grow and change. If I see her one day, how will I recognize her? I wouldn't know her, and she wouldn't know me."

"Allah knows what you both look like. Allah knows all. He will provide."

I was certain the woman was a charlatan who only wanted my money. "How much do you want?" I asked.

Her reply surprised me. "Nothing. If my prayers work, you can give me what you want."

I sensed a profound aura of peace about this woman, a quality of piousness. Her refusal to accept payment pending results, was the deciding factor; I had little to lose. "Very well," I said

She produced a worn half-sheet of paper from beneath her *chador*, and put it in my hands. "Read this prayer daily for one month. If within three months you dream of your daughter three nights. be certain you will meet again. You must continue with the prayer for the entire month." I vowed I would do as she said.

I returned home with the prayer hidden in my pocket. I read it constantly, and had soon memorized it. At the end of the second week, I dreamed I held Jasmine as I'd seen her last, that lovely infant with a head full of black hair and large eyes. I saw the crescent birthmark on her chubby calf. I awoke the next morning excited. A few nights later, I dreamed of her again. This time, she was a young, smiling girl, about ten year old. I called out her name, and she came running to me with open arms. Again, I knew her by the crescent moon on her leg. I spent that day smiling. Then, about two weeks later, I dreamed of a young woman in her twenties, with David's bright blue eyes and that same crescent moon on her leg.

I continued to recite the prayer daily.

The End

~You are invited to continue the saga of the Moon Trilogy, with Moon Child, Jolie's Story, Book 2 of the Moon trilogy and Moonlight, Book 3 of the Moon trilogy~

GLOSSARY OF PERSIAN TERMS

The following is not meant to be a concise Persian-to-English dictionary. This glossary has been provided solely to reference an understanding of Persian terms as they have been used in the context of this book.

A

ajab – how strange
Allah Akbar – God is Great
Alhamdo le'llah – praise Allah
alvot – womanizers; playboys
ammeh – paternal aunt
amoo – paternal uncle
arbob – landowner
aroos – bride
ayatollah – Muslim cleric of the highest order
azizam – my dear
aziz jon – precious dear
ayandehtoh seeya kardee – you've blackened your future

B

baakerreh – untouched; virginal
baalegh shodee – you've come of age
balleh – yes
band andoz – one who removes hair by threading
batche-heh-toh harram-zadeh hast – you're giving birth to a bastard
bebakhsheed – excuse me
beeya – come
beezahmat – please

befarmayeed – please, help yourself
beh darak – to hell with it
beh Ghoraneh Majid – to the holiest Quran
beh jonneh babat – I swear on your father's soul
beh jonneh khodet – I swear on your soul
beh jonneh man – I swear on my soul
beh Khodah – I swear to God
beh Quran – I swear on the Quran
beh omeedeh Khodah – may it be God's will
beh Toorah – I swear on the Torah
beraghks – (command to) dance
bereem – let's go
berreh bemeereh – may it die
bokharee – radiator
bokhorr – (command to) eat
borak'Allah – bravo; you did well
borro – go
borro aghab – go back

C

chador – long piece of cloth covering women from head to toe
chahar-shambe – Wednesday
Chahar-shambe Soree – party held the Wednesday before the Persian New Year
chai – tea
chai nabot – tea sweetened with crystallized sugar
chee begam? – what can I say?
cheeyeh? – what is it?
chera? – why?
chet chodeh? – what has happened to you?

D – F

Dayee – maternal uncle

dasteshoon dard nakoneh – may her hand not hurt (from having overworked)
deevoneh shodee? – have you gone mad?
dehatee – villager, one of a low caste
delam meesoozeh barosh – I pity her
eftekhar kon – be proud
ensha'Allah – God willing
ensha'Allah lanat beshee, bemeerree – God willing, I hope you are cursed and die
fadot sham – may I be sacrificed for you
fahmeedee? – did you hear?
fallgir – fortune teller

G

gaz – fragranced nougat candy made with the sap of desert plants
ghellyon – water pipe
ghorbonnet beram – may I be sacrificed for you
ghorbonneh shomah – I would sacrifice myself for you
ghormeh sabzee – stew of green herbs
Guillee Khoshbooee – (a poem entitled) "The Mud that Sat by the Rose"
guivehs – cloth slippers with soles of rubber

H – I

Haft Seen – seven symbolic items that commemorate the Persian New Year
hakim – doctor
halvah – hardened golden-brown candy surrounded by thin slivers of almonds
hammom omoomi – public baths
harram-zadeh – bastard child
harram-zadeh darree – you have a bastard child
hayah kon – be ashamed
heech kassee -- nobody
Hijrah – Muslim lunar calendar

J

jaa'haazeeyeh – dowry
ja'leb – intriguing, unique
jen – a mischievous, magical being
jendeh – whore
jonam – my darling
jon – dear
joon – dear (familiar form)
joonie – little dear
joob – canals that run along the streets of Tehran

K

kabob koobeedeh – skewer of ground meat
kabobee – kabob vendor
kardeem? – vulgar way of asking "have we had sexual intercourse?"
kee? – who?
keeseh hammom – coarse mitt used to exfoliate
kesafat – dirty, filthy
khafeshoh – (command form) choke; be quiet
khaleh – maternal aunt
khanomeh sangeen – well-behaved woman
khar – donkey
kharob dokhtar – damaged girl
kheja-lat kon – be ashamed
khob – well
Khodah – God
Khodah bozorgeh – God is great
Khodah 'hafez – God protect you
Khodah ham'rahet – God be with you
Khodah meedooneh – God knows
Khodah nakhad – may God forbid it
Khodah shahed – God is my witness
Khodah umresh bedeh – God grant her life
Khodara shokr/ shokre Khoda – thank God

khodiya – god (exclamation, not referring to the actual deity)
khok be sarresh – curse: dirt on his/her head
khok sheer – drink of sweet, watered rocket seeds
khoobeh – it's good
khoon – blood
khosh amadee – you are welcomed
khostegar – suitor
kookoo sabzee – omelet of sautéed green herbs
korsi – a table covered with blankets that is used in the winter. A brazier with lighted coals is set underneath the table to heat the room.

L – M

la paee – between the legs
longis – long sheets
madar jendeh – daughter of a whore
madar sag – bitch (daughter of a dog)
meerram – I'll go
mehree'yeh – Iranian form of alimony that is written into the marriage contract
mobarak – congratulations
mobarak boshad – may this be a blessed occasion
mommy joon – term of endearment Persian mothers often use to address their children *Muharram* – the first month on the Shiite Muslim calendar, a period of mourning that commemorates the death of Mohammad's son-in-law and his successors.
mullah – Muslim clergyman
mushallah! – well done! praise God

N

na ghabell – someone worth nothing; unworthy
najess – filthy; unclean
nakhare – no
noghl – sweet candies made of slivers of almonds covered with sugar and rose water

non – bread
nonneh barbarri – oval-shaped Persian bread, made of long strips of perforated dough
Nou Rooz – the Persian New Year

O – R

ob goosht – Persian chicken soup
omram – my life (a term of endearment)
pagosha – first time after that a bride and groom are guests of their parents as a couple
pas chera? – then why?
peesh-kesh – take it as a gift
roosaree – Muslim head scarf
roo sheshm – on my eyes; you humble me

S

saalom – a greeting
salamati – to your health (a toast)
samanoo – cooked wheat, used on Persian New Year as a symbol of God's grains, life's food*sangeen* – decent; clean
seeb – apples, used on the Persian New Year to symbolize harvest, plenty, and health
Seenzdah-be-dar – the 13th day of the Persian New Year. Families gather outdoors so as not to be caught by bad luck inside their homes
s'eer – garlic, used on the Persian New Year to symbolize nature and natural medicine
sekkeh – coins, used on the Persian New Year to symbolize wealth
serkeh – vinegar, used on the Persian New Year to symbolize cleanliness and hygiene
shah damaad – bridegroom
sharrm – shame
sheshm meezanan – they give the evil eye
shookhee meekonee? – are you kidding me?
shozdeh – prince

sofreh – large cloth spread out on the floor in place of a dining table
sofreh aghd – large cloth spread out on the floor, on which bride and groom sit during the marriage ceremony
sohan – circular pastry made of dried flour doused in honey
sombol – hyacinth, used on the Persian New Year to symbolize love

T

takhtenar – backgammon
talagh – divorce
tarroff – custom of declining a person's offer or invitation several times before accepting, to be polite
tokhmeh sag – son of a bitch
tomboon – loose pants traditionally worn by women as underwear
torsheed – to pickle, or get too old to marry
toyee? – is it you?

U – Z

ushes – hearty soups with meats, vegetables, rice or other grains, herbs and occasionally fruit
vazeer – a minister or advisor
vye – wow
vye barr man – oh my god!
zanamee – you're my wife

NOTE TO MY READERS

The challenged faced by the dichotomies inherent in biculturalism is one theme of **Persian Moon-Layla's Story,** Book One of the Moon Trilogy.

Immediately preceding the Islamic Revolution, I made one final visit to Iran. For the next six years, my law practice assisted Iranians thrown into major socio-economic and cultural transition as they sought legal status in the United States. When push came to shove, in the face of major upheaval, I found they proved to be a resilient people. Yet, there were scars as they juggled the culture that they were born into with the culture that they were thrown into.

I was fascinated as I watched Iranians – and particularly, young Iranian women – try to harmonize two diametrically opposed influences. On the one hand, they enjoyed new freedoms available to them in the Western way of life; on the other hand, Iranian cultural imposed certain traditional expectations on them.

My hope is that through reading this book, many might come to learn more about Iran before and after the Islamic Revolution and confirm the universality of human nature.

Thanks for reading **Persian Moon-Layla's Story.**

DISCUSSION QUESTIONS

Thank you for reading *Persian Moon – Layla's Story*. Here are some suggested topics for discussion:

1. When Layla, comes into her moon while playing with the boys and asks Zahra Khanom why she hadn't forewarned her, Zahra says, *Layla, I am your mother and I know what's best for you. You were too young to understand. Now you are a young lady.*
2. Do you blame Zahra?
3. Do you blame Layla's father for allowing her to play with the boys?
4. What was your own experience and that of other females you know when entering the moon cycle?
5. When Layla sees the blood on her shorts, *the boys knew what the red stain meant … If the taboo imprinted in their young minds hadn't forbidden them from speaking of such things to a girl … the boys would have explained it.* Yet, despite the taboo, they were also her friends *who protected her like a little sister*. When they realized she was scared, should they have explained what was happening to her?
6. Do you understand why Layla was forbidden to be alone with a boy from that day on?
7. Do you think Zahra's own story of how she met and married Hadi helped explain to Layla's the reason Layla had to stay away from boys?
8. The boys seemed happy to re-engage with Layla the very day she came into her moon. Did that surprise you? Discuss.
9. How do you think Fotmeh felt towards Layla?
10. Why do you think Layla bonded so strongly with her father from an early age?

11. After Lalyla joined her father for the meeting with his advisors, he praised her suggestions. Do you think they were objectively good suggestions?
12. Why do you think the writer describes the personalities of Shireen, Ferri, Parveen and other characters in the story, but not Layla's?
13. How would you describe Layla's character and personality?
14. Shireen is very different from Layla. Do you think that's due to her upbringing?
15. Ferri is very different from Layla and yet they are best friends. What draws Layla to Ferri? What draws Ferri to Layla?
16. Do you think Shireen grows to love Taymour? Does she remind you of someone you know? Explain.
17. What are the pros and cons of imposing sexual boundaries on a young girl based on scientific untruths?
18. Could Layla have somehow escaped from Rostam? Discuss.
19. What was your reaction to the character of Rostam when you realized he speaks of himself in third person?
20. If you were in Layla's marital situation, would you tell your parents?
21. Would you have taken Adam up on his offer of marriage? Why? Why not?
22. Would you say Layla is a pragmatist? A romantic? An idealist? A cynic? Something else? Explain.
23. Would you have reacted to Anthony at the restaurant in the same way Layla did? Was what Layla did in keeping with what you knew of her up to that point? Explain.
24. Can you understand how it could be that Layla had such a skewed understanding of what constitutes virginity?
25. Layla's views about Californian girls seems to change as she feels better about her UCLA classes. Discuss.
26. Professor Dubos believed that the key to longevity is resilience. Do you agree? Has that proven to be true in your life? Discuss.

27. Do you think dinner on Friday night Shabbos with David and his parents was a good idea for a first date?
28. Compare and contrast David's parents with Layla's parents.
29. At the Kline home, David advances his belief that prostitution and early marriages are the result of a culture's sexual repression. Do you agree?
30. How could Layla justify sleeping with David despite her upbringing?
31. If you were Layla, would you have accepted David's marriage proposal and gone to Israel with him? Does her reasons for rejecting him make sense to you? Discuss.
32. If Layla was certain she would not marry David, do you think she was right to sleep with him?
33. When Jasmine was born, Layla refused to look at her. Yet, she spent about two weeks with her before leaving for Iran and putting her in the care of her college friends. Discuss.
34. Does Layla strike you as a girl who could easily fool her parents?
35. Were you surprised when she was caught at the airport?
36. Why do you think Hassan, The Rat, was so loyal to Rostam?
37. Do you think Layla with reunite with her daughter? Why? How?
38. Does Layla change by the time the story ends? How?
39. Is Layla proactive in her life? Why or why not?
40. Do you think Zahra truly cared about Layla's happiness? Discuss.
41. Did you know of the hymenoplasty procedure? Do you believe doctors would administer that procedure in your country?
42. Does Setareh strike you as a charlatan? Will Layla reunite with Jasmine?

ABOUT THE AUTHOR

Guitta Karubian is the author of the Moon Trilogy, consisting of *Persian Moon: Layla's Story - Book 1;*

Moon Child: Jolie's Story -Book 2; and

Moonlight -Book 3.

She is also the author of *Target,* a highly fictionalized account of a legal case, and a book of poetry, *You, Me, and I.* She was the founding editor of the English section of an international niche magazine and has had short stories and poems published.

Ms. Karubian is a graduate of the University of California at Berkeley and Southwestern Law School. She is the mother of two children and lives in Los Angeles, California.

You can contact her at GuittaKarubian.com and view her website at GuittaKarubian.com.

Thank you.

BOOKS BY GUITTA KARUBIAN

The Moon Trilogy

Persian Moon - Layla's Story *Book*

Moon Child - Jolie's Story *Book 2*

Moonlight - *Book 3*

Target

You, Me, and I